THE VILLAGE VET

In Talyton St George, vet nurse Tessa Wilde is on the way to her wedding... It should be the happiest day of her life. But then her car hits a dog, and though the dog is saved thanks to the Otter House vets, her wedding is not. Animal welfare officer and part-time fire-fighter Jack Miller spends his life saving animals and people. As one of Tessa's oldest friends, he feels he has the right to interrupt her wedding and rescue her from a marriage that can only end in tears. But does he? Tessa is sure she doesn't need rescuing least of all by Jack.

THE VILLAGE VET

THE VILLAGE VET

by

Cathy Woodman

Magna Large Print Books
Long Preston, North Yorkshire,
BD23 4ND, England.

British Library Cataloguing in Publication Data.

Woodman, Cathy
  The village vet.

  A catalogue record of this book is
  available from the British Library

  ISBN   978-0-7505-3635-6

First published in Great Britain in 2012 by Arrow Books

Copyright © Cathy Woodman 2012

Cover illustration © Rachel Ross

Cathy Woodman has asserted her right under the Copyright, Designs and Patents Act, 1988 to be identified as the author of this work

Published in Large Print 2013 by arrangement with Random House Group Ltd.

Magna Large Print is an imprint of Library Magna Books Ltd.

Printed and bound in Great Britain by
T.J. (International) Ltd., Cornwall, PL28 8RW

To Tamsin for her brilliant ideas!
To Will for keeping cheerful!

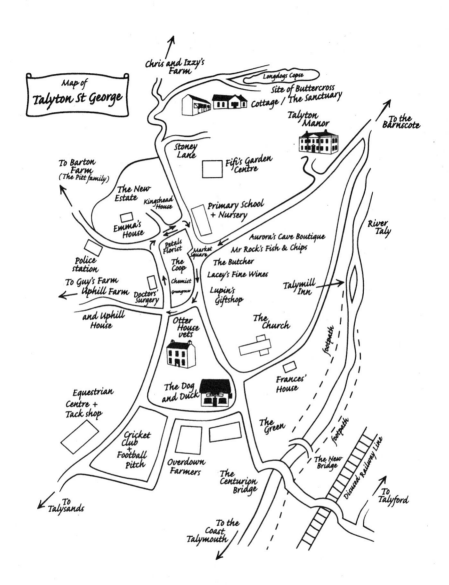

Map of
Talyton St George

Chris and Izzy's Farm

Longdogs Copse

Site of Buttercross Cottage / The Sanctuary

Talyton Manor

To the Barnscote

Stoney Lane

Fifi's Garden Centre

To Barton Farm
(The Pitt family)

The New Estate

Kingshead House

Emma's House

Primary School + Nursery

River Taly

Petals Florist

Market Square

Aurora's Cave Boutique

Mr Rock's Fish & Chips

Police station

The Coop

The Butcher

Lacey's Fine Wines

To Guy's Farm
Uphill Farm

Chemist

Grocers

Lupin's Giftshop

Talymill Inn

Doctors' Surgery

and Uphill House

Otter House vets

The Church

footpath

Frances' House

The Dog and Duck

Equestrian Centre + Tack shop

The Green

Cricket Club + Football Pitch

Overdown Farmers

The Centurion Bridge

The New Bridge

footpath

Disused Railway Line

To Talyford

To Talysands

To the Coast, Talymouth

Chapter One

This Year, Next Year, Sometime, Never

It isn't every day that I get to ride in a Rolls Royce, bowling along the Devon country lanes in the bright April sunshine with my dad at my side, singing 'Get Me to the Church on Time' in his rich baritone voice. His enthusiasm is infectious and I'm not sure which of us is most excited, me or him.

The chauffeur takes a right turn at the next crossroads, following the ridge of the steep wooded escarpment where I can just make out through the trees the gleaming meanders of the river, and the church spire and tower rising above the small town below. As the single-track lane widens to form a passing place, a dark four-legged shadow runs out in front of us.

'What the–!' The chauffeur slams on the brakes and time seems to slow right down as the car shudders to a standstill. There's an ominous thud, then silence.

'No, Tess,' my dad says, but I'm already out of the door, my dress hitched up around my calves and the heels of my shoes – my beautiful ivory wedding shoes – sinking into the mud at the side of the road as I go round to the front of the Rolls Royce to find a big black dog lying stretched out across the tarmac.

'Oh-mi-god,' I say, trying to dive forwards to help it, while my dad holds me back.

'No, Tess,' he repeats. 'It's too late. I think it's dead.'

Hollow with apprehension and shock, I stare at the dog, a handsome boy with a bloody nose and a small patch of white on its chest, willing him to be all right.

'He's alive,' I say with a sigh of relief as the dog lifts his head and gazes blindly towards me, his tongue hanging out from one side of his mouth and his ears floppy against the sides of his broad skull.

'He looks like he's seeing stars,' my dad observes as the chauffeur turns his attention to the dent in the front of the car, which has definitely come off worse. 'What are we going to do now?'

'He needs to see a vet,' I say, looking hopefully towards our driver.

'Never mind about the upholstery,' he says dryly. 'Let's get him into the car.'

Soon the dog is lying on the passenger seat with blood dripping from his nose, and I'm thinking that this isn't the most auspicious of beginnings. My dad looks like he could burst into tears and, thanks to his suggestion that we go for a spin first, which seemed like a great idea at the time, we're running more than could be construed as traditionally late.

'I'll drop you off at the church on the way to the vet's, and take the Roller to the garage for them to assess the damage before I come back to collect you,' the chauffeur says, putting out his hand to steady the dog as we negotiate the first sharp bend down the hill into Talyton St George, at which the dog sneezes, dousing the air with a delicate red mist.

'No, we must make the vet's the first stop.' I'm a vet nurse and I've helped out with enough road traffic accidents, or RTAs as we call them, to know that you can never predict the outcome. Sometimes it's the animals that look okay at first who don't make it in the end.

'She's right – we must go straight to Otter House,' says my dad. 'Do not pass "Go", do not collect two hundred pounds. Oh, Tessa, do you remember how we used to play Monopoly when you were a little girl? And Scrabble? You always won at Scrabble.'

'Dad, please, not now.' The words catch in my throat as I go on, 'You're making me feel sad.' It occurs to me that running the dog over could be a terrible omen, not that I'm superstitious, not really. It's just that I've been badly shaken up. So far my big day isn't going to plan.

It's Saturday, market day, and it takes a while to drive through the narrow one-way streets and Market Square, where the local traders are out in force, selling everything from free-range eggs and cider cakes, to country knitwear and carnivorous plants, but finally we reach the vet's, where the chauffeur stops outside on the double-yellow lines and heads into the surgery for assistance. I offer to help, but Dad insists that I stay in the car, and considering the circumstances, he's probably right.

I glance at my reflection in the rear-view mirror. My dark, almost black hair is pinned up in a bun with ringlets curling at my cheeks, my eyes sparkle with pearlescent shadow and my lips are stained scarlet, reminding me more of Snow White in *Snow White and the Seven Dwarfs* than myself. I'm the kind of girl who tends to stick with the natural look, my hair falling around my shoulders in waves, and I don't usually wear very much make-up. I love the effect though. I could be a Hollywood actress – Gemma Arterton perhaps, with a small stretch of the imagination.

I sit back and wait, gazing out of the window at the small crowd of people gathering on the pavement to admire the vintage Rolls and catch a glimpse of the bride. Glancing down at the bouquet in my lap, I allow myself a smile. That's me, Tessa Wilde, and today, as long as someone comes to collect the dog very soon, I'm getting married to Nathaniel Cooper, my best friend, lover and man of my dreams. All right, I'm twenty-eight years old and my dreams have taken a long time to become reality, but it's happening at last.

The chauffeur is back, opening the passenger door with a practised flourish for one of the vets from Otter House – Maz, one of the partners – to get the dog out of the car. In lilac scrubs and with a wedding ring dangling from a chain around her neck, she reaches in to slip a rope lead over the dog's head. As the rope tightens around his neck, he growls and throws himself out of the door, before staggering blindly across the pavement. Maz guides him towards the surgery, keeping a firm grip on the end of the lead, while the chauffeur returns to the driver's seat and, out of concern for the bride's sensibilities perhaps, lays his suit jacket over the pool of blood the dog has left behind.

'It doesn't take more than a couple of minutes to reach the church from here,' he says, restarting the engine, which rumbles and purrs like a big cat. 'I've never yet failed to get a bride to her wedding on time,' he adds, at which my dad looks like he might cry again.

'Please don't.' I reach out for his hand and give it a squeeze. 'The dog's in the best place.'

'I'm not upset about the dog.' His face is red, the effect of the champagne we shared before we left the family home, where I'd spent my last night as a single woman. 'Oh, I'm sorry, darling, I'm worrying you.' He unfurls a patterned hand-kerchief from his top pocket and blows his nose loudly.

'Dad, that's part of your outfit.' I start to chuckle, finding that I can't be cross with him. 'You're supposed to coordinate with Nathan and Mike.' Mike's the best man.

My dad apologises again. 'I can't help it. You might be all grown up now, Tessa, but you're still my little princess.' He turns and slides his arms around my shoulders without regard for my veil or flowers and gives me a bear hug. Tears prick my eyes as I clasp my hands behind his neck. 'I know your mum keeps telling me I should think of this as gaining a son-in-law, not losing a daughter, but I don't like the idea of giving you away.'

'I thought you wanted me to be happy?' I say softly.

'Of course I do,' Dad says, pulling back. 'Take no

notice of me. I'm feeling a bit overwrought.' He flashes me a grin. 'I shouldn't have had that drink.' After a pause, he goes on, 'Aren't you nervous? I was petrified when I married your mother.'

'I'm kind of nervous and excited at the same time. I'll be fine when it's all over.' I correct myself quickly. 'I mean, when today's over.'

'You only get married once. Well, that's what your mum and I did.'

'Did you ever have any doubts?' I ask him.

'About whether I was doing the right thing?' He shakes his head. 'None whatsoever, because I knew from the day I met her, just as you did with Nathan, that she was the one I was going to spend the rest of my life with, through thick and thin...' He pauses to pat his paunch, before continuing, 'Through fat and even fatter.'

I smile at him fondly. He would be more comfortable in drag. He was an actor, more often than not a pantomime dame, before the regional theatres closed through lack of funding. Now, in retirement, he writes stage plays and runs Talyton St George's Amateur Dramatic Group.

Comforted by my dad's ability to make a joke out of everything and by his conviction, as always, that everything will turn out right in the end, I turn my attention to getting myself and the dress out of the Rolls at the church, ably assisted by Katie, my chief bridesmaid and best girlfriend, along with two of Nathan's much younger nieces.

'Hi, Tessa.' Katie is about five foot five, the same height as me. She has green eyes and strawberry-blonde hair, and she looks utterly stunning in a pale pink, figure-hugging silk dress with buttons down the back. She kisses my cheek. 'Where have you been?'

Taking a deep breath of fresh Devon air that's laced with the scent of manure, I start to tell her about the dog.

'Tessa, I know you're mad about animals, but this isn't the time for a shaggy dog story, so to speak,' she interrupts. 'Apart from the mud on your shoes, you look fabulous, the perfect blushing bride.'

'I do feel a bit flushed,' I say. 'Have you got any concealer handy?'

'Trust me. You don't need touching up.' Katie moves closer and adds in a whisper, 'You have Nathan to do that later. That man is so hench.'

'I'm sorry?'

'Hench – enormously fit in this context. Keep up.' She gives me a gentle shove. 'You lucky thing. I'm so envious. You must be soooo excited.'

I touch my chest as we make our way up the path between the gravestones and memorials dedicated to the residents of Talyton St George who have gone before, feeling my heart racing beneath my fingers. The erratic rhythm has more to do with an imminent panic attack than excitement, however.

'Are you ready, Tessa?' Dad cuts in, offering me his arm.

I nod and hang on to him for dear life as we enter the church and begin the long walk up the aisle to the strains of the Wedding March, the music slurred and discordant, as though Nobby Warwick, the organist, has been down at the Dog and Duck to lubricate his pipes beforehand, something else I hadn't anticipated.

Dad walks stiffly past friends and family, and complete strangers from Nathan's side, in his morning suit and bow tie, the buttons of his coat looking as if they are about to pop and a red rash on his neck where he's been fiddling with his collar out of nerves. In fact, by the time we reach the end of the aisle where Nathan and his best man are waiting with the vicar, my father is clinging on to *my* arm, a tear glistening on his cheek. I stop and wipe it away with trembling fingertips, a small gesture that makes me smile because it reminds me of how I used to paint his beauty spot in the very same place before every performance during the panto season.

Reluctantly, Dad releases me and Katie takes the bouquet, stepping back as Nathan approaches.

'Tessa, darling, you're late.' Gazing at me with his cool grey eyes, he takes my hand and plants a single damp kiss on my lips. 'But you're worth waiting for. You look beautiful.'

'So do you,' I say gently. He appears pale underneath the deep tan he's been working on in preparation for the honeymoon, as if he hasn't eaten or slept for a week, yet Katie is right. Compact and muscular from regular, almost obsessive sessions in the gym, Nathan is enormously fit in more ways than one. Any woman would be proud to be marrying him.

'I can't believe how many people have turned up especially for us,' I say, looking around at the congregation, and spotting Nathan's parents who have travelled all the way from Spain and my great-aunt Marion who's made it here from her farm in North Wales in spite of being partway through a course of hospital treatment.

'It's going to be a great party,' Nathan says. 'I wonder if your maiden aunt will make it through the night, or whether she'll succumb from the excitement of it all.'

'Nathan, will you stop it?' I say, pretending to be appalled, but I know he's joking – my great-aunt might not be in the best of health, but there's a long way to go until I receive my inheritance, if she should choose to leave part or all of her estate to me. I don't care what she does with it because I've already inherited something from her that's far more valuable than money, her love of animals. 'Can't you be serious for once?'

'I'll try.' He pauses and my heart is melting as he continues, 'Today, I'll do anything you ask. This is your day and I want to make it special for you.'

I know he doesn't like me saying it, but it seems right, considering we're about to commit to spending the rest of our lives together. The words come tumbling out of my mouth. 'Nathan, I love you...' And it's here that he is supposed to echo the sentiment, because he has steadfastly refused to discuss it before, but all he can do is stare at the floor, shifting from one foot to the other in his squeaky new wedding shoes. 'Nathan, tell me you love me,' I whisper urgently. 'I need to know. I need to be sure.'

He looks up, raising one eyebrow. 'Of course I do, and you shouldn't have to ask that. It's a given.'

So he isn't going to say it even now, at our

wedding, I think as the organ stops, makes a single parping note and falls silent.

'Thank God for that.' Nathan rolls his eyes heavenwards. 'That was a bloody painful rendition.'

'Nathan.' I give him a look. 'No swearing in church.'

He smiles and I smile back, reassured in part that I'm doing the right thing. 'Tessa, are you ready?' the vicar asks from beside me.

'I'm ready,' I say aloud, although when I gaze at the altar in front of me I can't help thinking of sacrificial lambs.

Having introduced the wedding service, the vicar, a friend of the family, guides the congregation through a prayer and hymn with a deafening accompaniment from the organist. I sing along to 'Lord of All Hopefulness', but Nathan doesn't. He fidgets through the whole four verses, sometimes smiling, sometimes rolling his eyes, mocking the vicar, who is singing his heart out. His ability to have fun is one of the many things I love about Nathan, but I wish he wouldn't do it at other people's expense – and at our wedding.

We haven't been together for long, and sometimes I feel as if I've known him for ever, other times that I don't know him at all. Introduced by mutual friends six months ago, we met in a local pub, hitting it off immediately. He proposed on a romantic mini-break in Paris a few weeks later and I accepted. Nathan, who is the third serious boyfriend I've had – third time lucky, maybe – is different. I was born and grew up in this quiet country town and have never lived anywhere else but Devon, while Nathan has moved around, travelled widely and set up a successful business, importing and selling anything he believes will make him a profit and take him to his first million.

When we're together, he makes me feel special, although we aren't together anywhere nearly enough for me. There were a few awkward days at the beginning of our relationship when we were scratchy with each other because I thought he should be spending more time with me, while he thought I should understand that he was a busy man. I learned to let go while he carried on, on condition that he texted me regularly. It's a girl thing and I am a girl, I pointed out, at which he took me in his arms and said he could confirm that fact completely, and did, several times over.

At the beginning Nathan only had eyes for me, but I do wonder about him now. Am I mistaken or do his eyes keep drifting towards Katie's curvy rear? I expressed a preference for a less revealing version of the dress that she chose, but I gave in with good grace, wanting her to be happy, and she certainly seems happy, her gaze latching onto Nathan's now and again as if they are sharing a private joke. I've always wanted them to get along, but not quite as well as they do, I muse as the last notes of the hymn fade out and the vicar begins with the declaration. He looks from me to Nathan and back, smiling.

'First, I am required to ask anyone present who knows a reason why these persons may not lawfully marry to declare it now.'

There is an interval in which I can hear my

23

heartbeat leaping about, which is ridiculous, because there is absolutely no reason why Nathan and I may not lawfully marry, but before the vicar can continue smoothly onto the vows, there's a shout of 'Wait!' from the back of the church. 'Stop the wedding!'

At first, I don't understand what's happening.

'Jack! No, Jack!' There's a chorus of voices and a scuffle just inside the church door, followed by the sound of footsteps running along the aisle towards us.

I swing round, tottering on my heels, to find a tall, angry blond guy in tan chinos and a navy polo-shirt shaking off two of the ushers – one of my cousins and Nathan's brother – as he approaches.

'Well, well, well, if it isn't Jack Miller, your hanger-on,' Nathan says to me. 'I don't understand. You said he wasn't coming.'

'That's right,' I say, frowning. I did send Jack an invitation in recognition of the fact that he's been a friend of mine since I can remember, and with Nathan's assent and on the understanding that there was no way Jack would ever accept due to the disagreement he and Nathan had at the pub not long after Nathan and I first met.

There are occasions when honesty isn't the best policy and I wish I'd never mentioned to Nathan that Jack and I had had a teenage romance – an intense and all-consuming love affair that lasted until Jack went off to college – because it gave Nathan a good reason to dislike him. Unfortunately, the feeling turned out to be mutual and when Nathan made some jokey put-down about my muffin top, albeit a small one, Jack took it to heart on my behalf. Embarrassed by the way the two men were arguing in front of everyone, I asked Jack to leave, which he did, but not before telling me to think very carefully about what I was doing, a warning he repeated when I contacted him to let him know that Nathan and I were engaged to be married, not wanting Jack to hear it from anyone else first.

Why did I do that, you might well ask – because I suspected that he might still harbour feelings for me and I wanted to soften the blow, or to prove to myself that I had finally moved on, or both?

The next thing I knew was that Jack had gone away, not just out of town, but out of the country, to Asia, where he's been working with moon bears for the past four months.

'Hey, just a minute.' My dad tries to intercept Jack, but Jack pushes him aside with a thrust of one of his broad shoulders and confronts Nathan, who shrinks and steps back until he's almost swallowed up by the flower arrangement to the right of the altar. As the vase holding the flowers rocks ominously, the colour drains from Nathan's face and one of the little bridesmaids bursts into tears, I step in, pushing my way between the two men.

'Jack, what do you think you're doing?' My voice quavers with anger and confusion. 'This is my day and you're ruining it. You're wrecking everything!' I continue as the vase falls crashing to the floor, fragments scattering across the medieval mosaic tiles, and the congregation gasps as one.

'It's my right,' Jack growls back. 'Tess, let me

speak with you,' he adds, the expression in his brown eyes growing soft and beseeching. 'Two minutes in private. That's all I'm asking for.'

There's a pause and the congregation falls silent once more. I notice how rough Jack looks with his face unshaven, hair unkempt, and dark shadows under his eyes. Slimmer than when I last saw him, and sporting a deep tan and sun-kissed highlights, he looks decidedly well travel-led. I bite my lip, tasting blood. There was a time when I would have given him a hug to welcome him home: at this minute, I could kill him.

'Please...' His gruff tone reveals a raw emotion that twists through my heart like a knife, for Jack has always been the strong, silent type, unable or unwilling to lay his soul bare, and for the briefest moment I'm torn, but this is my wedding and Nathan is right beside me – apparently drawing his own conclusions about the situation, because I can sense his rising fury in the deep flush that floods his face and the tightening of his fists. 'I've been trying to get hold of you,' Jack goes on.

'Not now, Jack,' I say quietly, as Katie moves up to stand at my shoulder.

'Ask him.' Jack's eyes flash with anger as he nods towards Nathan. 'Ask him about the bit about forsaking all others.'

'I believe you'll find that that comes later,' says the vicar, trying and failing to defuse the situation.

'You're just fucking jealous, mate.' Nathan ducks forwards and aims a punch that glances across Jack's chin, making a hollow knocking sound. Jack lets fly with a right hook, catching

Nathan on the nose, at which he creases up, clutching his face. Blood drips through his fingers onto the broken china at our feet.

Katie touches my hand.

'We'll take one each,' she says brightly. 'That's enough, boys.'

When Jack moves to thump Nathan for a second time, I block him, telling him he'll have to hit me first, while Katie grabs Nathan's arm and drags him aside.

'You've broken my nose, you wa–' Nathan yells.

'It's nothing less than you deserve, you two-timing bastard!' Jack cuts in, touching the red mark that's appearing on his chin. 'I don't understand what they all see in you – you have all the charisma of a dead sheep.'

'Jack, will you please leave it,' Katie snaps. 'Leave it! None of this has anything to do with you. If you have any respect–'

A ray of light slants through a stained-glass window and onto the altar. I'm getting it now, but there has to have been a terrible misunderstanding. How can Nathan possibly be messing around with another woman when he's here right now, about to marry me?

'Jack, stop this,' I beg. 'Please don't go on embarrassing yourself in front of everyone. You've made a mistake in coming here.'

'Tess, it's you who's making a mistake, and it could be the biggest one of your life.'

'How can you say that to me? I thought you were my friend.'

'Somebody get him out of here,' Katie says. 'Get him booked into the funny farm asap. He needs to see a psychiatrist.'

'I'm sorry, one and all, this is a most unusual interruption,' says the vicar, making light of it in front of the congregation. 'We'll resume shortly. Come on, Jack, let's have a chat about this man to man.' He waves towards the organist. 'Some uplifting music of your choice, please, Nobby – take it away.'

As the vicar and my dad escort Jack off to the vestry, and the church fills with the trembling chords of 'Jerusalem', my knees grow weak and I fall sobbing into Nathan's one-armed embrace.

'Mind the suit,' he says, his words muffled by the handful of tissues he's pressing to his bloodied nose. 'We don't want to ruin the photos, do we?'

'You can have any blemishes airbrushed out,' Katie interrupts. 'I'm more worried about getting blood on the dress.'

I step aside, as my mum, dressed in an ice-blue suit and matching hat, joins us and gives me a hug. Usually, she's like sunshine – warm, bright and cheering – but on this occasion her expression is downcast and her lips are pursed with concern.

'What a to-do, darling,' she says as the guests are singing about England's dark, satanic mills.

'Did you know he was back?' I ask her, and when she nods sheepishly, I say, 'When?'

'I don't know exactly.' She shrugs. 'He came round to the house last night, asking to see you.'

'I was there,' I say, annoyed that I missed my chance to head this situation off, not that I expected it in the slightest. 'Why didn't you let him in?'

28

'It was very late, you were in the shower and the way he was, I thought it best that–'

'Mum, you should have told me.'

'And what good would that have done? You're marrying Nathan, so there's no point encouraging Jack in his hopeless pursuit. He's always liked you, Tessa, and I was afraid something like this would happen, that he'd come rushing in, trying to spoil things for you.' She lowers her voice, aware perhaps that everyone is listening. 'What was that all about anyway? Has Jack gone completely mad?'

'I don't know,' I wail. Nathan bought me a brand-new car only a few weeks ago – why would he go to all that expense if he has someone on the side? On the other hand, why would Jack make something like that up? Surely he can see that he's hardly likely to endear himself to me by attacking Nathan.

'Don't worry about it, love. We'll look back and laugh at this one day.' Mum pats my shoulder. 'I must get back to Great-Auntie Marion – she's been on the brandy already.' She hesitates. 'Shall I ask her if–'

'No thanks,' I say hurriedly. I don't need any more to drink; I need to keep a clear head. I pick up my bouquet from where Katie has left it on the steps up to the altar, and as my mum returns to the pews, Katie and Nathan move in to comfort me.

'Jack's jealous,' Katie says as Nathan slips his arm around my back, resting his hand on the curve of my waist. 'That's why he's doing this. It's one last, desperate attempt to stop you and

29

Nathan getting married.'

I shake my head. 'It's too way out, too extreme. Jack isn't like that.' He's cool, level-headed and good in a crisis. He's an animal protection officer and part-time retained firefighter. If he really knew Nathan was playing around, he would have come straight to tell me, not wait until the night before my wedding, or the wedding itself.

'I've never liked him,' Katie says, 'and this only goes to show I was right to trust my instincts. I always thought he was a bit of a stalker.' I feel my forehead tighten as she continues, 'He was always following you about.'

'I'll get him for this,' Nathan mumbles. 'My nose – it won't stop bleeding.'

'Do you need more tissues?' Katie fusses and frets. 'Would you like me to call a doctor or an ambulance?'

'That pathetic excuse of a bloke might need one when I get my hands on him,' Nathan fumes.

'Please calm down, darling,' I say, but he doesn't respond. He steps away from me, staring towards the vestry door, the muscle in his cheek tightening and relaxing with barely suppressed fury. Mike, the best man, moves around to stand between us and the vestry door.

'He isn't worth it, mate. He's just some small-town nonentity. Tessa, make your groom see sense, will you?' Mike grins. 'Don't hold back. Start as you mean to go on, because you'll be nagging him to death once you get that ring on your finger.'

'You have got it with you, haven't you?' Nathan says, his voice sounding stuffy and nasal.

30

Mike takes the tissues and puts an arm around Nathan's shoulders. 'Course I have. Calm down – it's all going to be fine.' He looks towards the vestry. 'Here they come.'

The vicar and my father return. I don't know where Jack is, where he will go, or whether he goes of his own accord or not, and I don't care. All I want is to get on with the wedding before I change my mind.

'Are you all right to continue?' the vicar says kindly.

I pick at the petals of the roses in my bouquet: this year, next year, sometime, never.

'Should we start again, right from the beginning?' the vicar asks. 'It's your choice, Tessa.'

'Let's start where we broke off,' I say, a little sharply. 'I'm sorry. That didn't come out as I intended.'

'Don't worry. You've had rather a shock.'

'I know.' If only the vicar knew that it isn't the shock that's bothering me; it's the doubts, the ones I thought I'd buried, now resurfacing like the bubbles in a chocolate fountain. I recall the first time I met Nathan, the dark hair, the tan, the signet ring and black Audi. 'I'm going to be the next Dragon in the Den,' he bragged. 'I'm on fire.'

'Tessa, stop spoiling the bouquet,' Katie says, relieving me of it for a second time. 'I want there to be something left for me to catch later on.' Her eyes shimmer with tears.

'Oh, Katie, don't be upset.'

'I'm not,' she gulps. 'I'm happy for you. Hey, stop that crying.'

'Am I doing the right thing?' I blurt out.

'It's too late for that. Let's go. Steve' – she turns to my father – 'come and give your daughter away. Nathan, you stand over there. Mike, check and recheck that you really have got the ring with you. We don't want any more glitches.'

Eventually, I'm right beside Nathan, inwardly thanking my chief bridesmaid for her organisational skills, or should that be her natural bossiness? Nathan is no longer bleeding to death as he claimed, the sole evidence of Jack's contact being a few flecks of dried blood on his upper lip. He keeps squeezing my hand and casting me glances, smirking each time, as if to say, I've got you now. My senses dull a little each time, the scent of fresh flowers becoming less distinct, the cross on the altar less bright, and the colours in the stained-glass windows less brilliant.

'Nathaniel Roderick Cooper,' says the vicar without emotion, 'will you take Tessa Gemima Wilde to be your wife? Will you love her, comfort her, honour and protect her, and forsaking all others, be faithful to her as long as you both shall live?'

I hold my breath during the long pause. I am not sure I can endure the suspense.

'As long as you both shall live,' the vicar repeats to help Nathan out.

'I do.' Nathan's voice is clear and cool.

It's 'I will'. You're supposed to say 'I will', I think as I breathe out and in again, feeling as if I'm about to drown. This ceremony isn't so much about marking the beginning of a new life, as the end.

Why am I getting married anyway? Aren't Nathan and I perfectly happy as we are, cohabiting in unmarried bliss? Well, no actually. I raise my eyes towards the vaulted ceiling at the painted bosses and fans of stone. We've had some terrible rows, and there was that text, a draft that I found on his phone when I just happened to pick it up to hand it back to him the other day. He said it was a joke to wind up one of his mates.

I turn back to him again. Will he love me and comfort me? He'll make love to me. There's a difference, and it isn't an entirely comforting thought. Will he honour and protect me? He protects me, making sure I'm never out after dark alone, but does that have more to do with possession and control than caring? What about being faithful to me for as long as we both shall live?

'Tessa,' the vicar says in a hushed whisper. 'Would you like me to repeat that?'

'I'm sorry,' I say. 'Yes, please. I wasn't concentrating.'

'It isn't the first time a bride has been overwhelmed with nerves at her wedding,' the vicar goes on. He clears his throat. 'Tessa Gemima Wilde, will you take Nathaniel Roderick Cooper to be your husband? Will you love him, comfort him, honour and protect him, and forsaking all others, be faithful to him as long as you both shall live?'

I stare hard into Nathan's eyes, searching for an answer. He cannot hold my gaze, and my heart plummets, dragging all my hopes for the future with it. How can I spend the next ten, twenty, thirty years with this man, if I can't trust him now?

'Tessa?' says the vicar. 'Tessa, Nathan needs an answer...'

Chapter Two

The Princess and the Frog

It's now or never. I look straight ahead between the towering stone columns beyond the altar, aware of the cool stillness inside the church, and the expectant silence from the congregation.

'I will not,' I say weakly, my heart barely beating.

'I beg your pardon,' says the vicar.

'I will not,' I repeat. 'I can't go through with this.' Plucking up all the courage I have left, I turn to face my groom. 'Nathan, I can't marry you.'

'Tessa?' His eyes grow dark and the blood drains from his face, giving him the look of a half-starved vampire, as the implications of what I've just said begin to sink in.

'I'm so sorry,' I go on, when his shock turns to devastation, and the church fills with exclamations of surprise and disbelief.

'Tessa, love?' I'm not sure whether Dad steps up beside me to comfort me or try to persuade me to change my mind, but I can't take it any more, all this love and attention, all this pressure and the overwhelming wave of guilt that I feel when I comprehend the magnitude of Nathan's grief. I've let him down. I've let everyone down, but it doesn't alter a thing. I can't change how I feel. I'm shattered.

With hot tears streaming down my face, I gather up my skirts, preparing to flee, but my wedding shoes with their elegant heels and slippery soles now plastered in mud were never designed for running, and I have to flick them off and pick them up before I can sprint down the aisle, covering the ground faster than Usain Bolt, as people press in on me from both sides, shouting 'Stop her!' and 'Let her go!' I keep running, stumbling into the porch where I bump into the chauffeur, who's having a sneaky puff on a cigarette.

'I'm sorry, I'm so sorry,' I gasp, as he holds one hand out to steady me.

'That was pretty quick – hey, where are you going?'

I don't know and I don't care. I shake him off and keep running on through the churchyard past the dark yew trees and graves and out through the gates onto the street, where I head down the hill until a paralysing attack of cramp forces me to stop with my back to the wall at the end of the iron railings. I take a few gulping breaths of oxygen, filling my aching lungs and clearing my head. What have I done?

'Tessa! Wait for me.' Nathan comes jogging up. Standing in front of me with his head tipped to one side, his face contorts like one of the gargoyles on the church. 'What the hell do you think you're doing?'

'I'm sorry, Nathan,' I keep repeating.

'You're crying.' Nathan's voice softens. 'Oh, come here, my darling.' He holds his arms out to hold me, but I shrink back until I'm squashed against the wall and he's treading on the front of the dress. 'You're all hyped up and emoshe. Why don't you take a few minutes then we'll go back inside? The vicar says he'll give us five.' His tone grows whiny and wheedling. 'All you have to do is say "I do", and it'll be over–'

'It's "I will",' I interrupt. 'How many times do I have to tell you?' But he isn't listening to me.

'My darling, all I want is to make your dreams come true. Come back inside,' he coaxes. 'Let's get that ring on your finger, so I can call you my wife. Think about it. In less than twenty-four hours we'll be on a plane heading far away from here for sunshine, sea and' – there's the briefest hesitation, but it's long enough – 'sand.'

'And sex. You were going to say sex.' I push him away, one shoe in each hand.

'What is it with you? I've bought you a house and a car, for goodness' sake, and the ring cost an arm and a leg. What more can you possibly want?'

'They're material things, and I'm very grateful, but I'm talking about being happy.'

'You were happy enough when I gave you the keys to the car.'

'I know, but a car doesn't last for ever.'

'It'll last a long time if you'd only look after it properly,' Nathan says, reminding me how he hates me leaving it outside the house, not parked in the garage.

'Oh, this isn't about cars,' I say, exasperated. 'It's about you taking the mickey out of every-thing: me, my great-aunt, all this joking about my expectations...' I hesitate, gazing into his eyes.

'Except it isn't a joke, is it?'

'Of course it is,' he says, but I can tell from the way he keeps glancing away from me that he's lying. It shouldn't come as a shock – he's often economical with the truth – but even so I can't quite believe that at the moment when you would have thought he would be baring his soul to try to win me back, he's still lying. It's as if I've been rudely awoken from a cliff-top sleepwalk to find myself on the edge of a precipice with Nathan's hand in the small of my back, about to usher me over.

'I'm not going back,' I say determinedly. 'I'll never be Mrs Cooper.'

Nathan raises his eyebrows, his expression suddenly dark as if a cloud has crossed the sun.

'I said I'm not going back, and I mean it, Nathan. I am not going to marry you.' I try to justify my decision so he can make some sense of it. 'It isn't just about you. It's me.'

'Tessa, this is stupid. You've been planning this day for months. You kept telling me, your friends, your family, the butcher, the baker – everyone – how you couldn't wait to get married.'

'It's difficult to explain, but I got swept up by the romance of it all. In the rush to make the arrangements, choosing the dresses and flowers, I kind of forgot what was important.' I pause, aware of the heave of Nathan's chest and the perspiration leaking from his forehead. 'I love you, but I don't love you enough–'

'Are you doing this out of some kind of petty spite because I won't say all that soft stuff, those three little words "I love you"?' Nathan says.

'I made a mistake, and I'm sorry,' I go on, without answering his question.

'You mean it then?'

'Yes.' I nod and Nathan's face crumples as if my message has finally sunk in. My sadness at what I'm doing to him knows no bounds.

'Let's have an April wedding, you said. You've made a right April Fool of me. You've stitched me up good and proper. You might as well have just killed me,' he sobs, stamping a small circle on the pavement. 'You're a cold, cruel bitch.'

'Nathan,' I cry. 'You'll thank me in the end. You'll find someone else.' If you haven't already, I want to add.

Nathan straightens his shoulders and wipes his eyes with his sleeve.

'How could you dump me at the altar, and in front of everyone?'

'I didn't intend to humiliate you.' I wish I could turn the clock back. I had doubts but I didn't have the courage to express them until it was almost too late, and I bitterly regret it.

Nathan changes tack.

'This change of heart is all down to that prat, Jack Miller, isn't it? Did you know he was back? Did you put him up to this?'

'No, no, no,' I keep repeating as Nathan continues, 'What exactly is he to you?'

'Nothing at all,' I say. 'Not now. You know we went out together for a while years ago. I told you, so why are you asking? We were sixteen, seventeen, then Jack went off to college and it was over.'

'Are you sure about that, Tessa? Katie seems to think you've been a bit more than friends since

39

then. Come on, Tessa. Admit it. It's common knowledge.'

'We were friends,' I confirm angrily, 'until I met you, in fact.' Nathan is desperate, trying to rationalise my decision, perhaps as much for the benefit of the crowd of onlookers that have assembled in the road to watch, as himself. He is the wronged man and I am the scarlet woman.

'You've been seeing him behind my back.'

'How can I have done? He's been out of the country for the past few months.' As I've said, the last time I saw Jack was when Nathan and I celebrated our engagement, after which he disappeared without sending so much as a text or a postcard.

'Don't act the innocent with me.' I notice how Nathan glances towards the crowd when he delivers this line.

'If you think I would do that, then you have a very low opinion of me.' I realise this is something I should have voiced before, Nathan's lack of respect for me as his fiancée.

'The right one though,' Nathan says, raising his voice so he could be heard from the Dog and Duck at one end of town to Lacey's Fine Wines at the other. 'You're a slag!'

'That's enough,' Katie says, stepping in with Mike, the best man.

'Too right,' says my dad, joining them. 'You leave my daughter alone.'

'What makes you think I'd touch her now?' Nathan spits with anger. 'She'd have made a slutty wife anyway.'

'How dare you?' Distraught, I hitch up my

dress and train and walk away, stubbing my toes on the pavement. My dad trots along beside me.

'Let's get a lift back in the Roller, Tessa.'

'I want to walk,' I say snappily. 'Leave me alone, Dad. I need to be on my own.'

'I can go and get the car from home, if you'd prefer to be anonymous.'

'It's a bit late for that, isn't it? I've jilted my groom at the altar and been told I'm a slag in front of my friends, family' – my voice rises to a scream – 'the whole town!'

'Where are you going?' Dad is struggling to keep up. I know he's trying to help, but I can't bear being alone with him because I can foresee the expression on his face, the abject disappointment that I have let him down.

'I don't know and I don't care.' Not stopping to pick up the shoe that I let fall from my fingers, I speed up, tearing along the street, past the terraced houses with their ridiculously small doors, past the police station and the pub, towards the river. The pavement peters out and I continue to follow the road, passing cars and caravans that are crawling in an almost stationary queue on the way to the coast, because it's changeover day at the campsites by the sea.

A couple of children shout and wave from a motorhome, 'Mummy, mummy, look at the lady in the princess dress!'

'It's the Runaway Bride!' yells a man from the car in front.

'The church is that way, my lover,' calls a man who's walking his dog. 'Hey, are you all right?'

I ignore him. I have this crazy idea of running

41

all the way to the beach and throwing myself into the waves, to be swept into oblivion, the epitome of the tragic romantic heroine, but, as I cross the footbridge and jog along the riverbank, I realise that my feet are hurting and it's still a very long way to the sea.

I stumble to a stop and look around me at the rolling green hills, the hazels covered with catkins, and the ancient oak trees in their spring attire. I turn my attention to the River Taly that snakes through the valley, its waters swirling with red Devon clay. There's a piebald horse tethered on the grass on the opposite side, and from somewhere along the bank below my feet, a duck squawks in alarm, drawing me towards it. I look over the edge. At the bottom where the steep slope joins the water, a duck is caught up in a plastic bag among the reeds, something that really shouldn't happen any more because the shops in Talyton St George no longer supply plastic bags for your shopping.

Inwardly ranting at litter louts, I make my way down the bank, sliding down on my bottom and sending the duck flapping a little way onto the water with the plastic attached to its wing. I take one step then two into the river, the bottom of which disappears suddenly beneath my feet, sending me headlong into the water. Gasping and plunging about, I grab for the duck, which makes one last squawk and flies off, leaving the plastic bag behind and me cursing circumstance, just as my dad's face appears over the top of the bank, his face filled with panic.

'Tessa, stop! Stay right where you are.' His feet

appear over the edge of the bank, and along with an avalanche of mud and gravel, he comes sliding down to join me, stopping just at the water's edge, holding out his arms. 'Let's get you out of there.'

'Dad, I don't need rescuing.' I try to rearrange my dripping headdress and veil while the dress floats in a circle around me, making me feel like a giant jellyfish.

'Let me be the judge of that.' Dad's hands are shaking. 'I hate to think what would have happened if I hadn't turned up.'

'What do you mean? I came down the bank to save a duck that was tangled in some rubbish.'

'Where's the duck now?' Dad says pointedly.

'It flew away.'

'Sure.' Dad shrugs. 'There's nothing to be ashamed of, Tessa. This will all have to come out eventually, so you can begin to deal with it.'

'Dad, I helped a duck,' I say, when it dawns on me that we are talking at cross purposes.

'I'll call the surgery – Dr Mackie will be able to prescribe you some pills and arrange some counselling. You need to talk to someone,' Dad continues.

'I wasn't trying to kill myself!' I exclaim.

'You weren't?'

'Of course I wasn't.' I start to shiver with cold. 'This hasn't been the best day of my life, but I have no intention of it being my last.'

'Thank goodness for that.' Dad smiles with relief. 'Come on, love. Let's go home.'

I wade back through the water, dragging the weight of the dress up the bank and along the path, hanging on to my dad's arm.

'I don't want to see anyone,' I say anxiously, but it's too late to worry about that because within five minutes, two dog walkers – the butcher's wife with her Great Dane and my parents' next-door neighbour with their spaniel – and a cyclist have given me strange looks, understandably since I'm walking along in a soaking wet wedding dress and no shoes.

'You can hold your head high. You've done nothing wrong.'

I smile wryly. I never could do any wrong in my father's eyes.

'What about Mum? I'm not sure I'm ready to face her, or the aunts and uncles. I feel so bad about dragging them all this way for nothing.'

'Don't worry about them. They'll get their free lunch.' Dad pats the back of my hand. 'We couldn't cancel the reception at the last minute so your mother and that sister of hers made the executive decision to go ahead with it to give everyone the chance to catch up.'

My parents' home, Kingshead House, is just off Market Square, and combines the advantages of living in the country with those of living in a small town. It used to be a pub and sometimes I fancy that the living room still smells of smoke and ale. I hesitate outside the front door beneath the overhanging porch, which is adorned with wisteria and fluted columns that stick out into the street, creating one of Talyton's glorious bottlenecks where traffic is both two-way and single-file. The sight of the spearmint-green render on the front of the building makes me feel slightly nauseous.

This isn't how it was supposed to be, I muse with a deep pang of regret. I was going to spend tonight at the Barnscote with Nathan in the honeymoon suite, and tomorrow I was flying out to the Maldives. I've been to the south of France, Tenerife and Portugal, but I can't imagine that I'll ever have the chance to go to the Maldives again.

'In we go, Tessa,' Dad says, opening the door.

After a hot shower, a sleep and a few more tears, I curl up on the sofa in the living room, wrapped in my dressing gown and sipping at a glass of warm whisky and lemon. The room is clean and tidy, but not modern. There are various paintings and sculptures by my mother in the room, and framed newspaper clippings and photos of my father as Widow Twanky and one of Cinderella's ugly sisters, with headlines such as 'He's Done It A-Dame' and 'Talyton's Leading Lady'.

Dad turns up with the house phone.

'It's Katie for you,' he says.

I shake my head, but he hands it over anyway.

'Tessa, where have you been? I've left hundreds of messages on your mobile,' Katie says.

'I'm not sure where I left it,' I mumble. Actually, I know exactly where it is: switched off on the windowsill in the shower room. Since checking my mobile after the wedding, I've discovered that Jack left hundreds of text and voicemail messages the night before, and he's been trying to get hold of me ever since.

'Oh, never mind that now. How are you? Do you want me to come over? I can probably leave Nathan in Mike's capable hands – Nathan's had

45

rather a lot of champagne.'

'He went to the reception? I can't believe he did that.'

'He wanted to be with his family and friends. Which is completely understandable,' Katie adds, as if challenging me to contradict her, 'and as the food and drink had already been paid for–'

'He thought he'd celebrate his narrow escape,' I finish for her, recalling the slag and slutty-wife comments.

'Oh, don't be silly. He's gutted. This was supposed to be his wedding night. He looks terrible.' She hesitates. 'I should have been looking after you, but you ran off and Nathan was in such a state. Well, I couldn't leave him, could I?'

I don't see why not, but I don't say anything.

'Katie, don't worry about coming over now. I've got my dad with me, and you've had a long day.'

'If you're absolutely sure.'

'Sure,' I confirm.

'All right, we'll go out for a drink sometime soon. How about tomorrow?'

'I can't face going out. I'll feel like everyone's looking at me.'

'We could stay in, drink some wine...'

'I've got no money,' I say, recalling that I paid for the reception on my credit card because Nathan's replacement card had got lost in the post, or so he claimed at the time.

'I'll bring a bottle.'

I can sense that Katie isn't going to take no for an answer, so I thank her and say she can drop round any time. My parents won't mind – they'll

46

probably be out anyway, knowing their insatiable appetite for social situations: parties, bridge nights, meetings of the Amateur Dramatics Group, who, even though it's April, will soon start writing and rehearsing the next Christmas panto.

Dad returns from the kitchen, bumbling in with eggs on toast and a tea towel over his arm, just like a waiter in a cheap seaside hotel.

'Oh no, thank you, I couldn't eat a thing,' I say when he offers it to me.

'Would you prefer a boiled egg with soldiers?'

'Dad, I'm sorry, I'm not hungry.'

'You need to keep your strength up. It might seem impossible now, but one day we're going to look back on today and have a good laugh.'

'I don't see how,' I groan, but I do take the plate, balance it on my lap and pick up the knife and fork, while my father plumps up the chintz cushions and plonks himself down beside me, the sofa creaking under his weight. 'Is this going to be one of your little talks?'

'It's always good to talk,' Dad says brightly. 'You go first.'

'You didn't approve of him, did you?' I say eventually.

'Nathan? No, I can't pretend that I did. You used to be so sensible, but he turned your head. Oh, I'm not surprised. He could be charming. Look at how he seduced your mother – not in the physical sense,' he adds quickly, eyes twinkling.

I recall Nathan taking me and my parents out to lunch at a rather exclusive fish restaurant on the coast. He won my mother over then and upset my dad by announcing our engagement

47

without asking him for my hand in marriage first. I remember how the conversation went.

'I didn't ask you because you would have said no,' Nathan said. There was a brief pause, during which you could have heard an oyster sliding down someone's throat. 'Steve, I understand because your daughter is a unique and special lady, and I am not worthy of her.' Nathan lifted my hand to show off the ring. He kissed my mother on both cheeks, and shook my dad's hand.

'Have you set the date?' asked my mother.

'As soon as possible,' said Nathan. 'I don't want to risk her changing her mind.'

Was that why he was in such a rush to get married? Was it a premonition? Dad brings me back to the present, saying, 'I know Nathan glowed in your eyes, all shiny and bright, but I always thought there was something of the night about him. Jack obviously thinks so too.'

'I didn't jilt Nathan at the altar on Jack's say-so,' I point out, a little annoyed at the suggestion that I'd actually listen to Jack, an old friend who has become a stranger. The decision was mine, and mine alone.

'But what he said gave you a nudge in the right direction,' Dad persists quizzically.

'My decision had nothing to do with Jack, nothing at all.' I will not admit it to anyone, but Jack's dramatic gesture did endow me with an extra shot of self-confidence, and Nathan's response failed to persuade me against my subsequent course of action.

'Whatever your reasons, Tessa, you did the right thing. Life isn't a rehearsal – it's the real thing.'

After a pause, my dad changes the subject. 'By the way, I rang about the dog. I knew you'd want to find out how he was.'

'You've made me feel really bad now. I forgot.'

'Not surprisingly.'

'How is he?'

'He's up and about. He's got a sore head, but Maz reckons he'll be fine in a couple of days.'

'Has the owner of the dog come forward?'

'Not yet, although you would have thought someone would have noticed by now. He's a big dog to miss. Maz was wondering if he could be the one that's been terrorising other dogs on the Green for the past few months. She's grateful that we caught him, even though we did have to run him over to do it.' Dad grins. 'He looks as if he's been living rough – ruff, get it, ruff, ruff, ruff.'

'Dad, you're barking.' I can't help smiling.

'That's better, Tessa,' he says. 'That's my girl. You know you have to kiss an awful lot of frogs before you find a prince.'

'That's just a fairy tale,' I tell him. 'I've kissed an awful lot of men I thought were princes and they've all turned into frogs.'

'Not all of them, surely. There's Jack.'

'What do you mean, there's Jack?' A flush of indignation spreads up my neck.

'I remember you two were always snogging on the sofa when your mum and I got home from bridge. There was never any sign of him turning into a creature of the amphibious kind.'

'Dad, you are so embarrassing.'

'I always hoped you two might get it together again one day, but I suppose there's absolutely no chance of that now.' I don't need to respond because my father continues, 'It's so out of character for Jack to draw attention to himself. At the club' – he means the Am Dram Group – 'he's very much backstage, as you know.' He pauses. 'By the way, he says he's very sorry.'

'You've spoken to him?' The idea of my father chatting with Jack upsets me – it seems disloyal somehow.

'I spoke to him at the church, as you know, and again when he turned up this afternoon with one of your shoes – you must have dropped it somewhere on your way to the river.' Dad sighs softly. 'He reminded me of Prince Charming bringing the glass slipper for Cinderella after the ball. Listen up.' Dad flaps his hands behind his ears, like a dog in a wind tunnel. 'They're on their way, your mum, your uncles and your aunts.'

I can hear Aunt Fifi's raucous laughter from here.

'Oh no, they're all out of their skulls,' I groan, holding a cushion over my face. 'Dad, will you excuse me? I'm going upstairs.'

'Go on then, love, but I can't promise I'll be able to keep them away. You know what they're like.'

Dad is right. I feel as though I'm lying in state when my mother and aunt turn up in my old room and sit on the end of my bed, one each side, my mum holding a glass of wine and my aunt clutching my teddy bear. They're both in their sixties and there's a strong family resemblance in their sharp, terrier-like features, but my mother dresses in casual tops, jeans and long boots, and lets her ash-grey hair grow long, wearing it pinned on the top of her head, whereas Fifi fights the ageing process by all means possible; keeping her hair short and coloured with blonde and copper highlights, she wears coordinating separates with matching shoes and handbags more suited to mayoral events, weddings – don't remind me of weddings just now – and school prize-givings than everyday activities.

'He is a right charmer,' Mum says, 'and more than comfortably off. Tessa, you would never have wanted for money.' She touches the corner of her eye. 'I thought I might be a grandmother by this time next year.'

'I'm sorry, Mum,' I say, my fingers tightening on the duvet, 'but it's my life. You would have been more disappointed if I'd ended up divorced and a single parent. I couldn't go through with it because I realised we didn't love each other enough to make it last. I loved him' – I bite back a sob '–but he couldn't say the same about me.'

'Men!' my aunt sighs.

'We shouldn't tar them all with the same brush,' Mum says. 'Look at my Steve.'

'I wish you hadn't – looked at him, I mean,' says Fifi with her customary sisterly tact (I'm being ironic). 'Steve's always been as poor as a church mouse.'

'I've always loved him though,' Mum says quietly, 'which is more than you can say.'

'Annie, are you casting aspersions on my marriage?'

'What's this about casting nasturtiums?' Dad waltzes in to join us. 'Oh, I see. Girls' talk. I'll

51

make myself scarce.' He rolls his eyes at me and I shrug back.

'Don't mind us, Steve,' says Fifi. 'We'll all be on our way downstairs in a minute, Tessa included. No buts,' she adds, aiming this at me. 'You mustn't be a party pooper.'

'That's right,' is my father's parting shot. 'Life might fall apart now and again, but the party must go on.'

'Fifi, I've had an extremely traumatic day,' I begin. 'I'd like some time to myself.'

'You must join us. We meet once in a blue moon for the odd hatch, match and despatch. Go on, Tessa, this could be your very last chance to see Great-Auntie Marion before she pops her clogs, and you must have some cake.'

'We brought the rest of the wedding cake back from the reception. I hope you don't mind,' says Mum, 'but it seems such a shame to waste it.'

'You can freeze one tier and use any that's left for making trifle,' says Fifi, getting up and taking my dressing gown down from the hook on the back of the door. 'There you are.'

Fifi and my mum virtually frogmarch me down the stairs and I spend the next few hours feeling like an exhibit at the zoo, being consoled by the extended family and jollied along by my maiden great-aunt over brandy and wedding cake until I'm so sozzled that I can almost believe the day never happened.

'That's right, dear,' Great-Auntie Marion says, patting my knee. 'You mustn't upset yourself any more – you can rest assured that we've all had a wonderful day.'

'I shall die an old maid,' I say with a theatrical flourish of my hand.

'There's nothing wrong in that,' my great-aunt says.

'I'm sorry.' I wish I hadn't mentioned dying either, considering that, according to Fifi, she's supposed to be on her last legs.

'It's all right. I've had a lot of fun as an old maid.' She lowers her voice and, glancing around the room, she adds, 'I've never been attracted to anyone of the male persuasion. It's so much easier to share one's life with women. I've always enjoyed tipping the velvet, if you know what I mean.'

I'm not sure that I do, but I have my suspicions.

'I'm sorry to hear you haven't been well,' I go on, changing the subject.

'Oh, I'm well enough,' she assures me. 'The doctors are keeping me going.'

What a day! The wedding car ran over a dog, the bride jilted the groom at the altar, the wedding cake is to be turned into trifle and my great-aunt has come out of the closet.

It's been the most devastating, yet bizarre day of my life. I wonder how Nathan must be feeling and hope he is all right, and then I start to worry about what I will do next. This morning, I had my future mapped out. Tonight, I have no idea what the future holds.

'You're in demand, Tessa,' my dad says, waking me the next day with hot whisky and lemon and some toast and honey, to make doubly sure that I won't catch a cold after my unplanned dip in the river. 'Are you up to seeing visitors?'

'I really can't face playing happy families again, not just yet,' I sigh, pulling the duvet up as far as my nose. 'Who is it?'

'I've got Nathan in the kitchen with your mum, and Jack on the doorstep. And don't frown at me like that. I had to let Nathan in because I didn't want them coming to blows, and you'll have to come down and speak to him because he refuses to leave without seeing you.'

'I don't want to see either of them. I've had enough of men – you excepting, Dad.'

'If you would just talk to them, they might both leave you in peace,' Dad says optimistically.

'Look, I can't do it.'

'Tess, love, you have to speak to Nathan at least.'

'Is he okay?'

'He's very upset.'

'After what he said to me yesterday in front of all those people?'

'He wants to apologise.'

'But, Dad, it won't make any difference. We're finished and the sooner he realises that the better.' My voice sounds harsh, but it's a cover for how I'm really feeling: pain and regret for not understanding before that Nathan and I don't love each other any more, if we ever did, and guilt, because I blame myself for making such a mess of things. It took Jack Miller to bring me to my senses.

'That's why you should have a word – to make it clear exactly where you stand, otherwise he'll be back here every five minutes, hassling you.' Dad turns and takes the robe off the hook on the back of the bedroom door, flinging it across the bed, where it falls on top of my head. 'Throw that on. I'll deal with Jack. You come down to see Nathan and clear the air.'

I make up my mind. 'Give me five minutes,' I say, and I fling on a pair of jeans and a sweatshirt, the ones I wore the night before the wedding when I was getting ready for the big day. I head downstairs to the kitchen, where Mum leaves Nathan and me alone. We stare at each other, unable to think of anything to say.

'You look pretty wrecked,' I begin, resisting the urge to give him a hug to console him, because I still feel for him as a human being, although he seems rather less than human at the moment. His breath reeks of alcohol and he's wearing the same clothes as the day before but without the tie and jacket.

'I think I'm allowed to,' he says, folding his arms across his chest and leaning against the worktop. He looks from me to the toe of his shoe and back. 'I've come to ask you if you'll reconsider, Tessa. I mean, just look at what you're throwing away.'

'I'm sorry?' I can feel my forehead tighten into a frown.

'I'm sure you are,' he says, misinterpreting what I've said. 'I heard you tried to drown yourself in the river – people saw you walking back through town with your father. You were soaked through.'

'Nathan, it wasn't like that,' I say, but he ignores me.

'You had good reason to want to top yourself, considering you thought you'd never see me again. But you're lucky because here I am, willing to give you another chance. You and me, we're good together.' He means in bed, I muse, as he goes on,

55

'I'm prepared to do anything to give it another go. We can still go on honeymoon, we can get married, a small do at a register office when we get back, just the two of us. How about it?'

'I don't understand why you're so keen on the idea,' I say, confused.

'We make a good team. I need you, Tessa.'

'What for?' I ask suspiciously. 'You don't seem to need me all that much – you don't spend a lot of time with me. I'm not sure you enjoy my company.'

'Of course I do. And I do spend time with you, as much as I can. I'm a busy man, working to make sure you have the best of everything, my darling.'

'I am not your darling,' I snap back. 'And you might be working all hours, but it's me who's been paying the bills recently.'

'I know I've had to ask you to use your credit card, but you know why that is – because my replacement card got lost in the post.'

'Yes, all right.' I hold my hands up, gesturing him to stop talking. 'You've already told me that several times over. When are you going to pay me back?'

'There's no need to worry about that when we're married.' Nathan walks over to me and grabs for my hand, but I step aside, putting the kitchen table between us. 'The investments I've made over the past couple of months haven't yielded a return yet – business is slow – but there'll soon be more cash coming in. I'm sure of that,' he adds in a far less confident tone than I'm used to hearing. His complexion is pale and shiny with sweat, and I'm

56

not sure if he's hungover, or really worrying about his money or lack of it.

Suddenly, I realise with a sinking heart that, although I imagined a clean break from my ex-fiancé, we are going to be entangled financially at least for a while until Nathan pays me back and we sort out whether or not we sell the house, or he buys me out and keeps it.

'Nathan,' I say firmly, 'you have to listen to me.'

'I am listening.'

'Yes, but you're not hearing what I'm saying, which is, I am not going to change my mind. I am not going to marry you, ever.'

'And that's your final decision?'

'My final decision,' I repeat for him.

'You'll regret this when I'm a multimillionaire,' Nathan growls.

'No regrets,' I say, as yet another realisation hits me right between the eyes: Nathan's frequent enquiries as to the state of Great-Auntie Marion's health and the size of my potential inheritance. (I caught him looking up land prices in Wales once.) 'I would never think of marrying anyone for their money,' I say coldly. 'Now, go away and don't come back.' Taking control, I direct him out through the back door, so there's no risk of him running into Jack if he's still at the front, but although I put on a show of emotional strength for Nathan, I am in tears when I sit down at the kitchen table, my head in my hands, because I got him so wrong. I thought he was marrying me for love.

Chapter Three

Hair of the Dog

I had a lucky escape. I have to keep reminding myself of that. I have plenty of support from friends and family, especially my dad, and I'm grateful, although I admit I don't always appreciate them.

Aunt Fifi has taken it upon herself to take me out today for a change of scene, and she's gone overboard with the nautical theme, wearing a navy dress printed with a yacht design, a jacket with an anchor brooch, a captain's cap, white deck shoes and matching handbag.

'Where's the boat?' I ask her, teasing her lightly when I join her outside my parents' house in my uncle's car after lunch.

'Oh, Tessa, I'm glad you've held on to your sense of humour.'

'I'm hanging on to it by my finger tips,' I say wryly. It's been three weeks since the wedding and I'm feeling worse, not better, more angry now than sad, especially having seen Nathan out and about in Talyton with a deep natural tan from where he soaked up the sun with Mike on what should have been our honeymoon. I glance down at my leggings, tunic-style top and flat sandals. 'Should I have dressed up? I can go back and change.'

'You'll do, though I don't understand young

people today – one's appearance should be a matter of pride.' Fifi sighs with regret. 'Mind you, when you have youth and beauty on your side, I suppose the clothes don't matter in quite the same way.'

'Well, you look great,' I say to cheer her up. She smiles briefly and changes the subject as a car horn sounds behind us.

'Dear niece, I'm afraid your wedding day will go down in the annals of family history. Who would have thought there would be fighting in church and blood spilled at the altar?'

'There wasn't all that much blood,' I point out, not wishing to be reminded but aware that Fifi's desire for a full inquest will have to be endured.

'So it turns out that Nathan was too good to be true.' Before I can ask her how she knows, she goes on, 'Annie told me about the money and, who knows, after that deceit, it wouldn't be impossible to imagine that he was two-timing you as well.'

'You said you liked him.'

'I did, but he misled us all, including poor old you.'

He certainly deceived me, I think. I discovered the full extent of his lies the day after the wedding.

'Your mother adored him and I thought he was the bee's knees. Your father was the only person to have any doubts.'

'He didn't say anything.' I shut my mouth quickly, recalling how Dad did try, but I didn't take it too well. 'Aren't you going to drive on?' I say above the cacophony of horns sounding from the cars queued up behind us, and the Co-op lorry

59

coming towards us. 'There are people waiting.'

'It's better that you've dealt with it now rather than go through a messy divorce. I hear he's left you in a bit of a pickle,' Fifi says, ignoring them. 'Tessa, don't glare at me like that.' She puts the car in gear and pulls out sharply. 'A problem aired is a problem shared. Your mum isn't the only person in the world who's talking about it. I've met with the WI and the local council, and you're currently top of the agenda – I don't mean officially. I'm referring to the latest gossip.'

'I hate that,' I say, grabbing hold of the seat as my aunt brakes to avoid an elderly woman who's struggling to cross the road with a heavily laden shopping trolley.

'Everyone will forget as soon as the next scandal comes along.'

So it's classed as a scandal now, I muse.

'Your face is a picture. I'm pulling your leg, metaphorically speaking.'

'I'd rather you concentrated on the road,' I say firmly.

'I'm trying to cheer you up, hence today's awfully big adventure.'

'This isn't going to take too long, is it?' I say anxiously. 'Only I've got so much to do.' I have a list ranging from contacting the bank manager at the branch in Talyton St George to arrange an overdraft to rewriting my CV. Thanks to Nathan, I need money. I need a job, and fast.

'Trust me. This is all to your advantage.'

'So, where are we going on this magical mystery tour?'

'You'll have to wait and see.' My aunt drives us

60

past the garden centre on Stoney Lane.

'I thought you might be going to ask my opinion on the latest fashions,' I say.

'Well, you weren't much use the last time. You have absolutely no style, Tessa.'

I bite my lip, suppressing a chuckle at the memory of standing in the country clothing section of the garden centre that she owns with my uncle, Fifi holding pleated skirts and khaki fleeces up against me. Clogs with ladybirds on them, chintz blouses and quilted jackets are not my cup of tea, but they must suit the clientele – the place is a goldmine.

'Oh, I hope you're as excited about this as I am,' my aunt goes on.

'I could be if only you'd tell me where we're going.' I'm smiling now, the most light-hearted I've felt since I discovered the extent of my debts. Nathan and I bought a house with a mortgage the size of the EU debt mountain, because although he said he had the funds to buy it outright, he wanted to keep them as liquid assets to invest in his business. Nathan insisted that both our names were on the paperwork, a touching gesture that made sure I had a vested interest in our home. It transpires that he cancelled our direct debit to the building society within a month of us moving in, and because he didn't have any funds in the first place, guess who is liable for the debt? It's me. And who not only paid for the wedding reception and all those bottles of bubbly that our guests drank their way through in my absence, but for the honeymoon too? Yes, me again.

When I returned to the house to collect some

61

clothes after the wedding, I discovered more unpaid bills, along with demands for immediate repayment with interest, and another day later, the bailiffs came and seized my lovely car because Nathan had failed to keep up with the hire purchase payments.

We were going to have a dog and start trying for a baby. I wonder if he meant that now, if they weren't all lies too.

'How is it going, living with your mum and dad?' Fifi asks as she drives along the country road out of Talyton St George. She turns into a long, narrow lane with passing places and has to pull in for a herd of about sixty black and white dairy cows on their way out from milking at one of the farms nearby. As they pass, one stops to investigate the bonnet of my uncle's new Volvo, leaving the damp imprint of her nose. Two more pause to raise their tails and deliver spattering pools of dung beside the wing.

I'm a boomerang kid, winging my way back to live with my parents at the age of twenty-eight. A week ago, I had my own house. Now, I have a massive debt to repay and nowhere else to go.

'I'm grateful to them for providing a roof over my head, but they're driving me mad,' I say.

'I thought it was supposed to be the other way round.'

'I'm not in the mood for socialising. They're always out in the evenings – which does mean that I get the television to myself – and then I lie awake wondering when they're going to come home. Inevitably, just as I've fallen asleep, they come falling through the front door, and the following morning when I'm about to hit the snooze button on the alarm, they're up and about, laughing and squealing, and fighting over the last painkiller, and who puts the coffee on.'

'Can't you move back into your house – temporarily, I mean? I don't see why Nathan should have the monopoly on it.'

'Until it's repossessed?' I bite my lip. It's a lovely house, a family home with five bedrooms, a study and landscaped gardens on the new estate in Talyton St George.

'You have as much right to live there as he does.'

'It triggers too many memories.' I have been back three times to collect my belongings, and each time I felt faint and sick. The house is a symbol of Nathan's deception.

'I think we might be able to help each other out, Tessa,' Fifi says.

'That's very kind of you, but I do have a plan.'

'Which is?'

'To respond to every ad for vet nursing vacancies and hope someone offers me a job as soon as possible.'

'But we don't want you moving out of the area again,' Fifi says, rather crestfallen.

'I'm not tied to Talyton St George any more. The house will be sold and that will be it.'

'What about your dad? He was delighted when you came back to live here.'

'From the way Dad carried on, anyone would have thought I'd been living on the other side of the world. I wasn't far away, twenty miles at the most. He does exaggerate sometimes.'

'Most times,' Fifi smiles.

'If I move out of the area, I can come back to join everyone for Christmas, for the Country Show, for the tar barrels and the wassailing.' Talyton St George has retained so many quaint – some would say bizarre – traditions.

'Neither of the practices here have got any vacancies. I've asked,' my aunt says. 'It's always useful to have contacts. Maz and Emma are such lovely people – Maz is committed to animal welfare, she's been very supportive of Talyton Animal Rescue.'

Aunt Fifi is chairperson of the local charity and has been since I can remember. I used to help out when I was younger, and that's what really inspired me to go into vet nursing.

'Otter House vets have two nurses already, and Talyton Manor vets, the large-animal practice, don't seem to have need of one at all. I tried to convince Alex Fox-Gifford, the principal, that he did, but he wasn't having any of it,' Fifi says, flicking the left-hand indicator on the car, and turning right into a narrow lane that I recognise from my volunteering days back when I was in my teens. It's a particularly narrow and twisty lane which peters out into no more than a farm track where the hedgerows press in on each side and overhanging tree branches catch at the car's paintwork.

'I thought I'd show you our new rescue centre,' Fifi says. 'I wanted to bring you here before, but–'

I cringe as I hear the chassis catch and scrape along the grassy ridge that runs along the middle of the rutted track.

'We're going to have to do something about the access,' Aunt Fifi comments as I keep a grip on my seatbelt and bite my lip to stop myself criticising the speed of her driving. 'The builder's truck is making it so much worse, especially when it rains, but it's a pity to have to spend money on asphalt when we could use it on refurbishing the rest of the kennels.' My aunt slams the brakes on as a rabbit crosses our path, and drives on more circumspectly until the track ends and a tall hedge of dog rose, hazel and brambles rises up in front of us, reminiscent of the impenetrable wall of thorns that grew up around the castle in the fairy tale of 'Sleeping Beauty'.

Fifi parks alongside a white truck loaded with pieces of wood and pots of paint, and printed with the logo, *DJ Appleyard: Quality Builder; for all your requirements* along the side. Emerging from the car, my aunt takes a call on her mobile from someone she knows on the local council, promises she'll phone them back and shows me a ragged gap in the hedge. Stepping through to the other side, I find I don't recognise the place even though I've been here before many years ago, and it's quite a shock to me.

To our left is the wood, Longdogs Copse, and to the right is a small paddock which is completely overgrown with weeds: docks, rosettes of ragwort and nettles. Beyond, there are some outbuildings, a barn open at one end, a shed, a row of cat pens and what we used to call the new kennel block. In the middle of the open space between them is the main building on the site. Buttercross Cottage, a quaint cob and thatch house with diamond leaded windows and flowers around the outside, has gone, destroyed in a fire one night three or four years ago. In its place stands an unprepossessing modern box of a bungalow with large windows, slate-grey render and a brown front door.

'That's a bit of an eyesore,' I observe.

Aunt Fifi has the grace to look a little embarrassed. I suspect she had something to do with it. She has influence, you see, she knows exactly how to run and therefore to manipulate the systems set up to maintain a fair and democratic community. If she isn't on one of the committees in Talyton St George, she'll have a crony who is.

'It's one of those things. Sometimes, I wonder if this place is cursed.' Fifi pauses. 'Gloria died in the fire, taking some of the animals with her. Alex Fox-Gifford, the vet, ended up in hospital. It was a terrible disaster.'

I remember Gloria Brambles, a strange old woman with pale skin, white hair, fingerless gloves, and a piece of amber containing some kind of insect hanging around her neck, both insect and owner trapped by circumstance. I used to help her out as a teenager when she ran the Sanctuary, supported by the volunteers and funds from Talyton Animal Rescue. My parents refused to allow me a pet because of their busy lifestyles and the cost, and Gloria took pity on me. She taught me a lot.

After Gloria's husband died, she began to shun the company of humans and turn towards the animals. She collected them compulsively and, because she couldn't bear to give them up for rehoming, she either invented various ailments for them, claiming they were too sick to go to new homes, as if she had Munchausen's by proxy, or she listed criteria for potential new owners that they couldn't possibly meet. She fell out with the volunteers, suggesting that they didn't know what they were talking about when it came to cleaning out kennels and walking dogs, and my Aunt Fifi stopped visiting altogether.

Ultimately, Gloria loved the animals too much. The Sanctuary fell into disrepair and the animals sat and suffered, until Maz tackled her about the welfare of the animals in her care. The night before Fifi and a party of volunteers were due to help remove some of the animals from the property, Gloria set fire to the cottage. She is supposed to have said that if she couldn't have the animals, then no one else could either.

I shiver at the sudden chill in the air.

Fifi says that she should have realised Gloria was too frail and infirm to look after the animals on her own. She should have insisted on the volunteers going in, or called an animal welfare inspector like Jack, or Andrea from the RSPCA, or arranged for a regular visit by a vet, but it was Gloria's property, so what could she do?

'Gloria didn't leave a will, which is odd, considering that her husband was a solicitor and she was an educated and intelligent woman. Everything went to the state when it could have come to us.' By 'us', my aunt is referring to Talyton Animal Rescue.

'I think she lost the plot,' I say.

'The people who bought the land after the fire were given planning permission for an avant-garde steel-framed house. We had reservations on the Council, but with the site being so far out of Talyton itself, who was going to worry about it? It's good to move with the times, and who was to say that this building wouldn't be admired as a valuable part of Talyton's heritage years into the future?'

'Where is it, though?' I say wryly. 'Where is this amazing building?'

'Unfortunately, the family failed to complete the build. They had some problems – a divorce, I believe – and ran out of money.' Fifi smiles. 'And that's where Talyton Animal Rescue has been able to step in. Do you recall the author Chastity Stubbs?'

'The romance writer?'

'Talyton's answer to Barbara Cartland,' says Aunt Fifi.

'I remember trying to read one of her novels. Dad used to leave them in the bathroom as reading material. She was pretty prolific, wasn't she?'

'She published four works a year from the time she was twenty-eight – the same age as you are now – to her seventy-eighth birthday when she put down her pen and retired.'

I wonder briefly if I should follow her lead, but I'm too cynical about love and the happily-ever-after to go there again. There will be no more silly romances for me. I recall the book was about a heroine who was as thick and wet as Dartmoor mizzle and one of those impossibly handsome yet arrogant alpha-male heroes who you would like to hit, not hit on.

'What has Chastity Stubbs got to do with the Sanctuary?' I ask.

'Although you didn't think much of her books, others loved them and she made a fortune from her writing. Sadly, she died recently in a nursing home down at Talymouth. She never married, maybe because of all that romance in her life. She never had children because, in spite of the hot sex–'

'Aunt Fifi.' I admonish her with a grin.

'She was ahead of her time. Some of the love scenes were rather steamy. She didn't stop at the bedroom door, which is probably why she was so successful. Anyway, Chastity left her estate to Talyton Animal Rescue with the express wish of re-establishing a rescue centre here for the benefit of all creatures, great and small. Although' – Fifi smiles again – 'we'll have to draw the line if anyone turns up with a giraffe or an elephant.'

'I didn't know about the legacy.'

'Tessa, I'm sure I've mentioned it to you, although you've more than likely forgotten. You have been otherwise occupied for the past few months.'

'Please don't remind me of what a fool I've been.'

'We've all made fools of ourselves from time to time. And talking of fools, where is DJ?' She hesitates, looking around. 'When we took him on as our builder, it was because he promised me faithfully that he'd complete the project – finishing off the house, renovating the kennels and constructing two stables in the end of the existing barn – by the end of April. Look at it. It's the beginning of May and it's ... it's a building site.'

We walk between a cement mixer and a stack of bags of builders' sand, two of them torn and spilling their contents onto the wasteland that surrounds the bungalow. Fifi stops, pushes the front door open and ushers me through.

'I should have known better, of course – I've never heard anyone say he's finished work for them on schedule.'

'Lastminute.com,' I say, smiling. I've seen DJ around Talyton before, working on extensions and roofing jobs.

'But he was cheap, and available, or so he said at the time.'

'Have you come to check up on me again?' A short, swarthy, dark-haired man in his fifties and dressed in paint-spattered overalls appears around the doorway – there is no door – at the far end of the narrow hallway. He winks several times as he approaches, paintbrush in one hand, mug in the other, but I don't read anything into it – it's a nervous tic.

'I thought your son was coming to help you today,' Fifi says.

'Oh, he'll be here tomorrow. Something's come up. He's gone to price another job.' DJ grins. I think he's enjoying winding her up.

'When are you going to finish the bungalow and be ready to make a start on the kennels? We have animals waiting. Our foster homes are full to overflowing. How long is this going to take?' Fifi asks, sounding strangely rattled. She's used to people taking orders without argument.

'As I've said before, Fifi, it'll take as long as it

takes, no less and no longer.'

'That isn't good enough. I notice the radiators haven't been fitted yet.'

'They'll be done tomorrow.'

'Tomorrow,' Fifi echoes.

'Tomorrow,' DJ repeats, as though he believes that if he says it often enough, it will become reality.

'I'm going to show my niece around,' Fifi says.

'Mind the paint,' DJ warns her. 'It's wet in places.' And he winks again, deliberately I think this time, as we pass him and head into the room beyond.

'What do you think, Tessa?' my aunt asks as she peruses the walls, which are painted a dull shade of mushroom. Not waiting for me to form an opinion, she goes on, 'You can use it as either the living room or main bedroom. We thought the room at the front would make a useful office combined with a reception area. There's another room slightly smaller than this one, a kitchenette and a bathroom. It's basic, but there's everything there that you need.'

'I suppose you'll need someone living on site.'

'That's the idea.' Fifi reaches out for my arm. 'So, if you can beg, steal or borrow a bed and a microwave, you can move in tomorrow.'

'Me?'

'Yes, you. Oh, darling, why did you think I brought you here? I can't find you a job as a vet nurse, so I'm offering you the position of manager in return for rent-free accommodation, the use of a vehicle and a salary of...' She mentions a figure that's much less than I could earn if I

71

returned to practice. 'I can't offer you any more than that. Chastity was a generous benefactor, but the money has to be eked out.'

'It's such a shock.'

'I can't say that it's the answer to all your prayers. It won't be much help with your financial position, but it does solve the immediate problem of finding somewhere to live.'

'Are you sure?' I gaze around at the house. It isn't up to much, that's true, but it's close to home and, as my dad would say, beggars can't be choosers. Finding new homes for stray and unwanted animals would be a fresh challenge, something different and potentially very rewarding, and it would give me the time and space to decide what to do in the longer term, but I hope this isn't special treatment. 'I don't want you offering me this opportunity because you feel sorry for me,' I continue.

'Tessa, you would be doing me and Talyton Animal Rescue a great favour. You're a qualified nurse, you care for animals and their welfare, and you're good with people.'

'I'm not so good at reading character,' I say ruefully.

'Some people are more devious than others,' Fifi says, and I wonder if she's thinking of Nathan or herself. 'If you can run a vet practice, you can organise the Sanctuary.'

'I haven't run a practice single-handed before.' I've dealt with difficult clients, grappled with smoking autoclaves and kept trainee vet nurses in line. I've babysat vets too, especially the ones straight out of vet school, some of whom didn't appear to know one end of a syringe from the other.

'You'll need to keep the volunteers in order and raise funds to keep the centre going.'

'I thought the committee did the fund-raising?'

'Oh, we do, but we'll need a lot of input from you. There'll be an open day and a ball this summer. That's what we've decided on so far.'

'It sounds fun.' It will keep my mind off Nathan and my money worries. It will give me a focus.

'I have a whole army of volunteers willing and able to help you out, and it's a year's contract, so you'll be secure for a while.'

'A year?' I say slowly. 'I'm not sure.' I start to backtrack as doubts come scuttling like rats into my mind. 'I haven't got any experience of running a rescue centre. I don't want to let you down.'

'I'm certain you wouldn't. Tessa, do think about it. You don't have to give me an answer now. Tomorrow morning will do.'

'That isn't much time.'

'We have animals waiting to move in. Our foster homes, as I said to DJ, are full. Other local rescue charities are chock-a-block. We are desperate. In fact, for the first time, we're thinking the unthinkable.' Fifi looks at me, her eyes growing bright with tears. 'We'll have to choose between them. Imagine that.'

'It won't come to that.' I rest my arm around my aunt's narrow shoulders. 'No vet I know will agree to put down a healthy animal, unless they're a danger to people or other animals.'

'It could happen,' my aunt insists. 'In all the years I've been on the committee, it's never been this bad. Look at the dog you took to Otter House.'

'What about him?' I feel a frisson of panic. 'I thought he was fully recovered and ready to go home.'

'He hasn't got a home, he's fit and healthy, and he's stuck at Otter House.'

'It's been three weeks.' Guilty for thinking of my own troubles and forgetting about the dog, I recall the soft expression in his eyes and the beat of his tail against the front of the cage when I dropped in to the vet's to see how he was a few days after the wedding.

'Wendy, our foster carer, offered to take him in, even though she has her full complement, a complete pack, but he tried to kill them all, so Maz had to take him back. She's rung round all the other rescue charities and put him on their waiting lists, but for now, he's...' Fifi pauses. 'Well, I suppose you'd call it kennel-blocking, taking up a bed that could be used for a sick patient. With that and his history of being a danger to other animals, I'm worried he's going to end up on Death Row, or the equivalent. Apparently, he's a strange dog. He's two or three years old at a guess, and because he's a Staffordshire bull terrier type, he'll be hard to rehome because of their association with pit bulls and other fighting dogs. You see, Tessa, that's where you come in. That poor dog needs your help – and he isn't the only one.'

'Look, this is all a bit sudden,' I say, torn. 'I do need time to think, Fifi. I can't give you a decision tomorrow – give me a few days.'

'I know you'll want to talk it through with other people, but I could really do with an answer as soon as possible.'

'I'll have a chat with Mum and Dad,' I tell her, but by the time Fifi's dropped me home after some dinner with my uncle at their house, my parents have gone out for a meal with friends.

I wait up for them for a while, making lists of the pros and cons of taking up Fifi's offer, and keen to share my news, but they don't arrive back until after midnight, by which time I've just fallen asleep. My mother decides to make pancakes with golden syrup, and my father knocks on my door to announce the fact.

'Come and join us, Tessa,' he shouts. 'No more hiding in your room like a princess in the tower.'

'Dad, you've woken me up,' I say, pulling the duvet up over my head. Suddenly, the Sanctuary appeals to me, a rural and isolated spot where I can retreat and find some space to think, somewhere that gives me a reason to get up in the mornings, somewhere I can make a difference, but I do join my parents in the kitchen over pancakes and a nightcap and discuss my options.

'I don't know what you were doing anyway, giving up your job like that.' Mum pours herself a second small brandy. She's changed into a white robe acquired from a stay in a hotel and pink fluffy moccasin slippers.

'I didn't give it up – it gave me up.' It was maternity cover, so I knew it wasn't going to last, although in my optimism I imagined there would be some way I could stay on.

'I'm referring to the job before that one, Tessa,'

Mum says sternly while Dad tosses the last pancake and fails to catch it, an action that results in loud guffaws of laughter and much clowning around with a bowl of suds and a mop. His laughter is infectious, and soon I'm laughing too, which gives me welcome respite from my preoccupations with money, or lack or it, and the uncertainty over my future.

I need a roof over my head and to work, but should I stay with what I know, vet nursing, or take a chance and accept the position at the Sanctuary?

Chapter Four

Horses for Courses

The next day, Saturday, I call Katie and arrange to meet for a drink in the afternoon.

'Where are you off to, Tess?' Dad asks, looking up from the paper as I grab my shoes and a bag. When I explain, he says, as always, 'Have fun, Princess. Make sure you're back by midnight–'

'Or else you'll turn into a pumpkin,' I finish for him. Smiling, I kiss him and go, meeting Katie outside the house. We stroll through town down to the river to make our way to the pub, Katie in full make-up, skimpy top and leggings while I'm in an oversized T-shirt and jeans. After Katie's given me a dressing-down for not dressing up, I tell her about Fifi's offer.

'You aren't going to take her up on it?' Katie says. 'You'd be mad to. You'll end up a glorified kennel maid and general dogsbody. A full-time position with part-time pay: that sounds to me like someone's taking advantage.'

'Talyton Animal Rescue's a charity.'

'That's no reason not to pay a living wage.'

'There's accommodation and use of a van.'

'A van, after that gorgeous Mini that Nathan gave you.' Katie chuckles. 'How cool is that? Not!'

'And I'd be working with animals, which I love,' I go on, as we're crossing the bridge that carries the traffic from Talyton St George towards the coast. Renamed the Centurion Crossing, it's the recreation of the old stone bridge that was washed away in Talyton's great flood of three years ago. We walk down the slope on the far side and join the path that runs along the riverbank.

'I suppose there's no harm in saying you'll do it for a while until something better turns up,' Katie says eventually.

'Ah, there's a hitch. Fifi wants me to sign up for a year minimum, so I can get the new centre off the ground. It isn't all about the animals. We'll be organising campaigns to raise money and attract volunteers too.'

'You said "we" as if it's a foregone conclusion and you've already made up your mind,' Katie says, raising one eyebrow.

'I've promised her my answer tomorrow.'

We make our way over the open field to the old railway line and clamber over the stile into the next field, where we come across a horse grazing beside the footpath. She's tethered to a post with a rope and chain in full sun with no shelter or shade, and has mown a circle of grass down to bare earth. As we move closer, I realise that she's more of a pony than a horse, a piebald cob, all black and white patches, with a long mane and an unbelievably thick tail that touches the ground. When she catches sight of me and Katie, she lifts her head and peers out through her forelock.

'She could do with some layers in that fringe,' Katie observes dryly.

'And a decent pedicure,' I go on, noticing how her stripy black and white hooves are long and ragged like an old man's fingernails. Her legs are swollen and some of the feather is coming off, and I can see her ribs and bony haunches. The lack of muscle and fat has given her a ewe neck that looks as if it's been set on upside down. I take another step closer and she backs away, turning her bottom towards us.

'I can't see any water,' I say.

Katie shrugs. 'I expect her owners come and give her a drink now and then.'

'She's a horse. She should have access to fresh water at all times.'

'Well, you know best, Tessa. I can hardly tell one end of a horse from another.'

'One end bites, the other one kicks,' I say, smiling. I grow serious once more. 'I'm going to have to report this.'

'Are you sure? It isn't really any of our business.'

'I can't leave it, can I? She looks as if she's being neglected.' I pull my mobile from my pocket, make an internet search for the number of the animal welfare officer, and I'm waiting for someone to answer when Katie gives me a sharp nudge. I look towards the stile where a large man, brandishing a stick, and a teenage boy in a cap are climbing over, yelling curses in our direction.

'I don't like the look of this,' says Katie. 'Let's get out of here.'

'It's the Maddockses.' I cut the call. Frank Maddocks, his girlfriend and his son live in a mobile home on a couple of acres of land behind Overdown Farmers, the wholesalers on Talyton St George's modest industrial estate. He's a wheeler-

79

dealer, poacher and smallholder, and I wouldn't like to meet him alone on a dark night.

'Leave my property alone!' Mr Maddocks shouts. He's about forty years old, dark-haired and at least six foot three. He stops right in front of me so I can see the pockmarks in his unshaven cheeks, and pounds the earth with his stick. 'What the bloody hell do you think you're doing?' His belly trembles beneath his check shirt and his jeans hang halfway down his thighs, the fabric ruckled over the tops of his brown work-boots. 'Too close and she'll give you both barrels up the arse.'

'We were just passing by, weren't we?' Katie tugs at my sleeve. 'Come on, Tessa.'

I stand my ground. 'She has no water,' I point out. 'How would you feel if you had nothing to drink?'

'She had a bucket last night. Some little toerag must have nicked it.' As Mr Maddocks approaches the pony, she puts her ears back and reverses until there's no slack left in the tether.

'She's in pretty poor condition too,' I persist, even though Katie has transferred her grip to my arm and is trying to drag me away. 'You can see her bones.'

'That's because you're used to seeing fat ponies. This' – he raises his stick and the mare flinches – 'is a working pony, not a field ornament, and don't tell me she has nothing to eat. There's grass everywhere.' He laughs, mocking me.

'She can't reach it,' I say, shaking Katie off.

'That's because of the tether,' he says sarcastically.

I'm just about at the end of my tether with him, I think, trying to work out how to deal with him.

'And I'm here now to move her along to a fresh piece,' he goes on.

'What about her legs?'

'That's a touch of mud fever, and she's under treatment for it – I use my own mixture, castor oil and zinc quite regular.' Mr Maddocks stares at me through narrow, deep-set eyes that remind me of a Dobermann and my heart thuds faster. I don't like him. He's a bully.

'I can report you, you know,' I say, aware that Katie is casting me warning glances as if to say, Shut up for goodness' sake.

'But you won't, will you' – he moves so close I can feel his spit on my face – 'because for a start you know you haven't a leg to stand on, and secondly' – he lowers his voice to a whisper – 'I know where you live, my darlin'. Your father's that poncey bloke, the weird one who makes a living dressing up as a woman.' He chuckles, revealing his stained and broken teeth. 'Hardly mutton dressed as lamb, is he? Ram dressed as mutton, more like. Anyway, you mind yourself.'

'Katie, did you hear that?' I look around wildly to find Katie backing away along the footpath. 'He's threatening me.'

'I'm doing nothing of the sort. I'm a peaceful man, a gentle giant.' Mr Maddocks gives his son a nudge with the end of his stick. 'I wouldn't hurt a fly. That's right, isn't it, Lewis?'

'Yeah, that's right,' the boy mumbles, keeping his hands in the pockets of his shorts and his eyes averted.

'Please, Tessa,' Katie begs. 'Let's just go.' As we walk away, she says, 'You aren't going to call animal welfare now – if you do, he'll know exactly who dobbed him in.'

'I can't just leave it. What if the pony died because we turned a blind eye? I could never forgive myself.'

'Well, at least wait until we're at the pub. I don't know about you, but I could do with a drink.'

At the pub, Katie heads for the bar to buy two white wines while I sit outside in the beer garden at one of the picnic tables and make the call to the local animal welfare officer. There's an emergency number because it's after midday on a Saturday, and as I start to leave a message so they can call me back later, a familiar voice cuts in. It's Jack Miller.

My instinct is to cut the call because he is the last person I wish to speak to, but the pony's welfare is at stake so I have no option but to continue, keeping my emotions in check and suppressing my rising resentment as memories of my wedding day come flooding back. Jack might have saved me from making a terrible mistake, but it doesn't make me feel any better about what he did. He had no right.

'Tess,' he says. 'It's good to hear from you.'

'This isn't a social call,' I say sharply. 'I'm phoning about a pony that's tethered down by the river.' I pause. 'I didn't think you worked for animal welfare any more. I thought you'd resigned.'

'I was lucky – when I came back from my travels I walked straight back into a job with Talyton Animal Rescue.'

'Does my aunt know anything about this?' I ask, suspicious now that Fifi has been up to her usual tricks, interfering in other people's lives.

'You can't be serious,' Jack says. 'Can fish swim? She's chair of the committee that appointed me. Not only that, your aunt knows everything that goes on around here.'

So why didn't she mention it to me? Not for the first time, I wonder about Fifi. She must have known that if I knew about Jack working for Talyton Animal Rescue, I would have turned her down flat.

'It's a bit of a sideways step, but I wanted to stay in the area.' Jack hesitates. 'Is this about the piebald mare, the black and white one?'

'I do know my horse colours,' I say, a fraction insulted.

'Of course you do. I didn't mean anything...' Jack's voice, familiar yet strange, smooth yet bittersweet like molten dark chocolate, trails off. 'Frank Maddocks keeps moving her on. The cricket club is up in arms because of the hoof-prints all over the pitch. I'm on my way home, so I'll come straight down to have a look. Are you with the pony now?'

'I didn't hang around.' In spite of my feelings for Jack, I warn him to be careful. 'Mr Maddocks was quite intimidating. I'm at the pub, the Taly-mill Inn.'

'I'll meet you there asap, Tess.'

Tess? He's always called me Tess, but the shortening of my name seems an overly intimate gesture from an old friend from whom I've become estranged.

'It's Tessa,' I say, the skin across the nape of my neck prickling with irritation.

'Okay, I'm sorry,' Jack says quietly. 'I'd be very grateful if you could show me where the pony is, or was. Frank is more than likely moving her on as we speak.'

Bother, I think, gazing dumbly at the screen as it turns blank. Events are conspiring against me.

'Are you all right?' Katie slides a glass of white wine across the table and sits down opposite me.

'That was Jack. Aunt Fifi rather conveniently omitted to tell me that he's working for Talyton Animal Rescue.' I take a sip of wine. 'She's made the decision for me. There's no way that I can move in to the Sanctuary now.'

'Don't be ridiculous. You can't turn down a job because of a man, particularly Jack. What's more, you can't keep going around looking like a candidate for *Ten Years Younger*. You really have to pull yourself together,' Katie says, stopping abruptly.

'Katie, what do you mean?' My fingers tighten on the stem of the wine glass.

'Oh, I'm sorry, it wasn't meant to sound like criticism. What I meant was that it's time you thought about moving on with your life.'

'It's been three weeks since the wedding, that's all,' I say, upset at her apparent lack of sympathy. 'Don't you understand? I've been through three weeks of hell.'

'All right, all right,' Katie soothes, touching my hand. 'I understand.'

I look at her, really look at her, and wonder if she has a clue.

'You need cheering up, Tessa. Let me get you another drink,' she goes on.

I glance down at my glass. It's empty.

'Thank you,' I say, smiling weakly.

'That's better. Don't let the bastards grind you down. Come on, you can relax now.'

'Not quite. Jack's meeting me here so I can show him where the pony's tethered,' I blurt out.

Katie picks up my glass. 'I'll get you that drink.'

When Jack turns up at the pub, Katie decides to stay behind while I show him where the pony is tethered. We walk in silence, the slight twitch of the muscle in his cheek betraying his awkwardness in my presence. Since I last saw him at the church, he's had a haircut and gone back to the clean-shaven look, and although I try to avoid looking at him at all, I do notice that he's wearing a green polo-shirt with the Talyton Animal Rescue logo, a pair of khaki cargo trousers and boots with odd laces, one black, one tan.

To my relief, there's no sign of Mr Maddocks and his son, but, as if to make me out a liar, someone has moved the post so the pony is grazing on a fresh area of grass with a bucket of water within reach.

'She was tethered over there.' I point out the bare patch of ground. 'I suppose you're going to say there's nothing you can do.'

'Let's not be too hasty,' Jack says. 'It doesn't do to rush in.'

There's something in the tone of his voice that makes me wonder, as I watch him take several photos of the mare and her environment from a distance, if he could be referring to me and the way I rushed into my relationship with Nathan. As soon as I accepted Nathan's proposal, I was bowled over and bowled along like a tumbleweed in the desert, unable to stop, to get a grip. Buying the dress, choosing the flowers, booking the church and the vicar: it was relentless. I realise it sounds like a pathetic excuse, but I didn't have time to pause to take a breath, let alone reflect on the consequences.

'Come here then, pony,' Jack calls softly, putting his mobile in his pocket. She gives him a warning flick of the heels to keep his distance. He hesitates and lets her settle before moving closer, keeping his eyes averted and his body side-on to her to reduce the level of threat, which makes me smile, in spite of myself, because no one could ever describe Jack as threatening. He's both soft-hearted and intensely masculine, an irresistible combination, but although he has many women admirers, he's not had a serious relationship since me, as far as I know. Not that he's a monk. He's had his share of girlfriends.

I gaze back towards the pony, one female who isn't impressed by Jack's manner and physical attributes, for she decides he's come close enough, spins around and runs towards him with her head down, charging like a rhino. With lightning-quick reflexes, Jack turns and legs it. The pony reaches the end of her tether and pulls up sharply, as if she knows exactly how far she can go, rears up and stamps her feet down twice, before standing there, tossing her head, ears back and grinding her teeth.

'That's one angry little mare,' Jack observes.

Like me, I think, amused at how she behaved

towards him. I admire her fighting spirit, and wonder what has happened to her to make her so feisty.

'I'm not going to get near her, am I?' Jack says ruefully. 'I'll go and have a chat with Frank to see if I can resolve this without taking further action.'

'Is that enough?' I say quickly.

'I don't see why not, if he agrees to call a vet to check the sores on the mare's legs. It's one of those grey areas that I come across all the time,' Jack explains. 'The pony's condition isn't great, but she isn't the worst I've had to deal with. It isn't a clear-cut case of neglect. There isn't enough evidence to prove in a court of law that Frank Maddocks has broken the Animal Welfare Act. Don't worry though: I'll be keeping a very close eye on him.'

But I do worry, I think. I hate to see an animal suffering.

As if reading my expression, Jack goes on, 'I'll be giving him a formal warning.'

'Can't you take the pony away?'

Jack shakes his head. 'Much as I'd like to remove all of Frank's animals, I can't.'

'Surely you can do something.'

'I don't make the laws.'

'That sounds like a cop-out to me.'

'My hands are tied,' Jack says simply. 'I do what I can. I can't do any more than that.'

'What's happened to you? Where's your compassion?' I want to stamp my foot in frustration on the pony's behalf. 'Do you want to know what I think?'

Jack stands with his arms folded and his head

to one side. 'No, but I'm sure you're going to tell me...'

'You've been in this line of work for too long. You've grown hard, uncaring and cynical.'

'How can you say that?' A shadow falls across his face. 'I take my job very seriously. I care, Tess. I care more than you will ever know.' He turns away and we walk back towards the pub, Jack several strides ahead of me until we reach the stile where he stops and waits for me to clamber over. I'd prefer him not to watch because I am not one of those lucky people who can do stiles with any elegance.

'Tess, I have something to say,' he says as I stumble off the wooden step on the other side. 'I'm sorry.'

'Sorry? Oh, if this is about personal stuff, Jack, I don't want to hear it.'

'Please, I need to get it off my chest.'

'I don't care because it's too little, too late,' I say bitterly. 'And you should be sorry for what you did to me, and the way you broke me and Nathan up.'

'I'm not apologising for that,' he says. 'What I'm sorry for is wrecking the wedding in front of all your family and friends. Listen–'

'Why should I?' I interrupt.

'I tried to contact you before, in private. I called you and texted you the night before. When you didn't respond I dropped by at your parents' house, but your mum wouldn't let me in.'

'Jack, you had no right to cause a scene.'

'I wanted to rescue you.'

'For goodness' sake, you're so melodramatic.

88

I'm twenty-eight years old – I don't need rescuing.'

'You saved me once. You saved my life.'

'If I hadn't been there, someone else would have stepped in,' I say, remembering.

'They didn't though. You did.' Jack holds out his left arm. 'There's the proof.'

'Jack, I really don't want to see.' I do look though – due to my interest in healing, of course, not because the sight of his taut, bulging bicep is irresistibly fascinating, all muscle and tendon. Leading down to the crook of his elbow and beyond is a long, purple scar, evidence of what happened at that party, the one Jack held for his friends to celebrate his sixteenth birthday when his parents were away celebrating a wedding anniversary in a hotel in Talymouth, and without their consent.

It was dusk on a warm summer evening, and we were dancing, drinking and kicking about in the garden. There was some horseplay going on between the boys, and I was consoling Katie on the fact that one of them whom she particularly liked had failed to call her as he said he would (it sounds like nothing, but it's the end of the world at the age of sixteen), when there was a yell and a crash, followed by the sound of shattering glass.

'Jack. Jack!' Someone swore. 'You're bleeding.'

Within a millisecond, I was at his side. He was sitting on the ground, surrounded by gleaming splinters, his hand pressed to the crook of his elbow and blood spurting out between his fingers.

'Call 999!' I shouted as I squatted down beside him. 'Jack, I'm here,' I said, looking around frantically for something to stop the bleeding.

'I feel … weird,' he muttered.

'It's okay,' I said, stripping off my vest.

'What are you...?'

'I'm making a tourniquet. Don't look,' I added, ferociously aware that his eyes were straying towards my bra. 'Now, let me wrap this around your arm.'

As I tied my vest around his elbow, an arc of blood hit my chest and a wave of nausea rose in my gullet. Jack winced as I tightened the material, applying as much pressure as I could, being careful not to drive any glass that might be in the wound any deeper or dislodge it and cause more damage, the single useful snippet of advice that I'd learned as a Girl Guide.

'There's an ambulance on its way,' Katie said, pushing her way through the assembled crowd. 'It'll be here in ten minutes and it's already been two minutes at least since I was on the phone,' she went on, reading my expression of near panic, 'so it's only going to be eight minutes, seven now...'

The tourniquet was dark and sodden with blood, and I needed another layer of material to bind over the top.

'Katie, give me your blouse,' I said, 'and your belt. Now! This isn't the time to pretend you're shy.'

Katie provided her blouse and one of the boys handed me a belt. I wrapped both items over the top of the makeshift tourniquet and tightened the belt above Jack's elbow. His face was growing pale, his skin clammy and cool. Trembling, he tilted towards me and fainted, and all I could do

90

was hold him in my arms, inhaling the sickly, mingling scents of musk, crushed tomatoes and illicit alcohol from a couple of bottles of elderberry wine that I'd filched from my dad's cellar.

'Stay with me, Jack,' I begged. 'Jack. Don't go to sleep!'

'Don't leave me, Tess,' he slurred.

'I won't leave you.' The words caught in my throat. 'I promise.'

I could feel him relaxing into me. I checked his breathing, which was almost imperceptible, like the kiss of a butterfly against my cheek, and an overwhelming sense of grief washed over me as I realised I was losing him.

'Jack's parents,' I called up to Katie. 'Has someone contacted his mum and dad?'

'It's here. The ambulance!' someone screamed. 'Let them through.'

The paramedics took over. The police arrived, and my dad turned up too, having been summoned by Jack's parents, who were making their way straight to the hospital. Dad took one look at me, handed me his jumper and said, 'All right, folks. The party's over.'

The party was over, but soon after, our romance began. I recall visiting him at his house once he was discharged from the hospital, taking him grapes for a joke, and sitting with him outside on a bench near the greenhouse from which his parents had removed all the glass as a safety precaution a little too late. I remember his scent of mint and recently applied aftershave, and how his arm – the good one – crept along the back of the bench and slid down onto my shoulders, and how

I turned and gazed into his eyes, my pulse bounding as I read the intensity of his expression, not one of brotherly affection this time, but desire.

He moved closer until our lips touched, igniting the fires of teenage passion, and that was that. We saw each other virtually every day, kissed a lot and gave each other little notes, presents and tokens until Jack went away to college, when we decided, by mutual agreement, to call it a day. It seemed the sensible thing to do, but it felt like the end of the world, and, until Nathan came along, I was never sure that I was over Jack.

'You saved my life,' Jack repeats, as we approach the pub once more. Is this why Jack feels that he owes me? Is this why he walked into my wedding? Is this why he's still hanging around?

'I don't want to remember,' I say firmly. I look at his expression, gentle, straight and inordinately sad, and my heart twists with regret. 'Jack, I don't understand. I didn't need some self-appointed knight in shining armour blundering in to rescue me. So what if my fiancé was sleeping with someone else? It was none of your business. And if you did it out of jealousy' – who's blundering now, I think, annoyed with myself for letting that idea slip out – 'then I'm sorry. Since we broke up and went our separate ways, I've never thought of you in a romantic way, not once,' I go on, my words drowning in the vehement sound of water rushing through the mill race alongside us.

'I heard you, loud and clear,' Jack says sharply, and with neither triumph nor satisfaction I watch him stride away into the bar and disappear. If Jack was lying about Nathan, then I am as bad as he is because I'm lying too.

Another memory flashes into my mind of when my parents were hosting a house-warming party. They hadn't done anything much to it, except clear out the glasses from the bar of the old pub, and drink the barrels in the cellar dry. Anyway, there were nine children, including me, Jack and his sister. The younger kids – I thought I was so mature, being one of the oldest at twelve – were continually pestering us for squash and biscuits, so Jack suggested a game of sardines.

'What do you think?' he said, addressing me and his sister, Libby. 'We can hide from this lot,' he added, flashing me a cheeky grin. Jack explained the rules of the game and elected Libby as searcher. When she began counting up to one hundred, we scattered. I hid in the cupboard in the spare room upstairs, sitting in the dark, listening to the footsteps and shouting from other parts of the house. One set of footsteps grew closer and the door opened, letting in a crack of daylight.

'Tess, is there room for a small one?' Jack said in a whisper.

'Course,' I said. 'Quickly,' I added as he scrambled in. 'How did you know I was here?'

'I watched you.' He pulled the door shut and sat down beside me, almost on top of me, with his weight against my leg. I remember sitting there unsure which leg was his and which was mine, tingling with pins and needles. I wished I could have stayed in that cupboard for ever.

Walking up past the willow trees in the beer garden, I return to sit with Katie, who's texting on her mobile. 'Anything interesting?' I ask her as she presses 'send'.

'I lead a very dull life,' she responds, dropping the phone back into her bag. 'How did it go with Jack?'

'It was pretty hopeless really. He isn't going to do anything for the pony apart from talk to Mr Maddocks, and I can't see any point in that.'

Katie frowns. 'I wasn't asking about the pony. I was asking about him and whether he said anything about what happened at the wedding.'

'He tried to apologise, but it's irrelevant now.'

'I reckon he made up that stuff about Nathan being unfaithful because he didn't want anyone else to have you. I don't think he ever got over you.' Katie casts me a sideways glance. 'I used to wonder about you too, before Nathan came along. You used to fancy Jack like mad.' I start to deny it, but Katie continues, 'We used to joke about it. Don't you remember? Before you and Jack got together, you used to hang around town, wishing you would spontaneously combust so he could rush in and rescue you. I'm surprised you didn't burst into flames – you were pretty hot for him. And when you broke up, you were gutted.'

'All right, maybe I was.' I hold my hands up. 'But I don't feel anything for him now,' I add hastily. 'Can we change the subject, please?'

We talk about the progress of the sale of the house – mine and Nathan's – Katie's work at the beauty salon and the salon's plans to diversify into male waxing. It's almost like old times and I feel much happier when I return to my parents' house later in the evening, where they are playing bridge with friends.

'Fancy a glass of rosé?' Dad asks me, throwing peanuts into his mouth.

'No, thanks.'

'Party pooper,' he calls after me as I head into the kitchen and extract a mug from the pile of dirty crockery by the sink, rinse it out and make myself a tea before going upstairs to my room to have a word with my aunt.

'You didn't tell me you'd taken Jack Miller on as animal welfare officer,' I say.

'Didn't I?' There's a long pause, too long, and I smile to myself when she continues, 'It must have slipped my mind.'

'Sure,' I say with irony.

'It really shouldn't concern you, Tessa. You'll be based at the Sanctuary while Jack's field-based. He'll be on the road most of the time.'

'I'll still see him though.'

'He'll be collecting and delivering animals, but I can't imagine that will be every day.' Fifi sighs. 'You really mustn't let your personal issues get in the way of what is a wonderful opportunity for you to get back on your feet. Of course, you'll have to settle your differences with Jack eventually.'

'There's no way–'

'Think of the animals.'

'I can't. I just can't. I don't want him anywhere near me.' I feel as though I've been deceived. 'Why didn't you tell me?'

'Because I knew what your reaction would be. You would have turned it down.'

'Yes, I would.' I hesitate. 'I am turning it down.'

'You must never let a man get in your way. Whatever happened to girl power?'

'I think you'll find that that went out with the Spice Girls,' I say, amused. My aunt likes to think she's in touch with modern culture, but she's several decades behind the times.

'Listen. Maz at Otter House has been absolutely wonderful, but she can't keep the black dog there at the surgery any longer, he has to be moved out tomorrow – and there are three orphaned ducklings that Mrs Dyer's Great Dane rounded up by the river that she's bringing with her because she hasn't got anywhere to keep them. So, whatever you decide, there will be animals arriving at the Sanctuary.' I hear the desperation in my aunt's voice, and I think of the black dog confused and abandoned in the kennel at the vet's. 'Tessa, they need you,' Fifi continues. 'We need you. For the sake of the animals, if nothing else, please, please don't turn this opportunity down.'

Chapter Five

Ducks in a Row

A couple of days later, I'm collecting the rest of my belongings from the home that was mine and Nathan's. I check I've picked up everything from the vast open-plan kitchen-diner, the one the estate agent described as perfect for the growing family when we bought the house, and I recall standing arm in arm with Nathan, my heart over-flowing with joy as I pictured the high chair pulled up close to the breakfast bar, the baby's bottle on the tray and the toys and teddies strewn across the laminate floor. There's nothing left in this room now that belongs to me, not even a single happy memory of my time here with my ex-fiancé.

With the very last box of make-up, paperbacks and shoes in my arms, I look back at the front of the house, at the windows glittering in the sun, and I feel sick with the realisation that that is all our relationship was, a façade.

'Hurry up, Tessa,' Katie calls from her car, which is parked on the drive. 'You said you didn't want to run into Nathan.'

'I don't,' I say quickly. 'Thanks, Katie.' I open the boot and place the box inside.

'What for?' she asks.

'For being such a great friend, going beyond

the call of duty, and acting as go-between. It can't be easy for you, either.'

'It's no problem. Nathan and I have what you might call an understanding.'

'Katie, you don't fancy him, do you?' I ask lightly, as I slide in beside her and close the door. I can't help wondering. 'You seem quite pally.'

'Of course I don't fancy him,' she says, scolding me for even suggesting it. 'We have absolutely nothing in common, apart from you.'

The more I think about it though, the more alike they are with their interest in health and the body beautiful.

'Oh, and a fondness for Formula One,' Katie adds, driving away.

'I didn't know Nathan liked motor racing.' I don't look back – I would cry if I did.

'He has a passion for it. He told me.' Katie raises one perfectly shaped eyebrow. 'I hope you don't mind that I'm still in contact with him, Tessa. If it's going to come between us, I'll de-friend him and delete his number.'

'You don't have to do that,' I tell her. 'Thanks for offering, but I don't want people feeling that they have to take sides on my behalf, and besides, it would make Nathan think he still mattered to me, when he doesn't.'

'That's the spirit.' Katie taps her nails – they're fluorescent pink this week – on the wheel in time with Beyoncé.

When we reach the Sanctuary, a scrawny black and white cat that's spraying up the side of one of the flower tubs next to the front door scarpers around the corner of the building and disappears.

'Is that an escapee?' Katie asks, as we start unloading the car.

'There aren't any animals here yet. I expect it's a cat from one of the nearby farms. I'll ask my aunt. She'll know.' I sigh deeply. 'She knows everything.' I unlock the door and let us into the bungalow, putting my things down to pick up the post that's piled up on the mat from the day before. 'Stick those boxes down anywhere,' I say. 'I'll unpack later.'

'Let's get it done now,' Katie says. 'I'll give you a hand.'

'You don't have to stay.'

'I want to. I thought you could do with some moral support when Jack turns up with the dog.' She pauses. 'When's the house-warming party?'

'You'll be the first to know,' I say, smiling.

'You know, this place isn't too bad. It has potential.'

'It isn't to my taste exactly, but I'm very lucky. It's out of the way and quiet, and I'm looking forward to a good night's sleep without being disturbed by my parents, although I shall miss them both, Dad especially.'

'I don't think it's going to be all that quiet,' Katie observes as the doorbell chimes the tune of 'The Lonely Goatherd' from *The Sound of Music*. 'Did your aunt donate that bell?'

'I expect so. It was obviously a line that didn't sell well down at the garden centre.' I chuckle as I head out to answer the door, where I find two earnest middle-aged (I'm erring on the generous side) ladies, dressed in sloppy sweat tops and joggers, jostling for position on the step.

'Hello, Tessa. What are you doing here?' says the taller of the two, who has short grey hair, a ruddy, broken-veined complexion, horn-rimmed glasses and fiercely white trainers.

'I'm moving in today. My friend Katie's here, helping out.'

'Oh?' the ladies say at the same time. They look at each other, passing unspoken messages between them. 'Is your aunt about?' the taller one says.

'She's supposed to be here, but there's no sign of her. I remember you from years ago when Gloria ran the Sanctuary,' I say, pleased to see familiar faces. 'You're Wendy,' I add, addressing the taller one, 'and you're Diane.'

'I'm in charge of rehoming and I foster dogs for Talyton Animal Rescue,' Wendy says, 'and Diane is currently treasurer of the committee.'

'We're the Tuesday gang,' says Diane, who wears her hair in a blonde shoulder-length bob and flat black moccasins with leather tassels.

'We're your volunteers for the day,' Wendy goes on, noticing me frowning.

'Are there any more of you?' I say, wondering what has happened to my aunt's volunteer army.

'It's just the two of us,' Wendy says, confirming my fears that the rest of the troops have either deserted or not been conscripted yet. 'Are you sure your aunt isn't here?'

'I can assure you she isn't,' I say as Diane slides her foot forward as if to step inside. 'I haven't seen her today.'

'It's unusual for Fifi to be so elusive,' Wendy observes. 'She usually loves being the centre of attention.'

'Well, it's pretty obvious why,' says Diane. Although she has the kind of figure you might associate with a jolly person, being well rounded and fully upholstered, she's actually a prickly character, and I'm not sure we're going to get along. She subjects me to an intense stare.

'I can let her know you want to see her,' I say, willing to help.

'I don't think that will be necessary. You see, I'm sure she knows that already and that's why she's avoiding us.'

'Is there some problem? Anything I can deal with?'

'No, no. We'll have to have this out with Fifi,' says Diane, her face flushed.

Wendy gives me an apologetic glance. 'Diane, let's not be rude to Tessa. This isn't her fault. What can we do? We're here for the day, until lunchtime,' Wendy elaborates. 'Then I have to get home to let the dogs out.'

'And I have an appointment with Dr Mackie about my asthmatics,' says Diane, and I start to worry about whether she should be volunteering at all in her overweight and breathless condition.

'I can walk dogs, but I can't do any lifting because of my arthritis,' Wendy says, as if she's keen not to be outdone.

'Well, every little helps,' I say brightly. 'There's plenty to do.'

'I'd like to look after the cats, the little darlings,' says Diane, at which I have to point out that there aren't any animals at the Sanctuary yet, although Jack is bringing a dog from Otter House.

'You could make a bed up for him in one of the

kennels,' I suggest.

'For the dog, or Jack?' Diane giggles. 'I wouldn't mind making a bed up for Jack Miller. He's a dreamboat.'

'Oh, you are naughty,' Wendy says. 'Never mind Diane,' she tells me, 'she has these terrible crushes.'

'He can crush me any time.' Diane fans her face. 'I'm having a hot flush – it must be my HRT.'

'What else can we do?' asks Wendy.

'My aunt's left a note in reception on the way in. The builder's finished the kitchen in the kennels, but he's left it in quite a mess. There are some pots of paint to clear out and the tiles need grouting, and the end of the barn needs clearing out ready for DJ to build the stables.'

'I'm up for a good old grout,' says Wendy.

'I'm exhausted already.' Diane wipes her brow. 'I could do with a coffee before we make a start. Do you have coffee?'

'There should be some in the kitchen here. DJ hasn't put the doors on the cupboards yet, so mind you don't trip over them. I'll carry on unpacking, so I can get rid of my boxes at least.'

'I shouldn't rush into unpacking just yet, Tessa,' says Diane.

'Is there a problem? If there is, I really think I should know.'

'Well, I suppose you're going to find out soon enough,' Wendy says. 'Tell her, Diane.'

'Much as I hate speaking ill of busybodies like your aunt–' Diane begins.

'Let's not forget that it's busybodies like Fifi who make the world go round,' Wendy cuts in.

'Without her efforts, we would never have got our hands on the Sanctuary. She has the animals' interests at heart.'

'It's a pity she doesn't have the same consideration for the people who are involved,' Diane goes on smoothly. 'Tessa, your aunt has ridden roughshod over the committee, making decisions neither with reference to anyone else, nor following the proper procedures.'

'She hasn't even told us that she's let you move in here, let alone installed you as manager,' Wendy says.

'There's been no by-your-leave, no discussion, no vote.' Diane shakes her head, high spots of colour forming on her cheeks.

'It's wrong,' Wendy confirms.

'It's more than that. It's a perfect disgrace.' Diane gazes at me, her eyes small and beady, reminding me of a malevolent hamster, the type that sits in the bottom of its box ready to bite before you have time to scruff up the loose skin at the back of its neck. 'You wouldn't have been my first choice. It would have been Jack.'

Jack again, I think, my heart sinking. Everyone loves him, apart from me.

'So where exactly do I stand?' I ask. 'I mean, have I got a job here or not?'

Having got this far, I find that I'm looking forward to the challenge of running a rescue centre more than I ever thought possible, of working with a team of animal-mad volunteers and the animals themselves, sick, distressed and unwanted animals in need of rescue, like the black dog who should be on his way to the Sanctuary

103

with Jack as we speak. I can't bear the thought of having the opportunity snatched away from me at the last minute because of some silly spat between the chair and the rest of the committee.

'I'm sorry, but we can't answer that right now,' Wendy says. 'You'll have to wait and see.'

'We'll let you know when we've spoken to your aunt,' Diane says more brusquely. 'Now, let's get on. Have you got any decaff? No? In that case, I shall have to drink tea. You do have tea?'

'I think so.' I hope so, I muse. I had assumed that volunteers would go out of their way to be accommodating, but I sense that Diane in particular is going to be a very demanding woman, and I'm actually relieved when I catch sight of Talyton Animal Rescue's white minivan – the one that I'm supposed to have the use of as part of the deal – arriving in the car park.

'That's Jack, your first unwanted animal,' Katie says, coming outside with me. 'Tessa, this must be so awkward for you.'

'I'll be fine. If I tell myself that often enough, I might just come to believe it,' I go on wryly. What with meeting Jack again and finding that I could be out of here before I've had time to settle in, it hasn't been the easiest of days so far.

Katie and I shimmy past Wendy and Diane, who remain standing on the doorstep but facing towards the minivan, Diane's mouth half open, I notice, as Jack jumps out and walks around the back. He flings the doors open, at which the black dog flies out on the end of a rope lead. Jack catches the end and pulls him up before he can make his getaway and return to his previous exis-

tence as a stray, terrorising the pet dogs of Talyton St George.

Jack, dressed in a sweatshirt and cargo trousers,
brings him across to me and Katie.

'Hi,' he says, looking directly at me.

'Hi,' I respond, struggling to find something to
say. He gives the impression he is finding this
situation as difficult as I am, but he deserves it, I
tell myself, although it's hard not to sympathise
with those beautiful brown eyes gazing deep into
mine (and I'm not talking about the dog's).

'I'll take him from here.' I hold out my hand
and take the end of the rope lead. The black dog
stands with his head down and his tail tucked
between his legs.

'Here's his discharge note from the vet,' Jack
says, handing me an envelope. I take it by the
corner as if it's stuffed with anthrax, and slip it
into my pocket.

'Aren't you supposed to book him in or something?' Katie says helpfully.

'Well, yes, eventually, I suppose.'

'Fifi has put some forms in the office. She said
we should use those.' Jack holds up his hands.
'Not that I'm trying to tell you how to do your
job.'

'I must go,' Katie says. 'I'll see you later, Tessa.'

'Thanks for your help,' I say, wishing her goodbye before I let the dog sniff at my arm and
stroke his short velvety fur, at which he shrinks
away. He is one unhappy dog.

'What's his name?' I ask, glancing up at Jack.

'He has no name,' he says gravely.

'Didn't the staff at Otter House give him one?'

105

I'm surprised, because it's usually the first thing that happens in a vet practice.

'They call him the black dog. I tried out a few names on the way over, but he doesn't respond to any of them: Dillon, Danny, Derek.'

'You've only reached the Ds,' I say, amused. 'What if his name begins with R? What about Buster? Did you try that one?' Why did I pick on that name? The black dog looks up at me and wags his tail half-heartedly. 'Buster isn't the coolest of names, I suppose.'

'He isn't the coolest of dogs. He seems a bit on edge, like that cartoon, *Stressed Eric*. How about Eric?'

'I prefer Buster.'

'The manager's choice,' Jack acquiesces. 'Like Buster, I know my place,' he continues dryly. 'Shouldn't he have some kind of card to attach to his kennel?'

'He's the only dog here,' I point out, miffed that Jack is so intent on telling me how to do my job.

'I'm thinking about the volunteers. They'll need to be able to record when they've fed and walked him.'

'All two of them.' In spite of myself, I smile. 'Fifi's army. I'll put something up later. Let's get him settled first.' I pick up the slack in the lead. 'Come on, Buster.'

He isn't impressed by his new accommodation, and it takes both Jack and me to coax him into the only kennel that's ready. There are supposed to be ten, but DJ has only got as far as the second one, where he's hanging the wire door on the front.

106

'I'm glad to see you're making progress,' I say lightly.

'You can't rush a good job, my lover,' DJ says, pausing to pick up a screwdriver from his toolbox.

'Um, I don't suppose you could fix the cupboard doors in the kitchen today?'

'I'll put that next on the list, but it may not be today,' DJ says, all seriousness.

'I was rather hoping to be able to make my breakfast tomorrow without falling over all that woodwork.'

'Your aunt wants me to fix up the stable first. That'll take a good few days because I've got to get a mini-digger in to dig out the floor in the barn, and then she wants a breezeblock partition, and that's got to be lined.' He grows defensive. 'And it's all very well her getting at me for getting backward with the work, when she's not exactly coming forward with the money. She owes me for materials.' DJ is one of those people who can't stay cross for long. He smiles. 'You'd better let me get on, in case you have any more dogs coming in today.'

I glance towards Buster, who's trotting up and down anxiously.

'It's all right, my lover. I'll keep an eye on him.'

'Thanks.' I fold my arms as I walk back to the bungalow with Jack, keeping an emphatic distance between us.

'You don't need to worry, Tess,' Jack begins. 'I won't be under your feet all the time. In fact, I'll make myself scarce as much as possible.'

'Whether you're here or not, it doesn't bother

107

me. I've been employed to run the Sanctuary and I'm not going to let personal differences get in the way of doing my job.' Okay, I think, I might not be here for long, but I'm not going to let Jack know that in case it should affect his opinion of my authority here.

'Message received,' he says in a low voice, but although I don't want to have anything more to do with him, I can't avoid interacting with him. There's the cat I spotted this morning, for example. Having worked in animal welfare for a few years before he took a sabbatical, Jack knows the area and the animals that live within it.

'That will be one of the feral cats,' he explains. 'After the cottage went up in smoke, some of Gloria's rescue cats ran wild and bred with the feral cats that were already here, and their offspring bred and their offspring too, and now the site is overrun with cats, but I'm on the case. I've arranged to borrow some traps from a friend of mine.

'The committee have managed to agree on one thing at least: to adopt a trap, neuter and release policy.' He hesitates, looking me in the eye, a small smile playing on his lips. 'I suppose I should run that plan past the new manager first.'

'I should, if you want to get on the right side of her,' I say lightly.

'I'll bring the traps up this afternoon. I might as well take advantage of this good weather to set them up.'

As Jack leaves, Mrs Dyer, the butcher's wife, brings the ducklings to me in a cardboard box.

'The mother abandoned them,' says Mrs Dyer

108

over tea and biscuits with Diane, Wendy and me. 'I took them back to the shop for the night, but I'm afraid my dog will snap them up if he gets anywhere near them. How old do you think they are?'

'Tessa, what do you think? You're the vet nurse,' Wendy says, turning to me.

'Your guess is probably as good as mine.' I peer into the box. They aren't the smallest of ducklings, or the largest either. 'About three weeks old, maybe?'

'Jack will know,' Diane says with confidence. 'I'll ask him when I see him.'

I'm beginning to feel that with Jack around, I have a lot to prove.

'Where do you want us to put them, Tessa?' Wendy asks.

I think for a moment.

'We aren't set up for ducklings, so we'll have to improvise. We can set up a pen in the barn with straw and a water tray. That will need to be filled with stones because we don't want the ducklings to drown – they might not be waterproof yet.'

'Gloria used to give them freshly cut dandelions and hang lettuce up for them to peck at,' says Wendy.

'How long will they have to stay here?' asks Mrs Dyer.

'We can release them when they're about eight weeks old and fully feathered,' I say. 'We'll have to find them a suitable pond.'

Under Diane and Wendy's instruction, I build a temporary pen with wire netting and hurdles in one end of the barn, the other end from the one

109

that DJ is supposed to be turning into two stables, and we release the three brown and fawn downy ducklings into it. They run about – I was going to say like headless chickens, except they're ducks – frantically taking in their new surroundings.

I offer to order some straw from one of the local farmers and pick up some grower's pellets. When Diane says that the charity will reimburse me, I'm too embarrassed to insist on payment upfront because I have no money, apart from the twenty pounds that my father lent me to buy groceries so that I would be set up in my new home here at the Sanctuary. Worrying that it looks as if I'm taking advantage of him, I go outside to phone Jack who says he'll pick up the ducklings' feed and a bale of straw as well as the traps. When I return to the barn, I find the ducklings have settled down and fallen asleep, lying on top of each other for warmth and security, and my heart melts.

'They're lovely, aren't they, Tessa?' Wendy says from her perch on an upturned bucket. 'Diane and I thought we'd keep an eye on them for a while.'

'I needed to take the weight off my feet,' says Diane, who's managed to find an old but serviceable deckchair.

I realise that I'm not sure how to handle the volunteers. I don't want to nag them when they're here out of the goodness of their hearts, but I can see that it's going to cost the charity a small fortune in tea and biscuits if they sit around doing nothing all day. Clearly there hasn't been much grouting going on, and I don't begrudge Wendy that because I'd rather be with the animals than making the finishing touches to the kitchen tiles too.

I have a lot to learn, I muse, and I'm not sure that I've done the right thing, taking the Sanctuary on. It isn't merely the challenge of dealing with Diane and Wendy, but the contact with Jack, which, so far, has been more than I anticipated. It appears that, whether I like it or not, circumstances are conspiring to push Jack into my path as much as possible, because he's back at four in the afternoon with the bits and pieces for the ducklings and three traps: wire cages with trip plates that the cats will set off once lured inside with some tasty food as bait, the doors closing behind them.

As Jack arrives, DJ is just going, leaving the cupboard doors on the floor, the kennels unfinished and Buster barking, unhappy at being left on his own.

'He'll get used to it, Tess,' Jack says when I suggest I go and see him. 'Surely, the more you keep fussing, the more fuss he'll make.' He pauses and goes on in a self-mocking tone, 'That's my compassion gone out of the window again.'

'I shouldn't have judged you the other day,' I begin.

'I do my best, within the constraints of the legal frameworks. Sometimes you have to follow the rules. You can't always follow your heart.'

'I'm sorry.'

'Forget it. I have,' Jack says with a shrug. 'I'll take those traps through to the kennel block.'

'I'll give you a hand,' I say, in penance for my

111

recent comments about his commitment to animal welfare. I carry one and Jack takes two and we line them up on the bench under the window in the kitchen. I leave the door open, because all the time that Buster can see us, he isn't barking.

'You don't have to help me,' Jack says, as I return from fetching a handful of old newspapers from the pile that Mrs Dyer donated as a thank-you for taking in the ducklings, using them to line the base of each trap.

'The ferals are my responsibility now.' I gaze out of the window, squinting in the afternoon sun, looking for cats, but find my attention drifting back to Jack and the way his hair curls as it touches the collar of his polo-shirt. I notice the determined set of his jaw, suggesting strength of character, so unlike Nathan's. 'What shall we bait them with? Cat food or tuna? I've got a couple of tins somewhere in the bungalow.'

'Cat food?' Jack raises his eyebrows. 'Times must be hard.'

'Tuna,' I say, relaxing when I realise he's being funny. He always did like a joke, a play on words, or a gentle teasing. 'I'll get some.' I come back from the bungalow with a tin and a fork. 'This feels really weird,' I begin. 'I swore I'd never speak to you again, yet here we are...' My voice trails off. I'm not sure I should have said anything.

'It would be impossible not to speak to each other, considering we're working together.' Jack's voice hardens. 'If you don't want to talk, don't feel obliged. I'd hate to think I was putting you out.'

'You aren't,' I say quickly. 'I mean, I'm only

112

chatting to you because – well, it would be even weirder not to.' I slip my fingers through the mesh of the trap nearest me and touch the trip plate. The door snaps down shut, making me jump even though I was expecting it. It's Jack's presence that is making me nervous.

Jack chuckles. 'Mind your fingers.'

'I'm not that stupid,' I say lightly.

'I know you aren't,' he says more seriously. 'You always were the clever one.'

'What do you mean?' The phone starts ringing. As I go to pick up the handset and answer, Jack finishes, 'At school you were the one who passed all the exams, teacher's pet, even though you spent all those hours in my bedroom helping me to revise.'

I try to ignore Jack's reminder of our shared past, concentrating on the person on the phone.

'What was that?' Jack asks as I cut the call.

'There are two blue-tit chicks on their way,' I say, unable to contain my excitement. The Sanctuary is up and running and the animals are already flocking to us in droves.

'How are they getting here? Flying?' Jack says. 'Sorry, that wasn't very funny, was it?'

'It was moderately amusing. With a little more practice, we'll soon have our own stand-up comedian.'

'You reckon?' Jack says, deadpan.

'Maybe, with quite a lot of practice...'

'I thought we'd put the traps in the garden behind the bungalow,' Jack says, changing the subject. 'The cats come in from the copse to look for food, they smell the irresistible aroma of tuna, and bingo, we've got them.'

'Is it really that simple?' I ask, picking up one of the baited traps.

'I hope so,' he says, bringing the other two. 'The last time I set up traps down on the industrial estate, it took three weeks to catch a single cat.'

As soon as we leave the kennels, Buster starts barking again, his bark turning into a haunting howl that tugs at my heartstrings.

'How will I be able to leave him like that all night?' I say aloud.

'Sometimes you have to be cruel to be kind. Give him a night or so and he'll be fine.' When I don't respond, Jack continues, 'I'll buy you some earplugs.'

We place the traps in the flower beds in the garden behind the bungalow, covering each of them with a towel so the cats don't feel too exposed once they're inside them, and we wait for a while some distance away to see if anything will happen. But Buster's barking is enough to put any cat off coming within a mile of the Sanctuary, let alone the garden.

'I'd better go.' Jack checks his watch. 'I'll be back first thing to check the traps. I've spoken to Maz at Otter House and she's ready and waiting to neuter any cats we catch overnight.'

'If we catch any.' I smile ruefully. 'I'll have to find a way of shutting Buster up.'

'Eric,' says Jack.

'Nice try,' I say, 'but it's Buster.'

Jack smiles back. 'I hope you don't mind me taking the van home for a few days – my Land Rover's out of action. Shout if you need it.'

'Okay,' I reply, suddenly aware of how isolated I am, staying at the Sanctuary.

'I'll see you tomorrow,' Jack says. 'Goodbye.'

''Bye.' I walk around to the front of the bungalow with him and watch him drive away. I stand there for a while, inhaling the pungent scent of tomcat from the tub of begonias beside me and listening to Buster wailing plaintively as if his heart is breaking. Soon I can stand it no more, and I go and let him out of his kennel.

'Hey, Buster.' He jumps up, landing his paws on my thighs. With his mouth open wide and tongue hanging out, he looks as if he's grinning. 'You can come and spend the evening with me, but you have to sleep out here.' I don't know why, but I wonder briefly with whom Jack is spending the evening and with whom he might be sleeping too. Don't go there, Tessa, I tell myself sternly. It's none of my business, and I'm not interested either...

Back at the bungalow, I notice Buster is bleeding from one of his front claws where he's been scraping at the kennel door. I make him stand in some salt water, dry his foot and dress it in a light bandage before sacrificing one of my socks, slipping it over the bandage to keep it clean and securing it with a strip of sticky tape, before Buster and I curl up together on the sofa with a few dog biscuits, a microwave meal for one and a glass of wine, interrupted by the arrival of the baby blue tits.

As with the ducklings, I'm not sure where to put them, so I take them into the bungalow and make them a nest of bathroom tissue in the incubator that someone on the committee has managed to beg, borrow or steal. They're both tiny and covered with downy feathers. One looks quite well, alert and bright-eyed, while the other is cool to the touch and very depressed. I arrange to feed them their first meal, hunting around in the barn where Talyton Animal Rescue has stored various items of equipment, cages and dishes, and finding three sets of fine tweezers, too rusty to be of any use, and a heated pad that doesn't work. At least the incubator is coming up to an acceptable temperature when I return indoors and search out the set of tweezers I use for plucking my eyebrows into some kind of shape. They will have to do.

I make up a dilute emergency rehydration solution of sugar, salt and water and use a make-up brush to dab it onto the edge of the chicks' beaks. Although I wasn't expecting the weaker chick to be interested, both of them drink, and I'm happy to go on to feed them with pieces of tinned cat food. The stronger chick gapes and accepts the food with great enthusiasm, continually gaping for more, while the weaker of the two refuses to open its beak until I stroke the food from the hinge to the tip until it gets a taste for the juice and eventually accepts a few tiny morsels.

Once they're fed, I cover the incubator to make it dark and leave them overnight in the reception/office. I walk Buster back to the kennels, but he stops outside the door with his tail between his legs and refuses to budge, looking up at me with those big brown eyes of his. How can I resist?

'Okay,' I say, glancing towards the kennel block

across the car park that's shrouded in darkness, 'you've won me over. You can stay with me, but don't tell anyone. It won't do my credibility as manager any good at all if we're found out.' I figure that if I put him back in the morning before breakfast, no one will ever know. Wagging his tail, Buster comes back to the bungalow, making me smile. If I'm honest, I'm doing this as much for me as for him.

My first night at the Sanctuary is very quiet, and rather long and lonely without my parents falling in through the front door in the early hours of the morning, or my dad turning up to chat over peanuts and a nightcap. I find myself alert to the unfamiliar sounds of the creaking gate, and the wind in the trees, but at least with Buster here I feel a little safer than I might otherwise. I think he'd soon bark if there was someone, or something, out there, not that I believe in baddies or evil spirits as such. It's because I was brought up in the pantomime tradition by my mum and dad that I have such a lively imagination for wicked witches, wolves and stepmothers.

The baby birds wake me at dawn the next day with joyful chirrupings. Shifting Buster's warm weight from my feet, I roll over and pull the duvet over my ears, but I can't block them out and I start to panic that they might starve if I don't answer their demands and feed them soon. It seems like a very long time since I put them to bed.

Buster thumps his tail against the duvet, making me smile at my sense of rebellion. My parents wouldn't let me have a dog, let alone one that slept on the bed. Not that Buster's mine, I remind myself. He's under my care until we find him the perfect home.

The baby birds continue to make a fuss, so I drag myself out of bed. I look out of the window onto the car park and find myself face to face with DJ, who's standing beside his truck. He gives me a small wave and I wave back before making a rapid retreat to grab my dressing gown to throw over my pyjamas. I make a mental note to remember to draw the curtains in future, something I didn't bother with because I have no immediate neighbours and I assumed I'd be dressed before anyone turned up at the Sanctuary.

'Do you want to go outside, Buster?' I ask, but he stays where he is, curled up on the end of the bed. 'You are one lazy dog,' I tell him. I get dressed, feed the blue tits, grab a piece of toast, drag Buster outside for a walk, feed the blue tits, clean out the ducklings and feed the blue tits again. Unsure how I'm going to keep this schedule up for ten hours, I call Fifi to ask her if anyone is planning to volunteer today because no one has reported for duty yet. 'I'm on my own with baby birds to feed,' I tell her.

'No one said this job would be easy,' she says.

'I'm not complaining – they're very cute. I'm just observing that if I'm feeding blue tits every half an hour, I'm not going to have time to do much else. I'd appreciate some help.'

'Oh dear, I'm afraid that you're going to be unlucky today. Diane came to see me last night to have a go about you working at the Sanctuary. I

118

don't know how on earth she weaselled her way into the office of treasurer when she doesn't seem able to put two and two together,' Fifi grumbles.

'She and Wendy said that you offered me the position without consulting with anyone on the committee,' I say, wanting to know the truth. 'I can understand why they're annoyed if that's the case.'

'Tessa, I hope you're not taking sides. Yes, I admit I didn't put it to the vote, but I had to move in a hurry because I didn't want you rushing off to work elsewhere, and you are the perfect candidate.'

'But not the only one,' I cut in. 'Diane mentioned the possibility of giving the job to Jack.'

'The silly woman! When she was in her teens, she fell off her horse, landing on her head. I don't think she's been right since,' Fifi says. 'Jack can't be field officer and manager. You can see for yourself that there's too much work for one person, and you can't do his job because you haven't his experience. And anyway, he has somewhere to live. He has his own house in Talyton. It's you who needs a roof over your head.'

'That shouldn't really be one of the criteria for giving me the job,' I point out. 'Don't you worry that Diane might take steps to remove you as chair after this?'

'I am one of the founder members. She wouldn't dare. Look, dear niece, I did what I had to do. If I'd put this to the committee, it would have taken them months to agree.' Fifi clears her throat. 'Diane will thank me for this one day.'

I doubt it, I think. If I wasn't in the thick of the

squabble, I would find it quite entertaining, the charitable ladies of Talyton St George acting most uncharitably towards each other.

'Oh dear, I'd better come over and see what's what after I've had a ring round to twist a few arms.' She pauses. 'Why don't you have a word with Jack when he comes to check the traps? He called me to let me know he's on his way to you.'

'I see...'

'It won't be for ever, Tessa. Those little birds will soon grow up and fly the nest.'

By the time Jack arrives, I'm feeding the blue tits yet again.

'Hi,' I say when he knocks and enters the bungalow – I left the front door open deliberately so I didn't have to stop partway through to let anyone in. 'How are you?'

'Good,' he says, coming to join me in the office area behind the reception desk where I've perched the incubator on the table.

'I've checked the traps and they're empty,' I go on. 'The cats around here don't appear to like tuna. I think we need to put something else on the menu.'

'Menu?' Jack frowns.

'That's what I said,' I say, half joking, half serious. 'I feel like the manager of a hotel, organising all these meals.'

Jack suggests pilchards for the ferals while I'm dangling the tweezers loaded with cat food above the second baby blue tit.

'I think that one's had enough,' Jack observes as the chick sits there with its beak firmly closed at last. He stands behind me, looking over my

120

shoulder into the incubator, so close that I can feel the warmth radiating from his body and his breath hot on the back of my neck. A tingle of irrational, unwanted and unexpected excitement rushes down my spine, spreading across my lower back. I dismiss it. It's nothing.

'In half an hour, I'll have to start all over again,' I say. 'I called my aunt to see if she could rally some helpers, but she hasn't come back to me. She said you'd been in touch with her.'

'It was the other way round. She was checking up on me,' Jack says, smiling. 'I'll ask Libby if she'll come and help you out later.'

'How is she?' Libby is Jack's sister who must be twenty-four or twenty-five now. She's lived with epilepsy for the past fifteen years, and as a consequence her family are very protective of her and she's still living with their parents.

'She's well at the moment,' Jack says. 'She hasn't had a fit for a couple of years now, but she still isn't allowed to drive because of her medication. She has a part-time job – you might have seen behind the till in the Co-op.'

'I have. I haven't really talked to her much though, only to say hi.'

'She gets bored sometimes. She missed so much school and she struggled through her college course. She isn't an animal person, as such. She likes them, but hasn't much experience apart from looking after the family pets. I think she'd enjoy helping out here though.'

'Come on, little one.' I pick up one of the baby blue tits to clean out the toilet tissue nest. The chick is so delicate that I'm afraid that I'll snap

121

its legs or crush its chest. The slightest movement of air ruffles the blue and pale yellow down on its body. 'Let's make you comfortable.'

'How are they doing?' Jack asks.

'I thought one was dying when I admitted them, but it's still here, alive and flapping.' I place the chick back into the nest alongside its sibling. 'There you go. You have a good snooze and I'll be back in half an hour. Keep eating like that and you'll grow big and strong.'

'You make a good mum – I mean, as in mummy bird,' Jack says awkwardly. 'Which flying school are you planning to send them to?' he continues, teasing.

'Jack!'

'It's good. It shows you care.' Jack hesitates. 'You know you've changed, Tess. You're quieter somehow, less happy...'

'It's hardly surprising, is it? Not so long ago, I was about to be married to a lovely guy' – okay, so there's a hint of the rose-coloured spectacles going on – 'when my whole life fell apart.'

'It isn't all that bad, surely?'

'I gave up a good job as head nurse at a practice in Exeter, thinking I'd soon be having babies. I did some maternity cover for four months before the wedding – Nathan didn't like it. He said he'd prefer it if I supervised decorating our house, but I knew I'd miss work if I gave it up altogether.'

'He must be doing pretty well for himself,' Jack says enviously.

'You haven't heard, have you? It was all a front. There is no money. Nathan set up his own business, but it failed. He's declared himself bankrupt

122

so he gets off virtually scot-free.'

'Really?' Jack's brow furrows. 'The bastard!'

'I'm left paying off my credit card bill for the reception and honeymoon which I didn't get to go on and Nathan did, and when the house is sold – it's on the market now – I'll still have a few thousand that I owe as my share of the joint mortgage. Thanks to Nathan, I'm drowning in debt.' I pause, wondering why I am telling Jack this when it has nothing to do with him.

'I'm sorry, Tess. You don't have to talk about it if you don't want to, but I'm here if you need a shoulder to cry on.'

'As a colleague,' I say quickly.

'Of course,' he says, in a slightly mocking tone of voice, and I kick myself inwardly for being so prissy.

'I'm lucky to have this job,' I say, changing the subject, 'although I have no idea how long I'll be staying here.'

'What do you mean? I thought you'd signed a year's contract.'

'I haven't seen any paperwork yet, and anyway, with the committee and my aunt at each other's throats, I imagine my contract could be cut short at any moment.' It all comes spilling out.

'Is there any way I can help?' Jack says.

'Pick me the winning lottery numbers, perhaps. I can't think of anything else.' I lean back with a sigh. If I close my eyes, maybe everything will go away. Including Jack. I open one eye. Maybe not Jack. It's good to have company, and he is good company, or do I just feel that way because he's the only company I have at the moment, the single person in my life who doesn't go on about the wedding and what a shame it was?

The Fray's 'How to Save a Life' is playing on the radio that I left on for the baby birds.

'I take it the dog stopped barking,' Jack says. 'You see, I was right when I told you to leave him alone.'

Should I enlighten him? 'Oh yes,' I reply. 'He was quiet all night.'

'Good. Look, I'll go and get Libby now,' he says.

'It'll be good to see her again,' I say, glad to have some space. It's rather warm inhere, and it has nothing to do with having my hands inside the incubator.

Chapter Six

Early Birds

It's the middle of May and I'm still here. The baby birds are more voracious than ever, getting through mealworms by the kilo, and DJ has finished the stables at last, although I'm still tripping over the cupboard doors and pots of paint. The apple blossom is on the trees and I've seen a little owl, nuthatches and a green woodpecker in the grounds of the Sanctuary. After a couple of weeks, I'm beginning to feel more at home and more convinced that I know what I'm doing.

Yesterday, Jack took the first feral cats – there are three of them – to succumb to the temptation of tinned pilchards in tomato sauce to Otter House vets for neutering, and today, Libby, who has been volunteering daily for the past week, is helping me out with the routine chores.

We're in reception, taking a break, although I'm still working, investigating ways to raise funds for the Sanctuary with a fun day and a ball, having discussed various possibilities with Diane and Wendy when they dropped by for a couple of hours at the beginning of the week, ostensibly to help, although I suspect it had more to do with keeping an eye on the place as it appears there is still tension between them and my aunt.

I have dismissed Diane's desire for a jumble sale

as too much work for too little return. Although she argued that the WI used to make lots of money from their jumbles, Wendy reminded her of the near riots that happened at the last one, at which someone broke their arm, tripping in the crush at the doors of the church hall, and two people were tackled for stealing jumble. A fun day and a ball sound far more entertaining – and much safer.

I glance away from the laptop, another second-hand donation to the Sanctuary, towards Libby, who sits very still on one of the office chairs that were given to us by a friend of Wendy's. You can tell that Libby is Jack's sister by the striking family resemblance in the light blonde hair, which she wears in a boyish crop, the brown eyes and the expressive mouth. Dressed in a pink T-shirt and fraying jeans with a white plastic apron over the top, she is stroking a well-endowed custard-coloured rat that sits on her shoulder with his long, naked tail draped behind her neck He was found abandoned under the footbridge over the river a couple of days ago.

'To think he would have starved if those people hadn't noticed him,' she says. 'They could have at least undone the cage door, so he could get out and search for food. He's so cute.'

I have to say I don't warm to him as I do to the dogs and cats. There's something off-putting about the twitching whiskers and red eyes. I wonder if I would like rats more if they had hair on their tails. He nuzzles at Libby's hair. Someone must have loved him once, just not enough.

'Why do people take on rats if they're going to

give them up?' I muse aloud. 'It isn't as if they live for ever. You would have thought they could stay the course.'

'Talking of courses, I think films like *Ratatouille* have a lot to answer for,' Libby says. 'If I was a little kid, I'd feel let down if I took on a real rat and discovered it was nothing like Remy and couldn't cook soup,' she adds with a giggle. 'I'm going to speak to our neighbour, if that's all right with you, Tessa. Ally has three sons and a dog. I do some babysitting for her now and then, and I know the boys would love to have another pet. What shall we call him though? He needs a name.'

'How about Nathan?' I blurt out.

Libby raises one eyebrow. 'Isn't he your ex?' When I nod, she goes on, 'Isn't that a little un-fair?'

'Nathan is a rat,' I say.

'I mean that it's unfair on the rat,' she chuckles, her face dimpling, 'but I think the name suits him.' She detaches the newly christened rat from her hair and lowers him back into his cage. 'He can stay indoors here for now, can't he?'

'I guess so,' I say with a sigh. Soon, there will be more animals living with me in the bungalow than in the rest of the Sanctuary put together, because I'm still smuggling Buster in to be with me every night. There is a steady stream of new arrivals, more animals turning up than leaving. In fact, Jack is carrying a bright red cat-carrier with the next one across the car park right now.

'Allow me to introduce you to Teddy,' he says with a smile, as he places the carrier on the desk.

'He's a tabby and white domestic shorthair, about two years old, and he's been living with his current owner for a couple of months. They saw him advertised online as needing a home and couldn't resist, but unfortunately for everyone involved, Teddy proceeded to make their elderly cat's life a misery, ambushing her on the litter tray and guarding the cat flap, so they decided he had to go, and here he is. He's all yours, Tess.'

'And mine, for now,' Libby says. 'I'll take him.'

'Thanks. I'll print off a record card and join you in the cattery in a mo.' I turn back to Jack. 'Are you collecting the ferals from Otter House later, or am I?'

'I'll get them,' he says, frowning, and I regret being sharp with him. It must have been an attempt to hide my reaction to his presence, because I'm still confused by him, by the difference between the man who strode up the aisle in the church, determined to wreck my wedding, and the man who is here now, rescuing stray and unwanted animals. 'Do you need a hand with Teddy?' Jack asks.

'I think Libby and I can manage one small cat between us.'

'Okay,' Jack says quietly. 'I'll see you later.'

Once he's gone, I join Libby in the cattery. Teddy is already in a run, hiding under a piece of veterinary bedding on his shelf with just his tail hanging down over the edge, the end twitching dangerously.

'I'm sorry, Tessa,' Libby says. 'I should have left him in his carrier so you could look at him first. There's something wrong with one of his paws –

128

he went ballistic, hissing and spitting at me when I let him out.'

I pick Teddy up, along with his bed, and examine him, wishing I had not been so quick to dismiss Jack, because I could do with his help. Libby doesn't have the confidence yet to hang on to a stroppy cat that's growling and lashing out in every direction, but I can see enough to confirm that Teddy has an abscess – one paw is swollen to twice the size of the others. I call Otter House to book him an appointment, wondering about the story that Teddy's owners have spun to Jack, and suspicious that this is more about them being unable to afford vet's bills than Teddy's alleged intimidation of their other cat.

'I'll have to call Jack to ask him if I can borrow the van,' I observe as Teddy heads straight back for the relative security of his shelf. Although I'm perfectly entitled to use the van, I don't like having to ask Jack, but that's how it is.

'You know, Jack's truly sorry for what he did,' Libby begins as she clips Teddy's record card to the door of his run. 'I wish you could forgive him, so we could all be friends again.'

'That's a little naïve, isn't it?' I realise I'm sounding harsh, but that's because I'm not sure I want to discuss it, but Libby is determined to stand up for her brother.

'He has the best of intentions' – Libby looks at me, her lips curving into a small smile – 'especially where you're concerned. He likes you, Tessa, and always has done.'

'He has a strange way of showing it,' I say grudgingly.

'He was gutted when he found out you were engaged,' Libby goes on.

So he was jealous, I muse, confused and embarrassed at the thought that Jack has feelings for me, that he might still harbour hopes of becoming more than a friend.

'I wish you weren't telling me all this, Libby,' I say. I feel awkward seeing Jack anyway, and this revelation isn't going to help. Does he really like me? I wonder. After Nathan, I'm not sure I want to find out. I shall never understand how the male brain works. 'Have you got a boyfriend, Libby?'

'No,' she says, her eyes soft with regret. 'I don't think anyone would have me.'

'What makes you think that?'

'It's my epilepsy.' She raises her hand to her temple. 'It seems to be under control at the moment with the drugs, but I could have a fit at any time. It would take someone incredibly special to take me on. I can't drive, I can't work full-time because I get tired and I'm not sure I could be alone with a baby or small child if I had kids...' To my alarm, because I hate seeing anyone upset, a tear rolls down her cheek.

'Jack said you were okay, that you hadn't had a fit for ages.' I watch her expression change. 'You have?'

'I was at work. It was nothing much. My hand started twitching and I couldn't use the till – it does, that before...'

'I see.' Libby doesn't have to spell it out.

'I've been in touch with my consultant and he's tweaked my medication. I hope it will settle down again. It's the electrical activity in my brain that causes it – the wiring went wrong somewhere along the line.' She pauses. 'I forgot, you'll know about that. I assume dogs and cats have fits.'

'They can do,' I say, 'but I'm more concerned about you.'

'I haven't told Jack because I can't bear him fussing over me. I know he means well, but he drives me mad. And I should have told you.' She stares at me, biting her lip. 'This always happens to me. You won't let me stay here now.' She rips her apron off and thrusts it into my hands. 'I'll go.'

'Libby, stop!' I run after her as she disappears outside, catching up with her partway down the track leading towards the lane. 'Please. Let's talk about this. I'm sure we can–'

I watch her stumble to a stop and slump down beside the hedge, sitting with her legs bent up and her chin resting on her knees, gazing straight ahead.

'Do you mind if I join you?' I say, sitting down beside her. 'Are you okay?' I ask eventually.

'As okay as I'll ever be.' She turns to me. 'Tessa, this is it. This is my life.'

'Tell me about it.' I pluck a blade of grass, idly wrapping it around the base of my ring finger as we talk.

'She said I could tell you,' I say to Jack when he returns from taking Libby home and visiting Otter House to drop Teddy off and collect the feral cats. (Teddy is staying the night at Otter House, having been sedated to have his abscess lanced and thoroughly flushed.) I'm in the kennels when Jack arrives, feeding Buster. 'She thought I'd say she couldn't work here if I knew, but that isn't the case. It's better to be prepared if anything should happen while she's here. Jack, please don't be angry with her.'

'I can't believe she kept it from me,' he says brusquely. 'What if she'd been here on her own?'

'She hasn't been on her own,' I point out, 'and she hasn't had a proper full-on fit either. She might never have another one.'

'But if she had, she could have been lying here hurt, or worse,' Jack says. 'If she has a prolonged seizure that goes on for more than two or three minutes, she could end up with further brain damage. Tess, I don't think you realise how serious this is. Libby could die.'

'I realise that,' I say after a pause, 'and it must be a terrible thing to have hanging over you – for Libby, you and your parents – but you can't stop her coming here.' I open Buster's kennel door and ask him to sit before I place the bowl of food – chicken casserole in gravy with a biscuit mix – in front of him. He dives forwards and gobbles it down. 'Libby loves the animals,' I go on as Buster chases the bowl across the floor in a frantic attempt to lick it clean.

'I'm not sure,' Jack says, shaking his head.

'Please, Jack. You need to trust her.'

'How can I when she's been lying to me? To our parents?'

'She says she's managing it. She's taking her medication as prescribed, and she gets a few hours' warning before she has a fit, so she can remove herself to somewhere that's safe. Jack, I'll

132

do a proper risk assessment, and as long as we make sure there's always someone else on the premises, and everyone knows what to do, there's no reason at all why she shouldn't volunteer.' I relax a little to try to lighten the mood. 'We need all the volunteers we can get.'

'I know.' Jack runs his hands through his hair. 'It's just that I can't bear the thought of anything happening to her. She's my little sister and I've looked out for her since she was born.'

'She's twenty-four,' I say. 'I understand where you're coming from, but you can't keep watch over her for ever. She has to be free to live her life as she chooses. If you forbid her to come here, you'll make her hate you.' I pause, remembering Libby's desire that I should treat Jack more kindly. 'Lecture over. Let's get these cats released back where they belong.'

'Maz says they're ready to go,' Jack says, and I breathe a sigh of relief that he's still talking to me. 'She's given them names, but it's pretty obvious which is which.'

I follow him out to the van where he's left the rear doors open to allow the air to circulate, so the cats don't overheat. He passes me one of the traps, and brings the other two over himself. 'The scrawny black and white one is called Scabby; the ginger one with its tail missing, No-Tail; and the grey long-haired one which is almost bald since they shaved it, Knotty.'

I have Knotty. He lies cowed in the trap, keeping his eyes on me, the enemy, and uttering a strangled yowl when I speak to reassure him.

As we take the traps around to the rear of the

133

bungalow, the early evening sun disappears completely behind the clouds and it starts to rain. The weather isn't ideal, but it's warm and the cats will be happier outside in their own surroundings, so Jack and I open the traps and stand back, watching and waiting, and it isn't long before two of the cats fly out and disappear into the bushes, whereas Knotty, who seems a bit slow, takes a few minutes to realise that only a couple of steps lie between him and freedom. When he does leave the trap, he stalks across the lawn, picking his paws up high as if he has an aversion to wet grass.

'He's a bit of wuss,' Jack observes, as the rain starts to turn his sweatshirt a darker shade of blue. 'I reckon he was a pet that's gone over to the wild side.'

'And I reckon we should go inside,' I say, water dripping down the back of my neck. 'Would you like some tea?'

'Are you sure?'

'I wouldn't have asked if I wasn't,' I point out lightly. 'Come on, I could do with a drink before I give the babies their last meal of the day.'

In the kitchen, having abandoned my shoes in the hallway, I search for mugs, finding two on the windowsill while Jack goes to the fridge for milk, passing so close I can feel the hairs on his arm. Trying to ignore the blip in my pulse and the vague ache in my chest, I pour the boiling water into the mugs. Jack passes me the milk carton, his fingers brushing lightly against mine. I glance up and he looks away.

The contact, intentional or not, is the last thing

I want, or seek, yet it sets up a ripple of longing through my body. In spite of Nathan, I miss being close to a man – any man, I tell myself sternly as I catch up the teabags and give them a good squeeze, not Jack in particular.

'You don't have to slum it in the office. You're welcome to join me.' I direct him to the living room. 'Take a pew.' I wish I hadn't put it that way – we aren't in church now. I sit on the sofa while Jack settles on the armchair, pink-faced, and I wonder if I've made a mistake in inviting him into my home. If he does, as Libby suggests, have feelings for me, am I encouraging him?

In another life, I might well be tempted to encourage him, I muse as I gaze at his unruly blond hair, his steady expression and the soft light in his eyes. Having been forced into Jack's company, I've been reminded that he is a very attractive man: handsome, not flashy; masculine, not arrogant. In addition, Jack is caring. There aren't many men who are interested in rescuing cats and dogs and ponies, and, thinking of ponies, I ask him if he's had any more to do with Mr Maddocks.

'I'm on the case,' he says. 'That's all I can say for now.'

'The pony's safe though?'

'I'm monitoring the situation.'

'Is that a euphemism for doing nothing?' I know Jack's hands are tied, but I can't resist pursuing the subject because I want to be sure he's doing enough. The pony needs help, even if she has a funny way of showing it.

Frowning, Jack shakes his head. 'I know where

135

she is and I'm making daily visits. I'm not ignoring it, if that's what you mean.'

'I'm sorry. It's just that I hate to think of her standing in some field up to her knees in mud in the rain, thirsty and starving because Mr Maddocks has forgotten her, or can't be bothered, whatever his reasons are.'

'Well, it isn't down to ignorance,' Jack says. 'He's kept all kinds of livestock for years. I think it has more to do with his chaotic lifestyle and lack of income.'

'I really think you should put the pony first. She behaves as if someone's beaten her up,' I point out. 'She's scared of people, but then you've seen what she's like,' I continue, backing down. Who am I to go telling Jack how to do his job?

'If you must know, Frank has taken her back to the smallholding he rents by the industrial estate – he's got her in a postage stamp of a paddock, so she isn't tethered at the moment. She has access to hay and water, and I've confirmed that Frank's made an appointment for Alex, the vet, to call in on him. I'm sure Alex will impress upon him the importance of keeping her in a dry and hygienic environment.'

'Will Mr Maddocks listen to him?'

'Everyone listens to Alex Fox-Gifford. He has a definite air of authority and he's persistent. Between the two of us, I think we can make Frank Maddocks see sense.'

I shake my head. 'It's so frustrating though. Why does it have to take so long?'

'It's the nature of the beast. Look, why don't I take you over to see the pony next time?'

'What about Mr Maddocks?' I'm not sure I want to see him again. 'Don't you ever worry about your safety? I know from working in practice that where animals are concerned, people's emotions are often running high.'

'Frank is all mouth. I'm not afraid of him. There are others I wouldn't have wanted to have met on a dark night, a couple whom I testified against in court in a case that resulted in them having their dogs taken off them and a lifetime ban on keeping animals.' Jack picks up his mug and sips his tea. 'I'll let you know when I'm visiting Dolly next – that's what Frank calls the pony. It's Dolly after his grandmother, the woman he thought was his mother when he was growing up as a boy. She was pretty rough too, by all accounts.'

'Why do you make excuses for him, Jack?'

'I'm not making excuses. His attitude is vile, but I have got to know him over the years. Welfare investigations aren't merely about the animals. They're about the people who are involved too, and many of them have issues with relationship breakdowns, substance abuse and poor mental health.' He falls silent for a while. 'Tess,' he begins eventually. 'I mean, Tessa—'

'Oh, you don't have to—' I cut in.

'I don't want to upset you – I've done enough of that already.' Jack smiles a small, lopsided smile that sends my heart into somersaults.

'Tessa doesn't sound right when you say it,' I say awkwardly. 'To be honest, it makes me feel as if you're talking to someone else.'

'I can give you a hand with feeding the birds.' He glances at his watch. 'I can stay another hour

137

or so.'

I want to ask him where he's going afterwards, but that seems too personal. We aren't teenage sweethearts any more. We're working together. As I have to keep reminding myself, this is a professional relationship.

'Thank you,' I say gracefully. 'There's so much to do.'

'Too much,' Jack agrees. 'Fifi needs to drum up some more volunteers. Is there some problem? There are rumours, according to Frances, the receptionist at Otter House, about unrest within Talyton Animal Rescue.' Jack clears his throat. 'They're accusing Fifi of nepotism because she gave you this job without consulting the other committee members.'

'Some of the original volunteers from Gloria's time here, who were keen to come back, have changed their minds, and there are plans afoot to make a challenge on the leadership. I don't know for sure, but I thought I'd let you know in case you want to forewarn your aunt... They're only rumours though,' he goes on, noticing my frown. 'Oh dear, I'm digging myself furiously into a hole like a rabbit on Red Bull.'

I smile at the thought, but I feel upset that people are talking about me and my aunt behind our backs. No one likes to be thought badly of and it affects others, like Jack and Libby, and the rescues. The fewer volunteers we have at the Sanctuary, the less time we can spend with each animal and the poorer their chances of being rehomed or released.

'I'll speak to my aunt,' I decide. 'I need to find

138

out what's going on. I might be able to persuade her to help out for a few hours too.'

'You mean, Fifi doesn't mind getting her hands dirty?'

'She's always willing to muck in.'

'But not muck out, as such.' Jack smiles again, lifting my spirits.

It's almost like old times, when we were friends, hanging out or chillaxing together. I sink down into the sofa. 'Tell me about the moon bears. What is a moon bear?' I ask.

'It's a black bear with a white patch that looks like a crescent moon on its chest. They're beautiful creatures, wild yet gentle and very intelligent. I had an amazing trip,' he says, 'and I'm glad I took the time out to do it, but the suffering of the captive moon bears is unbelievable.' He explains how they are caught and kept restrained in tiny cages so they can be milked for bile through metal pipes implanted into their bellies. It's a life sentence, and their lives are often cut short through stress and overwhelming infections.

'Why? What for?' I ask, wincing at the thought.

'Bear bile is a valuable commodity – it's believed to have medicinal properties, and although there are synthetic versions, people want the real thing. There are several charities involved in making a difference through rescue, rehab and education, but it's going to take time before the practice is abandoned altogether.'

'You seem very passionate about the cause,' I say eventually. 'Do you think you'll go back one day?'

'I'd love to go back permanently,' he admits.

139

'I'd set up a rescue centre like a shot, but this is home and I have Libby to think of. My parents aren't getting any younger and, in spite of what she says – and your opinion on the matter – she needs someone to look out for her.'

For once, I bite my tongue.

'I'll go and feed those chicks,' Jack says, getting up to feed the baby blue tits. I join him in the office, and just as they take their last mealworm, a car's headlamps come flaring through the window.

'Are you expecting someone?' he asks.

'It's Katie.' I recognise her car, an old Ford Fiesta. I dash out to the kitchen and rinse my hands before opening the door to greet her.

'Hiya, stranger, where have you been all my life?' I say.

'Has it really been that long, Tessa?' she says, grinning. 'I've been let down at the last minute so I thought I'd come and catch up with you. I've brought wine, chocolate and Robert Downey, Jr – well, not him exactly, but a DVD with him in it. I thought you might need cheering up.'

'So what's happened to the new man then?' I have to ask.

'New man?'

'There must be one: I've hardly seen you, you're looking great and you've lost weight.'

'Oh, I've had a lot on.' Katie stops abruptly and lowers her voice to a whisper. 'Hey, what's Jack doing here? Are you and he–?'

'Of course not.'

'I meant, are you talking to each other,' she says archly. 'What did you think I was going to say?'

140

'Hello, Katie,' Jack says, walking up behind me.

'Hello,' she says icily.

'I'll see you soon, Tess,' Jack goes on. 'I won't stop.'

I wish him goodnight and thank him for his help as he steps aside to let Katie pass before walking out into the rain.

'What on earth is going on?' Katie asks when the van disappears off down the track. 'Why are you letting him hang about here with you?'

'Because he works here, no other reason.'

'It's gone eight o'clock.'

'Shall I open the wine?' Trying to divert her line of questioning, I reach out to take the bottle from her.

'You know, sometimes I forget how good-looking Jack is,' Katie says, following me into the kitchen.

'So does he, I think,' I say, before wishing I hadn't.

'What did you just say?'

'Oh, nothing.'

'Yes, you did. I believe you've just admitted that you find Jack Miller good-looking.'

'Katie, I can appreciate his looks and hate him at the same time,' I say, amused. At least Jack doesn't make a big deal of his appearance, unlike Nathan, who is, or was, a walking encyclopedia of male grooming products.

Katie changes the subject. 'How are you getting on with living here in the middle of nowhere?'

'It's great.' I've had fun today with Libby and Jack, and the animals. I've enjoyed walking Buster through the copse, past the unfurling bracken, the beech trees and the ancient oak. 'Katie, I know you don't understand, but I'm doing something useful. I haven't thought about Nathan and the wedding, and I haven't had time to fret over the money, or lack of it either.'

'That's good, Tessa,' Katie says, frowning, 'but you don't have to pretend with me.'

'I'm not pretending,' I counter. 'I mean it. I've had a great day.'

She looks at me, her head to one side as if she thinks I'm slightly touched.

'I really don't think it's going to take me as long as I thought to get over it,' I say optimistically.

'You're being so brave. I know I'd still be in bits if I'd split with Nathan, and so publicly.'

'He isn't worth it. He's really messed up and I can console myself with the fact that as it was all so public, everyone around here knows exactly what he's like.'

'That's right,' Katie says cheerfully. 'No self-respecting woman will go out with him now.'

Chapter Seven

The Nature of the Beast

I planned to sneak Buster back to kennels the next morning before anyone else turned up, but I overslept, having drunk too much wine with Katie last night, finishing the bottle myself because she was driving. Libby is on the doorstep, wondering where Buster is.

'I thought he'd made a break for freedom.' She smiles as he jumps up and down barking at her, but when she approaches to stroke him, he stands stock-still, hackles up and tail down, and growls.

'Buster! No!' I tell him in no uncertain terms. 'That is not acceptable.'

'You sound like Supernanny,' Libby says, backing off. 'I don't think he likes me much.'

'I don't know why he did that,' I say, concerned. Is he protecting me? Is this a sign of persistent aggressive behaviour? Did he think Libby was going to hurt him? Would he have gone further than a growl, if I hadn't told him off? 'I took pity on him last night, and to be honest, Libby, I don't feel quite so sorry for him now.' I've redressed his foot because he ripped the dressing off while I left him unattended for a few minutes, and I've wrapped the whole thing in a plastic bag to stop it getting wet. 'Did Jack drop you off?'

'Yes, he's gone to visit that pony, the black and white one that belongs to Frank Maddocks.'

'Oh, I see. That's good to hear.' Why didn't he stop to invite me along as he said he would last night? I wonder. I shrug off an irrational sense of being let down. Jack knows that Libby and I have enough to do at the Sanctuary without taking time out to run around the countryside, glorious as it is on this sunny May morning, to look at ponies.

'Do you want me to take Buster back to kennels?' Libby says, sounding not entirely enthusiastic – unsurprisingly, given the mixed greeting he gave her.

'It's all right, Libby. There's no need to take your life into your hands. If you can get his breakfast ready, I'll bring him over in a couple of minutes. I've written up a new card to go on his kennel in case we have any more potential adopters to visit.'

'By the way, thanks for talking to Jack yesterday, Tessa. He listens to you.'

When I meet Libby in kennels, she's bringing Buster's water bowl from the kitchen. Wanting to avoid further confrontation, I take it and put it in the kennel with him.

'Can Buster be put up for rehoming yet?' Libby asks.

'What do you think?' I respond.

'Tessa, I don't have to think, I'm staff. I do as I'm told – most of the time.' She looks over my shoulder as I peg Buster's new card to the front of the kennel with a list of instructions for his daily routine. 'It's better than a hotel: twice daily walks and breakfast – is that full English or Continental?' She laughs at my hesitation. 'You take everything so seriously.'

'Someone has to make sure we get it right,' I say, a little hurt. Am I that serious, that dull? 'The bit about changing the water – it should be bottled, not tap, and preferably sparkling,' I go on, straight-faced.

'Really?' Libby stares at me. Her expression makes me chuckle.

'Okay, very funny. I get it,' she sighs.

'Going back to the subject of rehoming Buster,' I begin, 'I don't think it's going to be easy. For a start, we know he can't be rehomed where there are other dogs, due to his penchant for trying to kill every one he sees, as evidenced by his behaviour on the Green when he was free to roam... And I'm not sure he should be rehomed where there are humans of any age, considering how he growled at you,' I add. 'I can make as many excuses for his attitude as I like, but it doesn't change the fact that he has a problem.'

'I'm not sure I'll trust him now though,' Libby says, snapping the fingers of a pair of rubber gloves. 'He'll hardly endear himself to the general public by growling at them.'

I recall how Buster grumbled at the chauffeur when he took him into the vet's on the way to the wedding after his altercation with the car. I blamed it on him being in pain from his injuries and confused from the bump to his head, but I fear that this attitude of 'growl first, ask questions later' is more engrained in Buster's character than I first thought.

I watch him reinvestigate the kennel. He sniffs at the plastic bed and cocks his leg over the fluffy bedding.

'Never mind, house-training can break down when dogs are kennelled,' I say, but a wave of doubt washes through me. If I was dreaming of uniting animals with their perfect people, the reality of rescue is now beginning to set in. Buster has issues that mean he's going to need an extra-special home. Does it exist? Why should anyone step forward and choose a dog like Buster over some cute puppy?

We do have our first success later this morning though, thanks to Libby. I get to hand over our first adoptee to his new owner.

'There you go.' I give the rat, which is in a card-board box with ventilation holes and a securely taped lid, to one of Ally Jackson's boys. 'I hope you'll be very happy together,' I say. It seemed like a good idea at the time, but now I feel sorry that I associated my ex with this fiercely intelli-gent and playful creature.

'Oh, they will be,' says the proud and enlight-ened mum, standing beside her ten-year-old son. Ally is in her thirties and wearing a powder-blue trouser suit. 'Is there anything I can do to help the Sanctuary? I can't volunteer – I don't have time – but I am the roving reporter for the *Talyton Chron-icle*, and I could write a feature on some of the animals.'

'That would be great. We need all the publicity we can get,' I say. 'Thank you.'

'Don't thank me. I'm grateful to you because I have to fill the pages of each edition, week in,

146

week out, and not much goes on in Talyton, as you know.' She's smiling as she goes on, 'Sometimes, I pray for fire or flood, something dramatic to report, instead of stories of missing cats, school nativity plays and gallant grannies throwing themselves out of planes for charity.'

'All the best,' I say, as Ally posts a small donation into the box on the desk at reception. 'Keep in touch. We'd love to hear how Nathan's getting on.'

I watch them go before I return to the kennels, checking my mobile on the way to see if Jack's been in touch at all – not because I've missed seeing him so far today, but because I thought he'd want to let me know about the pony. Okay, who am I trying to kid? I like his company. Jack is completely straightforward and honest. He's kind too, and approachable. With Jack, what you see is what you get, and I hate to admit it, but I'm rather liking what I see.

There is no text or missed call on my phone, but I can hear a heavy vehicle rattling and banging along the track towards the Sanctuary. I pause in the car park, wondering if it's DJ coming to collect the mini-digger he's left outside the barn, but it's Jack driving a purple horsebox.

'What are you doing?' I shout over the engine, which sounds like a misfiring machine gun.

'Hop in,' he says, calling out from on high. 'We've got to go and pick up a pony.'

'How exciting,' I call back, before remembering that, if I go, Libby will be left here by herself. 'I should stay here, Jack. Libby and I have got too much to do.'

'Actually, I need as many hands as possible. There's a pony on the loose.'

'Frank Maddocks's little mare?' I ask, shading my eyes from the sun as I look up at him.

'I went to see her this morning. There was no one at Frank's place and the paddock gate was hanging open. I think Dolly's gone in search of some decent grazing.'

'Have you any idea where she is?'

'There have been a few sightings so far; the last one was of her trotting along the road near the Green. I should think she's given a few drivers a shock.'

'As long as no one's been hurt,' I say. 'I'll fetch Libby.'

When I return from the kennels with her, Jack is making a hash of turning the lorry round, making it judder and stall several times through a three-point turn.

'Do you want me to have a go?' I yell up to him. 'You can go back much further. You've got miles between the back of the lorry and the fence.'

Jack's head appears out through the window. He's looking flustered, his hair ruffled and his face red.

'I can't do it with you two watching,' he complains lightly, but Libby and I stay where we are, chuckling to each other and commenting on male drivers. 'I'm being ultra-careful,' Jack goes on. 'Alex Fox-Gifford lent me the box and I have to return it in one piece.'

'You'll be lucky,' I shout over the sound of the engine. 'It looks as though it's going to fall apart at any minute.'

Eventually, the lorry is facing towards the track. Libby and I move around to the passenger side and climb in, Libby letting me go first to take the seat next to Jack.

'Age before beauty, Tessa,' she says cheekily.

'Thanks for that,' I say, smiling as I fasten the seat-belt. 'Are we going?' I ask Jack as he struggles to put the lorry into first gear.

'Patience, Tess,' he says, glancing shyly towards me. The lorry rumbles forwards and bumps its way along the track down to the lane, the dashboard vibrating so violently that it dislodges the paperwork Jack's left on top.

'I hope we don't meet anything coming the other way,' Libby observes as she picks up the papers and tries to put them back in order.

'So do I,' Jack says.

Down by the river, there's a strong police presence, for Talyton anyway: one police car with flashing blue lights parked on the Green and a lone policeman running after a piebald pony across the field beyond. Jack turns in and parks the lorry on the Green as well.

'My aunt isn't going to like this,' I observe, noting the tyre tracks in the damp grass. 'The council will be up in arms.'

'Think of it as our contribution to the community: if the council is fussing about a bit of mud, they won't be poking their noses into anything else,' Jack says. 'I put a new front door on my house before I went away, and now they want me to apply for retrospective planning permission. Can you believe it?' He pauses, looking back towards the bridge across the river where Fifi is

149

getting out of the Volvo. 'I know I shouldn't be rude about your aunt, but here comes the Gestapo to tell me to shift the lorry.' He jumps out and makes for the stile. 'You deal with her, Tess. Libby, you're with me.'

Fifi comes stumbling through the grass in her heels.

'Darling, Tessa, I heard there was a drama on the Green, and I had to come,' she says, touching her throat as if she's slightly breathless. 'What's going on?'

I point to where the pony is cantering off way into the distance with the policeman – I think it's PC Phillips – still chasing after her and gradually falling behind. Apparently realising that he's on a hiding to nothing, Jack and Libby are coming back to the lorry.

'I thought we'd try with a bucket of feed,' Jack says. 'Libby, there's one in the back of the lorry along with a couple of lunge-lines, a head-collar and a chifney.'

'You know you shouldn't have parked on the grass,' Fifi says, while Libby hunts for the equipment. 'There's the beer festival and Britain in Bloom competition coming up, and the Green must look pristine.'

'I'm sorry, Fifi,' Jack says politely. 'I didn't want to obstruct the traffic by parking on the bridge, and it's imperative that we catch this pony before she causes an accident... You do understand,' he adds, as if he's challenging her to argue back.

'Oh, of course, Jack,' my aunt says, giving in, but there is a wicked twinkle in her eye when she continues, 'Speaking as a member of the council, the grass is top priority, but as chair of Talyton Animal Rescue, the pony must come first. What can I do?'

'If you had your running shoes on, I would send you off after PC Phillips.' Jack glances down at her feet. 'You aren't going to get very far in those.'

'There must be something I can do. I'm not one of those people who can stand and watch.'

'Actually, there is,' he says, looking towards the stile where PC Phillips is struggling to get his weary legs over the top and down the other side. 'You can keep Kevin occupied here. Talk to him about traffic calming or something. He hasn't a clue when it comes to horses. He's chased Dolly almost into the next county, and if we're not careful she'll end up on the main road to Talymouth.'

'Why is he here anyway?' Fifi asks.

'Two reasons. Firstly, to seize the pony on behalf of the police.' Jack glances towards me. 'The fact she's strayed is like a gift. It's a great way of getting her away from Frank Maddocks just as it looked as though there wasn't enough evidence to make a case against him. Secondly, it's good to have a police presence in case Frank should turn up, not that he's likely to in the immediate future. He isn't answering the mobile number I've got for him, and when I called in at his mobile home his son said he'd gone on holiday with his girlfriend, to Spain, he thought, or Turkey.' Jack smiles briefly. 'Geography doesn't appear to be his strong point.'

'Isn't he worried about Dolly?' I ask.

'He said she was nothing to do with him. It was

151

up to his father.' Jack greets PC Phillips as he staggers towards us, clutching his hat and rubbing his sweat-soaked hair into spikes.

'I'm not as fit as I was,' he gasps, looking down at his muddy uniform. 'I'm going to have to take up running. You're the expert, Jack. How are we going to catch the little sh–' He stops abruptly at the sight of my aunt. 'Ah, good morning, Fifi.'

'Hello, Kevin,' she says. 'Mind your language, dear boy. Remember you're not mixing with common criminals now.'

'I apologise.' He blushes. 'It's that pony. I've let it wind me up.'

'It's all right, Kevin,' Jack says. 'I have a plan. There's a gap, in the hedge she must have forced her way through. If you can wait near the stile, you can head her off if she comes back in this direction, but be careful not to stand in her way – she's built like a tank. Find a stick to wave at her, or make a lot of noise to frighten her off. In the meantime, Libby, Tess and I will take the gear and see if we can tempt her to come to us.'

'I can't see how that's going to work,' says PC Phillips.

'I'm depending on her being hungry,' says Jack. 'Come on, then. Let's go.'

We share the equipment between us. Jack carries a head-collar and rope, and a bucket half filled with pony nuts. The bucket is bright purple, like the lorry. Libby and I bring the rest, walking along the path beside the river for some distance before we catch sight of Dolly, who's standing in the shade of an oak tree, her head down, eyes half closed and resting one hind-leg.

152

'We'll stop here,' Jack decides in a low voice. 'Now, remember not to chase her. If she gallops off again, just turn around and walk back the other way. If we spook her she'll be through the next hedge and into the garden at the back of the pub, and from there it's hardly any distance to the main road, and you know how fast the traffic travels along there.'

It's true, I think. I blame it on the grockles, or tourists, who aren't familiar with the road, gaining speed along the long straight sections and scaring themselves witless at the hairpin bends on the hill down into Talymouth.

'Why don't Libby and I stand along the hedge-line and flick the lunge-lines at the pony if she tries to make a break for it?' I suggest.

'You can try,' Jack says. 'I'll approach her with the bucket. Be patient though – I might be some time.'

Libby looks at me. 'Rather him than me,' she mouths.

Jack plants the bucket a few metres from the pony and stands a little way back, side-on to her, his shoulders slumped and eyes averted in order to appear non-threatening as he did before. He might have convinced himself, but he hasn't convinced Dolly for she opens her eyes and raises her head, flaring her nostrils and snorting with alarm, a sound that sends a flock of pigeons flying out from the branches above her, making her leap forwards in fright and taking her closer to the bucket. She knows what it is and she's interested, but it takes her ten minutes to decide that it's safe to put her nose inside it and start

153

snaffling up the nuts.

'Good girl. You're doing so well, Dolly,' Jack says in a voice that would seduce any female. Well, it would work for me, if I was looking for a man, which I'm not, although I find myself transfixed by the way he gradually and quietly moves in to the pony's shoulder to reach out and scratch her withers before laying the lead-rope over her neck. He waits for a moment for her to lift her head from the bucket, and slips the head-collar over her nose before taking advantage of Dolly's decision to dive back for more pony nuts, lifting the strap behind her ears and fastening it at the side of her head.

I give him the thumbs up, not wanting to scare the pony by cheering and shouting, and we begin to make our way across the field back towards the Green, taking the shorter route along the old railway lane, Jack leading Dolly ahead of me and Libby. At least, that was Jack's intention, but before he gets there, the pony catches sight of some sheep grazing in a small flock on the hillock to our right. Either that or she's suddenly decided that recapture was not on her agenda. She arches her neck and sets out at a trot, tearing the rope from Jack's hands, swinging her rump as she passes and landing both barrels on Jack's behind.

'She got me!' Jack shouts, as Dolly thunders back towards me and Libby, the rope tangling around her front legs, without deviating from her chosen path. We jump aside to let her pass before running over to Jack, who stands, grimacing and clutching his rear. 'She got me,' he repeats.

'What's the damage?' Libby says, half serious,

154

half laughing at her brother's discomfort. 'Show me.'

'No way, sis,' he says, shaking his head.

'Won't you have to report it as a work-related accident?' she teases.

'It's nothing,' he insists. 'Now, where's that bloody pony?' She hasn't gone far, having returned to the shelter of the oak tree, somewhere she appears to feel relatively safe. 'I shouldn't have relied on a head-collar. I should have put her in the chifney.' Jack looks towards me. 'You've got that, haven't you? It's the leather headpiece with the thin metal bit attached – the kind of bit they use for leading racehorses and colts to stop them rearing and getting away.'

I hand it over, wishing him the best of luck and wondering if we're ever going to catch her.

It's another two hours before Jack gets Dolly back to the Green and another thirty minutes to load her into the lorry, by which time I'm not sure who is sweating the most, the people or the pony. It's a relief when we return to the Sanctuary. Jack parks the lorry and Libby goes to make some cold drinks, feed the baby birds and let the dogs out, while I shut the gate onto the track, making sure the catch is secured so we don't risk losing Dolly again. Together, Jack and I open the ramp at the back. The pony stands behind the partition, rolling her eyes, tossing her head and pawing furiously at the floor. Her coat is dripping with perspiration and the air is rich with the scent of dung, sweet meadow hay and hot horse.

Jack enters quietly.

155

'Hey there, Dolly. Let's calm it down, shall we? You're going to love this place.' He glances towards me, and adds, 'I hope.' He unties the quick release knot before I take the clip off the partition and swing it open for him to lead the pony down the ramp – or, as it turns out, for her to lead him. She hesitates at the top and throws herself off, yanking the rope from his grip yet again.

'You are one ungrateful pony!' Jack shouts, losing his patience with her at last. I don't blame him. She's infuriating, and doesn't she know it, trotting about the car park, holding her head and tail up high, snorting and showing the red flare inside her nostrils. She has one blue eye and one brown, and she doesn't look anything like a lumbering cob now. She's light – and surprisingly quick – on her feet as she grabs a mouthful of begonias from the tubs that Fifi donated from the garden centre, before spinning around and cantering towards the paddock, where she stops and nudges at the gate.

'There doesn't appear to be much wrong with her legs, after all,' I point out. 'She's like a racing thoroughbred.'

'I think we need the bucket again,' Jack says, heading off around the back of the lorry. He takes some time and, assuming he's having trouble finding the bucket, I decide to give him a hand.

'Jack,' I call as I run up the ramp. 'I think I saw it underneath the saddle racks.' I stop at the top. Jack is standing half hidden by the partition, facing away from me with the bucket slung over his wrist, his trousers and pants halfway down his thighs, his torso twisted as he tries to examine his

156

buttocks. I don't know where to look, but it's too late to pretend I haven't noticed.

'Oh, I'm sorry,' I say at the same time as Jack looks up, registering my presence, his expression like that of a shocked sheep. He tugs his trousers up to cover his modesty, blushing furiously to the roots of his blond hair.

'I was just checking the damage,' he says quickly. 'I thought she might have drawn blood.'

'Would you like me to have a look for you,' I say brazenly. 'I can give you a professional opinion.'

'No, thanks, Tess. I'm okay. Dolly's bruised my pride more than she has my' – he fumbles rather sweetly for an appropriate description of the affected area – 'bottom.'

'I bet you'll be tender for a couple of days.'

'Yeah.' He fastens his fly and the buckle on his belt, before exiting the lorry with me. 'I thank my lucky stars that the pony wasn't wearing shoes.'

Dolly is still at the paddock gate and we manage to persuade her through by rattling a couple of mints in the bottom of the bucket. Jack unclips the lead-rope, leaving the head-collar on so we can catch her for the vet when he comes.

'Perhaps we should have left her in one of the new stables,' I say as Libby joins us with glasses of orange squash. 'That's what they're there for.'

'She's used to being out,' Jack says. 'We don't want to make too many changes at once, otherwise she'll get colic.'

'What happens next?' Libby asks. 'Can she go straight up for rehoming?'

'I'm afraid it's more complicated than that,' Jack replies. 'Mr Maddocks will be given a week to

157

come and claim the pony and pay a release fee. If he can't, or won't, the police will send her to the horse sales, where she'll be auctioned to the highest bidder. That's how they defray their costs.'

'I don't see how you can possibly let Dolly go back to that man,' Libby says, staring at her brother, and I echo her feelings on the matter.

'Believe me, I'm doing my best,' Jack says gruffly. 'Let's concentrate on making her safe here before we worry about what happens to her in the future. Have you checked the fences, Tess?'

'I'll do it now, and I'll fill the trough.'

'Let me do that,' Libby says. 'I want to look after Dolly. I've always wanted a pony, but Mum and Dad wouldn't let me have one.'

'You can, if she stays,' I observe, watching Dolly whinnying and galloping about, her mane and tail flowing behind her. 'I don't think she likes it here.'

'She needs some company,' Jack says, addressing me.

Don't we all, I muse, afraid that I am beginning to crave Jack's company a little too much. I gaze at him more fondly than I thought possible after what he did at my wedding. The drama and excitement of catching the pony is not the only thing that made my heart beat faster today.

Chapter Eight

Special Delivery

It's three days since we caught Dolly and brought her to the Sanctuary, and we haven't been able to get near her since. The trick with the bucket isn't working because, with all the grass in the paddock, she isn't hungry. Libby tries to tempt her over with a carrot, but Dolly isn't stupid.

'That didn't work,' Libby says, coming over to join me where I've taken it into my own hands to sweep up some of the builder's sand that DJ hasn't got around to clearing up yet. 'Do you want a hand moving some of those tools?' she goes on.

'I wouldn't mind. DJ hasn't shown up yet.' It's gone eleven and I'm not sure he's going to today.

'He's started work on another job,' Libby says. 'I saw his truck parked outside one of the houses in Silver Street this morning.'

'Oh, great. That's just what I need, and it explains why he isn't answering his phone.' I pause. 'We've got the Fun Day at the beginning of June – less than a fortnight away. It isn't going to be much fun if this place looks a mess.'

'It won't. We'll all muck in,' Libby says, picking up a shovel that turns out to be in two pieces. 'Where shall I put this?'

'In the far end of the barn or in the shed. Any-

159

where as long as it's out of sight.'

We're partway through our task when the postman turns up in his red van. He isn't our usual postie, I notice when he jumps out with a sheaf of letters. He's much younger, for a start, in his mid-twenties and good-looking, with short brown hair, hazel eyes and a lightly tanned complexion.

'Hi,' he says, smiling. 'I'm Ash. I should have been here hours ago – I have a special delivery for you.'

I notice how he automatically turns to Libby, not me, and I feel like I'm butting in when I introduce myself.

'I'm Tessa, the manager here... And this is Libby, one of our volunteers,' I go on, when Libby just stands there, staring at him in his navy T-shirt and shorts with a standard reflective Royal Mail waistcoat over the top. Perhaps I should go on to clarify that she's our only volunteer, because, like DJ, Diane and Wendy haven't shown up either. Perhaps I should also give her a nudge: she's making herself look completely transparent, playing with a lock of her hair and popping her eyes at him, but it seems that Ash is equally taken with her.

'I feel like I've met you somewhere before,' he says eventually. 'I live down at Farley's End.'

'I'm from Talyton St George,' says Libby, with a small frown.

'I've probably seen you in town then. There's no reason for anyone to visit Farley's End – there's nothing there except a farm, five cottages and a derelict chapel.'

'Were you ever a Young Farmer?' Libby asks.

160

'The post,' I cut in.

'Ah, yes.' Ash hands me the letters, at least a tree's worth, forwarded from my parents' house and defaced by my dad's handwriting (I never did sort out my change of address when I moved in with Nathan). I think it is Dad's way of letting me know that I'm neglecting him, and I make a mental note to invite him over with Mum sometime soon, perhaps for the Fun Day and dinner afterwards. I'm well practised in preparing meals for the animals, but my cooking isn't so hot, and I tend to make a dog's dinner out of even the easiest of Delia's recipes.

Ash turns back to Libby. 'Didn't you use to go swimming at the pool in Talymouth? I was a lifeguard and a Dolphin.'

Libby blushes. 'That's right. I remember now. I used to hang around there with my friends.'

'Um, is there anything I have to sign for, only I'd like to get on,' I say. 'Ash, you said you had a special delivery for us?'

'I almost forgot,' he says, turning towards his vehicle. 'It's in a box in the van. Oh no, it isn't.' I follow his gaze, alerted by the lilt of panic in his voice. There's a cat, a black and white one, standing on the driver's seat with its paws resting on the edge of the part-open window. 'It must have forced the lid open. I thought I'd stuck it down well enough.'

'Don't open the door,' I tell him as he makes for the van.

'I thought Postman Pat was a fictional character, but look at you and your black and white cat. You're just like him.' Libby grins.

161

'Yeah, but I don't have the silly hat and three fingers on each hand,' Ash counters. 'It's all right – I've heard all the Postman Pat jokes today. My mates have been winding me up since they found out I'd picked up a cat on my round. I found it in the back of the van – it must have jumped in and hitched a lift somewhere. The trouble is I'm not sure where to deliver it back to, so I thought I'd bring it here. Can you take it?'

'Yes, of course. Libby, would you mind getting one of the carriers from under the desk in reception?' She bustles off and returns with a white wire basket, and we spend five minutes coaxing the cat into it before we can settle it into the cattery in the pen opposite Teddy's. I check it quickly – it's a girl. Hopefully, someone will notice she's missing and give us or the local vets a call, or, if she's lucky, she'll be microchipped and we'll be able to reunite her with her owner. It doesn't look as though she's been living rough – she's too well fed.

Once Ash has gone, Libby clips a record card to the cat's pen.

'I've given her a temporary name,' she says.

'What is it?' I ask.

'In tribute to Postman Pat, it has to be Jess.' Libby looks at me. 'At least that's cheered you up, Tessa.' She returns to tidying up after DJ, while I remain in the cattery to spend half an hour or so with Teddy. I tell everyone that it's all about his rehabilitation, helping him to be the best pet he can be, but it's more about me taking time out for a sneaky cuddle.

When the phone rings, I tuck it awkwardly between my chin and shoulder, so I can keep hold of Teddy while I answer the call.

'Talyton Animal Rescue here.' Teddy butts his cheek against my face – he's been much happier since he came back from the vet's. 'How can I help?'

'I can't hear you very well.' The woman at the end of the line sounds mature and well spoken. 'There's a lot of interference.'

'It's all right.' I try to persuade Teddy to go back into his pen. 'It's a cat purring.'

'A cat?' she says dismissively as he turns to make a run for it before I can close the door.

'Hey, come here.' I grab the phone with one hand and rugby-tackle the cat, grasping him around his middle before pushing him back into his pen, closing the door and slipping the bolt across. 'I'm sorry about that – Teddy loves his cuddles.'

'Cuddles?' I can hear the disgust in the caller's voice. 'Never mind, I wanted to ask you if you take in dogs.'

'We do, although we don't have much kennel space available at the moment.' DJ still hasn't completed the work in the kennel block. 'Did you want to come and meet the animals we have up for rehoming?' We haven't all that many yet: Buster, Teddy and a pair of crazy spaniels.

'Oh no, I don't want to rescue a dog. I want to hand one over to you.'

'Can I ask why?' I make every effort to sound sympathetic, but I guess I'm always going to find it hard to understand how anyone can give up their pet, except in the most extreme circum-stances.

'It isn't mine. It's my mother's. She's going in to hospital for an operation, and it's unlikely she'll ever return to her house. The nursing homes I've looked at won't take pets.'

'There's no way you can take your mother's dog on?' I say. Ask a silly question...

'I work full-time and I can't possibly take on a dog, any dog – and besides, Tia is used to having someone at home at all times. It wouldn't be fair.'

'Perhaps you could kennel the dog until you're absolutely sure your mother isn't going home,' I suggest. 'That way there's a chance they can stay together.'

'No, I've made my mind up. The dog has to go.'

I bite my tongue. It seems very harsh, and I wonder why she won't try harder to care for her mother's dog. I would in her position.

'You could have a dog walker drop in once a day while you're at work.'

'Tia doesn't walk any more, and to be blunt with you, she isn't my kind of dog. If I was going to go to the bother of having one, I wouldn't choose Tia. I'd opt for one with – how should I put it – a bit of personality.'

I'm worried now. The dog needs rescuing from this dreadful woman, but how am I going to rehome a dog of Tia's description?

'You'd better bring her over,' I say with reluct-ance. 'I'll be here all day.'

'Can't you collect her?'

'Have you got a car?' I say impatiently.

'I'm not taking the risk – Tia suffers from travel sickness, even on the shortest of journeys. And I can't possibly force her to walk to you. As I've

164

said, she doesn't do walks any more.'

'How old is she?' I ask.

'Eleven or twelve, thirteen maybe. I don't know – she's just a dog.'

It crosses my mind that Tia might be better off being put down. It's horrible to contemplate, but sometimes it's the fairest option. However, I don't want to force this woman into making the decision. She sounds as if she has absolutely no compassion for either the dog or her elderly parent.

'She's blind and doesn't hear very well, and I've no idea if it's because she's deaf, or completely senile like my mother. Well, tell a lie. My mother isn't completely senile – sometimes I think she puts it on to avoid talking to me.'

Give me strength, I think as she piles on problem after problem. I repeat my request that she bring the dog, but in the end I agree to send Jack with the van as soon as possible. The caller is not someone who is used to being denied.

After clearing the kennel next door to the crazy spaniels, I take five minutes out, choosing a dry spot on the lawn at the back of the bungalow, where I lie down on my back and squint up at the leaves on the cherry tree. The sun filters between them, warm on my skin. It's a beautiful day.

I stretch my arms, admiring the muscles I didn't know I had before working at the Sanctuary. I'm wearing a vest with lace trim, jeans rolled partway up my calves and a pair of particularly unsexy steel-toecapped walking boots. The position of manager is both character- and body-building.

On hearing a vehicle coming up the track, my

165

heart misses a beat, but regains its normal rhythm when I look past the side of the bungalow to the car park and realise that it's my aunt, not Jack.

'Well done, Tessa,' she says, brandishing a copy of the paper when I meet her out the front. 'You should have gone into PR. Look at this.' She opens the Chronicle at page two and shows me the results of my interview with Ally, who, true to her word, came out a couple of days ago with a photographer to take pictures of some of the animals. Teddy the cat was a natural poser, gazing into the camera while I held him in my arms, whereas Buster hated it, looking away before deciding he'd had enough, slumping down on the floor with his nose tucked under his paws. 'The ducklings are gorgeous,' Fifi goes on, and I have to agree with her, they really have the 'ah' factor. 'If they don't persuade people to come and have a look around at the Fun Day, nothing will.'

I was hoping the photo of Buster would make someone fall in love with him, but I'm doubtful now. He looks like a grumpy old man.

'So, how is it all going?' Fifi asks when we're finally alone together, having dropped Libby off at the Co-op, where she's been called in to do an extra shift, and brought me to the garden centre for a cream tea. It is one of her many missions in life to get some weight back on my bones, to turn me from what she describes as a skinny chicken into a fat bird.

'I thought you might have come up to find out,' I respond, wishing to let her know that I've

166

missed her help without sounding as though I'm criticising her lack of input. We are sitting at one of the tables in the coffee shop, surrounded by fronds of greenery and beside a stand of special offers – impulse buys of handy items you never thought you needed, like grippers to attach to your shoes so you can walk safely on ice, and fleecy sacks you can wear while chilling out on the sofa in the winter, shopping trolleys and support stockings.

'Oh, I've been rushed off my feet as usual. I'll drop by to do some more office work one day next week.' She pauses, gazing at me, her eyelashes long and thick with mascara and her lips an unnatural matt pink. 'Have Diane and Wendy been along to volunteer recently?'

'They turn up occasionally. They seemed keen to start with, but their enthusiasm appears to be waning. Libby's often about though.' I smile to myself. I reckon she'll be staying on at the Sanctuary for a long time yet, and not just because of her interest in the pony.

'And Jack? Is it working out between you?'

'I couldn't do it without him,' I say generously.

'I see. So you are managing to work with him, after all?' A smile plays on my aunt's lips. 'I knew you two would get along.'

'We get along for the welfare of the animals. We're very ... professional.' I find myself blundering on in my eagerness to prove that there is not and never will be anything between me and Jack, in spite of my aunt's apparent determination that there will be hearts and flowers.

'Jack's a lovely boy,' she continues. 'He's always

167

thinking of others before himself. He was called out to the Old Forge up at Talyford the other night. There was a fire, and Penny – you know Penny, with the assistance dog – was trapped in her studio. According to the gossip in the butcher's, Jack forced the window at the back and carried her out over his shoulder, would you believe it?'

Do I believe it? I know from experience that you have to take some of Talyton's spicier pieces of gossip with a pinch of salt, but this one seems genuine.

'When did this happen?' I ask.

'On Monday night.'

'Jack didn't say anything.'

'Well, he wouldn't, would he? As a retained firefighter, he would say that it's what he's paid to do for the members of our rural community.' My aunt smiles again and adds with more than a trace of irony, 'Why should he mention it to you anyway, Tessa? I wouldn't expect Jack to make small talk to me when our relationship was on an entirely professional footing.' She changes the subject. 'How's DJ getting on?'

'When I managed to get hold of him, he mentioned that he hasn't been paid,' I say as tactfully as I can manage.

'That's Diane's fault,' Fifi flashes back. 'She's treasurer. She's withholding the funds.'

'Can she do that?'

'She thinks she can.'

'But DJ's doing the work, so he's fulfilling his side of the contract. You can't not pay him.'

'I'm doing my best in the face of adversity.' Fifi

168

taps her spoon against the side of her teacup. 'Diane has always been a subversive influence on the committee and she's always had her eye on taking over the role of chair, not because she'll be any good at it, but out of envy.'

'Let's forget Diane for a moment. I'm worried that DJ will push off without finishing everything. The stables look great, but he hasn't hung the doors in the kitchen in the bungalow, or completed the last five kennels (there should be a row of ten), or lined the shed so it's useable. I'd like it all to be done before the Fun Day. It isn't long now and we're nowhere near ready to show it off to the public. I don't have time for DIY when I'm tied up with the animals.' I am beginning to panic. 'Is Diane being a pain about the money to get at you for taking me on here? Because that's the rumour, according to Jack.'

'I'm still chair of Talyton Animal Rescue. No one can do anything without my say-so.'

'Fifi, do you think I should leave? My leaving would solve the problem.'

'Don't even think of it. We'd never find anyone else of your calibre, and besides, we need someone there now. There are animals at the Sanctuary that need full-time care. I can't let you abandon them.'

'I could stay until the committee finds a replacement.' It would break my heart, but I would do anything to save the Sanctuary, and with the committee members falling out with my aunt, I can feel it beginning to fall apart.

'You are not going anywhere, dear niece. There's bound to be some unrest among the volunteers –

169

people don't like change. One day, they'll see sense, and in the meantime, we must go ahead with the fundraising events for this summer, otherwise the summer ball will end up as a winter one, and that will clash with the highlight of the hunt's social calendar, the Hunt Ball. I thought we'd go for September.'

'How can we go ahead with arranging a ball if the rest of the committee isn't onside?' I spread a dollop of clotted cream onto my scone before scooping jam from the dish on the tray in front of me. I was going to choose carrot cake because it sounds vaguely healthy, but as Fifi noted while I was deliberating at the counter, the garden centre's carrot cake should carry a warning: may contain traces of carrot.

'We'll worry about that later,' Fifi says. 'If we wait, everywhere will be booked up.'

'We need a half-decent venue that isn't too expensive,' I explain. 'You know everyone so I thought you might be able to strike me a good deal. I thought maybe I could look at the Talymill Inn, the Dog and Duck or the Cricket Club, or we could keep it simple with a hog roast at the church hall.'

'Oh no, you can't possibly expect everyone to make a splash unless you book somewhere far more exclusive,' Fifi says disapprovingly. 'And a hog roast? That will not do. That will not do at all. You'll be telling me you want to hold a disco in a barn, like the Young Farmers. Tessa, I am not wading through mud in my best shoes and sitting on a straw bale with a paper plate of greasy pig and slimy coleslaw. Ugh!'

170

'What about here, at the garden centre? You could donate the fee to Talyton Animal Rescue.' I warm to my idea. 'You know what you're doing. You've held dances here before.'

'Yes, tea dances for the over-eighties.' Fifi shakes her head slowly. 'Your uncle couldn't cope with the idea of partygoers' undertaking drunken antics among the gnomes, and I couldn't stand the strain of watching him getting more and more stressed out.'

'What kind of balls do you go to, Fifi?' I ask, pretending to be appalled. 'They sound completely wild.'

'Someone always ends up dancing on the table,' she begins, tilting her head to one side. 'You're so staid, Tessa. Don't you ever have any fun?' She hesitates. 'I'm sorry, you've been through so much recently. That was tactless of me' – she laughs at herself – 'as ever.'

The 'having fun' gene must have skipped a generation, I muse, thinking of my parents' antics, the pyjama parties, murder mysteries and post-panto celebrations.

'I'll make sure you let your hair down. We'll find you a dress and some decent heels, and a handsome man to accompany you. Cinderella, you will go to the ball.'

'Thank you, but–'

'No buts. I'll pay towards the dress and lend you a pair of shoes.' Fifi strokes her top lip as if checking for stray whiskers. 'I might have to leave the handsome man down to you. I'm sure Jack would be more than willing...'

'Jack,' I echo. 'I'll be too tied up with organising

171

the event to take part,' I say, but I feel a frisson of excitement at the thought of being among all those people, dressed in black tie and glamorous dresses, drinking champagne and dancing. I picture myself holding on to Jack's arm as I greet the guests on behalf of Talyton Animal Rescue before he leads me onto the dance floor, spins me round to face him and slips his arm behind my back... Okay, I can't imagine the next part because I can't dance to save my life, but it involves some bodily contact – chaste bodily contact, you understand, but contact all the same.

'Tessa?' Fifi brings me back down to earth. 'You haven't been listening to a word I've said. You appear to be terribly distracted.'

'I'm sorry,' I say quickly. 'I'm back...'

Fifi gazes at me, bemused, as if to say, But you haven't gone anywhere.

'Where does the hunt hold their ball?' I ask. 'Couldn't we try there?'

'Alex Fox-Gifford hosts that at the Manor and, to be honest, it's a little run-down; all very well for the horsey set, but not what I had in mind.' My aunt leans towards me. 'I think you should call the hotel in Talymouth, the one on the seafront that has a ballroom.'

'Won't that be too expensive?'

'That's what I'm trying to say,' Fifi says, exasperation etched across her face. 'You should ring them to find out how much it is per head and check availability in September. It would be such a coup if we got that venue. Go on, Tessa. Call them now.'

I have to deal with it when I return to the

172

Sanctuary, however, because Jack phones me to let me know he's on his way there, having picked up Tia the dog, and I have all the keys. My aunt drops me off, giving me time to give the baby birds their afternoon tea before Jack arrives about twenty minutes later.

'Tessa, I've brought you a new resident, but judging by the look of her, I don't think she's going to last very long. She's pretty ancient,' Jack says brightly, looking out of the open window of the van and slapping the outside of the door with the palm of his hand in rhythm to the music playing on the radio.

'So this is Tia,' I say as Jack hands me the paperwork. I scan down the form that Tia's owner's daughter has completed on her behalf.

'The old lady has lost her marbles so the daughter has power of attorney. It's all above board...' Jack pauses. 'I don't hold out any hope of you finding a home for this poor old thing. I almost stopped at Otter House on the way to have a chat with Maz or Emma, but I thought you'd better have a look first.'

It's one of the reasons Fifi took me on. Because I'm a vet nurse, I can make the initial assessments on every animal we take in, thereby, in some cases, saving the charity money on vet's bills. Not in Tia's case though.

Jack opens the door and swings his long legs out of the van before walking around the back in a navy polo-shirt and combat trousers that fit snugly across his muscular buttocks. I try, but fail, not to look. He opens the rear doors, slips a rope lead over the dog's head and lifts her down.

173

'Meet the lovely Tia,' he says.

I approach the hugely overweight roan cocker spaniel that's bulging with fatty lumps and bumps that shouldn't be there, and hold out my hand to her. She sniffs it vaguely then stands with her head down and tail tucked between her legs, much like Buster did when he first arrived at the Sanctuary.

'You poor old thing,' I say gently. 'Jack, let's get her into kennels so I can give her the once-over.'

'I wish you'd do that for me,' Jack says, touching the small of his back. 'I could do with a once-over. She weighs a ton.'

'Be careful what you wish for,' I tell him with mock sternness. 'I might find I have to be cruel to be kind.'

'Yes, I'd prefer you to miss out the bit with the thermometer to be honest,' he jokes.

Tia waddles along behind us, puffing and panting, her tongue hanging out and her overgrown nails clacking on the floor on the way to the kitchen in the kennel block. Suppressing the urge to invite Jack onto the table for a full examination and maybe a back massage, I ask him to lift the dog up for me, where she stands like a statue.

'Go on then, nurse,' Jack says, smiling. 'Do you want me to restrain her for you?'

'I don't think she's going anywhere fast.' I check Tia over, examining her mouth, nose, eyes and ears. She reeks of halitosis, greasy skin and infected ears, so much that she makes me retch. 'I'm going to have to book her in to see one of the vets. She's in a terrible state.'

'Do you think anyone will take her on, a dog of

174

her age and in this condition?' Jack asks tentatively. 'She might not last much longer.'

'She's a sweet dog.' Mild, by which I mean she has an almost non-existent persona. 'There must be someone out there who will love her.'

'That's one of the things I like about you, Tess. You're always so bloody optimistic,' Jack grins.

'Not always,' I say. 'Put her into the kennel next to the spaniels. I'll contact Otter House to book an appointment for tomorrow. Can I have the van?'

'I can take her.'

'No, it's all right. I'm happy to do it.' To be honest, I could do with having a break from the Sanctuary. It's more a lifestyle than a job. I stroke Tia's floppy ear through the dense mats of hair. She can't have been brushed for years.

'I'll drive you there,' Jack says.

'Jack, really, there's no need. Anyway, I could do with picking up a few groceries at the same time. I've got a list as long as my arm of things we need for the Fun Day: drinks, a banner and balloons, which reminds me, I must get in touch with Jennie to ask her if she'll donate some cupcakes.'

'We could run up to Overdown Farmers for dog and cat food too,' Jack says.

I give in graciously. 'That would be useful. Thanks.'

'I'll be here at eight.' With one easy move, Jack wraps his arms around the dog and lifts her back down to the floor. He hands me the end of the lead and Tia follows me into the kennel where I squat down beside her and slip the rope over her head.

'Good girl. I'll get you some dinner.' I turn to Jack, who towers above me, his combats smeared with dried mud and grass stains. 'Do you know what she has? Dried food or tinned, or a mixture?'

'I asked, but she didn't have a clue.' Jack folds his arms across his chest. 'It looks as if Tia eats pretty well anything from the size of her. She'd make a handy coffee table for someone.'

'Jack, that's mean,' I say lightly.

'Sometimes you have to laugh or else you'd cry. Besides, the dog isn't offended – I don't think she can hear. Or see,' he adds, as Tia takes a stumbling step to the left and bumps her nose on the wall.

'She needs a guide dog,' I say. I walk her out to the run and make sure she's checked out the bowl of fresh water and the bed I've put together for her, a plastic one that's raised off the ground so it's draught-proof. She clambers stiffly onto the top of the cushion inside it, turns around a couple of times and lies down, trembling and whining, her nose tucked into her tail. 'It's such a shame that this had to happen to her. She's petrified.'

Jack hands me a crumpled tissue.

'Thanks,' I say, blowing my nose. 'I've got a touch of hay fever. It must have something to do with the straw I put down for the ducklings.' I don't know why I have to hide my feelings from Jack when he seems almost as upset for Tia as I am. 'Do you think it's fair to leave her in a kennel?' I ask him. 'I doubt she's ever been away from home before.'

'I'll feed her, and see if she settles.' Jack fetches

176

a bowl of dog food, which makes Buster next door want some and he starts to bark. 'He's getting more confident.'

'I've been doing a lot of work with him.'

'I wish someone would give me that much attention.'

'Don't I talk to you?' I say archly.

'I wasn't just thinking of talking,' he says, making me blush.

I try to make light of it, continuing, 'I'll take you for a walk if you like now and again. You'll have to be on a lead though!'

'I wouldn't run away, Tess,' he says in a low voice, and although I don't quite catch it, I think he adds, 'I promise,' and my heart flutters briefly like a butterfly settling on a flower.

'I think Jack's trying to seduce me, but a man's promise doesn't mean anything, does it?' I say to Buster much later when I'm taking him out for one last stroll around the copse. We walk up the hillside, past the stand of conifers and mature trees, stopping at the top to look at the view of the sun setting behind the hills in the distance, and I wonder if Gloria Brambles ever came up here to do the same. It's beautiful. Buster tenses, sniffing the air, and a deer leaps across the path only a few metres away from us before disappearing into the bushes opposite. I squat down beside Buster with my arm around his neck, considering myself to be, in spite of everything, a very lucky woman.

How could anyone do such a thing? Hanging on to Buster by the collar as he strains to get to the crate on the doorstep the following morning, I count the heads that peer nervously out of the top. There are three of them: gorgeous puppies with floppy ears, wavy golden coats, long tails and oversized paws.

'Please, Buster, leave them alone,' I say, losing patience with him. 'You can't have them for breakfast and that's that. Come on.' I drag him away and shut him in the bedroom, so I can assess the new arrivals. They have apparently been abandoned overnight without anyone – even Buster – noticing until about ten minutes ago, when he began snuffling about at the front door.

'You poor little things.' I bring the crate in-doors, worried they might jump out, but they are too confused, happy for the attention yet appre-hensive, as well they might be with Buster's style of welcome. I yell at him to stop when he starts scratching at the bedroom door, asking to be let out. He doesn't like other dogs and he isn't all that keen on people, but solitary confinement doesn't suit him.

I pick the puppies out one at a time, two girls and a boy, and give them each a cuddle, breath-ing their scent, which reminds me of damp earth and Marmite. They nuzzle at my hands and lick my nose, making me smile. Although their pot bellies suggest an infestation of worms, and they have a few fleas between them, overall they're in good condition, which makes it seem even more incomprehensible that anyone could do such a thing. I glance out of the window where the clouds scud across a blue sky. At least they chose a warm night.

I decide to take the puppies to the kennels and call the vets to see if they can give me a longer appointment this morning, but they are fully booked. It isn't a problem though – it never is for them – and they promise to fit the puppies in with Tia.

'Call yourself a guard dog,' I tell Buster when I return to the bungalow. 'You're all mouth and no trousers. You didn't make a sound last night.' He looks up at me, all sheepish. 'I don't mean it,' I say, apologising. 'Come on, let's go for a–' I don't have to say the word, because he's off, scampering around the bungalow like a demon, leaping up and down and barking to go out. I don't have much time before Jack turns up with the van to go to the vet's, so I don't bother to get dressed, taking a stroll around the paddock in my wellies and dressing gown and quickly returning Buster to his kennel, only to find Jack coming across the car park towards me.

'Hi, Tess.'

My heart sinks, because there may be some truth in my aunt's opinion that there are times when one really should keep up one's appearance, and this occasion might just be one of them.

'What time do you call this?' Jack says, tapping his wristwatch.

'I'm all behind.'

'I should say so, like the cow's tail.' He smiles.

'We should get going,' I say. 'Maz will be expecting us.'

'Don't you think you ought to get dressed first?' Jack says, amused. 'You seem to be in a bit

179

of a flap.'

I explain about the new arrivals as we get ready to leave. I'm sure he can manage the trip to the vet's by himself, but it's a good excuse to spend time with Tia and the puppies and, if I'm honest, with Jack.

'What have we here?' Maz says, her wedding ring on a chain around her neck and a pen tucked into the pocket of her paw-print top, when we're squeezed into the consulting room at Otter House. She looks into the crate that Jack has placed on the table. 'A veritable squirmish of puppies? How sweet!'

'Someone abandoned them on the doorstep at the Sanctuary last night,' I say. 'I don't understand why Buster didn't bark.'

'You mean the black dog,' Maz says, stroking the puppies with both hands. 'I expect he thinks he doesn't need to bother now he's got his paws firmly under the table. Are you any closer to finding him a home yet?'

'He lives with you, Tess,' Jack points out when I shake my head. 'He might as well be your dog.'

'It's part of his rehabilitation,' I say, grinning.

'Sure,' Jack says.

'I've heard that one before,' Maz says, picking one of the puppies up out of the crate and hugging it to her chest. 'You vet nurses are so predictable, making the same excuses to take unwanted animals home.' She plants a kiss on top of the puppy's head. 'You won't have any trouble finding homes for these guys. You'll have people fighting over them.'

'We have a waiting list for puppies. It's a shame

180

so few people are looking for adult dogs,' I observe.

'Do you know anything at all about their background?' Maz asks.

'I found a note tucked in the side of the crate. They were the last of a litter of nine and surplus to requirements. They're seven weeks old, their mum was a cocker spaniel and their dad a Standard poodle.'

'So they're cockapoos,' Maz says, smiling.

'I can't keep up with all these odd crosses,' says Jack. 'A dog is a dog, as far as I'm concerned.'

'It's very fashionable at the moment,' Maz says, 'but it's gets confusing when people start crossing the crosses, a cockapoo with a springador, for example. It's supposed to reduce the incidence of breed-related genetic conditions like hereditary cataracts and hip dysplasia, but I can't help wondering if it will end up multiplying them and making the situation worse.'

She goes on to examine the three puppies and pronounces them fit and healthy before giving them their first vaccinations to help protect them against infectious diseases during their stay in kennels. Jack returns them to the van while I talk to Maz about Tia.

'I'd be ashamed if I were her owner,' I say as Tia plants her bottom heavily on my feet. 'The elderly lady who had her has been ill, and no one in the family appears to have taken responsibility for the dog.'

Maz suggests that we weigh her on the scales in the waiting room, where it takes the two of us to lift her on.

'I don't believe it.' Maz presses the reset button three times. 'No, that's right. Don't listen, Tia,' she goes on, turning to me, and adding in a low voice, 'She's gross.'

'How much does she need to lose?' I say, trying to read the display.

'At least one third of her body weight, and I'd really like to see her become half the dog she is.'

'I don't know anything about her history, whether or not she's always been overweight. Jack thought that she used to be one of Talyton Manor's patients, but she can't have been to see a vet for years.'

'She seems a sweet enough dog – by nature I mean, not by smell. I'm not sure I'm going to be able to bring myself to kiss her.' Maz chuckles as we take Tia waddling back to the consulting room and heave her onto the table. 'Some of my clients think I'm mad kissing my patients.'

She talks through her findings as she examines the dog. 'She has a nasty infection in that ear, and her mouth is disgusting. Most of those teeth are going to have to come out. I'll scale and polish the rest and put her on some antibiotics. We'll give her a pedicure while she's under anaesthetic and trim the mats from her ears, paws and tail. Maybe a bit of pampering will make her feel better.'

'Thanks, Maz,' I say, sorry that I have to leave Tia with her. 'Best of luck, old dog,' I tell her as one of the nurses comes to take her through to the kennels to await her dental.

'I'm not intending to kill her,' Maz says, sounding slightly affronted.

'I know you'll look after her,' I say. She hasn't

182

been at the Sanctuary long – only a day – but I already feel as if she's part of the family there, my extended family, and she's old and not in the best of health.

'Go on, Tessa,' Maz says, smiling, 'call after three and I'll let you know what time you can collect her.'

Jack and I head back to the Sanctuary to settle the puppies in one of the kennels before going out again for the shopping. Much later, when Jack has returned Tia, looking drunk and disorderly, to the Sanctuary, I try to cheer her up with some boiled chicken chopped into tiny pieces. When I drag her into her kennel, she looks as though she might hang herself, she's so depressed, so I take her off to the bungalow with me to join Buster, leaving the puppies curled up together asleep with a ticking clock to mimic the comfort of their mother's heartbeat. Although I'm worried that Buster will turn on her, it seems as though he knows what she's been through and recognises in her a kindred spirit, because he sits by her bed, watching over her while she sleeps off the anaesthetic.

However, when I wake in the middle of the night, I find them both on the end of my bed and the duvet damp around my feet. When I switch the light on and discover that Tia has been dribbling from both ends, my heart sinks, because there appears to be more to this abandonment than meets the eye. Who will take on a depressed old dog that's obese, smelly and incontinent? How on earth will we find her a new home?

Chapter Nine

Wild Horses

The pony will not be caught. Libby, Jack and I try for another week – one person at a time, so as not to overwhelm her – tempting her with carrots, apples, mints and pony nuts, but to no avail. It isn't until the eighth day, when I'm regretting not putting her into one of the stables in the barn, that she deigns to put her head in the bucket and let Libby snap a lead-rope to the head-collar to bring her inside. She baulks in the doorway, but with Jack shooing her in from behind she walks in and I can close the stable door on her with a sigh of relief.

'She's a nightmare,' I observe. 'It's no wonder Mr Maddocks couldn't look after her properly – she probably wouldn't let him.'

'Well, I suggest you call the vet and the farrier out today while we've got her trapped,' says Jack.

'Yes, boss,' I say sarcastically, 'I'll get that organised. Well done, Libby. You are the Sanctuary's secret weapon, Talyton St George's very own horse whisperer. What did you say to her?'

'That she's a good girl, and then I let her think that coming in was all her idea, and I took my cap off because she didn't like it.'

'Mr Maddocks's son was wearing a cap,' I say. 'I wonder how he treated her.'

'I don't like to think about it,' Libby says. 'Shall I give her some hay and water?'

'Good idea.' It will help her to settle if she hasn't been in a stable before. 'I have to go and make some phone calls, if you're okay here.'

'And I have things to do,' says Jack, walking away.

'I'm fine,' Libby says. 'I'll keep an eye on Dolly for a while, then I'll go and feed the birds.'

'I expect they're cheeping for elevenses by now.' I smile ruefully. 'The baby birds are our most demanding residents, continually calling for room service, but they won't be here for ever. We won't know what to do with ourselves when they fly the nest.' I'm joking. I'm sure we'll have plenty to do through autumn and winter, finishing off the projects that DJ has abandoned. He texted me this morning to confirm that he's had enough.

'Where's Jack going?' Libby changes the subject at the sound of the van starting up and driving away.

'I don't know,' I say somewhat sharply. 'I'm not his keeper.'

'I wasn't suggesting you were. All I–'

'I know,' I cut in. 'I'm sorry. I'm feeling a bit overwhelmed at the moment with DJ going and the vet's bills coming in.' And I braved it to look at my bank account last night, not a good idea as it turned out. 'Look, I'll catch up with you later. I need to have a word with Diane and Wendy.'

They've turned up to help today, and I don't want them disappearing off to have their hair done, or let the dogs out, before I've spoken to them about various issues that have arisen – the Fun Day and rehoming criteria for a start. Everyone seems confused, telling potential adopters completely different stories, some that they can't have a kitten if they have children under the age of five, others that they can. It isn't good advertising for the Sanctuary. It puts people off.

'Your aunt and I didn't used to agree about the rehoming criteria for the rescues,' Diane says, dunking a biscuit into her second or third mug of coffee as we sit with Wendy outside the barn in the sunshine. 'I always supported Gloria's view that there should be no compromise.'

'Surely there's no such thing as the perfect home though,' I say. 'You have to make allowances, otherwise the animals will end up here for the rest of their lives.'

'That's what happened when Gloria was here,' Wendy points out. 'Many of the dogs and cats ended up staying here, a few because they had special needs, so to speak, but most because she couldn't bear to let them go.'

'She was a wise woman,' Diane says. 'These poor creatures have already had tough times. What is the point of letting them go to homes where they aren't going to be looked after properly? I'll give you an example. We wanted to rehome a dog with a chronic ear infection who needed long-term medication and, although the potential owners assured me they could pay for it, I felt from the state of their house that they'd struggle and the dog would suffer as a consequence.'

'You can't make judgements like that,' I say. 'They could be too busy to keep the place tidy,

186

not penniless.'

'Ah' – Diane peers helplessly into her mug, into which her biscuit has disappeared – 'but being busy is another barrier to taking on an animal. If they're too overstretched to tidy their house, then they're too busy to walk a dog, as far as I'm concerned.'

'Well, we can't be too strict,' I say. 'If we don't rehome our current intake, we can't accept any more, and that's that.'

'There are still more outbuildings for conversion,' Diane argues.

'That isn't the point,' I say, frustrated by her attitude. 'If we have too many animals, we can't look after them properly. And don't tell me we can always enlist some more people to help – we have too few volunteers as it is. What's more – and I don't want to get involved in the politics of it all – we can't convert any more buildings. We haven't got a builder: DJ's left.'

'Blame it on your aunt,' Diane cuts in. 'You need to have a go at her.'

'I've already spoken to her.' I rang this morning after I read DJ's text. 'She says she has no authority to unfreeze the money. It's down to the committee.' I believe that, like the charity's assets, Fifi has been frozen too – frozen out. 'Diane, I'd really appreciate it if you could pay DJ, with interest, and persuade him to come back to finish the projects he signed up for before Saturday. It's a health and safety issue for our visitors. If the place isn't tidied up, I'll have to cancel the Fun Day.'

Diane takes this very calmly. I'm afraid that she has nothing in her life apart from pursuing her ambition to take over as chair of Talyton Animal Rescue, whereas my aunt has too much and is in danger of losing her position because she hasn't the time to sort it out. I allow myself a smile. There's no way that Diane and Fifi will ever agree because they both want the same job.

'I can't talk to DJ,' Diane says. 'He was Fifi's choice. She's made a habit of riding roughshod over the rest of us, and it has to stop.'

I sigh inwardly. The stress is getting to me. If I were a bird, I'd be pulling my feathers out.

Unfortunately, the vet can't be with us until late afternoon, by which time Jack has taken Libby home for her shift at the Co-op. Alex Fox-Gifford, tall with silvering dark hair and fierce blue eyes, arrives at four in his checked shirt and navy cords, carrying a stethoscope and visit case.

'Hi,' he says, 'how's it going?'

'Well, thanks. How's business?'

'Brisk, although we're always busy this time of year. Maz has been telling me that you've been turning up at Otter House so often recently that you should take out a season ticket.'

Alex and Maz are married, Talyton St George's golden couple, according to my aunt.

'I wish there was something that could cut the cost... I'm not complaining,' I go on hurriedly, 'I know what's involved, running the surgery, paying for staff and buying drugs.'

'I expect you're keeping them in doughnuts,' Alex says.

'I don't have any doughnuts, but I do have biscuits. Would you like some tea or coffee?'

'I'd better not. I'm planning to be back in time

188

to pick up George from nursery.' George is Alex's son. 'Where's this pony?'

'She's this way, in the barn. Jack arranged for the police to seize her when she was reported straying on the roads. You know Mr Maddocks, the owner, don't you?'

'I've had the pleasure of meeting Frank Maddocks on many occasions. He will keep tethering his animals on our land. My father used to keep hassling him until he moved them off, but I just don't have the time or the inclination.'

When Alex and I reach the stable, Dolly takes one look at us and turns her bottom in our direction, the end of her tail trailing through the straw.

'I'll keep out of the way until you've caught her,' Alex says.

I grab the lead-rope that Libby's left hanging beside the door, and walk in, outwardly confident and inwardly petrified, my heart knocking against my ribs.

'Come here, Dolly.' My voice emerges as a high-pitched squeak. I'm not particularly confident around ponies. I had some riding lessons at the riding school, but to my parents' relief I didn't catch the pony bug.

'Dolly?' I stick my hand in my pocket and rustle a sweet wrapper, which makes her turn to face me with her ears pricked. I take out a mint and hold it in the palm of my hand. Dolly takes a step forwards, extending her neck until I can feel the breath from her flared nostrils, followed by the slightest touch of her lip when she picks up the mint and crunches it between her teeth. I take out a second one and, as she reaches out for it, clip the rope onto the ring under her chin.

'Gotcha,' I say quietly and, with a sense of triumph, I lead her towards the stable door. 'All right, Alex. Here she is.'

'Thanks, Tessa.'

When Dolly spots Alex on the other side of the door, she stops dead and utters a loud snort as if to say, 'Uh-oh, it's the vet!'

'How does she know?' I say. 'Has she met you before?'

'I've never treated her. Frank doesn't have a vet – he does everything himself with various pills and potions, drenches and medicine balls that he creates from recipes he finds in ancient veterinary texts... I wonder if she doesn't like the smell of cows?' Alex adds, sniffing at his sleeve. 'I've been vaccinating some calves.'

He opens the stable door, at which Dolly spins round, taking me by surprise and showing Alex her heels.

'I'm sorry,' I say, turning her back to face him. 'Did she get you?'

'She tried to take my kneecaps out,' he says, grimacing as he flexes and stretches one leg. 'Have you a bridle for her?'

I shake my head. Jack's taken the chifney.

'In that case, it might be a good idea to wrap the lead-rope around her nose to give you a bit more control.'

Fumbling with the rope, I loop it around Dolly's nose, pull it tight and hang on to it, digging my heels into the straw.

'I've got her,' I say, more confident that I can

hold her now, but Dolly has other ideas. When Alex approaches a second time, she rolls her blue eye at me and shakes her head, tearing the rope through my hands before charging at him, stopping dead to rear up and slam her front feet down just centimetres from the toes of his boots.

Standing his ground, Alex growls at her, 'That is not funny, pony,' and to my amazement, she takes a step back.

I apologise for not being able to hold her, checking the stinging tracks of the rope burns across my palms.

'I think she has it in mind to kill me,' Alex says darkly. 'I knew I should have sent Justin, my assistant, in my place. Let me go and draw up some sedative.'

'How on earth will you get that into her?'

'I have a cunning plan.' Alex chuckles. 'Don't panic – I've never had a pony beat me, and I'm not going to let Dolly break that record after all the years I've been in practice. She's a nasty piece of work, much like Frank Maddocks, a real witchy mare.'

As manager of the Sanctuary, I feel responsible for Dolly's disgraceful behaviour, and I realise how a parent must feel having a naughty child: somehow, it reflects on you.

'What will happen to her if she's like this?' Suddenly, I feel quite low, as I did with Buster. I don't expect Dolly to be in the slightest bit grateful, but I didn't imagine she would be so aggressive and, frankly, unlovable. 'I suppose she'll end up being put down.'

'Tessa, give her a chance,' Alex says. 'There are

plenty of ponies that don't like vets, and I should know.'

'I don't like going to the dentist,' I say, 'but I don't try to kill him.'

Alex returns from his four by four with a needle and syringe loaded with sedative.

'If you can get hold of the end of the lead-rope and walk outside so you can hang on to her over the stable door, I can shoot this into the muscle at the side of her neck.' Seeing my hesitation, Alex goes on, 'You can feed her some more mints to keep her mind off the needle.'

His plan works and the sedative goes in, although the needle stays embedded in her neck when she jumps away.

'I can retrieve that when she's sleepy,' Alex says. 'It doesn't matter.'

'Do you think it will work?' I ask anxiously. Sometimes animals are so wound up that no amount of sedative will have the desired effect.

'If we're quiet and don't disturb her,' Alex says, and we wait in complete silence until Dolly lowers her head and starts to doze, her eyes half closed, sweat forming in silvery beads across her coat – a good sign that the sedative is taking effect. Alex opens the stable door and ushers me in to stand at Dolly's head.

'I could have given her a bit less,' Alex observes as he checks her over, listening to her chest, examining the scabs on her legs and frowning when he looks at the state of her feet.

'I've called the farrier,' I say. 'He's coming out this evening as a special favour.'

'I would let him know she's dopey now – leave

192

it too long and she'll be back on form. I suppose the alternative is for me to leave you some sedation for when he comes, but you mustn't give her another dose within twenty-four hours.' Alex stops abruptly. 'I apologise. I'm talking to you like you're a client, not a vet nurse.'

'I'm not all that clued up on ponies, but I have looked up mud fever because I'm assuming – although I know I'm not qualified to make a diagnosis – that's what's causing the scabs on her legs.'

'That's correct. I'm going to run the clippers over them to remove all that feather, so you can get her skin really clean. I'll record her details so the police can apply for a passport, I'll microchip her and give her a first vaccination. Jack said that as far as he can find out, she hasn't been registered or vaccinated before. Oh, and I need to check her teeth as well.'

Alex records the mare's markings on a sheet: her patches; the broad and crooked blaze down her face; the positions of the distinctive whorls where there's a change of direction of the lie of the hair, like human fingerprints. He fills in the rest of her details: mare, approximately ten years old; breeding unknown. He scans for a microchip but there isn't one, so he injects a chip about the size of a grain of rice under the skin in Dolly's neck as I stand beside her, sensing the steam rising from her body and wondering what other indignities she has been subjected to throughout her life.

Alex goes on to fit a gag, a metal contraption with leather straps with which he can ratchet the pony's mouth open so he can check her teeth.

'These haven't been looked at for a long time, if ever,' he observes. 'She's got some nasty hooks at the back. It's no wonder she isn't keen on being led about in a head-collar – she's really sensitive because the hooks have dug into her gums, forming ulcers, and you probably know yourself how painful they can be.' He grabs a bucket, fills it with water from the outside tap and takes a rasp to Dolly's teeth.

The sound of metal grating across the rough edges until the rasp runs smooth makes my toes curl and I'm relieved when, red-faced with effort, Alex drops the rasp into the bucket one last time to rinse off the fragments of enamel.

'All done,' he says. 'Can you stay with her for another half an hour or so? She should be wide awake by then.'

'No problem,' I say, thanking him.

'Is there anything else I can do while I'm here?'

'I'd normally ask Maz, but seeing that you're here, would you be able to check a stray cat for a microchip? She's in the cattery. She's called Jess.'

'Will do,' Alex says.

He returns a few minutes later, excited at having discovered a microchip, which means we have a chance of reuniting Jess with her owner. He promises me he'll leave me the details in reception, so I can make contact with them.

'I won't charge for the cat, and you needn't worry about the bill for this one,' Alex says, nodding towards the pony. 'At the moment, the police are responsible for all of Dolly's expenses.'

'Alex, I really don't want this pony to go back

194

to Frank Maddocks or for auction. No matter how nasty she is, she doesn't deserve that. Can't you support Jack in making a case against him? You're a vet. Can't you write a report on what you've seen today?'

'I'm willing to support Jack if he has a go, but this pony's a borderline case. She shows signs of neglect, but she isn't in immediate danger.' Alex looks at me with compassion and understanding, as I grow tense with frustration.

'Then the law's an ass as far as I'm concerned.'

'You're going to come across this all the time, working in rescue. Talk to Jack.' Alex leaves some treatment for mud fever and instructions on how to use it, but nothing will soothe my concerns for the pony's future.

When the farrier leaves, Dolly is still asleep so I pick up a bright red brush from the bucket of grooming kit Libby has left outside the stable, and start brushing the tangles out of Dolly's mane, which comes down below the point of her shoulder in stripes of black and flaxen. It's very satisfying and takes my mind off everything, even Jack. Dolly begins to wake up from her drug-induced slumber, shakes her head and flicks her mane, and I have to brush it all over again.

I decide to leave her in the stable, giving her a flake of hay to keep her occupied overnight before I take Buster and Tia for a short stroll to the copse. I don't go all the way round because Tia struggles to put one paw in front of the other. When I turn back towards the bungalow, Buster hesitates, flicking his ears back and uttering a short sharp yelp of alarm. I follow his gaze towards the hedge, the hairs on the back of my neck pricking with unease. Something, or someone, is watching me.

I take a few steps towards the hedge, Buster pulling forwards on the lead, Tia sitting back on hers, until I feel like I'm being stretched in two. Suddenly, there's an orange flash, like that of the evening sun being reflected in a lens, and a scuffling sound. Buster starts barking hysterically.

'Buster, it's nothing,' I tell him. 'You have an over-active imagination,' I add, finding it easier to blame the incident on the dog than analyse it in any depth. Was it a deer? Or a fox? Was there someone watching me, or was it just a falling branch that set Buster off?

On the morning of the Fun Day, a sunny day in the beginning of June, Jack and I are hanging the banner I bought across the gap in the hedge where the cars come through from the track. Standing precariously on a chair – so much for health and safety, but desperate times require desperate measures – I take the banner out of its wrapper and hang on to one end while Jack walks the other over to the stepladder on the other side, the banner unfolding to reveal the words ... Happy Birthday!

'Oh no, I've got the wrong one,' I shout. Jack turns. 'What am I going to do? It's too late to go and get another one.'

To my consternation, Jack starts laughing.

'It isn't funny,' I say, but his laughter is infectious, and soon I'm laughing too, along with Diane, Wendy and Libby, who turn up to see what the fuss is about. My aunt is disapproving.

196

She likes things to be just so.

'I'm sorry,' I say. This isn't a great start. Perhaps I should have gone for a later date to give us more time to prepare as I originally planned. I'd decided against it because I thought we needed to get as many people – potential adopters and volunteers – through the gate as soon as possible.

'Let's hang it anyway,' Jack says, winking at me as if to say, Don't listen to them, Tess. 'It doesn't matter – we'll turn it back to front and put up some balloons. People are coming here to meet the animals and have a look around the Sanctuary.'

'And eat cake, I hope,' I say, turning to look at the trestle tables lined up outside the bungalow and laden with cupcakes, brownies and flapjacks.

It's a slow beginning to the Fun Day, but by midday our guests are arriving, keen to have the guided tour. Diane, deciding that she's too exhausted to remain on her feet, sits at the cake table, sampling each variety while she takes payment, and Wendy takes responsibility for making tea and squash. Fifi meets and greets the visitors as they turn up, which means Jack gets to do the tours, Libby runs the face-painting and I deal with anything else, which includes reuniting 'Jess' the cat with her owner, who turns out to be an employee of my aunt at the garden centre.

'This is Maddy Carpenter,' Fifi says, introducing me to a woman in her sixties. Tall with sinewy arms and long bony fingers, and dressed in a green sweatshirt and tight jeans, she reminds me of a Venus flytrap. 'She's been in plants for years.'

'Hi,' I say, realising that my aunt means the

197

'Plants' section of the garden centre, the covered area outside that's too hot in summer and like the Arctic in winter, where Maddy's skin appears to have weathered to the consistency of deeply wrinkled leather.

'I've come for Kitty,' she says, smiling and lifting the carrier she has with her to show me. 'The postman picked her up by mistake.'

It takes me a moment to realise she's talking about the cat we called Jess.

'Come with me,' I say, sidestepping a fast-moving child who's toddling around the car park, making animal noises, and I take her to the cattery where Jack is introducing Teddy to various people, including my mum and dad. Jack seems pleased to see me, and waylays us en route to Jess's pen.

'Tessa, help me out here,' he says. 'What would you look for when choosing a cat?'

'It's easy,' I say. 'Generally, dogs aren't fussy, but cats are pretty discerning creatures. You don't choose them. They choose you.' I chuckle as I pass by. 'I'm not sure that was much help, was it?'

I pause outside Kitty's pen to unlock the door – we've padlocked them so they can only be opened by me, Jack or one of the official volunteers, to reduce the risk of escapes.

'How many times do I have to tell you not to accept lifts from strangers?' Maddy says in her broad Devon accent. 'She's done it before – she hitched a lift in the Argos lorry. Thank goodness I had her microchipped.'

I let Maddy into Kitty's pen, where she collects the cat up and pushes her head first into the carrier. Kitty has other ideas, reversing straight back

198

out. Maddy tries again. This time, Kitty arches her back so there's no way she'll fit through the entrance of the carrier.

'Would you like me to try?' I say, stepping in to join her, but she's already trying to post Kitty in tail first, which doesn't work either: Kitty digs her claws into her owner's sweatshirt and uses it as a ladder to scramble onto her shoulder. I help to extricate the cat's claws from the sweatshirt and lift her down. I turn the carrier on its end, and before Kitty has time to plan her next move, I pop her in, bottom first, and quickly shut the door.

'Bingo,' I say.

'That's a good trick,' says Maddy. 'I'll try that one next time, because I'm sure there will be one. I keep telling her, if she must have a change of scene, she could at least hop on a bus – that way she can do a round trip and save me picking her up each time.' She thanks me for looking after her and apologises for interrupting the Fun Day.

'There are cakes on sale and if you would like to join our happy band of volunteers' – okay, I admit I'm exaggerating here because they aren't that happy together – 'there's a book in the office where you can leave your contact details.'

'I'll have a look at the cakes,' she says, 'but I couldn't help out here. I'd want to take them all home with me.'

I smile to myself because I feel exactly the same.

By four, the Fun Day comes to a close. My aunt awards the prizes to the winners of 'Guess how many mealworms the baby blackbird can eat at one sitting' and the 'Follow the paw-prints treasure hunt', the winner of the latter being a boy I recognise from earlier in the afternoon, who asked me if we had any crocodiles for rehoming. I suggested he tried a specialist reptile rescue centre. There's no way I want the responsibility of keeping dangerous animals on the premises. It's bad enough having slightly touchy characters like Buster and Teddy here, and I suppose I should include Diane and Wendy in that number too because Wendy in particular has been scratchy with me today, over the fate of the tins of dog food that Libby has collected in the box she set up for donations in the Co-op. In Wendy's opinion, the tins should be shared equally between the Sanctuary and her foster dogs, whereas Libby thinks they should all come to the Sanctuary. I side with Libby, seeing it was her idea. This doesn't go down well with Wendy, who leaves early to go and let her dogs out.

By five there's hardly anyone left, just me, Jack, Libby and my parents, Katie having declined my invitation for drinks and some food at the last minute. Dad is helping me out in the kitchen in the bungalow, where I'm cooking a chilli and rice. He grabs a spoon from the drawer to test the chilli.

'Is it hot enough?' I ask.

He slaps his lips together and shakes his head.

I throw in another sprinkling of dried chilli. Dad takes another spoonful.

'No,' he says. 'It needs more.'

'Are you sure?' I don't trust his judgement: he has cast-iron taste buds.

He has another taste, and another.

'What do you think of the Sanctuary?' I ask him.

'You're very lucky,' he says, confirming what I already know. I'm incredibly fortunate, for, in losing the house and the money I did have, I've fallen a long way, yet somehow managed to land on my feet, like a cat. 'It does smell a little peculiar though,' he goes on. 'In the living room, there's a distinct air of yeast-ridden codpiece.'

'I don't know what that is,' I say, blaming it on the neighbouring farmer and his muck spreader rather than the real culprit, who is unaware of her role in the matter. Tia is still leaking a little, in spite of the drugs that Maz prescribed for her, but I'm hoping that when she loses some weight and her muscles are toned up with more walking, I'll stop finding puddles and wet patches around the bungalow.

'I've heard from Great-Auntie Marion,' Dad says, changing the subject. 'She wanted me to thank you for inviting her to the wedding; she said she had a wonderful time. She also said she's having tests for cancer. I thought you might like to give her a ring for a chat sometime. She's afraid the next time the family meets, it will be for her funeral.'

'How morbid,' I say, but I make a mental note to call her sometime.

'Hey, Tess, you have to come and see this,' Jack says from the kitchen doorway.

'I can't at the moment,' I say.

'You'll love it, and it won't take long. Two minutes of your time, that's all.'

'I can look after the chilli,' Dad says.

'As long as you promise not to eat it all while I'm gone. It's no wonder you've got a barrel there, rather than a six pack,' I say, prodding him gently in the belly.

'All right, I promise, love.'

'Dad, stop crossing your fingers – you have your hands behind your back.' Laughing, I join Jack, following him out to the barn where Libby, dressed in jeans and a white T-shirt, has tied Dolly to the ring outside.

I open my mouth to speak, but Jack raises one finger to his lips and shakes his head almost imperceptibly. I remain silent, watching Libby start to brush the pony with a special bristle brush that she bought for her, beginning behind the pony's ear and running the brush in sweeping strokes across her neck and shoulder, following the lie of her hair before moving down her front leg. As the brush touches the pony's knee, Dolly stiffens, clamps her ears back and stamps her foot as if Libby is a pesky fly.

Catching my breath, I make to take a step forward ready to warn her to be careful because I remember how Dolly behaved with the vet, but Jack stays me, one hand on my arm.

Libby starts again, neck, shoulder and down the front leg. Dolly is calmer. She moves the brush further down Dolly's leg to her fetlock, at which she tosses her head, fighting the rope, rears up and slams both feet down just as she did with Alex.

'Hey, Dolly, that's enough,' Libby croons. 'I'm not hurting you.' She gives her a rub behind the ear and offers her a Polo mint, which she has no

202

hesitation in accepting. With utmost patience and quiet movements Libby starts brushing again, repeating the process seven times in all, after which Dolly decides it isn't worth arguing any more. She relents, allowing Libby to brush her all over, even her feathers. 'Good girl.' Libby gives her another Polo. 'That's enough for today. We want to end on a good note, don't we? Tomorrow, we'll see if you'll let me pick up your feet to practise for the farrier.'

The blacksmith has been out to trim Dolly's feet, but he managed only one before he took umbrage and decided he'd deal with her only under sedation. Even with Dolly under the influence, both Libby and the blacksmith looked as if they could do with sedation themselves by the time they had finished all four.

Jack and I move towards her, Jack keeping back, perhaps remembering the kick up the backside that Dolly delivered when he was trying to lead her across the field to the railway line.

'Wow, Libby,' I say. 'What did you say to her?'

Libby grins. 'Sweet nothings. Whispering is definitely more effective than shouting as far as Dolly's concerned.' She scratches the pony's withers, and, in response, Dolly arches her neck and nibbles at Libby's sweatshirt with her top lip as if Libby is another pony, indulging in some mutual grooming. 'I think she's going to be all right in the end. Do you think we'll be able to ride her one day?'

'I don't know,' Jack says. 'I doubt Frank Maddocks would have broken her to ride – her knees would buckle under his weight. Besides, I doubt

203

she'll be here long enough for you to find out.'

'What do you mean?' Libby's face falls. 'Oh, I know you talked about her being sold... I suppose I'd hoped she might have to stay. If Mr Maddocks appeals against the police's decision to seize her, it will slow everything down. She could be here for the winter.'

'Wishful thinking, sis,' Jack says. 'How many times have I warned you against falling in love with unsuitable or unavailable...' He pauses.

'Ponies,' Libby finishes for him, a small smile on her lips. 'Never. You've often mentioned un-suitable men though.'

I wish someone had warned me against Nathan, I think, gazing at the soft light in Jack's eyes as he goes on to suggest that she shouldn't grow too attached to the animals at the Sanc-tuary.

'You can care about them, but you have to be prepared to let them go,' Jack says. 'By all means spend as much time as you like training her. If you can tame Dolly, she'll have a good chance of going to a great home. As she is, I'm not sure anyone will want her.'

'I know that,' Libby says, sounding exasperated now. 'You are so patronising sometimes. I'm not ten. You really don't have to treat me like a child any more. I don't need your constant protection, Jack. It's suffocating.' She stamps her foot, much like Dolly does when she isn't happy. She turns to me as she unties the pony and walks away with Dolly ambling along next to her, calling back over her shoulder, 'I'm sorry, Tessa, but it really pisses me off.'

'Tess, did you see?' Jack says. 'How did she manage that?'

She has a way with animals, I think, as does her brother. A delicious quiver of longing darts along my spine. Jack has a way with women too...

Chapter Ten

Lonely Hearts

I'm back at Otter House one morning with Tia and Teddy, beginning to feel as if I'm spending more time at the vet's than I did when I worked as a vet nurse.

'Hi, Tessa. Can't you keep away?' Maz jokes, as she calls me into the consulting room. 'I hear the Fun Day was a success. I've had several clients talking about it.'

'We raised some money, but we didn't rehome any of the animals. Mind you, who would want to rehome Teddy and poor old Tia here?' She has a second ear infection now, on top of everything else, and whenever she shakes her head, she leaves a trail of brown spatters – at first I thought it was gravy – across the freshly painted walls. Cuddling up with her is like snuggling up with a well-loved yet musty teddy bear.

'I don't know what to do with her.' I stroke her as she stands trembling on the consulting-room table.

'We'll get that ear cleared up. Somebody will come along. Give it time.' Maz kisses the top of Tia's head. 'Does she mind being in a kennel?'

'She hates it – I've never seen a dog so depressed. I've taken pity on her, and she's living in the bungalow with Buster, who seems happy to coexist with her as she's no threat to him what-soever.' I grin. 'I'll have to put a limit on my com-passion though, otherwise there'll be so many dogs indoors I'll have to move into one of the kennels myself.'

'Have you thought about doing a golden oldie offer? You could say that Talyton Animal Rescue would pay a contribution to her vet bills once she was in a new home, because they're only going to escalate. That might tempt someone to take her on,' Maz says as she looks down Tia's ear and gently cleans it out.

'It's worth a try. I'll work out the relative costs of keeping her long-term at the Sanctuary or paying towards her bills later on.'

Maz squirts ear drops down Tia's ear and massages it for a moment. When she lets go, Tia shakes her head, covering Maz's paw-print top with yellow splashes

'Spot the deliberate mistake.' Maz chuckles. 'I should have held on to her head for a bit longer. Keep those drops going in for a few days and bring her back on Monday.'

I lift Tia gently down to the floor.

'Who's next?' Maz asks.

'Teddy.' I let go of Tia's lead and let her wander around the consulting room, sniffing at the cup-boards – searching for food, I imagine – and bumping into table legs, while Maz takes a look at Teddy, who, since the abscess cleared up, has acquired a skin infection under his neck.

'That's nasty,' Maz comments. 'I'm going to prescribe more antibiotics, but I'd like to take some blood to test for the feline leukaemia virus and the feline immunodeficiency virus if that's all right with you. Hopefully he's negative, but I think we need to know what we're up against. As you know, either of those viruses can damage the immune system and make him prone to bacterial infections, among other things.

'You can't rehome him with other cats if he's positive for either virus because both are transmitted by biting and close contact – mutual grooming, for example. I'm not saying he'll have to be put down though,' Maz says quickly. 'I've rehomed positive cats very successfully.' She pauses. 'Can I ask you a favour, Tessa?'

'Of course,' I say, tickling Teddy's chin.

'Izzy's tied up in theatre with an emergency and our other nurse is off today. Are you happy to hang on to him while I take the blood?'

'As long as I can wrap him in a towel. He's prone to hissy fits.'

'I've noticed,' Maz says wryly. She shows me a scar on her forearm. 'He did that the last time he was in to have that abscess drained. I should have been more careful. He isn't a bad cat though.'

'You'll be trying to tell me he does it because he's misunderstood next. No excuses, Teddy.' I go on to wrap him particularly carefully, pinning him down on the consulting room table, while leaving one front leg free for Maz to access for the blood sample. As if intent on proving us both wrong, Teddy doesn't put a paw out of place.

'I'll let you know the results as soon as I get them.'

'Thanks, Maz.'

I take Tia and Teddy back to the Sanctuary, wondering if we'll ever manage to rehome any of the rescues. It hadn't occurred to me before that it wouldn't be anything but straightforward. However, the animals arrive with the problems that turned them into unwanted pets in the first place: Buster's aggression towards other dogs, Tia's age-related conditions, and potentially for Teddy an incurable infection that could shorten his life.

I lift him out of the van and return him to the cattery where he jumps up onto his shelf as if there's nothing wrong with him, and, instead of hiding under his bed, he sits there, blinking at me. I bite my lip. I can't advertise him until we know the outcome of the blood tests, but I need to take steps to advertise the others.

'How about "single black male"?' I say, writing notes on the back of an envelope while Libby and I take a break in the office with coffee and biscuits, and a kitten, later on. Libby is hand-rearing a feral that a member of the public handed in the other day. She's about four weeks old, tortoiseshell and white, cute but fairly wild and highly infectious to our other cats because she has a nasty bout of cat flu, hence the reason for keeping her isolated in a cage in the bungalow. It's debatable whether I should have agreed to take her in at all – she's going to cost a fortune in vet's bills and probably end up back out in the wild, but the other option was ... well, you can probably guess, and I couldn't contemplate that.

When Libby cleans the kitten's eyes and nose, she mewls and wriggles in protest.

'Ouch! You're a feisty little thing,' Libby says, glancing at the scratches on her hand. 'I'm sorry,

Tessa, what were you saying?'

'I was wondering if I could start the ad with "single black male"?'

'Can you say that?' Libby asks.

'It's a true statement,' I point out.

'Okay, go on.' Libby pops the kitten back into its basket. 'I've had no experience of Lonely Hearts columns or internet dating, I'm afraid, so I'm not much help.'

'Hey, hang on a moment,' I chide. 'I haven't either, and I don't intend to.'

'Maybe I should give it a go,' Libby says mournfully. 'My friends are in serious relationships and getting engaged, one is pregnant, and I feel as if I'm being left behind. There aren't many eligible bachelors left in Talyton St George.'

There's Nathan, I think, but I wouldn't suggest him as potential boyfriend material to my worst enemy.

'What about Kevin, the policeman?' I say to Libby. 'I don't know if he's attached or not, but he seems okay.'

'For a man in uniform, I don't find him a particularly arresting sight,' she says with a grin. 'No, we used to go to school with him, if you remember.'

'I don't,' I say, racking my brain.

'You see, he wasn't that memorable then.'

'Libby, you have plenty of time. Don't rush it.' I pause. 'Now, where was I?'

'You were composing an ad for Buster, our special needs dog.'

'I don't know what you mean,' I say protectively. 'He's amazing: loyal, sensitive. I'll put that

210

in. How about "single black male, good-looking and affectionate, gsoh, seeks one-on-one forever relationship with lady (preferably), no children, no pets"? Should I add an age group?'

'Does age matter?'

'A more mature lady might not be able to keep Buster under control out walking on the lead.'

'That will depend on her build as much as her age,' Libby says, laughing. 'Are you going to add that this lady needs to be in possession of a fuller figure? Tessa, I think you need to make it less specific.'

'What about Tia?' I go on. 'How do I make her sound really appealing? "Overweight, elderly female with her own teeth (just seven remaining), looking for that special someone..."'

'I think you have to emphasise what she's been through to gain the sympathy vote, so people can't resist offering her a home for her twilight years.'

'It's sad, isn't it? No one ever picks Tia out when they come to look for a dog, because she's always the one cowering at the back of the kennel. She hates it in there.'

'Which is why you're always taking her over to the bungalow with Buster,' Libby points out, her expression one of amusement. 'You should take them both on, Tessa.'

'I can't have one dog, let alone two. It isn't a good time for me. I haven't got the money to pay for food and vet's bills at the moment. I'm going to be paying my debts for a very long time, years at this rate, probably decades.' I change the subject. 'So, do you want me to put an ad in the

211

Chronicle for you too? They might have a preferential rate, a three-for-two deal.'

'No way, Tessa.' Libby pretends to look appalled.

'So are you looking for love, or not?'

'I'm not looking as such.' She blushes. 'I was hoping love would come to me.'

'You mean, as a special delivery?'

'I might do.'

'You could do a lot worse than Ash,' I say, thinking of Nathan.

'What about Dolly?' Libby changes the subject quickly. 'Do you know what's happening to her, officially, I mean?'

'There's some dispute between Jack and Mr Maddocks, who's appealing against the seizure.'

'How can that be right?' Libby's eyes grow moist and her lip trembles. 'How can you rescue her and then throw her back into a situation where anybody with enough money can take her?'

'It isn't my decision, Libby. The court has to decide whether she was legally seized, or if Jack has enough evidence to take Mr Maddocks to court for breaking the Animal Welfare Act.'

Jack didn't follow protocol, which is partly my fault, I think with a twinge of guilt. If I hadn't made my feelings about the pony so clear, perhaps he would have taken the time to get the paperwork right.

'I won't let her go to auction,' Libby says in a hollow voice. 'There's no way.'

'We might not have a choice.' Suddenly, I feel weary because Libby's right. Selling Dolly would be a travesty. It goes against everything we do at

212

the Sanctuary. We can't let it happen, but what can we do? 'I will do my utmost to prevent her being sold on,' I continue, 'but she can't stay here for ever. There'll be other ponies.'

'Dolly's special,' Libby says.

'All our rescues are special,' I counter. 'You know the best thing you can do is to keep working with her so she learns to trust humans again. That will give her the best chance of finding a good home.' I've had mixed feelings about Dolly throughout her time with us, but I'd love to see her happily settled, not just for her sake, but for Libby's too.

I put the ads that Libby and I have composed in the Lonely Hearts section in the *Chronicle*, and Ally writes a piece with Buster and Tia's photos in there too.

Buster is doing well. He hasn't growled at anyone since the incident with Libby. All he wants now is somebody to love him, and I do everything I can to give him a chance. I keep the details on his kennel updated, and when I show visitors around the kennels I always stop and spend time beside him, talking about his virtues: how he loves to walk in the copse (on the lead, because he refuses to come to call); how he adores sleeping on your feet on the bed at night, something that will be of great benefit on cold winter nights (some visitors like this, whereas some don't); how he can pick out the word 'biscuit' in ordinary conversation (and drools on the carpet in response); and how he picks up his bowl when he wants feeding. I try to convey the right blend of canine intelligence and cuteness to appeal to as many people

213

as possible, but he gets no offers. Neither does Tia.

It's a Monday morning in early July. I didn't use to like Mondays when I was in practice. Either I was exhausted from working with the duty vet or I'd been out clubbing with Katie over the weekend, and inevitably Monday was our busiest day as clients had waited to bring their pets during the working week rather than disturb the vet, or in some cases to avoid paying the out-of-hours fees, which they didn't understand were not related to the time of their emergency appointment but were on a sliding scale, depending on how much they annoyed the vet. Actually, there was only one vet who was particularly irritated by clients ringing to demand to see him just when he was about to eat, his bad temper inversely proportional to the level of sugar in his blood.

It's different here at the Sanctuary. I'm on my own, which is great, except for when I get that sense that someone is watching me. It's become a regular occurrence every third or fourth night, and I'm grateful for Buster's presence. The other thing I love about being here is that I'm the boss. There is no one telling me what to do and when to do it, except – I smile to myself – the baby birds. They are still pretty demanding, tweeting all the time, a bit like Katie, who has discovered the joys of Twitter, following hundreds of celebrities as though she knows them personally. I wish I had the time, but if I did, I wouldn't waste it.

It's a warm, sunny day, so I find some outdoor tasks that need doing: I empty and scrub Dolly's

214

trough clean of algae and snails and refill it with fresh water, leaving the hose to run while I hammer a couple of nails into the fence by the gate where Dolly has pushed through to nibble the longer grass on the other side. When I turn back to the trough, Dolly has picked up the end of the hose between her teeth and is nodding her head up and down, spraying water everywhere.

'Dolly!' Laughing, I walk across to take the hose back. She drops it and flicks her heels up at me. 'You are a strange pony,' I say lightly, noting the shine on her coat, the flesh that's covering her ribs and pelvis, and the size of her belly. 'When will you realise that we're on your side?'

My mobile rings as I stick the end of the hose back in the trough. It's Maz, asking if we can take in a stray cat. I tell her that Jack will collect it from the surgery tomorrow and update her on Teddy, who turned out to be harbouring the feline immunodeficiency virus in his body, which explains why he's prone to other infections. It also makes him more difficult to rehome, as he has to go as a single indoor cat. Wendy texts immediately after I've finished speaking with Maz, saying she'll be over to do the baby bird rounds at lunchtime and walk the dogs, and at the same time a car turns up with another animal needing a home.

The woman who brings it introduces herself as Yvonne, and she works with Libby at the Co-op. I show her through to reception, where she teases apart the torn tissue in the bottom of a washing-up bowl to reveal the tiniest baby bird with a yellow beak, fluffy down, and stubby wing and tail feathers with stripes that are just beginning to show.

Although my head is saying, Oh no, not another one, my heart is melting.

'It's a house martin,' Yvonne explains, saving me the potential embarrassment of having to take a guess. 'The parents built a nest high in the eaves of the house. I came home with the shopping to find the nest on the patio and this little creature lying dead, or so I thought. He was cold and wet, but when I picked him up, he moved. I thought he was going to die anyway and I thought about asking my son to, you know, help him along, but I couldn't do it, so I put him in a box on the boiler and within half an hour he was cheeping for food.

'My son went on the internet to find out what to feed him, my daughter picked up mealworms and cat food from the pet shop on her way home from the stables, and we took turns feeding him every one to two hours during the day from about six in the morning until nine at night. I hope we did the right thing.'

'It looks like you've done a great job. I wouldn't normally have expected one this young to survive such trauma. It's going to be a while before he's strong enough to fly.' I pick him up to check him over, at which his head bobs up on the end of his scrawny neck, his beak open wide.

'That's why I've brought him to you,' Yvonne goes on. 'He's constantly hungry. I thought he was cute at first, but he's taken over my life. When I went to work on Friday, I took him with me because I was worried he'd starve. My boss gave me an ultimatum, and that's when I realised

I couldn't be his foster mum any longer.'

'I know exactly where you're coming from,' I say, with a rueful smile. 'We have several babies here already: a couple of blue tits that are ready for release, blackbirds, sparrows and a robin, so he won't be on his own. No sooner have we finished feeding them, they want feeding again.'

Yvonne smiles back. 'I hope you have plenty of help.'

'We're always looking for volunteers,' I say hopefully.

'It isn't for me. I like to do my bit for the Brownies – I'm Tawny Owl for the local pack.'

It was worth a try, I think, as I pop the bird back into the bowl where it crawls back beneath the tissue. So far, everyone I've asked has turned me down.

'There's plenty of it because I didn't want him to hurt himself on the journey,' Yvonne says.

I fill in what I can of an admissions form and ask her to sign the house martin over.

'You can write his name in the box. He's called Vlad, after Klitschko, the fighter. We called him that because he won't give up, although there was a moment when I wished he would,' she adds with good humour. 'I've driven twenty miles to bring him here, that's a forty-mile round trip, I've been feeding the' – she swears lightly – 'thing for four days and I've been under his spell the whole time. He's the first thing I think about when I wake, and the last when I go to sleep... If I go to sleep,' she amends. 'I've been worrying about him all night, wondering if he'll still be alive in the morning. I thought having a baby was bad

217

enough, but having a chick is so much more time-consuming, don't you think?'

'I don't know – I've no experience of babies.' I feel a pang of regret at being a single woman with no immediate prospect of a steady boyfriend, let alone a baby, when Yvonne goes on to thank me and asks if she can keep in touch to see if Vlad makes it. I give her a card with a note of the bird's admission code.

During my morning walk with Buster, I call Katie for a chat. She has five minutes between facials.

'I don't suppose there's any chance you could come over for an hour or so tonight to give me a hand. It's just that as soon as I've done one round of baby bird feeding, they're ready for the next meal. Please, Katie. I'll pick up a pizza and a bottle of wine from the Co-op.'

'I'm sorry, I'm out tonight,' she says. 'Before you ask, it isn't a date. I'm meeting a friend for a drink.'

'Anyone I know?'

'One of the girls from the salon; she's been having a tough time with the boss. He's harassing her and I've told her she doesn't have to put up with it. She wants to talk through her options.'

'Oh, okay.' I smile to myself. 'You're becoming quite the Good Samaritan.'

'I could come over for a couple of hours this afternoon, if that's any use to you. It's my half-day.'

'That would be great, thanks. I've got to pop out for some more dog food sometime, but I'll make sure I'm back before three.'

I feed all the baby birds and go out in the van with a shopping list: cat food and litter, dog food, mealworms, diet food for Tia, more disinfectant – Talyton Animal Rescue should have shares in that – and pony nuts and a net of carrots for Dolly. I pick up everything we need in Overdown Farmers before I start driving back through town and down onto the bridge over the river, where I catch sight of a man in waders, thigh-deep in the water below, his blond hair gleaming in the sun. It's Jack.

On impulse, I turn left onto the gravel just past the end of the bridge, stopping the van beside the Land Rover that Jack's parked there. I jump out and cross the Green, stopping on the riverbank. Jack is standing with his back to me, stripped to a navy vest, bracing himself against the power of the river, a swan hook in one hand, his other hand guiding a swan towards the reeds at the edge. The swan, an adult, is clearly sick, paddling weakly against the current with its head held low over its back a couple of metres beyond him and just out of reach, while a couple of dog walkers watch from the new bridge, the footbridge a little way downstream.

Jack wades into deeper water, following the swan. It begins to drift back slowly towards him, at which he reaches out with the hook. Although it appears defeated, the swan has plenty of fight left in it. It stretches its neck and flaps its wings, sending up glittering splashes as it struggles away, settling back on the water, tantalisingly out of reach once more.

Jack waits before making a second attempt and

a third. On the fourth, he manages with a practised swing of the hook to catch the swan's neck when it tries to fly up again, hissing with annoyance and fear. This time, Jack draws the swan in close until he can reach over and use his hands to catch its neck, then grasp it across its body to restrain its wings, before lifting it from the water and tucking it under his arm to bring it safely across to the bank to the applause of the dog walkers.

'Well caught, Jack,' I call.

He looks up and smiles, and my heart lurches as he strides up the bank in thigh-length waders. I try to avert my eyes from this stirring sight – I hadn't realised that waders could be quite so ... compelling. I focus on the swan instead, a big bird with crisp white feathers, apart from those on its head that have been stained a reddish-brown by the iron deposits at the bottom of the river.

'Hi there, Tess,' Jack says, the muscles in his arms rippling while he tries to keep the swan under control.

'What a gorgeous creature,' I say.

'Do you mean me or the bird?'

I glance up at Jack's face. He's grinning broadly, so I think he's joking, but I blush anyway. I can't help myself. Like the swan, Jack is gorgeous, inside and out.

'You've turned up at just the right time,' he says. 'I could do with a hand getting this young lad into the bag. It's along here somewhere – I've paddled further than I realised.'

'How do you know it's a lad?' I ask, over the sound of the swan's continued hissing and snorting. It might be a mute swan by name, but it's far from that by nature. It is able to communicate its feelings all too well.

'I've been watching a pair of swans down here. This is their first year together and the pen, the female, is sitting on some eggs on a nest downstream from here. This is the cob. You can tell from the size of the basal knob, the black swelling on the upper bill that stretches up to the forehead. It's bigger in males than females.'

I walk along the bank to collect the bag and pick up Jack's keys and wallet before I help him wrap the swan.

'That's got it,' Jack says at last, as I finish fastening the straps on the bag around the swan's body, distracted by the sensations of being so close to him – Jack, that is, not the swan. His scent, an aphrodisiac combination of aftershave and the outdoors, tempered with the earthy smell of river water, fills my nostrils, and the sound of his voice close to my ear, and the occasional touch of his skin against mine as our arms come into contact while restraining the swan, makes my pulse beat faster and sends my imagination into overdrive.

'What's wrong with me?' I say. 'I mean with the swan. I'm talking about the swan.'

I'm aware that Jack is looking at me, one eyebrow raised.

'I thought you were supposed to be a vet nurse.'

'I'm getting out of practice,' I say, when he shows me the lump about halfway down its neck. 'What do you think it is? A fishing hook?'

'Almost certainly. I see these injuries from time to time, along with the odd case of lead poisoning and swans that have flown into power cables. Anyway, I'm going to run this one straight to the seabird sanctuary at Marsh. This one needs to see a specialist.' Jack hesitates. 'Why don't you come with me and have a look around?'

'That would be interesting, but–'

'It isn't far, and we could stop for a bite to eat on the way back.'

'I ought to be getting back.'

'Tess, it's Monday and you've worked all weekend. You're allowed a lunch break at least.'

'Are you hinting that I should get out more?' I say, archly.

'Well, yes, I think you should ... as long as it's with me.'

'Ha ha,' I say with mock weariness. He's joking again. He tips his head to one side.

'How can I persuade you, Tess?'

'With your natural verve and charm?'

'I'm glad I'm going up in your estimation at last,' he chuckles.

'Well, you are doing your best with all these heroic rescues to impress me... I'm being ironic, of course,' I add quickly.

'And I wouldn't expect you to be anything but.' Jack picks up the swan and we start walking towards the vehicles in the summer sunshine. 'So, are you coming or not?'

'Oh, I don't know.' I'm tempted. 'Wendy's doing lunch for the baby birds and Katie's coming to do her bit of volunteering at three.'

'Katie?' Jack's tone hardens. 'You're still friends then?'

'Of course.'

222

'Okay.' Jack nods thoughtfully as I continue, 'We always will be. She's the best mate anyone could have, and whatever happens, we'll always stand by each other. I don't know what I would have done without her when–' I stop abruptly, not wishing to revisit the wedding and the weeks after it, and perhaps a little in denial about the fact I haven't seen nearly as much of her recently. I don't blame her. I've been consumed by my role at the Sanctuary. It's taken over my life, so much so that I can't remember when I last went anywhere, apart from into Talyton. How sad is that? I think, smiling to myself. How sad am I?

'Oh, go on,' I say. 'Why not? I'll join you.'

'Great,' Jack says. 'Shall we take the Land Rover or the van?'

We settle for the van. Jack drives while the swan hisses its displeasure in the back, but it's one of the lucky ones. When we arrive at the seabird sanctuary which is situated on an area of coastal marshland near the mouth of the River Taly, there's a vet there who anaesthetises the swan straight away and removes the hook and fishing line that have caught in its food-pipe, or oeso-phagus. Having been assured that the swan will recover with antibiotics and painkillers before he's released into the company of other swans, Jack and I are given the guided tour, before returning to the van and driving back through the small village of Marsh, where Jack stops at the pub.

The Three Cups is a typical Devon country pub built from pink cob and thatch that has weathered to the colour of mushroom gills. There is a single seagull perched on the chimney stack at one end and a flock of them swirling and swooping in the sky above, making plaintive cries. Inside, where the air smells of cold woodsmoke and real ale, it's so gloomy that you can hardly see the elderly man stooped almost double behind the bar. At first, I think he's looking for something, a glass or bottle, but he doesn't become any taller when he takes our order of a pint of prawns to share, fresh bread, cola and a lager shandy.

'It's very quiet here,' I observe when we're sitting outside at a rustic picnic table overlooking the small harbour at the back of the pub. 'Where is everyone?'

'This is off the beaten track. I think they get a few tourists visiting the seabird sanctuary; otherwise they rely on trade from the locals and the sailing club. I like it.' Jack squints in the bright sunlight, looking out towards the sea. I follow his gaze, observing a pair of large, dark birds diving into the water and disappearing before bobbing up again some distance away.

'Are they cormorants?' I ask.

Jack shades his eyes with his hands.

'No, they're similar, but a bit smaller and slimmer than cormorants. They're shags.'

'They're what?'

He turns to me, his expression flickering with humour. 'Why are you blushing?'

'Am I?' I touch my cheeks, which are radiating heat at the thought of intimacy with Jack. Shags! I give myself a silent telling-off. How childish. 'It's the wind.'

I pick up a prawn from the glass in front of us and examine it, regretting my choice. Pink and plump with a hard carapace, black eyes and various stringy appendages, it doesn't look that appetising.

'Look, you peel it like this.' Jack takes it from me and shows me how to peel the shell from the flesh, leaving the juicy body of the prawn, which he hands back, placing it on my open palm. 'Go on. Try it.' Laughter bubbles up in his voice. 'It won't bite – the head's gone.'

It tastes salty and sweet, fresh from the sea, although I still think as the juice trickles down my chin that I should have gone for something less messy, like a cold beef sandwich.

Grinning, Jack passes me a paper napkin. 'What do you think?'

'They're delicious,' I say, although I'm having trouble eating. Jack's presence makes me lose my appetite – in the nicest possible way – and I can't help wondering how his lips would taste right now. I turn away and gaze towards the boats in the harbour, small dinghies and fishing boats that are knocking gently against the harbour wall as the tide comes in, lifting them from their muddy berths. Jack was right. I needed a break. And I'm disappointed when he suggests that we get back to Talyton so he can check on the swan's mate and pick up the Land Rover.

'Won't she starve without the cob to bring her food?' I ask.

'The pen should be able to rear the cygnets by herself. It's a shame, but that's how it is. The cob can't be released until he's well again.' Jack pauses. 'I'll keep an eye on the nest. I always do after those kids threw the eggs into the river a

225

couple of years ago.'

'I don't remember.'

'It was headline news in the *Chronicle*,' Jack says lightly. 'We caught the little sods. Frank Maddocks's son was among them. We could have prosecuted because swans are a protected species, but it was a first offence and they were young lads, so they got off with a caution.'

'Dolly's well away from that family,' I observe. 'She's put on some weight now and seems very content pottering around in the paddock unless the flies are bothering her, when we bring her in.'

'I was thinking we should take her off the grass every day,' Jack says. 'She's verging on being too fat now.'

When we arrive back in Talyton St George, I let Jack out of the van. He wants me to see the swans' nest, but although I'm tempted, I decline.

'I guess I'll see you in the week,' I go on hesitantly, wishing the day with Jack could last for ever. 'At the Sanctuary,' I add quickly, in case he thinks that, like the shags, I'm fishing.

'I doubt I'll be able to keep away.' He gives me a long look, his eyes simmering with... Don't go there, I tell myself, looking away to fiddle with the tuning on the radio, but it's too late. In spite of my determination to blank it out, I've known it all along: Jack Miller is more than a little in love with me, and I with him.

Chapter Eleven

Hungry Birds

How do I feel about it? I ask myself later. Excited, flattered and ecstatically happy, yet I hesitate to look further ahead. In spite of claiming that I'm going to remain single for the rest of my life, I enjoy Jack's company and I can't imagine living alone at the Sanctuary for ever, sharing the crusts of my soldiers between Buster and Tia when I'm eating boiled eggs for breakfast, and taking them for extra walks to stop me from curling up on the sofa and vegging out in front of the TV every night. I know I shouldn't let my experience with Nathan put me off completely, but I'm not sure. Should I give Jack some encouragement, some sign that I'm interested in taking things further, or will that make life too complicated?

Part of me says, Why should things work out between us a second time round? Part of me says, Why not? I hesitate though. It seems such a big step.

'You're very quiet, Tessa,' Katie says when we're feeding the baby birds the same afternoon. I'm not sure how useful she is as a volunteer, because I got back to find Wendy showing her how to do it, yet I'm sure I've shown her before. 'Did Jack upset you again?' She holds a mealworm in tweezers just above Vlad the house martin's gaping mouth. 'I hope he isn't being a pain.'

'A pain?'

Vlad cheeps and stretches his neck until he can't possibly extend it any further.

'Katie, concentrate. Vlad wants his tea.'

'Oh' – Katie looks down into Vlad's box – 'so he does.' She releases the mealworm and it misses, landing on Vlad's back, at which he utters a series of angry cheeps.

'Try with a fresh one,' I say, smiling. 'I'll clean him up afterwards.'

'I'm not good with birds.' Katie grimaces. 'I prefer hairy animals.'

'Like?' I go on for her.

She glances back at me, eyes sparkling. 'I'm not saying.'

'So there is someone? Go on, you have to tell me about him now, otherwise I'll die from the suspense.'

'Tessa, I don't want to jinx it by talking about it.'

'Well, you've given me a clue at least. He isn't bald.' I'm excited for her. She has never made any secret of her desire to settle down, and I used to feel guilty when I was with Nathan because I had all the luck and she didn't. 'He hasn't got a hairy back, has he? Ugh.'

Katie giggles. 'You know me. If he has – and I'm saying "if" because I'm not going to give you any clues – I can soon sort it out with a bit of wax.'

'It's hardly a clue, is it?' Vlad cheeps yet again. 'He's asking for more, Katie,' I say, giving her a nudge. 'That bird is never satisfied.'

'Like someone else I know.'

'The new man,' I giggle.

'Tessa, I'm not going to talk about him, no matter how much you try to persuade me.'

It's a shame, I think. Usually she's as keen to tell me about her love life as I am to find out.

'He's married. That's why you won't tell me who it is.' Katie doesn't deny it when I continue, 'Please, be careful, and don't believe him when he says he's going to leave his wife.'

'You're the one to talk about being careful,' Katie counters. 'All this time you're spending with Jack, you'll only lead him on.'

'Maybe I want to.' I take the tweezers and load them with another mealworm so I can feed Vlad myself.

'No, you don't.' Katie raises her perfect eyebrows. 'Look at him.'

'I have and he isn't at all bad.' Massive understatement. He is gorgeous.

Katie stares at me as if I'm slightly touched. 'You definitely need to get out more. What's that saying, all work makes Jack a dull boy? Jack Miller is soooo boring. All he thinks about is rescuing animals.'

'And people,' I add, thinking of the way he cares for his sister, and his role as a retained firefighter. I don't know about his ability to put fires out because when I'm with him all he does is fan the flames. 'Isn't that enough?'

'He doesn't go out anywhere–'

'By anywhere, you mean to clubs,' I cut in.

'And he drives that battered old Land Rover and he doesn't have a clue about how to dress or look after his skin...' Katie pauses. 'I'm sorry, but, as your friend, I'm being frank with you to stop you making yet another mistake.' Her expression relaxes into a warm smile. 'This is silly, isn't it? We are going to have to agree to disagree. You go out with Jack, if it makes you happy.'

'That's just it though,' I say. 'How do I know it won't ruin our friendship? Mine and Jack's, I mean.' Katie doesn't respond when I go on, 'I think I would go out on a date with him – if he asked me.'

In spite of the Fun Day, and my and Libby's creative adverts for the rescues, the Sanctuary becomes increasingly overcrowded over the summer, possibly because it's holiday time and fewer people are looking to take on animals. We could do with an extension on the kennels, or even better a new kennel block, but it all costs money, money we just don't have when I add up the general running costs. It would help, of course, if the charity would agree to release the next tranche of funds from the author's legacy, but that is still under negotiation. There is money there now, but it won't last for ever, so I need to make sure we continue to raise cash to keep the Sanctuary going.

It isn't easy though. The ball's coming up in less than three weeks' time, and I have thirty pairs of tickets left to sell before we break even.

'You are coming to the ball with Ash, aren't you, Libby?' I ask her when we're together in the office, catching up with some paperwork and making a list of animal food and medicines I

230

need to order in for the next couple of weeks. Libby is supposed to be arranging a couple of home visits for me.

'I'm still waiting for him to ask me,' she says, her cheeks flushing.

'That's an old-fashioned view of romance, isn't it?' I respond. 'Why don't you ask him? The ball will be over by the time Ash gets round to it.' He's lovely, don't get me wrong, but although he's quite the jolly postman, he's also jolly slow. Some days our post doesn't arrive until after three.

'I'll see,' Libby says, and I know from the tone of her voice that she won't.

I click the end of my pen and threaten to speak to Ash myself if Libby won't do it, although it occurs to me that this is rather hypocritical of me, because I haven't yet plucked up the courage to ask Jack if he'll be my partner at the ball. I'm guessing he hasn't asked me because he's afraid of being rejected.

Picking up my notepad, I change the subject. 'Look, I've got another dog needing a kennel today because a young couple have decided they can't cope with a dog and a new baby. What is wrong with people?'

'You can be so judgemental sometimes,' Libby says brightly. 'Just wait until you have children and I'll remind you.'

'There's no way I'm having kids now,' I say defensively because it brings back memories of Nathan and his promise that we'd have a family.

'You will,' Libby says, her eyes twinkling with amusement. 'Now, what are you going to do about this dog?'

'I don't know.' I bury my face in my hands. They smell a bit doggie, even though I've washed my hands several times since I groomed Tia and cleaned her ears. 'I might be forced to turn it away.' I utter a long sigh. 'Sometimes I hate this job.'

'Rescue will always be like this,' Libby says sagely. 'You have to accept that there's a limit to what you can do. There'll always be too many animals needing help.'

'It's so sad though, and soul-destroying.'

'If it's a small dog, it could become an honorary cat,' Libby suggests.

'The cats won't like it.' I look across the office to the large dog cage in the corner where the feral kitten is making a steady recovery from cat flu and becoming quite tame. We've christened her Towie, and I think there's a good chance we'll be able to rehome her instead of letting her back out with the other cats that are living wild around the Sanctuary, if we can afford to pay the vet to fix her eye, and by that, I mean remove it.

At the moment, it doesn't appear to bother her because she's playing with a piece of screwed-up paper, skedaddling sideways across the cage with her tail stuck up in the air like a bottle brush before crouching, ready to pounce and kill.

'Or it could become an honorary pony if we penned it in alongside Dolly,' Libby goes on, warming to the theme. 'What kind of dog is it?'

'It's a mini chihuahua, what the Americans call a teacup dog.'

'Ah, that sounds very sweet.' Libby pauses. 'Couldn't you keep it with you, Buster and Tia?'

'I've already thought of that. No, Buster couldn't cope with another male in the house.'

'That could be inconvenient in the future to say the least, unless you're talking about male dogs in particular, rather than males in general. Buster's presence could have dire consequences for your love life.'

'I haven't got a love life,' I say quickly. 'Really, I haven't, and I don't want one.'

'Methinks you protest too much.' Libby tilts her head, a bit like Tia does when she's expecting you to give her a biscuit. 'It hasn't escaped my notice that you've been spending a lot of quality time with my big brother recently, swanning about with him, so to speak.'

'Very funny.' I shouldn't encourage her. I return to the problem of the dog. It might be the size of a teacup, but it's still a dog, and it needs somewhere to live, and I can't double it up with another of our canine guests in case they play too rough with it. 'I'm going to call Wendy to see if she can possibly foster another dog.'

It is a phone call I look forward to with some trepidation because Wendy and I haven't spoken since our silly fall-out over her entitlement to the donations of dog food from the box that Libby set up by the till in the Co-op. I have no quarrel with any of the committee. In fact, I can see only too clearly where they are coming from. It should have been a joint majority decision to take me on to work here, not Fifi acting alone.

'I'm sorry, Tessa, but you understand my position,' Wendy says when I explain my request.

'Can't we put our differences aside for the sake

233

of the dog?' I ask quietly.

'Oh, those aren't the issues. I'm up to my quota. There is no room at the inn, and it's all I can do to cope with the ones I already have. I rehomed one last week, but as soon as she went, another came in.'

'You haven't space for just one more?' I beg. 'He's the tiniest chihuahua.'

'A big dog inside a little one,' Wendy observes. 'I don't think so, Tessa.' I can tell from the tone of her voice that, as a true dog-lover, she's beginning to weaken. 'Can't you wait a week or two until one of the others has gone?'

'I don't think so, not when the husband is telling us that he will hold us to blame if the dog eats their baby before I can find someone to take it in.'

'How ridiculous is that!'

'I know, but I think he's genuinely upset and ashamed at having to get rid of the dog. He's probably very fond of it.'

'I suppose it won't require much food, or space on the sofa, and I won't have to walk it far with those little legs.'

'So, you'll take him?'

There's a long pause.

'I haven't said that exactly.' I can tell that she's smiling as she utters a self-mocking sigh. 'I'm such a soft touch, aren't I? Tessa, tell them that if they can wait until next week, that will be perfect. If not, then I'll squeeze him in.'

'I'll see if I can put them off for a few days,' I say, thanking her. 'What would I do without you, Wendy?'

'I'm sorry to have been a pain,' she says. 'I've had enough of all the petty arguments and bitching that have been going on. You're doing a great job and it's time we all stopped taking sides and worked together for the sake of the animals.'

'That's lovely to hear. Thank you.'

'Unfortunately, there are still some on the committee, and I'm not naming names' – although I can guess, I think wryly as Wendy continues – 'who cannot be persuaded to change their minds.'

'Well, I wish everyone could agree,' I say. 'I'll be in touch about the dog very soon.'

It is too late to put the owners off. According to the wife, as the baby screams in the background, the husband is on his way to the Sanctuary with the dog, known as Mad Max. I cut the call and phone Wendy back to arrange to take him over to her later.

The dog, dressed in a T-shirt with a Mucky Pup logo, comes with a wardrobe complete with clothes on hangers, two pairs of bootees and three bling-encrusted collars and leads. When the husband drops him off, he's crying.

'I don't want to do this. It feels like the worst kind of betrayal, but my wife is adamant, and she's right really… It's for the best,' he repeats, as though he's trying to convince himself. 'The baby is up every night with colic and we're both exhausted.' He kisses the dog several times, and by the time he can bring himself to leave him, I'm in tears too.

I take Max to Wendy's after I've dropped Libby home in the afternoon. I drive the van because Jack is away on a training course, and Max whines all the way. When I pass the church in Talyton St George, I find that although I think of the wedding and Nathan, it's not with the same pain as before.

Wendy's home, an impressive pebble-dashed Edwardian house, is in one of the roads in the older part of town, and I can tell before I walk up the drive with Max in my arms that I'm at the right place as a cacophony of barking dogs assault my ears.

Wendy opens the front door a couple of centimetres.

'Get back, dogs. Oh, do please be quiet! How many times do I have to tell you it isn't the postman?'

The door closes and reopens to let me in. Wendy, dressed in summery dog-walking clothes – a saggy blouse and floral cotton trousers – shows me through to the living room at the front of the house. It's decidedly shabby and an odour of bad eggs pervades the air. There are dogs everywhere, every single one perched on the furniture, including a snooty-looking Afghan hound, two Labrador crosses, a Dobermann and three terriers. There are blankets and throws draped over the sofa and chairs, and various rubber toys and bones scattered across the threadbare carpet.

'Take a pew, if you can find one. Off dogs. Off!' Wendy flaps her arms. The Dobermann comes trotting over to investigate, but the rest remain where they are. Wendy picks up one terrier and plonks it gently on the floor. It makes to jump back up.

'No, Gary!' she shouts, but it doesn't take any

236

notice, resuming its place.

'Don't worry. I can't stop for long. Where do you want him?' I say, nodding towards the dog that cowers in my arms, shivering and showing the whites of his eyes.

'Pop him down on the floor – I expect he can stand up for himself.'

I put him down and he stays there, his body low to the ground and his tail tucked tight between his legs.

'I'm afraid he's been rather spoiled,' I observe. 'I have his wardrobe in the back of the van.'

'Dogs should be allowed to be dogs. I don't hold with all this dressing up and treating dogs like surrogate children, but lots of doggies do have coats nowadays.'

'No, I mean a wardrobe: a box with doors and a hanging rail for his clothes. I'll bring it in for you.' I look around at the dogs on the sofa and chairs and smile to myself. Wendy spoils her canine foster family too, just in a different way.

'Take that T-shirt off him, Tessa,' she says. 'He's embarrassed.'

I remove it, aware that I'm squatting on the floor in a sea of hair, before stepping back to see what Max will do. He does nothing until the Dobermann, a massive black and tan dog with eyes sunk deep into its skull, comes forward to sniff at him, when he utters a low growl. The Dobermann continues to take liberties, sniffing first one ear then the other, at which Max, unable to contain himself any longer, lets out a furious yap and attaches himself by his teeth to the end of the Dobermann's nose. The Dobermann shakes his head violently, flinging Max off onto the rug by the fireplace. Undaunted, Max goes back in for more.

'No, Max,' I say, imagining carnage and yet another costly trip to the vet.

'It's all right.' Wendy touches my arm. 'Let them decide who's boss.' She chuckles as the Dobermann yelps and jumps back and Max stands feet square, head and tail up, facing him with his teeth bared. 'I reckon he can take care of himself, don't you?'

It seems that he can, for he proceeds to patrol the room, examining his new surroundings while the other dogs watch him with interest and from a respectful distance.

'He's going to be all right,' says Wendy. 'There'll be queues of people lining up to adopt him. He won't be here for long.'

I think of Buster and Tia, and wish I could say the same for them, but when I get back to the Sanctuary, my aunt, who has turned up for a couple of hours, is showing a couple around the kennels. She introduces them as Mr and Mrs Nelson. Mr Nelson is in his late fifties while Mrs Nelson is a few years younger. Some of our visitors struggle to choose a dog – big dog or little dog? Pedigree or mongrel? Puppy or adult? – but the Nelsons know exactly what they are looking for: a small terrier-type dog, preferably a Jack Russell. However, it's Buster who catches their eye.

'Can we go in with him?' Mrs Nelson asks.

'Let me get him out for you,' I say, not wanting to risk a confrontation between Buster and the

husband over Buster's territory. I hand him over, watching him sniff at their hands before they take him for a stroll in the copse. I wait for them to return, crossing my fingers in the hope that this will be Buster's lucky break.

'We love him,' says Mrs Nelson. 'He isn't quite what we were looking for, but he's adorable.'

'I'm very fond of him,' I say, biting back a sudden pang of regret at the thought that I'm putting my baby up for adoption.

'Will he fit in the back of the car?' says the husband. 'That's my only reservation.'

'Of course he will,' Mrs Nelson says, giving him a look that means, Shut up, I want this dog.

'He isn't all that big,' I point out.

'Can we try him in it?' says the husband.

'Of course.' I frown. It seems a strange request, but if it helps Buster find a good home...

It turns out that Buster does fit into the back of their car and, therefore, Mr Nelson agrees that he will fit in with their lifestyle. They enjoy walking and cycling, and evenings in, and they seem perfect – too perfect, I wonder, or am I just looking for an excuse to keep him?

I arrange a home visit with them for the following week, and stifling my doubts, I return Buster to his kennel, stopping to stroke his silky coat as he gazes up at me, hopeful that I'm going to come back for him when I retire to the bungalow later. Could I keep him? I wonder briefly. I can't afford to keep myself, let alone a dog, and if I took Buster on because I've become attached to him, what would stop me taking on others? I could end up with a menagerie, like some of the nurses I used to work with in practice.

'I think you'll be happy with the Nelsons,' I tell him. 'Your future now depends on the outcome of the home visit, but don't worry, I'll make sure you have everything you could possibly want and more, a special home for a very special dog.'

I glance into Tia's kennel, where she's lying curled up in her bed with her nose buried in her fluffy tail. Visitors constantly reject Tia because of her age and her health problems, and I can understand their worry that they'll grow to love her and lose her soon after. It's like adopting a granny: it isn't a great long-term prospect. She'll end up spending the rest of her life here, and what kind of existence is that? I try to remain optimistic. It looks as though Buster has found himself a wonderful forever home. Hopefully, there will be someone out there for Tia.

Chapter Twelve

Top Dog

I find that clearing the droppings from the paddock is always a good time to take stock. I work
in the bright sun, my skin prickling with heat and
perspiration even though I'm dressed in only a
vest top, shorts and wellies. I use a scraper and a
scoop, and a wheelbarrow with a wobbly wheel.
Like the mountain of droppings balanced on the
wheelbarrow, my position at the Sanctuary is
precarious.

DJ has moved on, out of pocket. Diane and
Wendy have apparently abandoned their prin-
ciples and, in spite of what Wendy said when I
dropped Max off with her, they show no sign of
returning to volunteer on a regular basis. Fifi and
the committee are at loggerheads. I have invoices
from both of Talyton's vet practices awaiting payment with interest, and I know for a fact that Jack
paid for the last purchase of dog food from Overdown Farmers, and my aunt has been bringing
supplies of coffee, tea and milk from the coffee
shop at the garden centre. Towie, the kitten, is
sitting in the cage in the office, as if she's on Death
Row, awaiting a decision on whether I can justify
the expense of removing an eye from a feral kitten,
who might make a great pet, or might not. You
could argue, on a practical rather than an emo-

tional level, that there are many more feral kittens out there, in spite of our trap, neuter and release policy, and the charity's money – if and when it comes – would be better spent on neutering.

I don't know what to do. I am working all hours because there are more animals here than Libby and I can cope with, and on top of that, I have a ball to organise and admin to deal with.

And then there's the problem of what to do about Jack. Now that is a more intriguing challenge. There is no doubt that we are growing closer again, but this time it is different. I don't think I can honestly say we're 'just friends'.

I push the loaded wheelbarrow over to the corner of the paddock where we are creating a muck heap of extraordinary dimensions for a single pony, run the barrow up the plank to the top and tip out the muck. I survey the scene from my vantage point, watching the buzzard that soars in the sky over Longdogs Copse, one of the ferals that is patrolling the hedgerow among the cow parsley, brambles and nettles, and a vehicle, the postman's red van, which is heading this way on the lane.

Not Jack then, I muse. I check my watch. I haven't seen or heard from him in all of four hours. I must stop thinking – no, obsessing about him – because if the committee have their way, I could be moving on very soon to who knows where without him.

'Letter for you, Tessa.' Ash brings an envelope over to me.

'Thanks,' I call from the top of the heap.

'I'll leave it here.' He balances the letter on the

gatepost, and with the next breath of a summer breeze, it floats down and settles on top of the water in the trough. 'Oh dear, you didn't see that happen, did you?'

'If it's another bill, then no, I didn't,' I say grinning as he flicks the water from the envelope and brings it over to the muck heap, stopping halfway along the plank to place it directly in my hands.

'How's it going?' he says.

'Great, thanks. Would you like to offer a home to one of our residents? We're running short on space.'

'I'd love to have a dog one day.'

'What kind of dog?' I say, wondering if I can tempt him to consider adoption in the more immediate future.

'One that doesn't bite the postman, obviously,' he chuckles. 'It won't be for a while though.' He pauses, colour rising in his cheeks. 'Is Libby here today?'

'I'm afraid not. She'll be sorry she missed you,' I go on, grabbing the opportunity to play Cupid, and perhaps sell a couple more tickets for the ball. 'Are you coming to the ball? You must have seen the flyers.' I've posted hundreds, probably more items than Ash posts through letterboxes in a week. 'You should ask Libby – she's always talking about you,' I say, planting the idea in his head.

Blushing furiously, he tells me he'd better get on, before he walks sideways down the plank, attempts the leap over the puddle at the base of the heap and lands with one foot up to his ankle in foul black liquid manure. 'Oh, shit,' he swears.

'You're right – that's exactly what it is,' I say brightly. 'You're a country postie – you should be wearing wellies.'

'Too late,' he says, with a rueful grimace. 'I'm going to feel a right idiot, going around smelling of muck all day.'

'You can wash it off before you leave – there's soap by the hose outside the barn.' I give him a wave. 'Bye.'

While Ash is driving away into the hills towards the moor, I open the soggy letter and read it with a sinking heart. The Talyton Animal Rescue Committee is calling an extraordinary general meeting and specifically requests my attendance tomorrow night at 7.30 at Wendy's house. This is it. This is the end. Diane and her cronies have decided to terminate my term at the Sanctuary because Fifi's contract isn't valid. I assume the worst.

The following day I turn up at the meeting, filled with trepidation. Diane sits at the head of the table in Wendy's dining room, pouring tea and carving slices from a caraway cake before the formal proceedings can begin. Wendy is present, of course, along with Frances, the receptionist from the Otter House vet practice, dressed in a psychedelic tunic top and trademark ash-blonde wig that reminds me of candyfloss twirled around a stick, and four other ladies from Talyton St George. There are hairs in the tea and hairs in the cake, and Max the teacup dog jumps up on my lap for a cuddle, moulting a few more hairs onto my black trousers for good measure.

'I have someone interested in taking Max,'

Wendy says, noticing his head pop up over the top of the table. 'Hopefully, he'll be gone by the end of the week. The others will be relieved to see the back of him – he's definitely top dog, a bit of a bully, in fact.'

Diane calls everyone's attention by banging an auctioneer's gavel against the table.

'Welcome to what is only the third extra-ordinary meeting of our illustrious organisation's history,' she says, before running through the list of those present and those who have sent their apologies. 'Fifi Green... Where is she?'

'Um, I don't think we invited her,' Wendy says, pulling out a pen, along with several poop-a-scoop bags and dog biscuits from her pocket, before she starts taking the minutes. 'In fact, Diane, you expressly told me not to invite her. She's still in the doghouse.'

'Isn't that rather irregular?' says Frances. 'She is chair, after all.'

'There are enough of us. We're quorate,' Diane says, 'seven good women and true.'

I stroke Max, running my fingers through his coat and catching a flea, which I snap in half between my fingernails. Should I mention it to Wendy? I decide not.

'Firstly,' says Diane, 'Fifi's position, as we've said before, is untenable. As chair, one cannot continue to impose one's wishes on the members of the committee without listening to their views, so, I put forward the motion that this committee has lost confidence in the chair and therefore the chair should be deposed.'

There are a couple of gasps and an 'Oh no'.

'Can we do that?' asks Frances.

'Let's vote,' says Diane, ignoring her. They vote on paper slips, dropping them into a box, which is passed around the table with great ceremony to Frances, who takes them out, counts them and writes notes on another piece of paper that she passes on to Diane. It gives me the impression of a secret society with strange rituals and its own rules.

'Those in favour, seven,' Diane says, raising one pudgy hand in triumph. 'I shall let Fifi know.'

'Are you going to suggest she remains as an ordinary committee member?' Wendy asks. 'It would be a shame for all her experience to go to waste. She's been good to Talyton Animal Rescue over the years.'

'She's very loyal,' Frances adds pointedly, I think.

'This is no time for sentimentality,' says Diane. 'I move that we nominate a new chair and place our votes today. None of us wants this ship to sail on rudderless, do we?'

'Can't we do that at the next meeting?' says Wendy. 'That will give us time to canvass opinion.'

'We must have this settled,' Diane insists. 'It's really important for the future of Talyton Animal Rescue that we have someone with the right credentials at the helm, someone who has served selflessly on this committee for many years, a "people" person – because this isn't all about the animals, you know – and someone with initiative who isn't afraid to speak her mind–'

'You mean you, Diane,' Wendy cuts in. 'You're describing yourself.'

Diane beams at her. 'So I accept that as your nomination, Wendy,' she says, continuing quickly before Wendy can respond, 'Thank you for your insight. You know that, if I'm voted in as chair, I shall serve this wonderful committee well. Are there any other nominations?' She looks around the table, glaring at each person in turn as if daring them to name anyone else.

They don't, and Diane is elected unopposed.

'It's time I left.' I get up, keen to escape because I feel that even by being here, I'm being disloyal to my aunt. She's always been good to me. 'I have to get back to let the dogs out.'

'Of course you do,' Wendy says. 'How remiss of us. But wait, we haven't discussed your situation yet. You were supposed to be top of the agenda. Please, sit down and hear us out.'

'Well, Tessa,' Diane says, turning to me as I return to my seat, and I feel myself beginning to wilt under her gaze, much like a potential apprentice in the boardroom with Sir Alan Sugar. 'I have had reports, personal communications' – the hue of her complexion deepens from pink through to scarlet – 'that you are a reliable, dedicated and selfless manager, a paragon, in fact.'

I can't help wondering if she's being sarcastic as she continues, 'The lovely Jack Miller–'

'Please, do stop swooning and get on with it,' Wendy says, interrupting. 'Diane, you think you're such a cougar.'

The other ladies laugh raucously. Diane glares at them, before continuing, 'You're just jealous. Some of us have it and some of us don't.'

'So, what did Jack say?' Frances asks.

'He said that he thought Tessa should remain at the Sanctuary, a recommendation indeed. I have a very high opinion of Jack Miller.'

My neck grows hot at the thought of Jack putting a good word in for me.

However, Diane goes on, 'There is no escaping the fact that Fifi had no right to give you the position of manager–'

'I understand,' I say. I can contain myself no longer. 'I'll pack up my things and leave in the morning.' I pause, my chest tight with disappointment at the thought of leaving the Sanctuary, a place where I feel I belong. 'All I ask in return is that the committee agrees to reinstate the financial support immediately, along with the volunteer rota, because if you don't the very animals you're trying to rescue are going to suffer. I can't and won't be held responsible for all this intrigue and petty infighting. I came to the Sanctuary in good faith. It wasn't some plot between me and my aunt. It was her suggestion, yes, but there was no malice intended. She knew I was more than qualified for the job and I was available to work straight away.'

As Diane opens her mouth to speak, I raise my hand.

'She should have discussed it with you first, but to be honest, I can see now why she didn't. Some say my aunt is haughty and overbearing and used to getting her own way, but I imagine she didn't ask your opinion because she guessed what it would be. I thought you were a group of like-minded individuals determined to improve animal welfare, but you're more like a council of war.'

'Is that all?' says Diane, her eyes glinting, no doubt with annoyance at my outburst.

'It isn't,' I confirm, and I go on to talk about Buster, Tia and Dolly. 'I'm glad I had the opportunity of meeting them, and giving them the chance of a happier life.' Brushing a tear from my eye, I fight to control the tremor in my voice. 'I'll always support the Sanctuary in the future, wherever I am, because it means a lot to me.' I think of the animals, of the countryside, of Libby and Jack. Of course, I think of Jack. I can hardly stop thinking about him.

There is a long pause, during which Diane clears her throat and turns to Wendy.

'I think we need to talk about this,' Wendy says. 'Do you mind, Tessa?'

I scoop Max up and go to leave the room to let the committee members continue their deliberations without me; I've no intention of staying.

'I'll go now. I've said what I needed to say.'

'No, stay,' Wendy says, talking to me as if I were one of her canine charges.

'I really do need to get back to let the dogs out,' I explain.

'Please, give us five minutes,' Wendy insists. 'Make yourself at home.'

Reluctantly, I wait in the sitting room, hovering with Max and reading the titles on the bookshelf: *Let Sleeping Dogs Lie, In Defence of Dogs* and *The Curious Incident of the Dog in the Night-Time*. There is no room to sit down even if I wished to: as before, there are dogs sprawled out on every horizontal surface. Soon, Wendy asks me to rejoin them.

'Go on, Diane,' she says as we sit down again. 'You must speak – you're chair now.'

'I owe you an apology, Tessa,' Diane says, touching her chest. 'I have allowed my differences with your aunt to prejudice me against you, against the best interests of the charity and the animals we rescue, and I'm sorry.' She glances around the table. 'We're all sorry,' she adds to a general murmur of agreement from the committee. 'You've spoken most eloquently, if I may say so, about how much the position of manager means to you. Your devotion is most touching, and so we have voted overwhelmingly to invite you to stay on at the Sanctuary for as long as you wish.'

I can stay. My spirits lift as Diane continues, 'I've been a little arrogant, thinking I can run the show myself. Nobody can. Talyton Animal Rescue is a team, and we need people like you on our side.'

'Thank you,' I say, 'but what about my aunt? Is she still part of the team?'

'Don't worry, Tessa. I'll make sure she understands her position,' Diane says. 'Have a small glass of elderflower champagne with us. We can have a chat about the home-check visits. I need to show you the ropes.'

'Oh, I don't think that will be necessary.' I was rather hoping Jack would come and do some with me. 'It's common sense, isn't it?'

'Have you done any yet?'

'I've got one coming up – someone's offered Buster a home. As for the rat, I didn't do a visit. The boys who adopted him know more about rats than I ever will.'

Diane frowns. 'You still have to visit.'

'Why? My time and the charity's money can be put to better use.'

'You know, you are more like your aunt than I realised.' Her expression relaxes into a smile. 'I'm sorry, Tessa. The Sanctuary means a lot to me.' She looks towards Wendy, and adds, 'To all of us.' She pauses for a moment. 'When are you going?'

'I've made an appointment for three o'clock on Wednesday – tomorrow.'

Diane's face falls once more. 'You shouldn't have done that, Tessa. Always offer them a time slot, between nine and one or one and five, or even better, make an unannounced visit, and that way you'll catch them out if they're at work when they say they aren't.'

'Are people really that devious?' I say, weary of Diane's paranoia. She loves animals, but appears to have little faith in human nature.

'Oh, I've seen it all,' Diane claims. 'Just you wait and see.'

The following day, Diane and I head down to Talysands in the van to make the home visit on Buster's behalf.

It's lovely. The Nelsons are keen to adopt and the wife has had dogs before. The house and garden are spacious and immaculate. Can I see Buster living here? Yes, but it breaks my heart to do so because I've done something really stupid – I've grown overly fond of him, as I fear I have done with Jack, a situation not helped by the fact that he put a good word in for me with the committee.

While Diane interrogates them about how they

251

feel about muddy paws and dog hair, the pros and cons of a bones-and-raw-food diet versus feeding a proprietary brand of dog food, and their ability to stump up for any vet's bills Buster might incur as he grows older, I tick off the boxes on the paperwork that she insisted I bring, along with a clipboard and pen.

Diane's questioning becomes quite personal, talking about the couple's working hours (Mrs Nelson is a lady of leisure, which is perfect), what they do in their spare time, how often they go on holiday and how much they drink. I frown at her. What business is it of ours?

By the time we've been there for half an hour, Mr Nelson is clearly growing impatient.

'Do you need me any longer? Only I have a tennis match at four.'

'We prefer to see the whole family together,' Diane says.

'We've seen all we need to see,' I say, cutting in. 'I'm sorry we've kept you.'

'It wasn't this intrusive when we went through the process to adopt a baby,' he grumbles lightly. 'We gave up in the end though. It was too much, wasn't it, love?'

His wife nods.

'Well, I don't see why you shouldn't have Buster,' I say, feeling sorry for them. 'You've ticked all the boxes. Congratulations.'

Mrs Nelson smiles broadly. 'Oh, thank you. That's so exciting. When can we pick him up?'

'How about tomorrow?' I say, thinking that will give me a chance to say goodbye. 'Any time.'

'That went awfully well,' says Diane on the way

back to the Sanctuary. 'That dog has really fallen on his paws.'

'I hope so. I'll be glad to see him settled,' I say, my fingers tight on the steering wheel. I'm not sure I like this part of my new job, especially when the Nelsons ring me later to delay collecting Buster for a few days while they have someone in to put up a new garden fence.

Back at the Sanctuary, I phone my aunt to let her know about the meeting, assuming I've given Diane long enough to speak to her beforehand.

'I would have known if there'd been a meeting,' Fifi says, her tone hollow with disbelief and shock. 'I'm chair, and no one calls a meeting without me.'

'I'm telling you, I was there,' I say. 'I'm sorry, but I thought you should know. Diane has been elected to replace you.'

'They can't possibly do that,' my aunt blusters. 'It's against the committee rules.'

'Rules that no one sticks to,' I point out. 'If you go accusing Diane of breaking the rules, I reckon she'll turn round and tell you that you have done the same in taking me on at the Sanctuary without a vote, or even calling a meeting.'

'Tessa, whose side are you on?' My aunt's voice is cracking as if she's about to cry, and I want to go round to give her a hug. I know how important status is to her. To Fifi, losing the chair of the Talyton Animal Rescue Committee is like losing a limb, but I have to be practical.

'I'm really sorry, but if I'm to be an effective manager, I can't get involved in the politics. I can't be seen to be taking sides. You do understand?'

'Of course I do. I'm not stupid, although they're

doing their best to make me look a fool.' My aunt sighs deeply. 'I'm beginning to think that it's all too much trouble. Sometimes it feels as though everyone's against me.'

'I'm not. I appreciate everything you do for me and the rescues,' I say. 'You'll be coming up to the Sanctuary soon, won't you? And you'll continue to help me organise the ball? I really don't think I can do it all myself and I'm not confident that anyone else will step in.'

'Yes, I won't abandon you, Tessa.' Fifi's voice brightens slightly. 'If nothing else, making a success of the ball will prove that they can't do without me.'

I wish her goodbye, grab some lunch and head off to the cattery where I meet Jack to give Teddy his daily dose of antibiotic. Jack's wearing light stone combat trousers and a navy polo-shirt with the welfare logo in red on his left breast. Standing close to him outside Teddy's pen, I can see the pulse in his neck and the shadowy dip between his collarbones. Tearing my gaze away, I turn to look at the cat, who's snoozing on his shelf.

'It's all right for some,' I say. 'Look at him – he's so lazy.'

'It's the first law of energy conservation, isn't it? Cats are great physicists – they know that energy is neither created nor destroyed, so they will always use the minimum amount of energy possible,' Jack says. 'Have you heard of the law of inertia in relation to cats?'

'Jack, I wasn't great at physics at school.'

'It's the one that goes, a cat will tend to remain at rest unless acted on by some external force, such as the rattle of a box of cat biscuits.' He chuckles. 'You do know the difference between cats and dogs?'

'Oh yes. Dogs have owners, whereas cats have staff.'

'How was the home check?' Jack changes the subject, brushing my hand as he passes me a strip of tablets.

'Can't you tell?' I say, glumly. 'Buster has new owners.' I bite my lip, my eyes watering as I think about having to let him go.

'That's great,' Jack says. 'Buster will have a wonderful life.'

'I know that it's the right thing to do, but it's so hard.'

Jack touches my shoulder. 'You'll still have me,' he says lightly.

'Are you flirting with me?' It's flattering, and I can't help smiling.

'Maybe,' he says. 'Are you going to catch this vicious beastie or am I?'

'I'll get him.' I take the towel from the hook outside. 'Come on, Teddy.' I wrap the cat in the towel, making a parcel of him, leaving just his head and tail sticking out. 'There you go. It's a wrap,' I say, handing him to Jack, who holds him while I pop a tablet down his throat. 'All done.'

'That was painless for once,' Jack observes, returning Teddy to his pen. He shuts the door, hesitating as if he doesn't want to leave me. 'Tess, do you still think about Nathan? I mean, I'm sure you do. It isn't something you get over just like that–'

'Oh, what do you know?' I interrupt, trying to

save both of us further embarrassment.

'I know what it's like to have a broken heart.'

I look Jack straight in the eye, challenging him. 'Do you?'

'I met someone while I was away.' He pauses. 'Why am I telling you this?'

'You can't not tell me now,' I say, finding that I want to know this Jack, the person he is now, much better. 'Who is she?' I ask, tentacles of jealousy taking a grip on my heartstrings at the thought of Jack with this unknown woman, Jack kissing her, making love to her...

'Who was she?' Jack corrects me, his expression mournful. 'I liked her a lot. She was one of the charity workers. She was married and ten years older than me, good reasons for pushing her away, but there was something there that I couldn't resist.'

'Oh, Jack. I'm sorry.'

'Don't be. When I was with her, it was as though nothing else existed.' Jack smiles ruefully. 'It was pretty intense but it would have burned itself out if I'd stayed any longer. It shouldn't have happened. I shouldn't have let it happen.'

'Don't beat yourself up about it,' I say, surprised at his admission. Jack's always been so well behaved, so good.

'I felt lonely and rejected.'

'Because she ended the relationship?'

'No, I think I fell for her because I was very unhappy. My heart was already broken before I met her.' He hesitates. 'Have you any idea why I left Talyton?'

'Because you wanted to volunteer with the

moon bears. You've told me that already.'

'I went when I heard you were engaged to Nathan,' Jack says harshly.

I stare at him as he continues, 'The bottom kind of fell out of my world. I thought I'd accepted that we would never be together, but you getting engaged made it final somehow. I decided I couldn't stand staying around to watch you getting ready for the wedding. I thought I'd feel better thousands of miles away.' He shakes his head slowly. 'It made no difference. You were out of sight, Tess, but never out of my mind.'

Joy and happiness bubble up inside me. No one has ever said anything so romantic to me in my life, but where does this leave us? I wonder. Jack ducks towards me and touches his lips to my cheek.

'I'll catch you later,' he says, leaving me standing there, stupid with desire, touching the very spot where he kissed me and wondering what will happen next, and when.

Chapter Thirteen

The Runaway Deer

It's early the following Saturday afternoon, late August, and I am alone at the Sanctuary, having shown the last of the day's visitors, a family with young children, around the place. They didn't offer to adopt one of the rescues, but the parents did drop a generous donation into the box at reception, perhaps as a forfeit for their offspring's behaviour. I asked their boys not to put their fingers in the hamster cage, at which one of them asked why, promptly sticking his finger through the bars. That's why, his mother said as he let rip an ear-splitting wail. I don't think he could have made any more fuss if the hamster had taken his finger off and, as it was, I had to dig out the first-aid kit to find some antiseptic and a plaster to staunch the flow of blood. (I'm being sarcastic – the wound was like a paper cut.) Anyway, they left not long ago, heading for the Minor Injuries Unit in Talyton St George to see if the victim of the attack needs antibiotics or a tetanus jab, while I fill in the very first entry in the accident book, leaning against the desk at reception.

My mobile vibrates, making me start. It's Jack.

'Hi,' I say. I've been wondering where he is and what he's doing. I suppose you could say that, after his confession, Jack has become my obsession. I can't eat or sleep for thinking about him. The feelings I have are far more intense than anything I felt for Nathan, yet neither of us has made any further move towards the other. I suppose it's better this way, keeping the status quo, but sometimes I wish Jack would take the initiative and ask me out.

'Tess, I'm going to come and pick you up on the way in to Talyton,' he says in a tone that brooks no argument. 'We need as many hands as possible – there's an injured deer on the loose. As far as the police can tell, although they can't get that close to it, it's in a pretty bad way. Can you bring some kit with you? I've left the stretcher in the back of the barn. If you wouldn't mind picking it up...'

'I'll find it.' I don't mind at all. Deer or no deer, I'd do anything for Jack. I'd walk to the ends of the earth for him, if only he'd ask.

'Thanks. I'll be with you in five.'

'Did you mean five minutes or five seconds?' I ask him when he turns up, the van screaming to a stop as it enters the car park. I fling the stretcher into the back, jump in alongside him, and he immediately performs a lurching three-point turn. 'Where's the deer?'

'It's running along the main road. The police have set up a rolling road block to stop the traffic, but they can't stop the deer. It's heading straight into town and it's absolutely petrified.'

I clutch hold of the seat as Jack puts his foot down hard on the accelerator and shoots off, jolting down the track.

'Luckily for us, it's a roe deer, not a red,' Jack goes on, 'otherwise we'd have no chance of handling it. Either Alex Fox-Gifford or his assistant, Justin, are on their way with a dart gun in case we have to tranquillise it.'

I glance towards him as we drive on into Talyton. He's totally focused on the task in hand. If anyone can catch this deer, Jack can.

'This is where you could do with some blue lights,' I observe when he has to pull onto the pavement at the end of Fore Street because the road is jammed with cars, holiday and weekend traffic heading out to the coast.

'Unfortunately, we're not allowed them on our own vehicles,' he says, getting out of the van, 'but yeah, they'd be useful in this kind of situation.' He grabs the stretcher, passes me a couple of blankets and a bag and we run towards Market Square, Jack with his mobile pressed to his ear in full emergency rescue mode, strong, capable and heroic – and very fit, I think, struggling to catch my breath as I try to keep up with him. We push through the crowds in the square where people have got out of their cars to see what is going on, attracted by the sight of not the usual one police car, but two, and several police officers who have gathered outside the ironmonger's shop.

Jack walks straight up to them.

'Animal Welfare,' he says. 'Where's the deer?'

'In there,' one of the policemen says. 'The vet's gone in to try and catch it.'

Jack pushes the door open and I follow. As we enter, a bell rings and a parrot screeches from a perch beside the counter. There's a scuffle from the room beyond and the sound of voices.

'Oh dear,' Jack says to me. A smile flickers

across his face. 'Get it?'

'Ha ha,' I say. 'Very funny.'

'You don't seem convinced,' he says lightly, before moving on through the shop, stepping over boxes of nails and screws that are strewn across the floor. Mr Victor, the proprietor, a man of small stature and wide girth, balding on top and wearing an old-fashioned brown shopkeeper's coat and glasses with thick, circular lenses, appears in the entrance to the room beyond.

'You'd better wait there,' he says curtly. 'The vet's trying to dart the damned thing. Look at the mess it's made. Why did it have to come in here?'

Mr Victor isn't renowned for his good temper, and at the moment he is definitely not a happy man. I glance behind me, noticing the overturned display of brooms, mops and buckets in the shop window. The parrot moves sideways along its perch, bobbing its head up and down in a threatening manner, before it opens its beak and speaks. It takes a couple of repeats before I understand that it's telling us to go away in no uncertain terms.

'Captain, that's enough,' Mr Victor says, his cheeks turning pinker than a hot dog's tongue. 'Not in front of the lady, thank you.' He turns to me. 'You're Steve's daughter, aren't you?'

'That's right.'

'Your dad was in here this morning for batteries, long-life double As,' he goes on.

'It's okay to go through, Tess,' Jack interrupts. 'Justin's managed to dart the deer.'

'You'd better go and get it out of here, before I have it for venison,' Mr Victor says.

261

Jack and I head through the back to the garden, a tiny walled area of paving slabs and potted geraniums, where we find the vet squatting down and pulling a dart from the rump of a reddish-brown deer that's about the same size as a border collie. It lies on its brisket with a glazed expression on its face. It has a black nose, small antlers and big brown eyes that are ringed with long lashes, the kind Katie's clients at the salon would kill for.

'What do you think, Justin?' Jack asks.

Although I know Justin is a vet, he doesn't look like the sort you might find in the stories of James Herriot. He has to be in his mid-twenties yet looks younger, and wears a stud in one ear and his hair gelled up at the front. When he turns to face Jack, I can see the multicoloured logo on his black T-shirt: *Feed the Fire*.

'He's completely stressed out. He's got a nasty injury to the left hind-limb, probably a result of jumping through a wire fence, and I'm not convinced he hasn't fractured the right one. I can't understand how he ran this far.' Justin hesitates. 'I'm reluctant to go straight for euthanasia – he has a lot of fight left in him – but it's going to be a long haul if he does pull through. Have you got the time and space to nurse him up at the Sanctuary?'

'Of course,' I cut in, desperate for this beautiful creature to have a chance of life. 'We wouldn't turn any animal away.'

'In that case, we'll get him up to the Manor so I can knock him out properly, X-ray the leg and see what I can do with this wound,' Justin decides.

Jack unrolls the stretcher, placing it alongside the patient. 'He can travel in the back of the van. He'll be safest in there.'

'Mind the legs,' Justin warns me as I move to assist. 'They kick pretty hard.'

'Tess knows a bit about deer,' Jack says. 'She's a vet nurse.'

'That's cool,' says Justin with a brief smile. 'You'll be able to help me out at the other end with the surgery. Alex doesn't believe in paying for a nurse as well as an assistant.'

'As long as you don't expect me to wash up at the end for nothing,' I say lightly, looking forward to getting back into an operating theatre even for a little while.

Jack takes the deer by the antlers, while Justin and I support the front and back ends respectively. As we lift it onto the stretcher, it starts to panic, in spite of the effects of the tranquilliser, kicking out like mad until Jack wraps its head with a towel so that it can't see me passing the straps around its body and tightening them up. Once the deer is secured, Justin and Jack carry it out through the shop into the square, where the crowd begin to clap and cheer, setting the deer off again.

'Quiet, please,' Jack orders sharply, and the noise subsides. 'The sooner we get this poor thing out of here, the better. Open the van, will you, Tess?'

'The key, Jack,' I say. 'You must have the key.'

Holding the back of the stretcher with both hands, Jack glances down towards his trousers and grimaces. 'Um, it's in one of my pockets.'

Great, I think. Until now, I've been maintaining a strictly 'no contact' policy, doing my best to keep my hands off him so as not to fuel the passion that is gently simmering between us when we are together, and now he's asking me to look through his pockets.

'Hurry up, Tess,' he says, looking at me with an expression of amusement at my discomfort. 'I'm not asking for a strip search.' He glances towards Justin who grins back, as though he's worked out the reason for my hesitation, and I feel a rush of heat flooding up my neck. Am I that transparent?

'Which pocket?' I ask. Jack's trousers do have rather a lot of pockets.

'I'm not sure. Try the back right.'

I move up behind him, pull the top of his pocket out with one finger and peer in. 'Nope.'

'Try another one.'

If this wasn't a critical situation for the deer, it would be funny, I think, embarrassed at having to grope Jack to find the key to the van, and it's a relief to find that when I do discover an object in his front pocket, it is indeed his key ring, a plastic representation of a moon bear.

My face continues to burn when I unlock the van for Justin and Jack to slide the stretcher into the back.

'I'll travel with the patient,' I say, keen to be able to sit in the dark to let my blushes subside.

'Okay,' Jack says. 'I'll shut you in. We'll see you up at the Manor.'

'Don't drive too fast,' I say quickly.

'Don't worry. I'll be gentle with you,' Jack calls back, and a tiny yet delicious shiver runs down

264

my spine, a yearning for Jack to be as gentle with me as he likes. Not for the first time, I wonder what it would be like to kiss and be kissed by him once more, not a peck on the cheek, but full-on, mouth-to-mouth resuscitation.

It's hard to remain detached and professional when you're waiting for someone to make the first move, I muse as I check the deer's heartbeat, touching its chest to see if it's still alive. It's been a while since we rescued the swan, and one thing is clear: something has to happen and soon because the tension is almost too much to bear.

Half an hour later, having put thoughts of Jack aside, Justin and I are working on the deer at the Talyton Manor practice. The operating theatre is not what I'm used to, being an ordinary room off the office above the stable block at the manor. There's a sink for scrubbing up, a bench with an autoclave on top for sterilising instruments, a cupboard with various kits wrapped in green drapes and labelled with tape, and an operating table that has a piece of timber jammed underneath it because the height adjustment mechanism has failed.

'Alex and I don't do much surgery,' Justin explains. 'We refer most things, although the boss is looking at moving the practice to one of the outbuildings on the other side of the manor house. He's been waiting for months for planning permission to redevelop it. It'll be great once it's done though, if I'm still here.'

'Are you moving on, then?' Jack asks, looking on.

'This is my first job. Eventually, I'll want to

look for a partnership or set up on my own.'

I tweak flow rate on the intravenous drip, while Justin checks the X-rays of the deer's back leg on the laptop he's set up on the shelf alongside the operating table.

'There's no fracture, just bruising, which means we're okay to go ahead and look at this wound.' Justin fills a kidney dish with cotton wool and dilute antiseptic, using it to rinse the deer's other back leg, the lower part of which has no skin left on it, the shiny white tendons and network of dark blood vessels completely exposed. 'There's nothing left to suture, so we'll have to go for repeat dressings to let it heal by secondary intention, i.e. on its own. It'll be a long, slow job, although it will heal eventually, as long as the deer doesn't succumb from something else. Sometimes post-capture myopathy can set in, where the muscles break down because of the effects of stress or infection.'

'Do you think it's really the right thing to do?' Jack asks.

I know what he means. The deer is stressed out already and redressing the limb every few days isn't going to help, but – I check the patient's reflexes as I lighten the anaesthetic slightly, turning the dial on the vaporiser – he has beautiful eyes – deep, dark and captivating, much like Jack's – and I really don't want to lose him.

'It's up to you, Tessa,' Justin says, turning to me. 'You're the one who will be looking after him.'

'What do you think of his chances?'

'I wouldn't like to say.' Justin pulls open one of the drawers in the cupboard and several rolls of bandages, the soft fleecy kind used for padding legs, spring out across the floor. He collects up a selection of dressing materials and places them on the operating table. 'Sixty-forty, as long as he gets through the next couple of weeks when the risk of myopathy or muscle damage is highest. I'll give him selenium and vitamin E to try to prevent it, along with a shot of antibiotic. He'll have to be tagged to show he's received medication, and it will be up to you to decide if he can be released back into the wild or not at the end of his treatment.'

'That won't be such a problem,' says Jack. 'I've got a contact with a herd of rehabbed deer on a country estate about twenty miles from here, if it comes to that.'

'Let's go for it then,' I say. I'll take the flak if there's a problem with paying the bills. I don't mind. It will be worth it, if the deer survives. I assist Justin with cleaning and dressing the wound before turning off the anaesthetic gas completely to allow the patient to recover consciousness, crossing my fingers and praying that he will wake up. In the meantime, Jack answers his mobile.

'That was Libby,' he says, smiling. 'She's wondering where we've got to.'

'Where is she?'

'She's with your aunt. They heard we were tied up with the deer, and decided to head up to the Sanctuary when Libby's shift finished at the Co-op. They're doing the supper round and they're going to let Buster and Tia out for five minutes before they go home.'

'That's very kind of them,' I say. 'Don't get me

wrong, I love the baby birds, but it's great to have a break.'

'I wouldn't describe this as a break,' Justin says, frowning.

'Oh, it is when you've been at the Sanctuary all day,' I assure him. I change the subject. 'How are we going to transport the deer?' He's beginning to stir, his ears and limbs twitching, and his eyes beginning to focus. I check his pulse. It's almost impossible to count and I don't like it: a rapid pulse is a sure sign of stress. I place a fresh towel over the deer's head to cover his eyes.

'Has Alex got my crate somewhere?' Jack asks. 'I left it here a while ago.' He looks at me. 'The last deer didn't make it.'

'I think it's in the storeroom,' Justin says. 'I'll get it.'

Five minutes later, Justin returns, struggling through the door with a wooden crate. He places it on the floor, and Jack and I lower the patient inside and secure the lid. There's a brief scrabbling sound, followed by silence.

'Let's get him to the Sanctuary,' Jack says. 'Thanks, Justin.'

'Where are we going to put him?' I ask as Jack drives us back to the place I'm beginning to call home. I sit beside him this time, the deer in the crate in the rear of the van.

'You're the boss.' Jack glances towards me, smiling. 'You decide.'

I give him a playful nudge. 'Keep your eyes on the road, please.'

'And I could ask you to keep your hands to yourself,' he teases back.

'So, are you?' I say boldly. I don't know what has got into me today.

'Am I what?'

I assume that he's changing gear to make the turn up the track to the Sanctuary, but his hand deliberately brushes against my fingers. The contact is electric and very distracting.

'You know very well.'

'You have to be explicit,' he says in a low and suggestive tone, and I'm certain now that we're on the same wavelength.

'Are you asking me to keep my hands to myself?'

'That would seem a little hypocritical of me.'

Because? I want to ask, but we're back at the Sanctuary and Jack's attempting to reverse the van around the side of the barn. 'You're going to hit the–'

'Tess!'

I bite my tongue.

'I thought the deer could go in the shed on the far side of the barn,' Jack suggests more seriously. 'That's out of the way.'

'I'm not sure what state it's in.' Diane and the other volunteers cleared it out for the hedgehogs. It's a good idea though: the less contact the deer has with humans, the better. 'I'll have a look.'

Jack stops and turns off the engine. I jump out and open up the shed, sliding the bar that keeps the door shut so that it swings, or rather scrapes, open.

'It's a bit rickety,' I say.

'It's what?' Jack calls from the back of the van.

'I'll get some straw, a flake of hay and a bucket

of water, and drape a sheet across the window. It will have to do.'

'You'll have to suggest Talyton Animal Rescue pay for some state-of-the-art deer accommodation,' Jack says. 'I've visited a wildlife rescue centre where they had stables with air-conditioning, dimmer switches and deer-cams. The animals lived in luxury.'

'I'm afraid that won't be happening here anytime soon. Although the committee's agreed in principle to release the funds, there's a legal process to go through and it's taking some time.'

I set up the shed for the deer before Jack and I carry the crate inside. I close the door behind us and Jack opens the side of the crate. Immediately, the patient rolls out, struggles to his feet and staggers blindly towards the wall, slamming his antlers against the timber. Jack and I make a rapid retreat, almost falling over each other on the way. We stop outside and, together, slide the bar back across the door.

Jack peers through a gap in the timbers.

'What's he doing? Is he okay?' I ask, resting my hand on Jack's shoulder as I stand behind him.

'He's up.' Jack pauses, his muscles tensing under my fingers, before he turns to look at me, face to face and disarmingly near with a wicked glint in his eye. 'What do you think we should do now?'

'We should come back in an hour or so to check on him,' I say quickly.

'And in the meantime?' Jack raises one eyebrow, and it's here, my senses heightened with anticipation and desire, that I should and could have tilted my head just a fraction closer and pressed my lips to his, except the deer appears to have other ideas, thwarting any imminent passion by battering his way through the shed wall, his antlers and one cloven hoof emerging from the hole he's made.

With a sigh of resignation, Jack tugs his polo-shirt over his head and drops it onto the deer's head in an attempt to subdue it before wrestling it down as it emerges completely from the hole in the wall, when he hangs on to it by its antlers, the muscles in his arms taut and bulging as he waits for it to settle. He glances towards me.

'I'm sorry, Tess. I usually wait to kiss a girl before I start taking my clothes off.'

'I should hope so.' I can't help giggling at his cheek and it feels as if we've both managed to drop our baggage at last: the resentment and misunder-standings over the wedding, and our differences in opinion over how to tackle the welfare of animals like Dolly.

'If you don't want this, you must say so now and I'll never mention it again,' he goes on, his chest heaving with the effort of keeping the deer from escaping. 'Actually, don't worry about giving me an answer this minute – I can't hang on to this guy much longer. Where are we going to put him?'

'I don't know,' I say, tearing my eyes from the few curls of blond hair that adorn the lightly tanned skin between Jack's pectorals. He doesn't carry much spare flesh on him. 'The dogs will scare him to death and he won't fit in with the cats. How about one of the stables? I can turn Dolly out in the field, if you think it'll disturb the deer having the pony right next door.'

The pony seems surprised to see me when I turn up with her head-collar, a state of mind that I take advantage of, bribing her with Polo mints to catch her before I lead her, without argument or barging, out to the field where she puts her head down to graze straight away.

'Hurry, Tess,' Jack calls. 'I'm getting cramp.'

'I'm hurrying,' I call back. I throw down an extra flake of straw and more hay before returning to help Jack carry the deer, a struggling bundle of sinew and hoof, into the stable where we lower him down and make a run for it, closing the top and bottom doors before he can fly out after us. I can hear him leaping about, slamming himself into the walls.

'Poor thing, I don't think he's going to make it,' I say miserably. 'I wish he had died before, or I'd asked Justin to put him to sleep. This is awful.' As I face the stable door, my chest hollow with regret, I become aware that Jack is close beside me, his fingers sliding over my hand.

'You shouldn't be so pessimistic when he's got this far. You should never give up... I did once,' he goes on softly. 'I gave up on something, someone who was the centre of my universe.' He clears his throat, and I'm afraid to ask him to explain in case he's talking about someone other than me, because all I can focus on at this moment is being the warm sun in the centre of Jack's existence. Tessa and Jack, Jack and Tessa: my heart begins to beat a chaotic rhythm as his fingers tighten around mine.

'You can't predict the future,' he says, keeping

hold of my hand all the way back to the bungalow, and I can't stop glancing down at his hand
and my hand joined together, and my spirit is
soaring high like a buzzard above the fields, and
I can't stop believing that Jack, the boy of my
dreams and man of my reality, and I are on the
verge of something wonderful, because, in spite
of all that's happened, I'm still a romantic at
heart.

I'm dizzy and breathless with joy, but I'm not
going to rush things this time, so I'm not disappointed when he relinquishes my hand to let
me unlock the door where Tia and Buster let
loose barking and scratching on the other side.

'Jack, you don't have to stay,' I say, hesitating on
the doorstep. 'I can keep an eye on the deer.'

He frowns. 'I want to stay, if it's all right with
you.'

'Of course it's all right.' I smile wryly. There's
nothing I want more.

I push the door open, at which Buster greets
me as if I've been away for four weeks, not four
hours, huffing and puffing, wagging his tail and
wiggling his whole body. Once he's turned his
attention to Jack, with whom he's only marginally
less overenthusiastic, Tia wanders across to sniff
at my knees and lick my hand in welcome.

'I wonder if Libby's fed them.' There are empty
bowls on the floor in the kitchen, so I assume she
has. I don't think Tia would let her forget. 'Would
you like a drink, Jack?'

'If it wasn't for the deer, I'd take you out for
dinner,' he says. 'We could go later.'

'I can do eggs on toast.' While I'm hunting for

the frying pan, Jack gazes out through the kitchen window where the sun is beginning to set behind the hills.

'I can't believe you never feel lonely up here,' he says, and I nod towards the dogs who are sitting beside the cupboard where I store their food, making out they've never been fed in their lives.

'I'm hardly alone, am I? I never have a moment's peace.' I pause. 'It is a bit creepy here sometimes though.'

'What do you mean? Ghostly? It's probably the spirit of Gloria Brambles haunting the place, checking up on you,' Jack says brightly, but for me, it isn't something to joke about.

'I don't believe in ghosts. It's more of a feeling of being watched.' I shrug off the anxiety that causes a temporary quickening of my pulse. 'Oh, it's nothing, just my overactive imagination, and anyway, if there was somebody out there, I have Buster and Tia to watch over me.'

'A runaway and a blind dog,' Jack chuckles before growing serious once more. 'Tess, if you're ever in the slightest bit worried, you can call me any time. I mean it.'

'Thanks.' I pull a loaf of bread out of the fridge. 'How many eggs would you like?'

After eggs on toast with butter and black pepper, Jack and I sit down on the sofa together. Romantic or what! Actually, not, because Tia and Buster are perched between us, Buster leaning in to me, nudging me each time I stop stroking his tummy, and Tia panting like mad, emitting heat like an oven. She's far too hot, but she refuses to give up her place.

'How is your aunt?' says Jack, over Tia's head. 'I haven't seen her for a while. Are there still problems between her and the committee? What's your position?'

Position? I shift on my seat, my brain mulling over the possibility of a double entendre. I can't help it. I am getting totally carried away by the idea that, by the end of the night, Jack is going to kiss me.

'Are you safe here?' he goes on.

'I don't know. I mean, I'm not getting paid.'

'You aren't? How are you managing?'

'Eggs on toast every night,' I say, smiling. 'It's all right. I have a very healthy diet now. My dad gives me eggs, and Fifi drops by with bread from the garden centre.'

Eventually Tia relinquishes her place on the sofa. Jack, I notice, slides his arm along the back towards me. Buster notices too. He cocks one ear, rolls one eye back and growls a long low warning: she's mine, don't touch.

'Buster, I don't need you protecting my honour.'

'Well, I don't know about that,' says Jack. 'You don't know what designs I have upon it, Tess.'

'You think you're so funny,' I say dryly.

'I'm not joking this time.'

'You aren't?' I gaze past Buster and look Jack straight in the eye. His expression is gentle yet I can feel my body responding to the hunger that lies behind it.

'I'll just let Buster out for a wee.' How to ruin the moment, I think as soon as the words come out of my mouth. 'I could have put that better, couldn't I?'

'Go on then,' Jack laughs. 'Perhaps I should come with you, in case there are any baddies out there.'

'I'll be fine, but you could go and check on the deer.'

'Are you trying to get rid of me?' Smiling, because he already knows the answer, he jumps up and disappears off outside while I let Buster and Tia out in the garden. I wait for them, musing on the theory that the amount of time it takes for a dog to go for a wee is directly proportional to the outdoor temperature and the amount of clothing being worn. It's turned quite chilly. I call them back after a few minutes, giving Buster a lecture on the way back to the living room.

'You can't go telling me who I can or can't see. Living with you is like living with my dad.'

'I can't blame him for wanting you all to himself,' Jack says, joining us once more, sitting down close beside me so I can smell his animal scent of musk and fresh air. This time, when he takes my hand, Buster remains silent, and Jack goes on, in a low voice, 'It's what I've wanted for a very long time.' He leans in and presses his lips to my cheek. 'It's what I've always wanted,' he whispers before kissing me again, this time on the lips. I slide my hands up around the back of his neck and lean into his embrace, my heart pounding and heat surging through my body.

'Me too,' I murmur, as my doubts and fears for the future fragment and disappear, being replaced by an overwhelming happiness, the like of which I've never experienced before, convincing me that this is the beginning of something really special.

Chapter Fourteen

The Morning After the Night Before

I wake with a jolt, lying under the duvet with Jack's arms around me, the morning light painfully bright and memories of the night before burning into my consciousness. Oh-mi-god, this is so bad – I gaze at Jack's beautiful face, at the golden stubble that adorns his cheeks and chin, at the curve of his lips as he sleeps – and yet it's so good.

I pinch myself because I can't believe it. I don't do this kind of thing, fall into bed with a guy on the first date. I correct myself. It wasn't even a date... I know how I should feel about waking up with Jack, but it's too late to be overwhelmed by a wave of virtue, and I salve my conscience, assuming that it won't be long before I can safely say that Jack and I are an item, that we are boyfriend and girlfriend, and then it won't matter.

As I lie there, revelling in the contact of his body against mine, I become aware of the sound of a vehicle turning into the car park.

'Jack.' I shake him by the shoulder. 'Someone's here.'

He mumbles an incoherent response, and I try again. 'Jack, we have to get you out of here.'

'Why, Tess? What for?' He props himself up on his elbow and frowns. 'Are you ashamed of me?'

I'm ashamed of myself, but I don't tell him that.

'I'd rather people didn't find out that you stayed the night. Not yet.'

'I don't understand.' He reaches over and plants a kiss on my lips. 'I thought you liked me. Tess, I'm very fond of you, and I don't care who in the world knows it, but if it makes you happy, I'll get up and make out I've just arrived... Or,' he adds with a wicked smile, 'we could pretend we aren't here, and make love all over again.'

It's too late for that. There's a knocking at the door that sets the dogs off barking, and a call of 'Yoo hoo, it's me, Tessa' through the letterbox.

Groaning, I rest my hand across my forehead. 'It's my aunt.' The thought of having to explain to Fifi is too much. I get out of bed, throw on a dressing gown and open the window wide. 'You go that way,' I whisper. 'I'll keep Fifi occupied for a couple of minutes – I'll tell her you turned up early to check on the deer.' I smile at his look of consternation. 'Go on.' I take as long as I reasonably can to walk along the hall to the front door, so Jack has time to retrieve his clothes.

'You took your time,' Fifi says sternly.

'I was in bed. I overslept,' I explain as my aunt, dressed in a red and white spotty summer dress and white shoes with red bows, hands me a hessian bag of provisions – bread, cheese and milk – keeping her eyes fixed on a point beyond my left ear, as if she's expecting to see someone appear behind me.

'I see Jack's here early.'

'Uh-huh?' I'm not sure how to respond.

278

'The van's around the corner.'

'Oh yes, that's right. He texted me to say he was coming in to check on the deer, the one that fled into the ironmonger's yesterday.'

'Everyone's talking about the Talyton stag,' Fifi says. 'His presence at the Sanctuary could be quite an asset. Ally Jackson can run his story in the *Chronicle* – there'll be plenty of visitors who will want to see him.'

'He's a wild animal,' I say. 'We can't have people looking in over the stable door.'

'We could set up a webcam,' Fifi says.

'I thought' – actually, I haven't been thinking about stags at all, but the idea has just popped into my head – 'that we might raise some money by having people pay a pound each to vote on a name for the deer. We could choose the best name and give a prize of chocolate, a certificate and a photo.'

'That's a lovely idea.'

'Why don't you come inside?' I say quickly, catching sight of Jack, who is skirting the edge of the car park towards the barn, his boots in one hand and socks in the other.

'Is there something wrong?' Fifi asks, her voice laced with suspicion. 'You aren't sickening for this summer flu that's doing the rounds? You're looking rather flushed.'

'Am I?' I touch my cheek.

'Your nerves appear to be playing up.'

'There's nothing wrong with my nerves, I can assure you,' I say, trying not to giggle as Jack gives me a wave before disappearing around the corner. 'Come on in. I'll get the kettle on, get changed and make some breakfast for everyone.'

'Would you like me to feed the babies first?' Fifi asks. 'That's what I'm here for.'

'We'll do them together later. We can talk about the final arrangements for the ball,' I say. (Diane didn't object when I told her that my aunt was going to continue to help me organise the ball, even though she was no longer chair. I think it suits Diane, who isn't keen to put herself out.) I check the time. It's eight o'clock and the birds usually have their first batch of mealworms or cat food at eight-thirty, or thereabouts.

I leave Fifi making tea in the kitchen while I throw on some jeans and a T-shirt, and run my fingers through my hair, thinking ruefully that I will have to do, and rushing back when I hear my aunt chatting to Jack.

'I'm afraid the choice of breakfast is fresh bread or more toast.' I say, handing Jack a mug of tea and hoping Fifi didn't spot my slip of the tongue. 'How is the patient?'

'Didn't you get my text?' Jack responds.

I check my mobile that I must have left on the kitchen worktop last night. I flick it on and check the message: *Dinner 2nite? Pick u up at 7☺xxJ*

'The deer's looking good,' Jack goes on. 'I left him nibbling at some hay. When did Justin say he'd be out to change the dressing?'

'In three or four days. After that, I should be able to do it myself.'

I tell Fifi about the extent of the deer's injuries and the damage to the shed over breakfast, which we eat in the living room with Buster and Tia sitting gazing at us, drooling at the sight and sweet scent of singed toast and jam. As we sit there, I notice a blackbird sitting on the lower branch of one of the apple trees, hopping back and forth and chirping, teasing one of the feral cats. The cat prowls around in circles with his eyes fixed on the bird, which stays tantalisingly out of reach. I am about to ask Jack about setting the traps again to see if we can catch any more when his mobile rings.

I notice how he frowns when he reads the number on the screen. He stands and holds up his hand to me. 'I've got to go. Thanks for breakfast.'

I follow him down the hall, everything that I wish to say to him stifled by my aunt's presence in the kitchen. 'I'll see you later.'

'Yeah. Cheers, Tess,' he says, before opening the front door and making a swift exit across the car park, driving past shortly afterwards in the van without a wave or an acknowledgement that I am there.

'He's in a hurry.' I jump at the sound of my aunt's voice right beside me. She must have crept up without me noticing.

'Oh, Fifi, you made me jump.' I stroke my throat, touching the track of Jack's kisses from the night before.

'That's because you're clearly preoccupied by something else, or someone else not so far away from here. Did Jack say where he was going?'

I shake my head.

'I expect he's been called out for a fire,' my aunt continues.

'I didn't hear his pager.'

'Well, he's always in demand. I don't know how

281

he does it.' Fifi pauses. 'Shall we go and feed those babies?'

'Yes, let's,' I agree, but nothing can take my mind off Jack. We woke up together and ate breakfast – okay, with my aunt as well – normal, everyday activities that a couple would do, but are we a couple, or are we better described as friends with benefits? I hope that in a few days' time we'll be able to consider ourselves as the former, and I can tell the world, my friends and family that I have a new boyfriend. I imagine the smile on my dad's face when I drop the fact that I'm Jack's girl into the conversation.

I text Jack when I'm out walking Buster in the copse: *Can't wait 2 c u l8r xT*. I debate long and hard about how many kisses to add, deciding one is appropriate. I don't think Jack will be easily frightened off, but I've had enough experience of men for that possibility to cross my mind, so I'm decidedly worried when I start getting ready for our date and he calls to say he can't make it.

'I'm really sorry, Tess, but something's come up. I hope you're not too disappointed.'

That would be an understatement. I'm gutted.

'Another time,' he says.

'Another time,' I echo. 'Make it soon.' I try not to sound desperate. 'You could call in later, if you like. I'll be here.'

'Not tonight. Look, I'll see you at the Sanctuary soon.'

What he says is perfectly reasonable. I'm afraid it's what he doesn't say that tells the story. He doesn't promise to make it up to me another time. I wipe the eyeliner from my eyes and wash my face before curling up with Buster and Tia on the sofa, stroking Buster's belly with one hand and caressing Tia's ears with the other. I tell myself that Jack isn't like Nathan and there's no way he would have cancelled our date without a very good reason, whatever it is. If only men were like dogs, the world would be a better place.

I don't see Jack for another couple of days. I text him because I can't resist, using the excuse of updating him on the deer's state of health, but he doesn't reply.

'I expect his mobile network's down,' Libby says when I mention it to her one morning while we're delivering hay and breakfast to the deer, before going to clean the kennels. Libby is protective of her brother, giving me vague answers as to his whereabouts.

'You aren't concentrating,' I tell her when she's trying to put on a disposable apron with one hand while texting with the other. 'I take it the course of true love is running smooth – you keep wandering around with a silly grin on your face.' I fill a bucket with hot suds in the kitchen sink. Libby grabs a pair of yellow rubber gloves and pirouettes around the room on tiptoes, her feet squelching in her wellington boots.

'Tessa, Ash has asked me to the ball. I'm soooo excited. I can't wait.'

'I'm pleased,' I say, smiling. 'I'm waiting for your brother to invite me.'

'Jack?' Libby says, frowning as she grabs a scrubbing brush.

'Oops. Perhaps I shouldn't have said anything,' I go on, but I don't mean it. I've been desperate to share my secret with someone who can keep it, at least until Jack and I decide to come out as a couple, so to speak. I trust Libby. She's become a good friend, more so recently than Katie, I think with a twinge of guilt. Although we're still in touch, there seems to have been a barrier between us since Nathan and the wedding.

I follow her into the first kennel with the bucket and a mop. Libby starts scrubbing the walls, writing the letters A-S-H across the surface in soapy water before wiping them out.

'Jack obviously hasn't...' My voice trails off before I pluck up the courage to start again. 'Jack and I have kind of got it together at last.' I go all Facebook on her. 'I don't think I'm jumping the gun when I say that we're in a relationship. Are you sure he hasn't said anything to you?'

'Tessa, Jack might be my brother, but he doesn't tell me everything that's going on his life.'

I dip the mop into the bucket, wring it out and make a start on the floor.

'I reckon I'm going to have to take the initiative. At least, being the organiser, I can keep a couple of tickets back if he leaves it to the last minute,' I say, thinking aloud.

Libby pauses scrubbing.

'Um, I think I'd wait for him to ask you. It's kind of traditional, isn't it, for the boy to ask the girl?' she goes on brightly.

'I didn't think you would be such a stickler for tradition,' I say, surprised by her attitude. 'Libby, you're really quite old-fashioned.'

'Well, it's a convention that's worked well for years.' She dips the brush back into the bucket.

'Perhaps you'd like to give your brother a nudge in the right direction for me and explain this protocol he has to follow.'

'Since when has Jack taken any notice of me?' she says, returning to scrubbing the wall with a vengeance. 'Have you had any votes for names for the deer yet?'

'There are some.' Ally Jackson put the competition into the *Chronicle* yesterday. 'I've had four suggestions by email and our recent visitors have filled in the slips and put them in the box in reception. Three people have gone for the same name. Can you guess what it is?'

'I know,' Libby says, 'Bambi. It suits him. He's so sweet.'

'Do you think so? Having watched him wreck the shed, I don't think it suits him at all. Conan is better, after Conan the Destroyer.'

'What will happen to him in the end?' Libby asks.

'It's too early to say. There could be complications with that wound on his leg, and there's still a risk he'll get over-stressed and come down with post-capture myopathy. If the wound heals and he stays healthy then we'll aim to release him back into the wild as soon as possible.'

'Wouldn't it be better to keep him? I don't like the idea of him fending for himself, or being run over or shot after all he's gone through.'

'He's a wild animal,' I say. 'He should be out with other deer, wild and free.'

'I suppose so,' Libby says. 'I'll cry when we let him go.'

'I expect I will too,' I admit. I am surprised how

285

emotional I get about all the animals. It's impossible not to get involved. In fact, I'm missing Buster and Teddy already, and neither of them has left the Sanctuary yet.

'We have a home for Teddy,' I tell Libby. 'He's going to live with a retired couple, an ex-admiral and his wife, in a house up on the cliffs near Talymouth.'

'I hope he won't be in any danger,' Libby says, immediately anxious.

'I've done the home check and I reckon that Teddy will fit in very well there. He'll be an only cat and he has an enclosed garden to play in.' Luckily, the virus in his body isn't causing him any major problems at present, and, according to Maz, it looks as though he could well live into a comfortable old age. 'The house isn't right on the edge of the cliff, if that's what you're worrying about, Libby. It's set quite a way back.'

'When's he going? I need time to say goodbye.'

'At the end of the week. They needed time to fit a cat flap,' I explain.

'What about Buster? He's going soon, isn't he?'

'He's supposed to be, but the Nelsons have delayed the date they're picking him up for a second time because they're going on a last-minute holiday and don't want to have to put him into kennels for the two weeks they're away.'

'That's fair enough, isn't it?' says Libby, dropping the brush in the bucket. 'It's better for Buster.'

'It is,' I agree, but it worries me that they've chosen a dog, yet put the holiday first. However, it means I don't have to angst about Buster leaving, because I know that letting him go will be one of the hardest things I've ever had to do.

Since the night we slept together, I've been on tenterhooks, hardly able to wait to see Jack again, but I've tried to carry on as usual. In the middle of the week, I'm swinging from euphoria to something akin to clinical depression. I'm in love, and it's making me slightly crazy.

Before I go completely mad, I make a mental 'to do' list as I work through the morning: post the latest orders for tickets, contact the band to confirm what time they're planning to arrive to set up and do the soundcheck, talk to the chef about the vegetarian option for the starter and, last but very much not least, talk to Jack, if I ever get to set eyes on him again. He hasn't been in touch since cancelling dinner, apart from giving me a brief wave from the Land Rover when he dropped Libby off yesterday.

Libby said he was rushed off his feet the first time I asked her where he was. One of the cygnets that had hatched in July from the nest by the river had collapsed in the reeds with suspected lead poisoning, and Jack had taken it over to the seabird sanctuary at Marsh. Without me, I thought, remembering our lunch overlooking the harbour and the sea beyond. He could have at least asked me, even if I couldn't get away. When I asked Libby for the second time, she said he was busy helping a friend in need.

'In need of what?' I said.

'Of rescue or something like that. You know what he's like, Tessa. He's always helping people.'

That's when it hit me: although I'd let myself think of Jack as my lover and potential soulmate, I didn't know everything about him.

Having stuck a stamp on the last envelope containing ball tickets, I decide to make my way to the kennels, but if I thought that being with the dogs would help take my mind off my preoccupation with what to do about Jack, it doesn't. Surely, it would cost him nothing to send me a text to let me know where he is. That he hasn't is preying on my mind. Is it because he's completely thoughtless, or is it because he doesn't want me to know where he is? Maybe he just doesn't understand what the other night meant to me.

I try to dismiss my concerns. I'm naturally suspicious because of what happened between me and Nathan. He was secretive about his business dealings and our financial situation, managing to hide the fact we were thousands of pounds in debt, so I'm bound to find it difficult to trust again. But Jack is not like Nathan and there is no reason for history to repeat itself.

To my surprise, Jack appears in the flesh just as I'm thinking about him, silhouetted against the door into the kennels. I'm sweeping down the concrete floor to kennel number three with a broom and bucket of diluted disinfectant, in readiness for the next occupant, the last one, Linford the lurcher, having been rehomed the day before.

'Hi, Jack. I thought you'd gone off me.' I smile out of relief at seeing him at last. 'Where have you been?'

'I've been a bit tied up.' Jack steps towards me.

'Tell me about it.' I exit the kennel and move in

288

his direction, assuming that we'll kiss – if not a full-on snog with tongues and the clash of teeth, at least a brush of the lips, brief contact to acknowledge what has gone on before and hint at what is to come. As I approach, though, Jack hesitates and ducks aside as if the sight of me, dressed in rubber gloves, wellies and a plastic apron, repels him.

'I'd have made a bit more effort if I'd known you were coming,' I say, forcing a smile 'I probably smell or something.' I raise one eyebrow, noticing that Jack isn't smiling back. 'You haven't bought your tickets for the ball yet,' I go on, and it's here that he's supposed to say in a sexy and ironic tone, 'Is that a subtle hint, Tess?'

'You still have some tickets, then?' is what he actually says.

'I've put a couple aside for you.'

'Thanks. Er, how much is it for two?'

I give him the figure, waiting for him to ask me to go to the ball with him, but he continues, 'I'm taking someone, a friend.'

'Oh?' I knew something wasn't right. Jack's face is shiny with sweat and he keeps looking down, scraping imaginary dirt from under his nails. 'Anyone I know?' I ask, a pulse of impending disappointment bounding in the back of my throat when Jack opens his mouth to answer.

'Her name's Karen.'

'Karen?' I fear that my voice says it all. I'm devastated.

'Remember I told you about the woman I met in Asia?'

'Yes?' The pain of loss and rejection is un-

289

bearable. 'You said...'

'I know what I said.' Jack gazes out behind him through the doorway as if he wishes he was out there in the hills, well away from me. 'She came to find me.'

'The day after we...'

Jack's brief nod of the head explains why he's been so evasive. It wasn't that I scared him off by falling into bed with him. It's because someone better turned up, and along with the initial shock that he's dropped me for someone else, comes anger.

'You bastard!' I lean against the broom, my fists clenched around the handle and forcing the bristles flat against the floor.

'She's left her husband and moved in with me,' Jack goes on.

It's all making sense now, the way Libby's been avoiding entering into any conversation about her brother.

'She had nowhere to go. What else could I do?' Jack shrugs. 'I should have told you before, but I couldn't bring myself to.'

'Yes, you bloody well should have done.' I am livid now. I throw the broom down, and I don't know what possesses me, but I grab the bucket and throw the contents at him.

'What the—' Jack stands there, spluttering, water dripping from his hair, his face and his clothes and forming a puddle at his feet. 'What the hell did you do that for?'

'What do you think?' I drop the bucket and it clatters across the floor.

'I'm trying to explain,' he says, exasperated.

With a shiver, he tugs at his shirt, lifting the fabric from his skin. 'You could have used warm water at least,' he adds, his tone softening.

'There are plenty of towels in the kitchen.'

'That sounds like one of your brighter ideas,' he says wryly. 'I'll grab one.'

I'd rather he left me alone, but he returns, drying his hair with a ragged beach towel. 'Are you all right?'

'What do you think?' I bite my lip. 'It was cruel to string me along like that when you had no intention–'

'It wasn't like that,' Jack interjects, but I don't give him time to elaborate.

'If you love her and it's meant to be...' Tears burn like acid down my cheeks. How typical of Jack to do the right thing!

'Tess, I wish things had been different. I'm so sorry.'

'Okay, it's fine. I didn't expect' – I begin to sob aloud – 'I didn't expect anything.'

'Tess, come here.' Dropping the towel around the back of his neck, Jack holds out his arms, but I turn away, embarrassed and ashamed for letting my passion for Jack overcome all sense of reason and restraint, and devastated that I misread the situation, mistaking his embrace for love. How does it go? A woman has to feel bonded to have sex while a man has to have sex to feel bonded. I'm gutted. I've been such an idiot, yet again. I don't understand men. I give up. I'm going to be a nun.

'I'm sorry,' Jack repeats.

'What are you sorry for? We had a fling, a one-night stand. These things happen.' I refrain from adding, Just not to me. 'You don't owe me anything. It was my choice. No one forced me...' I'll get over it. Maybe. One day. The words ricochet inside my head. It should have been me moving in with Jack, not this mysterious stranger. It should have been me! I dig my fingernails into my palms. I didn't know I could feel such agony.

Swallowing hard, I wipe my eyes and muster my remaining self-control.

'I'd better get on and finish up here,' I say, feigning normality. (I must have inherited some of my dad's acting genes after all.) 'I have a ball to organise.'

'What about you?' Jack says, his tone bright yet tinged with sadness. 'Who's the lucky guy taking you to the ball?'

'I'm not planning to dance.' I hear myself laughing like a madwoman. 'I've got two left feet and I could never get the steps in the right order when I did ballet.'

'I don't remember you doing ballet.'

'I was five or six, and my enthusiasm lasted three weeks. All I wanted was the tutu.'

Jack smiles. 'I can't see you in a tutu now.'

'What do you mean?' I glance down at my combats. Is he suggesting I'm a tomboy? Am I not girly enough for him? I never have been much of a girl. Is that why he doesn't want me? 'I'll be co-ordinating everything anyway.'

'You know how women grow old to be like their mothers. You're going to end up like your aunt.'

'Thanks a lot,' I say flatly. 'Look, I'm sorry about the water. Now, I need to get on. I really must finish up here.'

'What can I do?' Jack asks.

'Whatever you like,' I say, dismissing him. As long as you're out of my sight, I refrain from adding because I can't bear his presence any longer. It's too much of a reminder of my massive error of judgement. What was I thinking? That Jack was somehow different from every other man I've met? I bash the end of the broom into the corner of the kennel, knocking out the cobwebs and dust.

'I'll go and feed the baby birds for you.' When I don't respond, he adds, 'I'll catch up with you later.'

'Don't worry, if you have to get back,' I say. 'Everything's under control here.' Or it will be, when I can get a metaphorical lid on my emotions. I pause, listening to his footsteps disappearing off outside. How could he do this to me? I feel more depressed than I did on my wedding day. Within a few months, I have both hated Jack and fallen in love with him.

Later, once Libby and the other volunteers have gone home and I have the Sanctuary to myself, I go and give Teddy a cuddle and have a good cry. He purrs, headbutts my chin and kneads at my sweatshirt with his claws, making tiny holes across the shoulder, while his fur grows wet and spiky with my tears.

'Dear Teddy,' I murmur to him. 'We've found you a good home – I told you there was somebody out there for you. I'll miss you though.'

Teddy doesn't care and I wish I could be like him, happy with my lot. I pop him back into his pen, where he leaps onto his shelf with one lithe movement and curls up on his bed as if there's nothing wrong with him. I close the door and lock up for the night before returning to the bungalow where Buster and Tia greet me as usual.

'At least I can rely on you, and my friends,' I tell them, deciding to call Katie.

'Hi,' she says, answering the phone straight away.

'Are you busy?' I ask.

'Not tonight. I'm staying in to wash my hair. I had to find some excuse to spend some time at home – I've been out every night this week.' She pauses for a millisecond before rushing on, 'How are you, Tessa? Are you ready for the ball? I'm so excited. I've never been to a ball before.'

'Actually, I've kind of lost my enthusiasm for it,' I say, so despondent that I forget to ask her who she's going with.

'Is there something wrong? Has the venue fallen through or the band backed out?'

'The arrangements are going ahead as planned,' I say, 'there hasn't been a single glitch so far.'

'That's a relief,' Katie says. 'I thought from the sound of your voice–'

'It's Jack,' I blurt out. 'He's going to the ball with someone else. Can you believe it?'

'You mean, he hasn't asked you? Were you expecting him to?'

'Well, yes, and I'm gutted.'

'It's hardly the end of the world. I still don't understand how you can forgive him for the lies he made up at your wedding. Forget about Jack Miller. He isn't worth it.' She pauses before plunging on, 'You really need to get out more.'

'What difference will that make?' I say morosely. 'I'll never meet anyone who'll match up to him.'

'I don't know why you're so upset,' Katie cuts in. 'It isn't as if you've been going out with him or anything, unless there's something you haven't been telling me.'

'I slept with him,' I confess, after which there's a long silence.

'Are you completely mad?' Katie says eventually. 'You said you weren't going to rush into anything.'

'I know. I've been so stupid.'

'I didn't think Jack had it in him,' Katie breathes. 'And you? Tessa, what were you thinking?'

That's the trouble: I wasn't. I close my eyes, recalling the first touch – like a butterfly – of his lips against mine, his scent of musk, aftershave and coffee, the thudding of my heartbeat and the overwhelming throb of lust.

'Don't let this ruin everything,' Katie goes on. 'You were just getting back on track.'

'He's seeing someone else – he moved her in with him within twenty-four hours of sleeping with me. Well, Jack is the last mistake I ever make. I'm going to take a vow of chastity and become a nun.' I pause. 'Hey, Katie, who's your partner for the ball? Who are you going with?'

'Ah, I didn't like to mention it before because I didn't want to upset you...'

'Sock it to me,' I say, twisting the charm on my mobile until it snaps.

'I'm going with Nathan,' Katie says quietly.

'Nathan?' I don't understand. First Jack and

now Katie. It feels like a double betrayal. A pain cuts through my chest. 'How could you?'

'I'm sorry, Tessa, but it just happened. Nathan's my boyfriend.'

'You're really going out with my ex?' I can't quite believe it.

'I can't see anything wrong in that. As you say, he's your ex.'

'You know how he treated me.'

'Jack might have accused him of cheating on you, but there was never any proof,' Katie says in a tone of defiance.

'I know, but isn't the fact that he left me with all that debt enough to put you off? What on earth do you see in him, a vain, self-obsessed–'

'I don't know why you're being so mean about it,' Katie interrupts. 'You took him all the way to the altar before you decided you didn't want him. I had to pick up the pieces. He had no one else to turn to.'

'He had Mike. He had lots of other friends,' I say, exasperated with her. 'But then he always did have his eye on you, on either your boobs or your bum.'

'He's a man. That's what men do, and to be honest, Tessa, I think you're jealous.'

'Far from it,' I spit. 'I'm angry – not with Nathan – with you for being so stupid. He'll only take advantage of you, like he did me.'

'Well, he can't make me spend all my money – I haven't got any,' Katie says.

'You have credit cards,' I point out. 'I hope you haven't agreed to pay for anything.'

Katie falls silent, indicating to me that she has.

'Katie, you idiot.'

'I knew you'd be like this. Look, I don't expect you to be happy about it, but I can't help how I feel about him. He makes me feel–'

'Special?' I cut in. 'That's how he made me feel, but it was all talk. He soon started making excuses, spending more time at the gym or going away for business, so I hardly saw him.' I pause. 'How long has it been going on?'

'Hardly any time at all. A couple of weeks maybe,' Katie says quickly. 'And I know you don't believe me, but I was going to tell you,' she goes on, sounding hurt. 'You should have told me about Jack. We used to talk about anything and everything.'

'I know and I miss that,' I say, realising that we've been as bad as each other. 'All right, I'm sorry.'

'So 'm I.'

'Friends?'

'Friends,' she confirms, and we chat for a few more minutes before I take Buster and Tia out for one last walk as dusk is falling, returning Tia to the comfort of her bed, i.e. the sofa, before heading outside for a longer excursion with Buster. It's hard to explain, but Buster is a more willing confidant than Tia.

'So, Buster, you know I told you about Jack the other day. I thought it was on, but it turns out that it's all off.' The dog looks up and wags his tail as we follow the footpath at the edge of the neighbouring field out towards the lane before returning to the Sanctuary via Longdogs Copse. 'Jack has a girlfriend – I lucked out.' Buster starts sniffing around a clump of long grass and cocks his leg. 'Am I boring you? I suppose I do go on a bit about men, and the absence of eligible males in this part of deepest, darkest Devon.' I gaze around at the shadowy trees and the glimpse of the fields beyond where sheep are grazing. Why aren't there as many men as there are sheep around here?

'I'll soon be thirty and I still haven't met Mr Right,' I continue. 'You know, I reckon I'm like you, waiting for someone to love and love me back.'

Buster hesitates, diving towards the undergrowth alongside us at the end of his extending lead before stopping and standing stock-still, ears pricked and tail held out stiffly behind him. Seeming spooked, he growls a long slow warning, his hackles rising at the same time, before he utters a short bark.

'What is it, Buster?' I say, straining my ears to listen.

He barks again, telling whatever it is that's rustling about in the bushes to keep away.

'You silly dog, there's nothing there.' I make to drag him away, when I hear a cough. Buster hears it too, bounding towards the source of the sound and barking hysterically until the lead extends no further. 'Whoever you are,' I shout out over the sound of my heartbeat, 'go away! This is private property.'

I'm answered by the cracking of sticks and someone crashing through the bushes away towards the lane, and although I wasn't going to let myself be intimidated, I turn for home, walking quickly at first, then, when I can contain my fear no longer, running as fast as I can with Buster tearing along beside me. The faster I run, the slower my limbs seem to move and it seems to take an eternity to reach the bungalow. Once inside, I slam the door shut and bolt it top and bottom before closing all the curtains and blinds so no one can see in and, more importantly, I can't see out. I take the dogs into the living room and call my dad.

'Call the police while you're waiting for me,' he says, his voice filled with concern. 'I'm on my way.'

'Dad, there's no need,' I say, feeling a little foolish now.

'Nothing will stop me, dear daughter of mine.'

He turns up at the same time as PC Phillips and they take a walk together through the copse and check the outbuildings before returning to have a chat with me, PC Phillips writing everything down in his notebook.

'There are several sets of footprints, but no sign of anyone loitering in the copse,' he says.

'There are bound to be lots of footprints,' I say, sitting curled up on the end of the sofa with a cushion across my lap and one hand trembling on Buster's collar. 'We walk the dogs through there every day.'

'There are tyre tracks up to the gate into the copse – that's the one that comes in from the lane.' PC Phillips pauses. 'Have you any idea who might be motivated to do something like this, an ex-boyfriend perhaps?'

'What about Nathan?' Dad suggests. 'Does he

still bear a grudge?'

'I'm sure he does, but this isn't his style and anyway, I know for a fact that he has a new girlfriend. He's moved on. There is one person though: Frank Maddocks knows that Dolly's here at the Sanctuary, and he's aware that I reported him to Jack in the first place. I was there. He threatened me.'

'You didn't say anything, Tessa,' Dad says.

'He said he knew where I lived, that's all. Look, he was going to appeal against the way the pony was seized by the police, but he didn't have the grounds to do it, so maybe he's planning to steal her back.'

'I spoke with him a while ago and he doesn't want his property back,' says PC Phillips.

'Jack says it isn't so much that he doesn't want the mare. It's that he hasn't got the money to claim her.'

PC Phillips frowns, taking what feels like an age to respond. I glance at Dad, who rolls his eyes at me in sympathy. If the police constable's brain was a laptop, his superiors would have replaced it with a speedier version by now.

'If he was to take the mare, how on earth would he hide a pony around here?'

'He could sell her on or move her out of the area,' I say. 'I know she doesn't look all that much, but people would pay a premium for a coloured, weight-carrying cob like her. Okay, they might not be so keen if they got to know her, but if she was trained to ride or drive, she'd be a useful sort, according to Jack. Can't you go and have a word with him or something?'

'I'll have a drive by Frank's place,' PC Phillips says, 'but there isn't any evidence that he's been up here tonight. It's more likely that you disturbed some poachers. Did they have dogs with them?'

'I couldn't tell. It was dark and they were lurking somewhere in the bushes.' I bite my lip, willing myself to recall every detail in case I've missed a vital clue. 'No, I don't think they had any dogs. If they had, they would have barked when Buster barked.' I start to doubt myself. 'Perhaps it was a deer or a fox, after all.'

'Tessa, I've never heard of an animal having a smoker's cough,' my dad says. 'When I arrived, the first thing you mentioned was that you heard a man cough.'

'Yes, he did. It was a horrible hacking cough.'

'Well, there's no proof either way, so I suggest you keep in touch with us, Tessa, and take the usual steps to make sure you stay safe,' PC Phillips says, tucking his notebook and pen into his breast pocket. 'In the meantime, if you see or hear anything suspicious, don't hesitate to call me straight away.'

The incident has unnerved me and although I can't help wondering if he thinks I'm imagining it, on balance I'm pretty certain now that there is someone watching me, or the Sanctuary.

'I'll stay for a while, Tessa,' Dad says when PC Phillips has gone. 'Or you can come home with me,' he adds hopefully. 'Your mum and I miss you, you know, and there's always a bed made up for you.'

'You do believe me, don't you, Dad?'

'Of course I do. It isn't something you'd make up.' He stands up from the sofa and wipes his hands on his soft moleskin jacket. 'I wish I could get my hands on the little toerags, that's all.'

'You think it might be kids?'

'I wouldn't be surprised.'

'Where are you going?'

'To have one last look around. I'm not going to risk leaving my daughter's safety to Talyton's sleeping policeman, am I?'

'Oh, Dad, that's funny,' I say, relaxing for the first time since I took Buster for his walk. 'A sleeping policeman. Is he really that dozy?'

'I shouldn't be at all surprised if he's driven right past them on the lane.'

I stand up too, reaching out for Dad's arm. 'You aren't going wandering around the copse alone,' I tell him. I give him a look when he makes to argue with me. 'It would worry me sick. If they are poachers, they'll have guns.'

Reluctantly, he sits down again.

'As you won't come home, I'm going to stay the night,' he says. 'It's all right. I've made my mind up. I'll kip down on the sofa, if you've got a spare duvet or a couple of blankets.'

'You might end up with Tia,' I say doubtfully.

'I'll be fine,' he insists, 'and in the morning, I can go up to the copse and check that no one is there. It could have been travellers, I suppose, holidaymakers who couldn't get into a campsite at the last minute.'

It would be a relief if that was the case, I think, but it seems unlikely.

'I can give you a hand with the animals before

I go home, if you're on your own again. What's happened to the volunteers?'

'Libby's here whenever she can, while Diane and Wendy do a bit here and there. To be honest, Wendy isn't much help what with her arthritis and whimsical ideas about what she can and cannot do.'

'What about Jack? Has he been here today?'

I gaze down at the toes of my boots to hide the blush of shame and hurt that creeps across my face as I think of him.

'I'd be much happier knowing there was a man about on the premises,' Dad continues.

'Jack doesn't work here as such, Dad. He's out on the road, or in court acting as a witness for welfare cases, or he's fighting fires. He really isn't here that much.'

'Ah, he's such a hero,' my father says. 'He would make the perfect leading man. Have you let Jack rescue you yet, Tessa?'

'I don't know what you mean,' I say flatly, but he blunders on.

'Is Jack taking you to the ball?'

'No, Dad.'

'I expect he's too shy to ask.'

'It isn't that.' I force myself to meet my father's eager gaze. 'I'm surprised you don't know by now – I expect the rest of Talyton does. Jack has a girl-friend, an older woman, a cougar by all accounts, and he's already moved her into his house.'

'He hasn't? I don't believe it. Oh, Tessa, I thought...' My dad's face crumples as if he's about to burst into tears. 'I'd hoped that you and Jack would get together at last.' He wrings his hands. 'There must be some mistake.'

'There's no mistake.' I sit down beside him on the sofa. 'Dad, don't feel sorry for me. I'm not looking for love because it's far too soon after Nathan and, if I was, the last person I'd be interested in is Jack,' I go on, masking the effort that it takes to deny my feelings for him.

'You can't fool me, dear daughter,' Dad says, reaching his arm around me and patting my shoulder. 'You've always been a little in love with Jack Miller, and he with you.'

'If he was,' I say quietly, 'he isn't now and that's an end to it.'

Chapter Fifteen

The Sea of Love

It's the day of the ball at last, but first I have to say goodbye to Buster. I give him his breakfast and take him for a wander in the copse before putting him back in his kennel, hanging up his lead on the hook outside, and walking away for the last time without looking back, because I don't think I can bear to see his face again. I don't understand how it can feel so bad when I know I've done my best for him, finding him a forever home where he'll be loved and looked after. As I leave the kennel block, I hear him whine and scrape at the bars. Why does it feel like a betrayal?

I ask Libby to hand him over to the Nelsons when they arrive to collect him, and turn my attention to the rest of the rescues before checking on the final arrangements for the ball, the timetable and the items I've acquired for the auction of promises. Before I leave for the venue later the same day, I watch the last of the house martins flying across the sky on their journey south, and wonder with a lump in my throat if Vlad is with them, and what Buster is up to now.

Once I reach the hotel, I run through the arrangements with the manager before taking a couple of minutes in the cloakroom to touch up my lip gloss and flick the stray ringlets of hair back from my cheek. Katie styled it for me, penance perhaps for her going out with my ex, but it was a bit of a laugh, and I'm beginning to feel that I can forgive her and move on. As she said, it would be sad to fall out over a man, Nathan in particular.

I check my dress, which I bought with money my aunt gave me as a present, a simple navy gown that touches the floor with cross-over folds at the front set off with an aquamarine and gold belt. I strike a pose, stroking the clingy material over the curve of my waist. I'll do, but am I ready to face the guests arriving at Talyton Animal Rescue's inaugural ball? I can face most of them with equanimity, but how will I feel when I see Jack with his girlfriend? I take a deep breath and brave the hotel lobby where the guests are starting to arrive. Fifi and I greet them, while the hotel staff direct them to where they can leave their coats and to the bar, where we're serving champagne and canapés.

'You look lovely, dear niece,' Fifi says, giving me the briefest of hugs.

'Thank you,' I say, wondering if I've made a mistake on the tickets regarding the dress code. Both Fifi and my dad look as if they've come in fancy dress: Fifi as the lady in red, and my dad as an overweight emperor penguin. 'You look great too.'

'Is everything under control?'

'I think so. The band's done their soundcheck, the DJ's ready to go, dinner will be served as planned – except the chef's prepared a different veggie starter from the one on the menu – and I've taken Dad through the items for the auction of promises. He's stepped in as auctioneer after Mr Lacey had to drop out with laryngitis.'

'That's kind of him,' Fifi says.

'I did have to twist his arm.'

'Well, you've done a great job, Tessa.'

'It isn't over yet,' I point out lightly. Another minor glitch is the malfunctioning chocolate fountain, and the manager is attempting to source another one from the hotel at the opposite end of the seafront.

'There is one other thing...' Fifi says.

'Oh no, what have I missed?'

'I've tweaked the seating plan.'

'Fifi, why? I spent hours on that.' I drew up several versions, taking into account feedback from guests and my knowledge of which social group people belong to, keeping the horsey set, the bridge players and the actors from the Am Dram Group in their cliques as far as possible, and putting the whole of the committee of Talyton Animal Rescue together at the same table.

'You put us on the same table as Diane. I can't sit anywhere near that woman. I can't be in the same room as her.'

'You'll have to be,' I point out, my face dead-pan, 'unless you want to eat on your own in the bar. I can't please everyone and, besides, you all need to talk, so talk you will.'

'I've come here to enjoy myself,' Fifi says.

'Well, I suggest you get the business part of the proceedings over as quickly as possible.'

'That's why you put us together, isn't it?' my aunt says, in a moment of enlightenment. 'Tessa, that's most underhand' – she chuckles – 'I didn't think you had it in you to be so devious. You used to be such an innocent girl.'

'If you went back to the committee and served as an ordinary member, as they've invited you to, you would show that you're committed to the cause and not put off by all that petty infighting. You'll demonstrate your resolve and strength of character by rising above it, not joining in with all the bitching and catty comments.' I pause before continuing, 'So leave my seating plan well alone. If you move just one couple, it will set up dangerous perturbations elsewhere.' I don't explain, but it includes the possibility that I'd end up on the same table as Jack and I don't think I could bear that.

'Oh dear.' My aunt looks past me towards the door. 'Keep your chin up, Tessa.'

It's Jack, accompanied by his girlfriend, and Libby and Ash who look happier than ever, Libby in a short sleeveless dress with a flouncy hemline. I take a step back, hoping that Fifi will greet them while I hover in the background at the bottom of the white marble staircase that leads to the ballroom on the first floor, but it's too late. Jack catches my eye straight away with a somewhat sheepish glance, walking across hand in hand with the woman he chose over me. My heart plummets because although I was hoping she'd be like one of Cinderella's Ugly Sisters, some haggard crone with cataracts and no teeth, or what I imagine a cougar to be, a platinum blonde in an animal-print catsuit with pumped-up, artificial breasts, she's very attractive, petite and slender, with big grey eyes and elfin features.

'This is Karen,' Jack says awkwardly, introducing her to me. 'Karen, this is Tess.'

'Hello,' she says. 'Jack's told me all about you.'

Not all, I hope, raising one eyebrow towards him, and I detect the faintest sign of a blush in his cheeks.

'I expect we'll catch up with you later,' Jack says.

'I don't know what he sees in her,' Fifi says to me when they've moved on.

I can, I'm afraid. Her dress might be plain and her make-up understated, but a smile plays on her lips as she looks up at Jack, much like Buster looks – I correct myself – how Buster used to look adoringly up at me when he wanted his breakfast.

'She seems pleasant enough,' I counter, 'and she must be all right because she's into animal welfare like us.'

'She's old enough to be his mother.'

'There's no need to be kind to me,' I tell my aunt. 'She isn't that old.'

'Verging on too old to start a family. I wonder if Jack's thought about that.' Fifi sighs. 'Oh, who knows what men think? I've met many men and I'm none the wiser.'

I smile to myself. It's no secret that my aunt has had a few affairs of the heart during her marriage. In fact, I'm surprised my uncle's put up with it, although my mum says it's because they have an open relationship and my uncle has behaved just as badly, if not much worse, than her sister.

'Hi, Tessa.' Katie joins us, clutching Nathan's arm. I feel a sense of satisfaction when I see that he looks pretty wrecked already, his tie dangling from his collar, his face red and eyes bloodshot.

He's let himself go since I last saw him, but he's still the same: a nasty piece of work who virtually bankrupted me when he bankrupted himself. I can't stand him. I try to suppress the flares of anger that erupt at the sight of him.

'Welcome to the ball,' I say, acting my heart out. 'Katie, you look fab. I love the dress.' She looks stunning in a lilac gown, and all I can think is that she could do better than accessorising it with the rat on her arm.

Drinks are served, followed by a sit-down banquet, some dancing and an interlude for the auction of promises. My dad takes over the stage and the microphone to introduce himself, although most people here know very well who he is. I look around at the audience, hoping we haven't left it too late because many of the guests are looking pretty sozzled, but maybe they'll spend more than if they were sober.

'I hope you're enjoying this evening, having plenty of fun, and raising lots of money for Talyton Animal Rescue at the same time. Well, ladies and gents, girls and boys, dust off those wallets and loosen those purse-strings for tonight's very special auction of promises.' My dad pauses. 'We have to thank Tessa, my lovely daughter' – he looks across and I think, Please don't embarrass me – 'the best daughter anyone could have, who has begged, cajoled and fleeced the good people of Talyton St George for this wonderful variety of promises.'

Good people? I think. He's beginning to sound like Widow Twanky.

'Give yourselves a huge pat on the back for

your generosity. Now, where shall we begin?'

'Look at the list, Dad,' I say, bustling over to join him with my copy.

He looks at me. 'That's no good, love. I haven't got my glasses.'

'The first one is Jack,' I whisper to him. 'Go on.'

'Right, thank you, love.' I walk off the stage and Dad turns to the band. 'Drum roll, please. And our first lot is' – his voice booms across the sound of the drums – 'a slave for a day, our very own Jack Miller. Jack, where are you?'

I look towards Jack's table, but he isn't there. He's walking out from the door at the side of the stage, dressed only in a bow tie, dress shoes, a scarlet apron with 'All Yours' across the front and a thong, to applause and wolf whistles.

Blushing and bashful, Jack inclines his head to acknowledge the crowd, and stands with his feet apart and hands behind his back, awaiting his fate, which, when I look around at the eager faces, could be dire. I'm afraid he could end up being eaten alive.

'Okay,' my dad says, 'Jack says he has many attributes, but he's particularly handy around the house. He's good at DIY, can fit you a smoke alarm or make minor repairs. He can walk your dogs–'

'I'd like him to bring me breakfast in bed,' someone pipes up from the top table. It's Diane. 'Then run me a hot bath with bubbles.'

I watch Jack's expression. He's more likely to run for it than run Diane a bath, I think, amused, then I sober up, the ache of loss returning, seeping back into my soul. I don't believe I'll ever get over him. He'll always be the one that got away.

He doesn't escape Diane though. She starts the bidding – or, rather, tells her husband to – and keeps bidding until she's secured Jack's services, at which she insists on tottering onto the stage – with encouragement from the other members of the committee, I notice – in a clinging pale green dress and black patent T-bar shoes to check the goods for herself. Jack takes her prodding in good humour, but she won't let him go in a hurry, taking the microphone from my dad and holding herself upright, with her hand around Jack's back.

'I shall make sure I get my money's worth,' she shrieks. 'You'd better be prepared to work hard, young man.'

'Edward's money's worth,' Fifi calls out. 'It's your husband's money you've just spent. Go on, Diane. Make your speech.'

I catch my dad's eye. 'Hurry up,' I mouth. He needs to move the auction along because we're running out of time, and I begin to feel like Cinderella did, knowing that she has to leave the ball at the stroke of midnight otherwise her clothes will turn to rags and her carriage into a pumpkin. In fact, we have to finish by two, but the band still has to play one final set.

There's no stopping Diane, though, when she's in full flow.

'Fifi, you must join us on stage,' she says, 'and Wendy and Frances and the rest of our loyal members. We have an important announcement to make.'

The gaggle of women surround Jack, who

obliges by kissing each one in turn as Diane speaks of new beginnings for Talyton Animal Rescue.

'Tonight, the phoenix has risen from the ashes. We have had a tough few months and lost our way, but thanks to this evening...'

And a few bottles of champagne, I think.

'...we've put our difficulties aside. I would like to confirm that I have been elected as chair in the proper manner, while we have made Fifi, who has served us so well over many years, our honorary president.' Diane searches for me. 'Tessa, come and join us.'

'Oh no,' I say, but it's Jack who steps forward, offers me his hand and leads me onto the stage where Diane delivers her thanks for my work at the Sanctuary and confirms that the money has come through from the trust fund, ready to be spent on extending the kennel block and replacing the shed.

'And the vets' bills,' I finish for her.

'Hear hear,' Alex Fox-Gifford's voice calls from one of the tables at the back of the room.

'Dad, grab that mike, will you?' I say, as Diane is about to pass it over to Fifi. 'Don't let her get started.'

'But I have so much to say,' my aunt protests, and it's for exactly that reason that I want Dad to retrieve the microphone, because if my aunt gets going, she'll never stop.

The auction is a success, raising much more than I ever expected with the highest bid going for a year's supply of cupcakes from Jennie's Cakes and the least for a jar of Frances's prize-winning pickle. At the end, the band strikes up once more and my aunt clambers onto the table to dance with my mum.

'What's wrong with those two?' I ask my dad. A ticket for the ball appears to be a licence to misbehave, and the older their generation becomes, the worse they get. They are outrageous.

'I know what you're thinking, that they have no decorum,' he says with a broad grin, 'but those two girls certainly know how to have fun. Cheer up, Tessa. Why don't you have a dance with your old dad? Come on.' He holds out his arm. 'I won't take no for an answer.'

I dance, but my heart isn't in it. I should have been dancing with Jack.

Later, I check my watch as the band strikes up 'Hi-Ho Silver Lining' and most of the couples who are sitting at the tables take to the floor. It's approaching midnight and I don't want to be here when the slow dances start, so I make my escape, heading up the next flight of stairs to the balcony with a drink in my hand to look out at the sea glittering in the moonlight and the rocks that are humped on top of each other along the beach. On the lawn below, the committee – Fifi, Wendy, Diane, Frances and the rest, and my mum and dad – are playing mini-golf with fluorescent golf balls. I can hear their laughter and the occasional knock of a club hitting a ball, and I smile to myself. That's one thing sorted.

I lean over the railings, taking in deep breaths of salt air.

'Hey, Tess?' I jump at the sound of my name. 'Don't jump, will you?'

'Jack?' I say, turning to face him.

'I, uh, saw you walking up the stairs. Can I join you?'

'Feel free.' I take a sip of wine: Dutch courage. Keep it light, I think, my pulse flickering and dying again at the thought that Jack and I are alone together, but nothing can happen because he is with Karen. Where is Karen? I wonder. If I was Jack's girlfriend, I wouldn't let him out of my sight, not because I didn't trust him, but because I couldn't bear to be apart from him, even for a minute. I bite my lip. Is that why he took me up and dropped me? Because he interpreted my willingness to fall into bed with him as desperation and foresaw a lifetime with a girlfriend as clingy as a limpet?

'Hole in one!' someone screams from the mini-golf course below.

'That was my ball, not yours. You hit the wrong one.' It's Fifi and Diane bickering again.

'I didn't.'

'Did!'

'Oh no, she didn't,' my dad's voice joins in.

'Oh yes, she did...' There's more laughter and general agreement to go back inside, and silence descends.

'They're mad,' Jack begins. 'A slave for a day. It seemed such a great idea at the time.'

'Thanks for offering yourself up like that,' I say. 'I didn't realise you were going to dress up.'

'Dress down, I think you mean. Your dad thought it would be a bit of fun, and it probably was – for everyone else. Diane has wandering hands.' He smiles ruefully. 'How on earth am I going to survive a whole day with her?'

'I don't know,' I say, thinking that if he hadn't been with Karen, I would have put in a bid.

'It's a beautiful view from here,' he says, but he isn't looking at the sea. He's gazing at me, and I can't help wondering if he's slightly drunk.

'Shouldn't you be elsewhere?'

'Probably.' He clears his throat. 'Tess, I wish–'

'Don't,' I cut in quickly. 'Please don't mention it again. Whatever it was, it's over. I've moved on.'

'Have you really?' I can read disappointment in Jack's voice. 'You pretend you're so hard–'

'You took advantage,' I say harshly. 'That night...'

'I know that's how it looks now, but I didn't intend it to work out this way.'

'I suppose I didn't turn out to be the kind of lover you expected. I didn't quite do it for you,' I say bitterly.

'It wasn't like that. Tess, I never meant to hurt you.'

'Change the record, Jack. I've heard it all before.' I stare out to sea, wishing I was anywhere but here. 'What's wrong with you men? You're all so bloody predictable. Look at Nathan, hooking up with my best friend. Why Katie of all people?'

'They've been together for a long time,' Jack says quietly.

'Not that long, a couple of weeks, that's all.' I frown as I try to read Jack's expression in the near-darkness.

'It's quite a bit longer than that. Nathan has been living at Katie's flat since he was forced to move out of your old house when it was re-possessed.'

'How long?' I don't let him answer, continuing, 'Katie wouldn't lie to me.'

'She might to protect her reputation – what's left of it, anyway.'

'You never have had a very high opinion of her, have you?'

'With good reason.'

I look back at the sea as the clouds move across the moon, gradually blocking it out, so everything, the sky, the water and beach, grows black.

'What do you know that I don't? Jack, tell me.' Instinctively, I know he's telling the truth and Katie has been lying to me. 'Please don't leave me in the dark.'

'I wasn't going to say anything – sometimes it's better to let sleeping dogs lie.'

'Jack, please,' I repeat. I need to know.

'Your bridegroom was seeing Katie before the wedding.'

It takes me a moment to realise that he means before my wedding, the one that didn't happen, and it's as if someone has smashed the balcony away from beneath my feet. I grab the railings and hold on, my knees buckling in shock as Jack wraps his arms around me.

'Are you all right, Tess?' he murmurs.

'I'm okay. I feel a bit faint, that's all.' I force a smile. 'Too much champagne, I expect.'

'I've been watching you – you haven't been drinking.' Jack touches my cheek. I shouldn't, but I rest my head against his chest. 'I caught Nathan and Katie in Nathan's car the night before you were getting married, and they weren't talking, if you know what I mean.'

'Where? No, spare me the gory details.'

'I tried to call you, but you weren't answering your phone, and I went round to your house, but you weren't there.'

'I was at my parents' house.'

'Yep, I tried there as well, but your mum wouldn't let me in. She said you were washing your hair, or having an early night. Either way, it was a lame excuse.'

'Why didn't you text me?'

'I did, several times, and you didn't respond. I wrestled with my conscience all night, torn between opening your eyes to what your fiancé and bridesmaid were really like, and letting you continue in blissful ignorance. When I decided that I had to tell you, all I could do was crash the wedding. I didn't do it on impulse, or out of self-interest, much as that's what everyone would like to believe. Tess,' he goes on, hoarse with emotion, 'I did it for you.'

'But you didn't explain.' I start to cry, hot tears rolling down my face.

'No one gave me the chance, and you wouldn't let me near you afterwards.'

'You could have raised the subject when we began working together at the Sanctuary.' We've been so close, as close as a man and woman can be, and yet he never mentioned it.

'I didn't want to rake it all up again. You seemed happy enough and I didn't want to see you upset. Tess, I hate seeing you upset.' He pauses, reaching up to stroke my hair. 'Anyway, you seemed okay with Nathan and Katie being an item.'

'I did – for Katie's sake – and before this revelation.' I feel completely and utterly betrayed. 'How could she? How could Katie dress up as my chief bridesmaid and tell me how lucky I was, when all the time she was sleeping with my fiancé behind my back? She even told me how she couldn't fancy him in a million years because he wasn't her type. And why did Nathan do it? Wasn't I enough for him either?' I glance up at Jack's handsome face.

'Oh, why am I spilling my guts out to you? Go away. Go back to your girlfriend,' I say, pushing him away, my palms on his chest, 'though goodness knows, it's been a very long time since she was a girl.'

I hear the catch in Jack's throat as he steps back, releasing me from his embrace.

'I'm sorry. I'm being a bitch. She seems ... very nice.'

'Jack? Jack, are you there?' a voice calls from the bottom of the staircase.

'I'm on my way,' Jack shouts back, but the sound of footsteps draws close before he can make a move, and Karen appears at the top of the stairs.

'I've been looking for you. Oh,' she says, casting a questioning glance at me, before turning to Jack. 'Is everything all right?' she asks coolly.

'Everything's fine,' Jack says, and I'm grateful that he doesn't try to explain why I'm standing here in tears. I can see, though, from the look on Karen's face that he is going to have to explain why he's up here with me to her later.

'It's almost time for the last dance,' Karen says quietly, 'if you want to dance it with me.'

'Of course I do,' Jack says. 'Goodnight, Tess,' he adds gently.

I wait on the balcony, listening to their footsteps fade and the band playing a slow number, 'The Sea of Love', in the distance. I don't want to go back down, but I have to. I sneak downstairs to the cloakroom to wash my face and dry my eyes. To my horror, Katie is in there too, rinsing her hands and checking her hair. She gives me a half smile and asks me what's wrong.

'How could you?' I say, giving her a hard stare. 'You've lied and deceived me, your best friend.'

'What's Jack been saying to you?'

'You know very well. You've known all along. That's why you didn't want us getting together, because you were afraid he was going to drop you right in it. What did you think you were doing, sleeping with my fiancé and on the night before the wedding?' It sounds like some tacky soap opera: chief bridesmaid sleeps with groom. 'Why?'

'Because... Because... I don't know why. It just happened, he asked me to meet him, I thought it was about choosing presents for the bridesmaids, and one thing led to another.'

'Why didn't you say no, for goodness' sake?'

'I couldn't resist,' Katie says. 'I was flattered. Call me shallow, but Nathan said I had a cute bum.'

It's ridiculous, because the single thought in my mind is that he never said that to me. The bastard. Why did he go out with me in the first place? To me, he was a charming outsider and it was like choosing an exotic pet over a cat or dog. Although he said I'd have made a slutty wife, I don't think he meant it. I was wife material: caring, maternal and respectable, a woman you would be happy to introduce to your parents, whereas it was Katie who was the slutty one. There was a time just before the wedding when Nathan mentioned me signing a prenup guaranteeing him his conjugal rights twice a week. It was supposed to be a joke at the time, but I'm not so sure now.

'I'm sorry.' Katie steps towards me, holding out her arms. 'What's done is done. Friends?'

'Oh no, never again,' I say, turning away. 'I'll never forgive you for this.'

When I'm on the way back to the Sanctuary with my mum and dad in a taxi, my dad tries to console me.

'With friends like her, who needs enemies? They deserve each other.'

'Forget Katie and her tangled love life,' Mum says, her words a little slurred. 'That was a lovely evening, Tessa.'

'I think it was worth it,' I say. 'It looks as if we've raised at least three thousand pounds with the ticket price, auction and a couple of generous donations.'

'There'll be some major hangovers tomorrow morning,' Dad says.

'Everyone will be fine after a Bloody Mary and some aspirin,' Mum says.

'Would you like us to stay over?' Dad asks when we arrive in the car park. 'I think we should... It's very quiet out here in the countryside.'

'Hardly,' I say, hearing Tia howling in the bungalow. 'I'll be all right, Dad.'

'You haven't got the black dog any more.'

'He went this morning,' I say, biting my lip.

'I felt a whole lot happier when you had him living with you,' Dad says.

So did I, I think, but I don't admit it. 'You can make sure I get inside safely if that makes you feel better.'

My father escorts me to the front door and checks that there is no one inside and that the door is securely shut before he leaves in the taxi. I turn the TV on to make some noise and give Tia a hug without putting my face too close to hers, because in spite of all the bathing and treatment, she still smells of dog and ear drops, an improvement, I suppose, on her perfume before.

'It looks as if it's just you and me, old lady,' I tell her, and she wags her tail and squeaks with delight, just when I thought that nothing could ever again bring a smile to my lips.

Chapter Sixteen

Old Dog New Tricks

I received a text from Jack the day after the ball asking how I was, but I ignored it and I've been managing to keep my distance from him in the two weeks since, interacting only to deal with the rescues at the Sanctuary. The messages from Buster, or purporting to be from Buster, which I've been receiving and responding to since he went off to his new home have almost completely fizzled out. From receiving pictures on my mobile at least twice a day – of Buster enjoying breakfast, Buster playing ball, Buster having his paws washed, and Buster sitting, rather morosely showing the whites of his eyes, in his new bed, rather than on the sofa – I get the odd text message saying he's doing fine, and then nothing, until Mrs Nelson calls me one afternoon to say that Buster has gone missing. I dismiss her theory that he's been stolen from their back garden. It's far more likely that he's done a runner, but why when he's apparently so happy and settled with his new owners?

'You have called the police, the animal welfare officer, the dog warden and the local vets to see if any of them have picked Buster up, haven't you? When did you notice he was gone?'

'Last night,' Mrs Nelson says, and my heart

clenches in distress and anger.

'So you've left him wandering for almost twenty-four hours? He could be anywhere by now.'

'I'm sorry, my husband said not to make a fuss. Buster would come back for his food.' Mrs Nelson's voice breaks and my anger starts to disperse as I realise that she's just as upset as I am, if not more so.

'Where have you been looking for him?' I ask, my mind racing through the options for retrieving him.

'I had a drive around before and after work,' she says, before abruptly falling silent.

'You said you didn't work.'

'Well, I don't. Not much, anyway. I got the job after you made the home visit.'

She's lying, I think, feeling terribly let down on Buster's behalf. I wish I'd trusted my instincts and turned the Nelsons down when they started making excuses to delay picking him up from the Sanctuary. 'If he was my dog, I would be out there searching for him until I found him. I couldn't rest.'

'I'm afraid I have a confession to make,' Mrs Nelson says. 'He' – I assume from the way she says it, with ironic deference, that she's referring to her husband again – 'told me not to let on, but you're going to have to know that Buster just hasn't settled, and goodness knows, I've tried. He isn't my kind of dog.'

And she isn't his kind of person, I think with a flash of insight as she says, 'Buster is destructive in the house. Whenever I come back from work – I mean, shopping – I find something, my Lou-

324

boutins, a mattress or a leather couch, ripped to pieces. It's soul-destroying to walk back into the house and find it wrecked.' I make to interrupt, but she continues, 'I've spoken to a dog behaviourist, who says he has separation anxiety, a psychological problem that could be cured if we wanted to spend the time and money on it ... but we can't do it, I'm sorry. If he destroys anything else, my husband will destroy him.'

'Why didn't you let me know this before?' I say, aghast. Poor Buster – he must be so confused.

'I was too embarrassed to say anything. I felt as though we were letting you down – you seemed so fond of the dog.'

I am fond of him, I think, tears pricking my eyes. Buster, where are you?

'Thank goodness we never had kids. Buster and I have different aspirations and values – I prize my kitchen units while Buster doesn't. He's scratched those too. It's going to cost us a fortune to repair the damage he's caused.' I hear Mrs Nelson begin to sob down the phone. 'The house can be patched up, but I'm not sure I can say the same for our marriage. It's brought us to the brink of divorce.'

I get the message. 'So you won't want to have Buster back?'

'Absolutely not. I'm sorry, but his running away only confirms to me that he doesn't want to be here with us, and in a way, although I'm worried about him, it's a relief. I never want to see him again.'

Mrs Nelson appears to feel the same about Buster as I do about Jack, but I have no choice but to enlist Jack's help to search for the dog. He knows the area well and he has plenty of contacts. I put my faith in him. If anyone can find Buster, Jack can, and I call him straight away.

'I'm sorry, Tess,' he says when he comes to collect me in his Land Rover an hour later.

'It's one of those things,' I say dismissively, not wanting Jack's sympathy. When I explain that the Nelsons don't want Buster back, Jack is more forgiving of their behaviour than I am, suggesting that adopting a dog is like dating someone, moving in with them and making a commitment before finding out that you're not compatible.

'Where do you want to look first?' he asks.

'He used to hang out on the Green.'

'I had a quick look there on the way up, and I've asked a couple of the local dog walkers to keep an eye out for him, although they're all rather nervous, considering his previous form. I thought we'd go back there and have a look along the old railway line and the fields by the river. Alex Fox-Gifford has some sheep down there, so the sooner we get Buster back the better. We don't want him being accused of worrying the ewes, do we?'

'Or getting shot for it, you mean.'

'Alex wouldn't shoot a dog,' Jack points out. 'It wouldn't do his reputation any good, would it?'

'Oh, I can't bear this. What if he's been hit by another car? He could be lying injured, or...' I can't say it. Jack reaches across and rests his hand briefly over mine, a gesture of comfort and reassurance that makes my heart kick with regret and a fleeting desire for everything to be back as it was before Karen came back into Jack's life and turned mine upside down.

'We'll find him, Tess, even if we have to stay out all night. I promise.'

'You should more be careful about making promises you can't keep,' I say flatly when there's been no sign of Buster and Jack drops me at the Sanctuary a little after midnight, and then I realise I sound mean: he's spent hours out searching with me, the other volunteers that he rallied to help having gone home long ago. 'I'm sorry. I'm tired, that's all.'

'I'll see you safely indoors,' he says quietly, the darkness casting shadows across his handsome face, the sight of him tearing at my heartstrings. 'I heard about what happened the other week. You should have told me. You should have called me at the time.'

'Jack, nothing happened. Looking back, I wonder if it was all in my imagination.' I try to make light of it. 'I'm not scared. I can look after myself.' I keep repeating those words inside my head, hoping that eventually I'll come to believe them.

'I'll come with you to the door,' he insists.

'Really, it's fine. I have Tia,' I say, at which I recall that I used to have two dogs waiting for me, and Buster is still missing, and already my hopes for his safe return are beginning to fade. Stifling a sob, I jump out of the Land Rover. 'Thanks,' I wail as I run to the front door, fumbling for my key and trying to insert it into the lock.

'Tess, let me do it,' Jack says from behind me. 'Here...' He wrests the key from my fingers and

327

unlocks the door, touching the small of my back as he guides me inside and switches on the light. Tia is snoozing, outstretched on the floor. 'She'll never make a guard dog,' he observes.

'You're right. You can't teach an old dog new tricks,' I say, moving as far away from Jack as I can without completely disappearing into a different room.

'I'm sorry about Buster,' he says awkwardly, 'but we will find him. I know we will.' He makes to step towards me, holding out his arms, but I shake my head. My emotions are all over the place: I'm aching with worry for the lost dog, and still angry at myself for letting the Nelsons mislead me. What's more, I'm longing for a hug, but it wouldn't be right.

'I'd better go,' Jack says, after a pause. 'I must get back. I'll see you soon, Tess.'

As it turns out, we see very little of each other for the next few days, which is a relief to me. I take Tia down to the river and walk her around the Green every morning and evening; she's lost weight and is much fitter than when she first arrived at the Sanctuary. Even though I'm nervous after the incident in the copse, I stroll with her there regularly too, in case Buster should be making his way back to the rescue centre, but there's no sign of him, although sometimes I think I see his silhouette in the bushes along the edge of the path or disappearing into the shadows of the dense stand of conifers. I call and whistle, but he never comes.

Towards the end of the week, I'm still looking for him. At lunchtime, I return to the copse with

Tia for a short walk, Tia dragging along behind me.

'Come on, old girl. Hurry up.' The sky is darkening and I can hear the patter of the first spots of rain on the leaves of the silver birches and brambles along the path. Tia refuses to budge though, whining and keeping her nose stuck in the grass beside a fallen log. It isn't like her to make a fuss about anything, and her behaviour makes the hairs on the back of my neck stand on end. There's something wrong, a presence watching me from inside the bushes.

Apprehensive now, I go back to hustle her along, but as I bend over to take her by the collar, I hear a rustle and catch sight of the glint of a pair of tiny eyes and the silhouette of a pointed nose deep within the undergrowth. It takes me a moment to work out that Tia's found a puppy.

'Hey there,' I say gently, reaching through the thorny brambles to extricate it from where it appears to have become trapped, and bringing it out into the light, where I discover that it is, in fact, a fox cub, less than four weeks old, its reddish-brown fur like a jacket of fuzzy felt. Lost or abandoned, it's cold and weak and all it wants to do is curl up and close its eyes. It has given up the fight, and I can see that I'm going to have to do the fighting for it.

'Well spotted, Tia, but I don't know how you did it,' I tell Talyton's new search-and-rescue dog (I'm being ironic) as I tuck the cub inside my top to warm it up and carry it back to the bungalow. 'You're definitive proof of the existence of a sixth sense ... because the other five certainly aren't working properly,' I add as Tia bumps into the gatepost on the way out of the copse.

I send her back into the house without wiping her feet – probably a mistake because she's pretty muddy – before I jump into the van, still in my wellington boots. I turn the key in the ignition, and nothing happens. I try again, but the battery is flat. I glance across at the fox cub, wrapped in a towel in a cardboard box in the passenger foot-well. Now we both need help.

I call my aunt, but she isn't answering her phone. I call my dad – he and Mum are away visiting friends – and I can't ask Katie for a lift now that we're not speaking, which leaves me one last chance of rescue. Jack and I have been avoiding each other, and I don't want to ask him, but what can I do? I don't want to spend money on a call-out fee, and the cub needs to see a vet with some urgency if she's going to have any chance at all. (I've checked and it is a girl.) I make up my mind, and within twenty minutes Jack is driving me and the fox cub in his Land Rover to Otter House.

'Thanks for this,' I say grudgingly.

'You know me. I'm always happy to help,' he says, keeping his eyes fixed on the road ahead. 'How are you, Tess?'

'I'm fine, thanks,' I say, and then, after a long pause, 'How about you?'

'Not so bad.'

'And Karen?'

'She's okay, I think.'

I puzzle over this for a while, failing to come up with an explanation for his response. Jack only

330

thinks she's okay, I muse, which is odd when he lives with her.

'She's got a lot on her plate, dealing with the divorce. Her husband's being a sh–' Jack stops abruptly, as if he's revealed too much.

I feel sick with envy. I don't want to know. How can I possibly match her maturity and experience?

'Is there any news on Buster?' Jack says, changing the subject.

'Nothing at all,' I respond.

'Any more disturbances at the Sanctuary?'

'No.'

'How's the cub?'

I lift the corner of the towel and peer into the box on my lap. *Keep upright,* it reads on the side.

'About the same,' I respond.

Our conversation is stilted, as if we're unable to find anything to say to each other, and I'm relieved when we reach Otter House.

'What have we here, Tessa?' Frances the receptionist asks when I enter the waiting area. I find it difficult to explain that I'm pretty sure the cub is dying. My voice cracks completely, and I'm grateful when Jack takes over in his quiet and tactful way. Frances suggests that we take the cub straight through to the back of the practice, where Maz is preparing for an operation, so that we don't have to wait for Emma, the other partner, who's in the consulting room with another patient.

'You know where you're going?' she says.

'I know this place like the back of my hand,' Jack says cheerfully, opening the door for me to pass through into the corridor with the box in my arms. 'I've been here often enough recently.'

We meet Maz in the prep area, where she greets us in a set of scrubs and white wellies.

'I've admitted an emergency splenectomy,' she says, noticing me looking at her boots, 'and you know what they're like.'

'Messy,' I say, with a rueful smile, recalling the occasional bloodbath that I had to clear up when I was working in practice. 'I hope it goes well.' I put the box down on the bench and lift the cub out with the towel. 'I found this in the copse. Actually, I should give credit where credit's due. Tia found her...'

'She's pretty poorly,' Jack continues as my voice falters once more.

Maz examines the cub, opening her mouth to check her colour, tenting her skin to see how dehydrated she is, and taking her temperature, before grabbing the stethoscope that's dangling from the hook on the wall. Having listened to the cub's chest, she looks up, shaking her head.

'I'm sorry, this little one isn't going to make it. We could try treatment with fluids and antibiotics, but to be honest, I think she's too far gone.'

'Oh?' I gulp back a sob as I watch the cub sink onto her side and begin to lose consciousness. I so wanted her to live.

'I wish I could perform miracles,' Maz goes on. 'Izzy,' she calls to one of her nurses, 'can you fetch the blue juice? It isn't going to take much.'

How many animals have I seen being put to sleep? You become accustomed to the process, but I don't think it ever gets any easier, even though I know the cub is suffering and this will hasten the end. The nurse passes Maz a syringe and needle and she injects the drug straight into the cub's heart, meaning death is instantaneous and the cub's suffering is over.

I want to look away, but my gaze is drawn to the cub's belly as she lies on her side, the reddish fur fading through dusky gold to grey at her groin. The muscles across her shoulder twitch and her staring eye reflects the light from the examination lamp above.

I stifle a sob. Don't cry, I tell myself, not in front of the vet and the nurse – and Jack – but, as I step back and watch Izzy slide the tiny body into a tiger bag, named for its black and orange stripes, tears trickle down my cheek. Tasting salt in my mouth, I sense the pressure of Jack's arm sliding behind my shoulders, offering support and reassurance, and although part of me wants to hate him for what he's done, for taking me up and dropping me, I find that I like the contact. I lean back against him. I like it far too much.

'Thanks for dealing with the cub, Maz,' Jack says as I'm recovering my wits.

'Have you received any info about Buster, the missing dog?' I ask her.

'Nothing concrete,' she says, 'but you might want to keep trying the Green. One of my clients mentioned seeing a black dog by the river, not far from the bridge, early this morning when they were walking their dogs. It's all right, it didn't do anything. It didn't mount an attack, not this time.'

It is good news and bad news, I think: good that Buster is alive and well, because it has to be him, and bad that he's out there, at risk of returning to his unforgivable habit of picking on other dogs.

'I'll settle up with Frances on the way out,' I say.

'Don't worry about payment for today,' Maz says. 'I'm glad we could help.'

I thank her again as Izzy returns from having disposed of the cub's body. Although it's one of the downsides of the job, I envy her. The scent of the vet's surgery, disinfectant, surgical spirit and damp dog reminds me of how much I miss nursing.

'If you ever need a nurse, let me know,' I say. 'I'll do anything from the occasional shift to cover for sickness and holidays. I'd even consider a full-time permanent position, if one came up.'

'We don't have any vacancies at the moment. You're not planning to leave us in the near future, are you, Izzy?' Maz says lightly.

'You couldn't manage without me.' Izzy smiles.

'She's been here so long she's like part of the furniture, but I'll bear you in mind if we should need an extra nurse at any time. It's always good to have someone local.'

'Are you serious about returning to work as a vet nurse?' Jack asks when we're on our way back to the Sanctuary via the Green to see if we can find Buster.

'I've been burying my head in the sand recently. I have to find a way to repay my debts somehow. I can't carry on relying on charity, so to speak. I have to think about the future, buying a house of my own, paying in to a pension, all the boring stuff.'

'What about the rescue centre? What about your aunt?' Jack lowers his voice and adds almost imperceptibly, 'What about me?'

'What about you?' I say harshly.

'I'd miss you,' he goes on, sounding more confident.

'Well, that's tough.' I can feel the anger rising inside me. How dare he have the temerity to say he doesn't want me to leave because he'd miss me, when he's just gone off with another woman! 'You should have thought of that before, shouldn't you?'

In spite of my fury at his attitude, there's nothing I want more than to stay on – I glance at Jack and think, Apart from you. I want him more than ever. I yearn for the taste of him on my lips and his touch on my skin, but it's too late now. He's chosen her, hasn't he?

Life goes on and another week passes by. I remember to call Great-Auntie Marion, who sounds remarkably cheerful for a cancer patient on chemotherapy.

'I'm glad you rang, Tessa,' she says. 'It's lovely to hear from you.'

'How are you?' I ask.

'Not so bad... Well, not so good either,' she goes on. 'I've had to put the farm on the market, lock, stock and barrel, sheep included, I need to think of retiring to somewhere smaller and more manageable. But let's not talk about me. What about you? Have you washed that fiancé of yours out of your hair?'

'I certainly have,' I say.

335

'Good for you.' She pauses. 'That's our girl.'

I tell her about the ball and the animals at the Sanctuary, until I realise that she is no longer answering me. I tap the phone. (Why do I do that? Why will that make any difference?) A few seconds later, another voice comes on the line. It's a nurse who tells me I've sent my great-aunt to sleep.

'She tires easily,' she says.

I ask her to tell her that I'll call again soon, and then return to the office to join the fray.

There are no more sightings of Buster, but I'm kept busy at the Sanctuary with new arrivals – three hedgehogs, an unwanted family of mice that have multiplied because the owners didn't separate the boys from the girls, and a pair of cats handed in because their owners were emigrating – home checks and re-dressing Bambi's wound. It's been much easier since Diane, Wendy and the other committee members have mended their bridges with Fifi, and made a new rota for the volunteers. It helps too that the baby birds have flown and we're no longer tied to hourly feeding, so we've managed to catch up with some of the jobs that needed doing.

This evening, everyone has gone home, and I'm taking another look at Dolly because she hasn't seemed quite right all day. When Libby was preparing to go home with Jack, who had been working on the remaining kennels, fixing the front panels, she asked me to keep a special eye on her. I don't mind doing this while it's still light outside, but I'm not so keen when it gets darker and my mind starts playing tricks on me, spotting shapes, human figures, in the shadows at the base of the high hedges and under the trees.

The pony is not happy. She's been looking good up until now, with her long beard, dense feathers and winter coat growing through almost dappled over her rounded rump. Usually she's either grazing or dozing, but tonight she's unsettled, wandering around the paddock and stopping frequently to look at her belly, which is patchy with sweat.

I check my watch. It's half-six and outside surgery hours, so there'll be an extra call-out charge, but I really don't think this will wait until morning when Justin is due to come out and check on the deer.

Although I haven't had much experience with ponies, I have an inkling that she has colic. She is definitely not comfortable, and for someone who normally eats, well, almost like a horse, her behaviour is most odd. I hesitate to get in touch with Jack for advice, knowing that it will be like pulling scabs from partially healed wounds when I hear his voice again, but I do call him for Dolly's sake.

'I hope I'm not disturbing you,' I say lightly, overhearing a woman's voice in the background and automatically assuming that it's his girlfriend.

'It's no problem, Tess. Libby's cooking me dinner. She owes me for buying a new battery for her mobile. What can I do you for?' He sounds awkward, yet I find his bashfulness attractive, even sexy. My heart twists with the pain of unrequited love, because I do love him. I love Jack Miller – always have done and always will – and I didn't acknowledge it until it was too late. I think of my dad and one of his trite but true sayings: you don't know what you've got till it's gone.

'Tess, are you still there?'

'Yes. Yes, I'm sorry.' The sound of his voice made me forget what I was calling him for. 'It's Dolly. I could do with some advice.' I explain, and Jack tells me that it could be colic and that I should call the vet straight away.

'Get hold of Alex or Justin. Libby and I will be with you in five minutes.'

'That's pushing it,' I observe.

'I'll drive carefully, I promise.'

I call the Talyton Manor practice, hoping to get hold of Justin, the assistant, because the Sanctuary's outstanding bill is still gathering interest, but it is Alex who answers.

'I can always check on the deer at the same time to save you a call-out charge,' he says, making it perfectly clear that he hasn't forgotten about it.

'I'm sorry about the money,' I mutter.

'We'll sort it out sometime. I'll have to have a word with your aunt.'

'Please do. The funds should be on their way into the account.'

'Okay. Should I bring the dart gun to get near the pony this time? That's a joke, by the way. I'll be with you shortly.'

'Thanks, Alex.' I grab a coat and beanie hat and go outside, the air bearing a distinctly autumnal chill, to wait for Libby to arrive with Jack. It would be far better for Libby to approach Dolly than for me to try and more than likely fail.

When they turn up, Jack stands beside me while Libby catches the pony without any difficulty at all.

'How are you, Tess?' he asks, the warmth in his voice making my heart miss a beat.

'Fine, thanks.' Suddenly, though, I find myself on the verge of tears that I have to fight back, inwardly scolding myself for being soft.

'I can see you're really worried about Dolly,' Jack says gently, but he's got it wrong. Yes, I'm concerned for her, but this outburst of emotion is all about how I feel about him.

Libby leads the pony into the stable beside Bambi's. Dolly moves slowly, hesitating every few strides to switch her tail and kick at her belly.

'Come on, Dolly.' Libby strokes the pony's sweaty neck. 'What's wrong with her, Jack?'

'Alex is here. We'll find out soon enough,' he says, glancing towards me with a look, warning me to remain silent. I know why: Libby's very fond of the pony, and he's worried that if anything happens to her, the stress might set her epilepsy off again.

Alex marches up beside us with a stethoscope around his neck, a visit case in one hand and a box of plastic sleeves in the other.

'How is the patient?' he asks, looking into the stable. 'I take it you haven't checked her temperature...' A brief smile crosses his face in response to my raised eyebrows. 'It's all right. It's always better to let her kick the vet instead.'

'Can you give her anything?' Libby says, grimacing as Dolly rolls her eyes back and utters a low groan. 'Please, Alex. She seems to be in a lot of pain.'

'I'd rather not give her anything yet, unless we

absolutely have to. Let me see what's going on first. If you can turn her round, with her bottom facing me, I can examine her over the lower half of the door. I haven't forgotten how she tried to kill me.' When Alex reaches over the door with a gloved hand, Dolly puts her ears back and tosses her head before standing stock-still as though wracked by a wave of acute pain. 'How does the saying go? You can tell a gelding, whereas you have to ask a mare. Obviously, I don't ask her nicely enough.'

'Can I do anything?' asks Jack.

'I've got her. She's dying, isn't she?' Libby says, voicing my concern. Although there have been times I've wished her dead, I didn't mean it. I feel sorry for the pony, in spite of her attitude when she arrived at the Sanctuary, but I'm sorrier for Libby, whose lip is trembling as she tries not to cry in front of us.

'Not yet,' says Alex. 'She has plenty of years left in her.'

'It isn't colic, then?' Jack says.

'No,' Alex continues matter-of-factly, 'Dolly's in labour.'

It takes a moment for this fact to sink into my brain.

'She's having a foal?' I say stupidly.

'That's right,' Alex says. 'I don't know how I missed it.'

'I can't believe it. I mean, I had no idea.'

'I thought she was putting on weight because she was happy here,' Libby says with a broad grin, her cheeks pink with relief.

'Well, it won't be too long before you have the

340

proof right in front of your eyes. She's been in labour for a while.' Alex smiles as he pulls off his glove and drops it on the ground, which is just typical of a vet, I observe. They have a pathological inability to clear up after themselves. 'I think we should leave her in peace for half an hour or so to give her a chance to get on with it.'

'If you think that's okay,' Libby says doubtfully.

'Everything's coming along very nicely,' Alex confirms. 'I can take a look at the deer in the meantime, and I wouldn't mind a coffee, white with three sugars, and some of those biscuits that I had last time, the ones with the caramel through the middle.'

'I'll see what we have left,' says Libby, unclipping the rope from Dolly's head-collar. 'Coffee for everyone?' she goes on, her voice high with barely suppressed excitement.

'Please,' Jack and I say at the same time. 'A foal,' he goes on, his smile still having the power to make me melt inside. 'How amazing is that!'

'It's a bit late in the year. She must have been running with the stallion towards the end of last summer,' Alex says. 'Right, where's Bambi?'

'He's in the stable next door. Libby and I changed the dressing on his leg three days ago, so he's due a fresh one,' I say.

'We'll do that now so I can have a look,' Alex says, and we replace the bandages with new ones in the light of a torch. Alex confirms what I already know: that the wound is healing nicely from the edges in and there's no evidence of infection. He's optimistic that Bambi will go on to be released.

After coffee, we troop back to the barn together

in silence. All I can hear is our footsteps, whickering and the gentle shuffling of straw as we arrive at Dolly's stable. A lump catches in my throat as we look over the door to find the pony nuzzling at a wet bundle of black and white, still partially wrapped in membranes. 'Oh, there's the baby,' Libby sighs. 'Look, Tessa, it's beautiful. Dolly, you are such a clever girl.'

'What do you think, Alex?' asks Jack, putting his arm around his sister's shoulder and giving her a hug as she wipes her eyes on the sleeve of her fleece. 'You're the expert when it comes to ponies.'

'It's a little early to tell,' Alex says wryly, as the foal lifts its head, 'but it looks like it's nicely marked. I'll check to see if Mum's passed the afterbirth and make sure all's well, then we can leave them alone to get to know each other.'

'Thanks, Alex. I don't know what we'd do without you.' I feel really guilty about not being able to pay him on time. 'About the bill,' I begin.

'It's all right. Have this visit on me.'

'No, we couldn't possibly...'

'It's fine. Actually, I feel a bit guilty that I didn't even suspect the pony was pregnant I should have checked when I first came out to see her, considering her history. Call this my contribution to the Sanctuary. I'm sure there's never enough money.'

'Or enough space,' I add ruefully. 'I'm really grateful. We're struggling.'

'It doesn't help that you have another mouth to feed,' Alex says.

The foal is soon on his, or her, feet, drinking

from the mare. If I was concerned that Dolly might treat her baby in the same way she treats some of us, I was wrong. She adores it.

'She's very proud,' says Libby. 'What shall we call her? Him?'

'It's a colt,' Alex says. 'I had a quick look. He looks quite comical with that patch across his eye.'

'You aren't going to let yourself get too attached the foal as well as Dolly, are you?' I say lightly to Libby once Alex has left for home and Jack has gone to feed and clean out the cats in the cattery.

'I'll try not to, but this is fate, I reckon,' Libby goes on, busily texting on her mobile at the same time. 'Dolly will have to stay for a while longer, won't she? She can't travel anywhere with a young foal at foot.'

'She'll be here for the winter now,' I confirm. 'Who are you texting?'

'Ash, to let him know our news,' she says. 'This is the best thing ever.'

'So you're still together, you and Ash?'

'Yeah,' she says, smiling.

'Make sure you keep me posted,' I tease. 'I can hear wedding bells.'

Libby ignores that comment, and I notice her hand is twitching. When she sees me looking at it, she folds her arms, hugging the affected one to her chest in an attempt to keep it still.

'Are you all right?' I ask quietly, and then when she doesn't answer me for a second time, I go on, 'You have told Ash about your epilepsy, haven't you? I don't mean to nag, but–'

'I haven't and I'm not going to.' Libby's eyes flash with annoyance. Her mood has changed. 'You're as bad as my brother. Have I taken my medication? How am I feeling? Have I told everyone? I can change my status on Facebook and take out an ad in the *Chronicle:* Libby Miller suffers from epilepsy. Well, I don't. On a worldwide scale, my suffering is nothing. I can manage my condition. Give me some credit.'

'I understand that,' I say, as she continues, 'I'll tell Ash when it feels right. If I tell him now, I'll scare him off because he'll think I'm really into him, which I am...'

'Libby, he should know. It isn't fair.'

'Yeah, so we'll spend our time together with him watching and waiting for me to start twitching and frothing at the mouth. How cool does that look?'

'He needs to know the rules, like how long he can leave it before he calls an ambulance. Libby, how would you feel if it was the other way round?'

'I'd be petrified that he was going to die on me,' she says after a long pause for thought. Her lip wobbles and I'm afraid she's going to break down and cry.

'Exactly,' I say, putting my arm around her shoulders. 'Think about it.'

'I have, and I've made my decision to keep it from him for now. I'm prepared to take the risk. It's my life, my choice. And don't you dare say anything to either of them, Ash or Jack.' She changes the subject back to Dolly's baby. 'How do we start handling the foal?'

'Carefully, I should say. Dolly strikes me as

being the possessive type – she's bound to want to protect her baby. We'll have to take it slowly, one step at a time.'

How I wish Jack and I had taken it slowly, one step at a time. We should have gone out on a few dates and built up to the first kiss, not jumped into bed with each other at the first opportunity. He would have had time to get to know me even better than he already does, and realised exactly what he had to lose by dumping me for the cougar.

'Are you okay, Tessa?' Libby asks as we continue to watch the foal, which staggers shakily around to Dolly's head end and stands there so that she can nuzzle fondly at his face. 'Only you seem rather quiet tonight... What's up?' Libby goes on sternly when I don't respond. 'Are you still recovering from the ball?'

'That was weeks ago, and I didn't have a hangover, if that's what you mean.'

'You were one of the few who didn't have a drink or two.' Libby hesitates. 'So what is it? Didn't we raise any money?'

'No, we counted it all up and we made several thousand pounds.'

'You must be exhausted,' she says, probing.

'I'm not tired. Not really.'

'Is it Jack?' She takes my silence as affirmation. 'It is Jack. I don't know if it will make any difference, Tessa, but you should probably know that Karen's moved out and gone to stay with friends.'

'It makes no difference to me,' I say quietly. It's too late. I still have feelings for Jack, and I could so easily give in and go back to him if he asked me to, but it wouldn't be right. There's nothing to stop him letting me down again as soon as someone else catches his eye, and I'm not prepared to put myself through that kind of heartache again.

Chapter Seventeen

Nine Lives

Libby and Ash drop in regularly to visit Dolly and the foal, which they've named Apache. I leave them at the paddock gate with their supply of carrots late one afternoon and return indoors to have a shower after what's been a very long but rewarding day, playing fetch with the kennelled dogs and experimenting with a variety of toys with the cats. I smile to myself because that makes it sound as if I've spent all day playing games, when I've done all the feeding and cleaning out too. Working with animals is not a glamorous occupation.

I'm just letting Tia out in the back garden for a couple of minutes, when I hear Ash shouting urgently.

'Stay there,' I tell Tia. Checking the time on my watch on the way, I make a run for it back to the paddock, following the sound of Ash's voice.

'Libby's having a fit,' he screams from beside her, where she's lying on the grass at the base of the fence, her eyes wide open yet unseeing, her face red, saliva on her lips and her limbs thrashing about.

'Keep calm,' I say, looking to make sure she isn't going to hit her head on the gatepost, and checking the time again. 'Ash, talk to her, let her

347

know you're here.'

'Shouldn't we call an ambulance?' he says, his complexion as pale as Dolly's white blaze.

'Not yet,' I say as calmly as I can; I've never seen a human being have a seizure before. 'Trust me, Ash. I've done the risk assessment and she's okay for three minutes.'

'It must be at least that now,' he stammers.

'I timed it from almost when you started yelling.' I try to focus him on doing something so that he doesn't panic, although underneath I'm beginning to fear that we're getting close to the mark. 'Talk to her, Ash. Come on, that's your job.'

'I don't know what to say.'

'Anything, what you had for breakfast will do.' I begin to relax a little, noticing how Libby's body is growing limp and the twitches less frequent, and how her eyes settle on Ash's face, her brow furrowed as if she's trying to remember who he is. 'She's coming round,' I go on with a sigh of relief.

'Hi, Libs, guess what I had for breakfast?' Ash begins, before reeling off a whole list of foods: 'Cold pizza, curry, cornflakes, baked beans, eggs, a cereal bar, apple pie.' I raise one eyebrow when he glances up at me. 'I didn't have all of them today.'

'Ash,' Libby moans, groping for his hand. He links his fingers through hers and raises her hand to his lips.

'Thank goodness for that,' he breathes as she tries to sit up.

'Stay there,' I tell her. 'She'll be confused at first. Make her stay there, Ash. I'm going to get something for her to sit on and a glass of water. Do you want anything?'

'A double vodka, I reckon,' he says, with a small smile. 'No, don't worry about me.'

I deliberately take my time to collect up a glass of water and one of the deckchairs, giving Libby and Ash an opportunity to talk, while getting ready to console either of them if they should fall out.

As I approach, I hesitate, peering around the corner of the kennel block and catching sight of them sitting side by side, leaning against the fence with their legs outstretched. My heart sinks.

'You can't dump me because of this!' Ash shouts. 'It should be me dumping you for keeping secrets.'

'I can't let you dump me,' Libby argues. 'I'd never live it down. If you were a real man, you'd let me dump you.'

'But I've got grounds. You should have told me in advance so I knew what to expect. Libby, I've never been so scared.' Ash's tone softens. 'I thought you were dying. Why didn't you say anything before?'

'Because I thought...' Libby hesitates. 'I knew it would put you off. We're supposed to be dating, getting to know each other and having fun. You don't want to waste your time with me, watching and waiting and worrying about when I'll have the next fit.' She bursts into tears. Ash puts his arms around her. 'You know I could die.'

'Well, you haven't done yet,' he says, scrabbling around in his shorts pocket and pulling out a scrappy tissue, which he presses into her hand.

'There is always a risk...' she sobs aloud.

'Well, you've coped with it. I'm sure I can live with it too.' Ash pauses. 'Libby, I love you. If you think we're going to split up over this, you're wrong.'

I step out from my hiding place, feeling guilty for listening in on a private conversation, but relieved that they're talking. I walk across and hand Libby the water. I'm not sure she has need of the deckchair now.

'There you go,' I say lightly. 'How are you feeling?'

'I've got a bit of a headache, that's all,' Libby says. 'I think it's Ash who's feeling worse,' she adds, turning to him with a small smile on her lips, and I feel a stab of envy at their closeness and the way they mirror each other's movements. Even though they haven't been together for very long, they look like a couple of childhood sweethearts, and yet again it takes me back to Jack, and how we could have been like Libby and Ash if the course of love had run a little smoother for us.

I leave them together and return to collect Tia from the back garden where she has taken me seriously for once, still sitting exactly where I placed her in the middle of the lawn, a bee buzzing close to her face, tormenting her because she can't hear or see it, only detecting it when it makes a brief landing on top of her nose or behind her ear.

'Come on,' I tell her, touching her collar to let her know I'm here, and she struggles up and follows me indoors where I shower and retreat to make dinner, Ash and Libby dropping by to say goodnight before they leave.

Sometimes I think I'm going mad being here alone in the bungalow in the evenings, apart from Tia. I blame it on the pressure of running the Sanctuary and my mounting debts, because although the money is coming through from the charity's funds at last and I no longer have to shell out for cat and dog food, my salary doesn't even cover the interest payments. It's the first time too, when I look back over the past few months, that I've had time to reflect on the wedding and the anguish of losing my home. What's more, my dad came round a couple of days after I spoke to Great-Auntie Marion to tell me she'd died in her sleep. I didn't know her well, but I'm sorry.

It hasn't been all bad though, I tell myself, trying to stay positive. In fact, there have been some real highs as well as lows; the nature of animal rescue, I suppose.

The sound of a car outside makes me jump, but has no effect on Tia, who lies sprawled across the kitchen floor at my feet, licking and biting at her claws, an annoying habit of hers. I continue to feel edgy, more so now that Buster has gone, which reminds me with a pang of anxiety that he's still missing, either wandering the countryside, or lying injured or worse under some hedge.

It's gone seven and I'm not expecting anyone. Abandoning the stir-fry I'm cooking and leaving the lights off on the way, I look out through the office window to find Katie's car outside.

'What on earth does she want?' I grumble to Tia. I have nothing to say to her, and if she's come here for sympathy because Nathan's dumped her for someone else, as I expected he would all along, she's wrong.

She's broken the code, and it might sound like a squabble in the playground, but she went too far this time. Our friendship is irretrievable. I've moved on.

I'm so relieved though that it isn't a stranger, someone following me or watching me, that I answer the door.

'Yes?' I say, coming face to face with the woman who slept with my fiancé, looking pale yet defiant beneath her make-up.

'I have a surprise for you, Tessa,' Katie says.

'Haven't you given me enough of those already?'

'This is a nice one. I think you'll be pleased.'

'Is that Nathan with you?' I look towards the car. The engine's running and there's a shadowy figure in the driver's seat.

'It's all right. I told him to wait for me. I'm not staying.' She undoes the top button of her coat, a short lime-green mac, and refastens it once more, flashing the ring on her left hand.

'So that's it?' I say, annoyed now. 'You've come to gloat.' I start to shut the door on her, but she stops me.

'It isn't like that. I've brought you a dog. The one on the posters. You must have seen them – they're all over Talyton. I recognised him straight away: Buster, the black dog, who used to live here at the Sanctuary.'

'You mean, you've found him?' I say, light dawning at last. 'Where is he? Is he hurt?'

'Hey, calm down, Tessa. You seem more excited

about the dog than you ever were about any man. He's fine.'

'How did you get near him?'

'Nathan and I were walking to the pub when we came across him on the Green. He was chasing a squirrel. The squirrel went up a tree, and the dog went straight into it. While he was looking a bit stunned – like Nathan after he's had a few too many – we managed to catch him.'

'Oh, never mind Nathan, where's Buster?' I can't wait to see him again.

'Have you got a lead we can use?' Katie asks. 'We used Nathan's tie and a piece of string.'

I grab a rope lead from under the counter in the office and join Katie outside, where she's opening the side door of the car.

'No!' I shout, but it's too late. Buster – because there's no doubting that it's him – comes flying out of the car, and just when I think he's going to disappear across the car park and into the night, he skids to a stop, just like a cartoon Scooby Doo, turns and bounds towards me, squeaking with joy. He leaps up, wagging his tail and landing his paws on my midriff, almost knocking me off my feet. 'Buster! I didn't think I was going to see you again. Where have you been?' I say, half chiding him, half laughing with relief.

'I don't think he's going to tell you,' Katie says as I slip the lead over his neck.

I give Buster a massive hug before thanking Katie for bringing him back to the Sanctuary. Dolly has safely delivered a foal and Buster has returned in one piece. Perhaps life is looking up again.

'There's no need to thank me,' Katie says. 'I knew you were fond of him.'

'I was fond of Nathan once,' I say quietly.

Katie looks me in the eye. 'You weren't fond enough though, if you're honest.'

The smell of petrol fumes is beginning to get right up my nose. 'Who are you to talk to me about being honest when it was you who–?'

'Let's not go there,' Katie interrupts. She reties the belt on her mac, pulling it tight around her waist. 'Look, I hope the dog's all right – and you too.'

She looks exhausted, dark rings around her eyes and her face gaunt.

'How about you?' I say, relenting.

'I'm well.' She pauses as if wondering whether or not to leave it at that, but a small smile touches her lips, and she continues, 'I'm pregnant.'

I take a moment to respond. 'Was it planned?'

Katie shakes her head. 'I'm not sure I'll be able to cope with two kids: Nathan and a newborn.'

'You'll survive,' I say. 'You always do. Congratulations, by the way.'

Nathan sounds the horn, making Katie start.

'I'd better go,' she says, and I watch her return to the car before closing the door once more, bringing Buster inside with me. I let him off the lead and he goes mad, tearing around the bungalow, barking and sniffing and squealing. He runs up and down the hall and then into the front room, launching himself onto the end of the sofa where he sits, panting, as if to say, I'm back. I'm home.

Tia, who's been sleeping on the other end of the sofa, wakes and hauls herself up. Blinking, she stares blindly around the room before uttering a short, sharp, questioning bark. Buster responds by sliding towards her on his belly, leaning up to lick Tia's nose and mouth, giving her an enthusiastic greeting. She whines and licks him back and, within five minutes, they're lying alongside each other as if Buster's never been away.

'Hey, budge up. Make room for a small one,' I say, wanting to sit with them, but they refuse to move, so I try another tack. 'Buster, you must be starving. Do you want your dinner?'

At the word 'dinner' he jumps down, pushes past me and heads for the kitchen with Tia not far behind, rejuvenated by the return of her companion. Buster wolfs down his food before padding back to see me.

'You're like a boomerang kid. What am I going to do with you?' I ask him, over the moon to have him back, but already worrying about what is going to happen to him next. I decide against disturbing Jack with news of Buster's return until the morning. Instead, I take Buster outside to accompany me on my late-night tour around the Sanctuary, smiling when I glance down at his shadow at my heels. It's just like old times.

'Come on then, boy,' I say to him once I've given the other dogs – a collie called Dandy, a Lab cross called Colin, and Benson, an odd-looking brown mutt with one ear up and one ear down – their last biscuits. 'There's just Dolly's hay to go out in the paddock.' She needs extra fodder at the moment so she can feed her foal, Apache. I head round to the barn and move past the stables to the back where we're storing a ton of hay for the winter, clambering up onto the stack and pushing a bale off the top.

Buster utters a sharp bark.

'What's up?' I peer down at him. 'There's nothing there. You're making it up.' I slide back down, retrieve the bale that's bounced some way across the barn, prop it up against the base of the stack and take the knife to cut the strings, becoming aware of the sound of a vehicle rattling up the track. I hesitate, my pulse tripping into overdrive, as it approaches then stops somewhere outside and the engine cuts out.

I put the knife down, tucking it behind the bale before taking Buster by the collar and creeping out of the barn, switching the light off on the way and thankful that there's no moon tonight. Buster barks again.

'Sh,' I hiss. I can hear voices. There are two men and they're coming this way. I duck back against the kennel wall, pulling Buster close and praying he won't draw attention to us as the men's footsteps grow louder, and I catch the scent of cigarette smoke. No matter who they are, or what they're here for, they are up to no good. I glance around for somewhere to hide, like when I played sardines with Jack, making myself as small as possible, scarcely daring to breathe, but all I can do is stand with my back pressed against the wall. I fumble for my mobile, flick it on, type the word 'help', and I'm adding recipients when they come around the corner. I press 'send' and start to dial 999, but it's too late.

The flash of a powerful torch temporarily blinds me.

'There she is.'

'Don't touch me,' I say, hanging on tight to Buster.

'It's the manager. Where's your boyfriend, Jack Miller, the bastard who stole Dolly off me and almost broke my heart?'

'He isn't my boyfriend and he isn't here,' I say calmly.

'You're lying.'

'He isn't here,' I repeat.

'I'll have you then for what you done, aiding and abetting kidnap. This one deserves a good hiding,' one of the men says, and I realise as my vision returns that it's Frank Maddocks with his son. With a bloodcurdling growl that makes it clear he means business, Buster lunges towards them, sinking his teeth into the older man's leg.

'Get off me.' Cursing, Frank lifts his stick and cracks it across Buster's head, at which Buster lets go, only to go in again, embedding his teeth in Frank's groin, which only serves to enrage him further. He gives him another thwack with the stick and, this time, Buster yelps, sways and falls to the ground where he remains, not moving.

'Buster,' I scream, trying to get to him, but Frank's son has his hands on my shoulders, dragging me back.

'Buster!' I kick out to no avail, and my mobile goes flying, scattering into pieces.

'What shall we do with her, Dad?' the son asks, his teeth gritted with the effort of maintaining a vice-like grip on my flesh.

'We'll give her a good hiding, like I said.'

'I don't hold with duffing up a woman,' the son

357

says obstinately. 'Why don't we take her with us?'

'No, she'd be a hindrance. Lock her up,' Frank says gruffly, a cigarette between his rubbery lips. He's bent almost double with pain, but it's nothing to the pain I'm suffering with the dog lying there and me unable to help him.

'Where?' Frank's son forces me to shuffle around the corner of the building where he opens the door into the kennels and pushes me on through, our presence setting off a chorus of ear-splitting barks. Frank follows close behind, bashing the kennel doors with his stick in an attempt to shut the dogs up. When we reach the empty kennel at the end of the block, Frank's son shoves me roughly inside, knocking me off balance so I fall, hitting my head against the wall. While I'm sitting up and assessing the damage, he slams the door shut. Frank hands him one of the spare padlocks he must have picked up on the way in, and he slips it through the catch and clicks it shut.

'Have a nice life, you little bitch,' he says, laughing at his own joke.

'Let me out,' I say, struggling up and clinging on to the bars at the front of the kennel. 'You can't do this. You can't do this!' I repeat, screaming above the sound of the dogs, but the pair of them ignore me, walking away down the corridor, Frank tossing his cigarette into the kitchen before they disappear into the inky darkness. I run at the kennel door and slam into it with my shoulders, then my feet, but nothing happens. I turn my attention to the exit at the rear of the kennel that leads to the outside run, and curse my attention to detail when it comes to security, because that's locked too.

I'm trapped. In despair, I sink down to the floor, my back against the wall. The dogs have fallen silent, listening to the sounds from the car park, the rattle of a trailer, shouting and yelling. I can hear my heartbeat too, hammering like an express train confined in a tunnel. My body is hot with anger and fear. What is happening to Buster? What are they doing out there? When will someone find me?

As my eyes become adjusted to the dark, I can pick out the lines of mortar between the breezeblocks and the shine on the stack of stainless-steel bowls that have been left on the floor in the corner. I become aware too, of a change, the smell of burning and the acrid scent of smoke unfurling its way along the corridor towards me. It takes me a moment to work out that Frank's discarded cigarette must have set something alight in the kitchen, and it's now that I really start to panic. There are bags of dog food, stacks of towels and old newspapers out there, plenty to feed a fire.

I jump up again and begin to pace the kennel, thoughts of survival and of Gloria Brambles and the fire that razed Buttercross Cottage to the ground racing through my brain. It can't be happening again. The Sanctuary is fated.

As I pick out the sound of a vehicle driving away and Dolly whinnying frantically from the paddock, the dogs start to howl and I raise my voice to join them, wondering if I managed to send that text and if help will come in time.

The choking smoke swirls across the ceiling,

sinking slowly towards ground level and gradually filling the corridor, for what seems like hours, but it's probably only ten minutes before the sound of emergency sirens overwhelms everything else.

'Tess!' I catch the sound of Jack's voice in the distance.

'I'm here!' I rattle the bars again. 'I'm here!' I can't speak any more for coughing, but he must have heard me because a figure steps out of the smoke, dressed in a helmet and dark flameproof clothing with reflective strips and shining a torch. I'd recognise him anywhere from his voice and the way he moves, steady and confident. 'Jack, I'm locked in. There's a padlock.' I pull my T-shirt up around my mouth and nose while he forces it, shouldering the door open.

'Let's get you out of here,' he says. 'Can you walk?'

I nod to confirm it and he leads me through the corridor, past the kitchen door, which is now closed. By mutual agreement we pause to let the dogs out, dragging the collie into the corridor when he cowers in the corner, and sending the three of them outside, where they're rounded up by some of the many people that have arrived to help.

'Where's Buster?' He's my priority now that I'm safe, but Jack wants to send me to see a para-medic. I refuse point-blank.

'You've had a bump on the head. Tess, you're rambling. Buster is missing. You've been out searching for him, remember?'

'There's nothing wrong with me,' I insist, touching my temple, feeling the throb of a bruise

360

and the sticky track of congealing blood. 'Katie brought Buster back this evening. I was doing the last round of the Sanctuary with him when the Maddockses turned up. Buster went for Frank – he bit him twice. If he hadn't been here, if he hadn't launched himself at him, I'm not sure I'd be here to tell the tale.' I shudder, recalling how Frank's expression had been dark with revenge, his absence of compassion and his sheer determination to get whatever he came here for.

'Buster's intervention gave that extra moment of time, long enough for Frank's son to pull him back from the brink of actually hurting me. He beat the dog up instead.' I bite my lip when I notice him on the ground beyond the fire engine that's pulled up close to the kennel block. Maz is on her knees beside him, listening to his chest with her stethoscope, her hair gleaming in the beam of a set of emergency lights. Stepping over the hose that one of the firefighters is unrolling into the kennel block, I join her, sinking onto my heels next to Buster, who is lying on his side, ominously quiet.

'Is he...?' I begin.

'I don't know,' Maz says. 'Talk to him, Tessa. He isn't responding to me.'

'Buster?' My chest is tight with grief and fear that I've found him, only to lose him again. 'Come on,' I urge him. 'Please wake up.' Slowly and shakily, he lifts his head and gazes around him, a glazed expression in his eyes, and strings of drool dangling from his jowls. 'Buster,' I repeat, his name catching in my throat. 'Don't you recognise me?' I reach out and touch his paw, giving it a

361

squeeze, and he beats his tail twice against the blanket Maz has slid underneath him. 'Hi there,' I say, a wave of relief washing through me. 'You're safe now. I'm not going to let you out of my sight ever again.'

'That's better,' Maz says. 'He needed some TLC. I reckon that's another of his nine lives gone.'

He's a dog, not a cat, I want to say. It's cats who have nine lives, but it doesn't matter. Buster is merely dazed, not brain-damaged. My dog, my saviour, is going to be all right.

'I'm assuming you'll want to keep him here for observation,' Maz goes on.

'Yes, I'd rather you didn't admit him unless it's essential. Is it safe to move him indoors? He'll be more comfortable on the sofa.' When Maz agrees, I look around for Jack to confirm that we're all right to enter the bungalow.

'The fire's out,' Jack says. 'It wasn't much – a few towels and newspapers. The dogs are fine – they're in the stable next to Bambi. The cats are a little disturbed, but none the worse for all the noise and activity that's been going on.'

'And what about Dolly?' I ask. 'She was tearing about the paddock earlier.'

'She's going mad,' Jack says. 'The Maddockses have taken Apache.'

'Oh-mi-god, where is he? He'll starve without his mum.'

'He's in the trailer at the end of the track and I'm hoping you're up to helping me fetch him back.' He raises his hand to show me Apache's foal slip, the head-collar Libby has taught him to wear. 'I think we're going to be grateful that my sister has already started working with him.'

'Where's Frank?' I ask, apprehensive now that he might have got away.

'He's been arrested and taken to the station.' Jack picks Buster up and carries him into the bungalow where Maz and Tia can keep watch on him, before we jog down the track in the dark to the trailer that's been parked haphazardly against the hedge at its junction with the lane. Jack hands me the foal slip.

'Apache's used to girls,' he says, opening the groom's door in the side of the trailer and ushering me in.

'He's used to Libby,' I observe when the foal takes one look at me and panics, reversing and kicking at the ramp at the back.

'Steady there,' I soothe, holding out my hand for him to investigate. 'Am I really that scary?' I murmur.

'You can be, Tess,' Jack mutters from outside, making me smile. 'It hasn't escaped my notice that you've become much more confident about keeping the volunteers in order recently.'

As I relax, Apache seems to relax too, taking one step forwards, his head outstretched and his breath warm on my fingers. I don't rush him.

'Have you got him yet?' Jack whispers.

'Almost.' Apache takes another step, allowing me to scratch his neck before I slide the foal slip over his nose and fasten it behind his ears. 'Good boy.'

'Are you talking about me again?'

'Don't flatter yourself, Jack Miller,' I say, keeping

363

my voice down so as not to frighten Apache any further: he seems very upset and fidgety away from his mother, who's screaming for him in the distance. 'All right, you can let us out now.'

Slowly, he lowers the ramp. Apache waits, twitching and flicking his ears, ready to run if he needs to, but I've got him, and with gentle persuasion I lead him down the ramp and up the lane with Jack walking along beside me, all the way to the paddock, where the foal stops and utters a high-pitched whinny. Hearing him, Dolly comes galloping at full pelt towards the fence, skidding to a halt just in time, neighing and whickering and rearing up, desperate to get to her baby. Jack opens the gate enough for me to push Apache through and Dolly greets him, sniffing and grooming his back as he nuzzles her, looking for milk.

'Aah,' I say, a lump in my throat, when he latches on to drink, and Dolly stands with her head lowered and her eyes half closed, the sweat drying on her flanks. She might hate most human beings, but the mare makes a brilliant mum. I throw out some more hay for her before returning to Buster's side to relieve Maz so she can go home. PC Phillips joins me to take a statement and, just as he's leaving, Jack appears to tell me the fire brigade have finished damping down and they're clearing the scene.

'Thanks, Jack,' I say as I sit on the sofa beside Buster, stroking his ear. He sighs now and again, as if he's making the most of the attention, while Tia sits quietly at my feet, warm like a pair of furry slippers. 'Between you and Buster, you saved my life.'

'I was doing my job.' Jack smiles, his teeth bright in the subdued light. 'It's a tough job rescuing damsels in distress, but someone's got to do it.' He pauses. 'Are you sure you're okay?' I nod as he continues, 'I don't think you should be left on your own with that bump on your head. Is your dad on his way? Does he know?'

'I called him on the landline to let him know I was all right – he and Mum are away for my great-aunt's funeral. I feel guilty for not going, but I didn't feel I could leave the Sanctuary for a couple of days.'

'You should have said – I'd have stayed over.' Jack towers over me. 'In fact, I'll stay here now as your parents aren't here.'

'Will you sit down?' I say, too exhausted to argue. 'You're making the place untidy.'

He makes himself comfortable on the armchair and we talk.

'I knew someone was watching me,' I say, going back to all the times when I felt uncomfortable at the Sanctuary, thinking I sensed someone's presence, and to the occasion when I called my dad and PC Phillips came and I managed to convince myself that, if there was anyone there, they were poachers passing through. 'I kind of guessed it might be Frank Maddocks, but I thought he was out purely for revenge. I had no idea that he was waiting for Dolly to give birth so he could steal the foal from under our noses.'

'It was a stupid plan,' Jack says. 'I don't know how he thought he was going to rear Apache without his mother.'

'I reckon he would have taken Dolly too, if he

365

could have caught her.'

'Well, I'm glad we managed to reunite them before any damage was done.'

Tia shifts on my feet. Buster yawns and shows me his belly in a not-so-subtle hint for me to give him a scratch.

'Tess, is there any chance...?' Jack begins eventually.

'Chance?' I look up abruptly, our eyes locking. 'Chance of what?'

'Of us, you and me, starting again?' he goes on.

'I don't think so.' I pause, regaining control of my emotions, a tangle of hurt and resentment at the way Jack has behaved towards me. 'I can't believe you're asking. I thought we had something and you dropped me just like that for some other woman.' I hug Buster to my chest. 'Why would I risk having my heart broken for a second time?'

'I made a mistake,' Jack says, his voice tremulous, making me soften towards him, but I can't let him break through my defences.

'So, let me get this clear,' I say. 'This other woman with whom you had some kind of fling or romance comes strolling back into your life, and you invite her to live with you in your house, and then you say it was a mistake? I really don't understand.'

'I'm trying to explain. I didn't know what to do when Karen arrived on my doorstep with nothing but a suitcase and holdall. She was in pieces and had nowhere to go. What else could I do, kick her out onto the street?' He looks me straight in the eye. 'What would you have done?'

'I would have found her somewhere to stay, the bed and breakfast at Barton Farm or a room at the Talymill Inn.'

'I felt responsible for her. She was in a terrible state, crying all the time. I didn't want to let her out of my sight, in case...' Jack shrugs. 'I thought she was suicidal.'

'Either that or she was using emotional blackmail to get you back. Jack, whatever her motives and your reasons for getting together were – and I don't want to know the gory details – you could have had the decency to let me know, not left me hanging on... Oh, I remember, I rather threw myself at you. Why should you treat me with any respect?' I add bitterly.

'I was a coward. I didn't have the balls to tell you. Karen turned up out of the blue, and I kept promising myself that I'd make a time to meet you so I could tell you face to face because letting you down by text or phoning wouldn't be right. Tess, you didn't throw yourself at me. It wasn't like that,' he goes on, his eyes filled with hurt.

'Wasn't it?' I say defiantly.

'You know it wasn't,' he repeats. 'That night we spent together meant everything to me.'

'So much so that you disappeared off and moved another woman straight into your bed–'

'Tessa, I haven't slept with her,' Jack interrupts. 'Do you really think that I'd do something like that? I do have morals, you know. I'm not some alley cat.'

He didn't sleep with Karen, I think, my heart lifting slightly. It makes me feel marginally better, but doesn't negate the fact that he dropped me when she turned up, even if it was out of his over-active sense of responsibility and desire to rescue everyone and everything he meets.

'How can I get through to you?' Jack goes on. 'You are so bloody stubborn. While I was away, I made certain vows to Karen, stupid spur-of-the-moment promises that, if things had been different – that is, if she hadn't been married – I'd have looked after her, but it was a brief affair, something wonderful and unexpected, and it wasn't supposed to last.' Sighing deeply, Jack runs his fingers through his hair. 'This is such a mess.'

'Libby says she's moved out.'

'She knew I was in love with somebody else – you, Tess.'

'Me?' I shake my head, sorry for myself and for this woman who left her home and her husband, only to find out that Jack didn't love her after all. 'No, Jack. I'm not interested. Who's to say you won't do something like that again the next time your conscience tells you to offer shelter to another ex of yours?' A fleeting image of Jack opening a rescue centre for ex-girlfriends springs to mind.

'I haven't had that many exes,' Jack says, defending himself. He wipes his palms on his trousers. 'If you ever change your mind, I'll be ready and waiting.'

'Don't be silly,' I say, forcing brightness. 'You won't hang around for ever.'

'I've told you, I'm not going anywhere.'

Whereas I might be, I think to myself. Jack's declaration, the size of my debts and my near brush with death have made me realise I should move on. If I stay here, I'll end up mired in insurmountable financial commitments with Jack as a constant reminder of what could have been. Life really is too short. If I'm going to regain my independence and set myself up with a house and a pension, I have to do it now, not leave it until it's too late. It's time I took steps to escape, to get out of Talyton St George altogether and start anew.

Jack remains in the armchair, head bowed and shoulders hunched, and I'm torn between asking him to leave, and telling him to come over and hold me, and never let me go.

'Do you remember when you said at the Fun Day that you don't choose a cat, a cat chooses you?' he says. 'Buster must have picked up some feline traits, because it seems he's chosen you. He isn't going anywhere, is he?'

'You're right,' I say, relieved that we're on to another subject. Where Buster's concerned, I'm going to listen to my heart not my head this time. 'He's staying with me and Tia. I can't risk putting him through the trauma of another failed adoption. It wouldn't be fair on anyone.' I know I said I wouldn't take any animals on, but if I'm moving anyway, I won't be tempted again, unless I come across the odd stray with a good sob story when I'm back in practice.

'Buster's one very lucky chap, curled up with you like that,' Jack says, his face etched with regret. 'Remember what I said. If you ever change your mind, you know where to find me.'

'Jack,' I say gently, because I can see he's genuinely upset that I will never agree to get back with him, in spite of the fact that I'm aching to fall into his arms and forget everything for tonight at least. 'Can we talk about something else now?'

'Such as?' he says.

'How we're going to go about releasing Bambi if and when he gets the all-clear? The committee's latest plans for the Sanctuary? They've suggested creating a dedicated room for the baby birds that will inevitably arrive next spring.' I smile, and Jack gives me a small smile back as I go on, 'Where would you like to start?'

It takes a while for the conversation to flow, but it does, and Jack and I talk until dawn – as friends, and only as friends.

Chapter Eighteen

King of the Forest

A week later, my mind is unchanged, although I'm pretty certain Jack has been doing his utmost to challenge my decision, spending many hours of his spare time at the Sanctuary, repairing the fire damage in the kitchen in the kennel block and repainting, generally putting himself in my way. He buys presents for Buster and Tia, metal tags with my name and mobile number on them to go on their collars now I've adopted them officially.

I send off several job applications and wait for responses, but my concerns regarding my debts are solved by a visit from my dad, who turns up one evening with a bottle of bubbly to celebrate my change in fortune, created not by the fairy godmother but by the kindness of Great-Auntie Marion. She has left me a significant amount of money in her will, enough to pay off my current obligations with a little left over.

I have good friends, I have Buster and Tia with me, Frank Maddocks has been charged with attempted theft and assault, and Justin has confirmed that Bambi is almost ready for release. On balance, all is well, apart from the uncertainty between me and Jack.

We choose to release Bambi on a misty morning in early October when the weather is forecast to remain calm for a few days. The injury to his leg has healed, and although he's left with a significant scar, the vets have passed him fit for release. He can feed, move around normally and is in good condition; and, just as importantly, he's still wary of humans and domestic pets like Buster and Tia. We talked about carrying out a soft release, letting him out from the Sanctuary so he could take his time to leave us, perhaps moving into the copse and establishing his position with the deer already there, but in the end decided on a hard release in a quiet area of woodland on the Fox-Giffords' estate.

With Libby's help, Jack and I have managed to secure Bambi in the padded deer crate in the back of Jack's Land Rover, ready to go.

'Jump in, Libby,' Jack says, climbing in the driver's side.

'I'm not coming,' she says.

'But you said you were. You made such a fuss.'

'I've changed my mind. I think I'll be too upset,' she says, 'and anyway, three's a crowd.' She glances up at her brother with a smile playing on her lips. 'You and Tessa rescued him, so you should be the ones to let him go.'

'No, you must come along too,' I say quickly. There was a time not so long ago when all I wanted was the opportunity to be alone with Jack. Now I'm not sure that I trust myself with him. There's so much I want to say to him that is better unsaid, and besides, Libby shouldn't be left here at the Sanctuary on her own. She scared me when she had that fit, and I can understand why Jack feels so torn between letting her have her independence and wanting to watch over her.

'Libby?' Jack says.

'Don't worry. Diane and Wendy will be here in ten minutes or so. I'm going to get Apache to practise being led around the copse. He needs a proper education so he doesn't end up like his mum.'

'You're going to be one of those crazy horse owners,' Jack says with a mock sigh, 'unable to hold a conversation about anything apart from the price of hay and horseshoes.'

'I can't wait,' Libby says, grinning. Since the arrest of Mr Maddocks and his son, she's been in negotiation to buy Dolly and her foal, and next spring she's planning to move them to Farley's End, where Ash's mum rents a field for her elderly pony. Eventually, she's going to break Apache to drive.

'I expect Ash will drop in with the post too,' I say, realising why she is so keen to stay.

'I'll be fine,' Libby confirms, blushing a furious pink. 'Go on, and don't hurry back.'

'Come on, Tess,' Jack says, making his mind up. 'Let's go.'

I jump in, dressed in new boots and a waxed coat that I bought in Overdown Farmers.

'I've brought along some emergency rations – I'm not sure how long this will take,' he says, nodding towards the flask and bar of chocolate that lie on the seat between us as he turns the key in the ignition.

Travelling the short distance to the release site, I can smell Jack's scent of fresh aftershave and clean washing. Sick with longing and annoyed with myself for not being able to get over him, I gaze at Jack as he keeps his hands on the wheel and his eyes on the road, driving past the entrance to the Manor where we released the ducklings a few weeks ago, on the Fox-Giffords' pond, and continuing on up the hill with green fields on either side.

'This is it,' Jack says, turning left past the next hedge-line where the bushes are laced with silvery spiders' webs, and drawing to a stop in front of a log that has been left across the entrance to the wood beyond, where the trees are swathed in their fiery autumnal colours of red, gold and bronze. 'We'll have to shift it between us. Do you mind?'

I try to open the door, but it's stuck. I give it a shove and it still won't budge.

'Well, this is embarrassing,' I begin as Jack leans across me to pull on the handle, his arm brushing against me, the contact making the hairs on the back of my neck stand on end and my heart beat faster, as I recall his touch that night when we made love. For the briefest moment, he freezes as if the memories have come flooding back for him too, but the click of the door, like a hypnotist's fingers, snaps us back to the present.

'There you go,' says Jack. 'Simples.'

'When you know how,' I say drily.

'There's a knack to it,' he says, holding the door open for me so I can jump out and move round to meet him over the log, where the air smells of bruised grass, wet rot and leaf mould. It's sodden and studded with orange and grey fungi, and it's soon clear that we can't shift it between us. Jack reverses – with my assistance, of course – turns the Land Rover around so it's facing the other way, and ties a rope between the tow-bar and the single branch that remains attached to the log, before dragging it aside into the undergrowth so we can pass, driving on through between the trees until the track we're on divides into three.

Jack stops and frowns.

'Do you know where you're going?' I ask.

'According to the map, there should be a clearing up here somewhere.'

'I thought you'd been up here before to choose the release site.'

'I have. It's just that now... Unfortunately, one tree looks very much like another.' Jack drums his fingers on the wheel, and drops of rain begin to patter onto the windscreen. 'This isn't looking too promising.'

'We can't release Bambi in this weather, can we?'

'Let's give it half an hour or so to see if it stops. It'll give us time to find the release site.' Jack reaches across the back of the seat, his hand close to my shoulder as he turns to look through the canvas window at the rear of the vehicle to reverse, the wheels spinning in the mud then finding purchase, the Land Rover shooting back at speed.

'Be careful,' I say, 'the poor deer.'

'I'm sorry,' Jack says. 'I think it's this way.' He takes the narrower turning to the right that leads us to a small clearing where the grass is lush and long, parking under the trees at the edge. The rain turns into a downpour and it's looking increasingly unlikely that we'll release Bambi today.

'Should we go home?' I ask.

'Let's give it another ten minutes – as long as you don't mind waiting here with me...' Jack's voice trails off and I don't know what to say. Mind? In spite of everything, the wedding and the way he behaved over Karen, I love spending time with him, just the two of us – the deer shifts in the crate in the back – and Bambi. 'I don't want to go back to the Sanctuary,' Jack goes on, his voice rough like gravel. 'I like it here.' He glances across at me. 'Coffee?'

'Please,' I say as he picks up the flask and pours me a coffee into the cup.

'How do you take it?'

'Don't you remember?' I say, disappointed that he's forgotten when I thought we knew each other so well.

'I'm teasing you, Tess. White, no sugar. You see, I do know.' He pauses. 'Would you like a biscuit with that?'

'No, thanks. I'm not hungry.' My lack of appetite has more to do with the man sitting alongside me than the fact I had three Weetabix for breakfast.

'It's our lucky day,' Jack says eventually as the rain stops, the sun comes out and the clouds part above the trees to reveal blue sky. 'What do you think?'

'Let's go for it,' I say, keen to get out of the Land Rover to put some distance between us so I can make sense of the turmoil of emotion triggered by Jack's proximity, as well as release

Bambi from the confines of the crate as soon as possible. Jack gets out and comes striding around to the passenger side to open the door for me. I stumble as I jump to the ground, literally falling into his arms. He steadies me, holding me by the shoulders, and the world stands still. When I dare to look up, his eyes are fixed on mine.

'Thanks,' I say, pushing him away, unable to bear the intensity of the contact any longer. I turn my attention to the clearing itself. I can picture Snow White lying in her glass coffin in the centre, the poisoned apple with the bite taken out of it alongside her. I poisoned myself for anyone else after Jack. I wish it had never happened, yet I'm also glad that it did. 'Let's not keep Bambi waiting any longer.'

Together, we haul the crate out of the back and lower it to the ground. We make a good team, I think, watching the taut sinews in Jack's arms and the strength in his shoulders that could sweep a princess off her feet and onto a shining steed, as he takes most of the weight. My gaze transfers to the muscular tension in his thighs, imagining them wrapped around the aforesaid steed and then around the princess as he takes her into the forest to have his wicked way with her. Oh, how I wish I believed in fairy tales.

'There we go. Are you ready?' Jack asks me. 'You can do the honours.'

'We should do it together,' I say, taking his hand and placing it on the catch on the front of the crate, leaving my fingers on top, sensing the warmth of his skin. We unlatch it and slide the door open before retreating, hand in hand, to the other side of the clearing to give Bambi some space. I stand next to Jack, watching the crate, yet aware of the man beside me, the rate and depth of his breathing and the tension in his body, matched by my own, confirming what I already know: that I still fancy him like mad.

I force myself to concentrate on the crate.

Bambi's shiny black nose appears, followed by his eyes and ears. Suddenly, he dashes forwards, scrambling out of the crate and regaining his composure once his feet touch the grass. He trots away towards the bracken, floating across the clearing on his impossibly slender limbs, his head held high and his ears flicking back and forth with uncertainty.

For a moment I think he's going to disappear, but he hesitates and turns his head, gazing towards me and Jack with those achingly beautiful brown eyes, as if to say goodbye.

'Good luck,' I whisper, trying to be strong, but as I catch sight of the last dapple of his coat merging with the shadows of the wood, I start to cry.

'Hey, Tess.' Jack releases my hand and slides his arm around my shoulders, gently pulling me round to face him, and hugging me to his chest. 'He'll be all right. It's for the best.'

'I know,' I say.

I focus on the mole on Jack's neck through a blur of tears and listen to the deep rumble in his throat as he goes on, 'This is what I love about my job, letting them go.'

Letting them go, I echo silently. If I leave now, I'll be letting Jack go too, along with my dreams of a future at his side.

'It's the best feeling,' Jack says.

'Almost the best.' There, I've said it. I've broached the subject at last. 'There are other things in life, apart from rescue, I mean.' I bite my lip, tasting blood.

'Such as?' Jack holds me closer. 'Go on. Tell me.'

'Jack, we need to talk,' I begin, but I can hardly speak, overwhelmed with love and desire, and fear that now he might have changed his mind and not want me any more. 'I'm very fond of you.'

'As I am of you,' he says quietly.

'It's more than that,' I stumble on. 'I can't stop thinking about you, from the moment I get up in the morning to when I fall asleep, and when I do get to sleep you're always in my dreams.'

'Not bad dreams, I hope.' When I look up, his eyes are glinting with amusement. 'Is that it?'

'Is that it?' I try to push him away, but he stands rock solid. 'I've just spilled my guts and all you can say is, "Is that it?"'

His expression grows serious. 'If only you knew how long I've waited for you to admit that... What's made you change your mind?'

'I had to tell you,' I say. 'I'm about to hand in my notice at the Sanctuary.'

'You can't do that,' he says hoarsely.

'Well, I can,' I say, 'but I don't have to.'

'What are you talking about? You aren't making sense.'

'What I'm trying to say is that my decision depends on you, Jack.'

'You'll have to explain.' He releases me from his embrace, takes my hand and leads me to the Land Rover where we sit side by side, perched on the flap at the back. 'Go on, then.'

'For the first time in ages, I have options,' I begin. 'I'm on the shortlist for an interview at a practice in West London.'

'London? That's miles away. You'd hate it.' Jack touches my face and tucks a loose lock of hair back behind my ear. It's a tiny, heart-melting gesture that makes me want to cry all over again. 'I thought you were settled at the Sanctuary. I've heard you calling it home. And what about your parents, Tia and Buster, me and Libby, your aunt?'

'I can take them with me – the dogs, I mean. Mum and Dad can visit – they'll enjoy the nightlife.' I don't mean to be flippant, but it's my way of coping with an awkward situation in which I feel I'm exposing myself in a most intimate way.

'What about the animals? The rescues?'

'They'll have you and Libby, Diane and Wendy–'

'You said you had options,' Jack interrupts harshly. 'What are the alternatives?'

'My great-aunt has left me a substantial inheritance, enough to pay off my debts, which means I'm not under pressure to find a job that pays me a living wage just yet, so...'

'You don't have to leave?' Jack finishes for me.

Shaking my head, I lean into him as his arm creeps around my waist.

'Please, don't leave,' he whispers. 'You're very special to me, Tess. I'd do anything for you, absolutely anything, walk over hot coals...'

'Wouldn't you put them out first?' I say, my heart beating faster. 'You are a firefighter, after all.' And a lifesaver, I think, remembering how he led me through the choking smoke in the kennels on the night that the Maddockses kidnapped Apache.

'Since I found out how Nathan and Katie were treating you, and saw how sad you were when you first came to the Sanctuary, all I've wanted to do is rescue you, Tess,' Jack goes on, pausing when I make a show of gazing into the distance, as though I'm searching for something. 'What are you doing?'

'Looking for the shining steed, the chainmail and the lance,' I say with a small smile. 'Jack, I don't need rescuing.'

'I know that. You can stand up to anyone,' he says ruefully. 'Let me put it in a different way. I don't want you to leave. Talyton Animal Rescue needs you, the animals need you.' He takes a deep breath. 'I need you. Tess, my darling, I love you. I've always loved you. I've made mistakes, but I'll never let you down again. I promise.'

'Jack–'

'Sh,' he says. 'Let me finish.' He leans in and touches his nose to mine, gazing softly into my eyes. 'I want to make you happy. Will you let me…?'

'Yes, Jack.' Unable to restrain my joy, I slide my hands around his neck and press my lips to his. 'You know, I can make a special exception for you. You can rescue me any time…'

The publishers hope that this book has given you enjoyable reading. Large Print Books are especially designed to be as easy to see and hold as possible. If you wish a complete list of our books please ask at your local library or write directly to:

Magna Large Print Books
Magna House, Long Preston,
Skipton, North Yorkshire.
BD23 4ND

This Large Print Book for the partially sighted, who cannot read normal print, is published under the auspices of

THE ULVERSCROFT FOUNDATION

THE ULVERSCROFT FOUNDATION

... we hope that you have enjoyed this Large Print Book. Please think for a moment about those people who have worse eyesight problems than you ... and are unable to even read or enjoy Large Print, without great difficulty.

You can help them by sending a donation, large or small to:

**The Ulverscroft Foundation,
1, The Green, Bradgate Road,
Anstey, Leicestershire, LE7 7FU,
England.**
or request a copy of our brochure for more details.

The Foundation will use all your help to assist those people who are handicapped by various sight problems and need special attention.

Thank you very much for your help.